THE CHERRIES

Faith, hope, happiness
Does she dare?

First Published in Great Britain 2019 by Mirador Publishing

First edition: 2019

A copy of this work is available through the British Library.

ISBN: 978-1-912601-75-2

Mirador Publishing
10 Greenbrook Terrace
Taunton
Somerset
UK
TA1 1UT

The Cherries

By

D. B. Carter

Dedication

To my wonderful Rebecca, who has so patiently supported me and believed in this book. The only true achievement of my life is to have been loved by you all these years.

To my beloved sister and parents, who I so wished had lived to read this. It was in the pain of your passing that 'The Cherries' was forged.

To Daniel, Leona, Dee, Jane, Sandra and so many others. Thank you, my dear friends, for all your encouragement.

To my children, who have shown me who I want to be when I grow up.

Chapter 1

The bright sunshine made the car intolerably hot. Marian took her eyes off the road for a few moments to glance at her daughter, who had been sleeping in the seat next to her almost from the point they had joined the motorway some three hours beforehand. She reflected that her hopes that Susan was going to be great company for the journey were somewhat optimistic, but that teenagers, even late-teenagers, loved to sleep.

Eyes back on the tarmac monotony stretched ahead of her, Marian saw a signpost marking the next services a mile ahead. She spent the next thirty or forty seconds debating whether she needed to stop for a break, made her decision and flicked the indicator to pull onto the slip road.

As the car slowed, Susan stirred in her seat and groggily opened her eyes.

"Are we there already?" she croaked.

"No, sleepyhead. I'm just stopping at the services. We've still got a couple of hours to go."

Susan grimaced a bit and picked up the bottle of flavoured water she had brought for the trip. She grimaced even more when she drank from it.

"Ugh!" she exclaimed loudly. "That is disgustingly warm! This whole car is an oven." She stabbed at the air conditioning button. "Why won't this thing work?"

"I don't know, darling. I can't afford to have anyone even look at it for the moment. You know how things are. I'm just grateful the engine works."

Susan scowled out of the window as her mother pulled into a parking space which seemed to Susan to be an almost ludicrous distance from the services themselves. Both women climbed wearily from the car and stretched before making their way to the facilities.

"I'm nipping to the loo," said Marian, "are you coming too?"

"No, I'm fine."

"Are you sure? It's at least another two hours from here."

"Mum, I'm fine. You're just getting old," Susan teased, "I'll get some drinks. What do you want?"

"Oh, a small coffee for me, please."

By now they were passing through the sliding entrance doors and they parted ways. Susan went to the takeaway restaurant and ordered a small coffee and the largest iced cola that they sold.

Returning to the foyer, she saw her mum emerge from the toilets and gesture that she was popping into the newsagents. Susan stood patiently, or as patiently as she knew how, slurping on her drink and people watching. She observed a couple of lads in the small amusement arcade playing a motor racing simulator and wondered to herself why anyone would want to take a break from driving by playing a driving game.

Turning, she caught sight of her reflection in the window and frowned even more; dark hair scraped back into a ponytail, voluminous dungarees over a white t-shirt and a pair of scruffy, cheap trainers. Not that she cared about her appearance, just that she didn't like to think about it. Seeing her mum making her way to her, dressed immaculately, makeup perfect, hair flawless, Susan doubted whether anyone would realise they were related.

Marian took the coffee Susan held out to her and eyed the gigantic drink her daughter was drinking.

"Thanks, darling… are you sure you don't want to pop to the loo?"

Susan sighed loudly.

"No," she told her mother firmly. "Now let's get going."

Marian said nothing, but took hold of Susan's arm and gave it a loving squeeze as they walked across the car park. There was a little patch of grass with a picnic table in the shade of a small tree nearby and the two women sat there to eat some sandwiches which Marian had bought from the service station shop. They said little, not least because the sound of the traffic from the motorway was still quite loud, even at a distance. Susan slipped off her trainers and felt the cool air on her bare feet as she sat on the bench, knees straight. She slowly lowered her feet to the ground and savoured the sensation of the blades of grass against her soft pink soles.

She slurped at her straw. The cola was pretty much finished, but the ice cubes had begun to melt and it was still refreshing.

Marian looked at her, and was so disturbed at the amount of liquid that her daughter had consumed that she decided she needed to go to the loos again for herself. But she also knew that Susan would be annoyed. "Only a couple of hours," she said to herself. If only she had known that her daughter was also secretly wondering if she shouldn't nip back to use the Ladies, but was too stubborn to admit her mistake.

So, they got back into the aging Citroen and re-joined the motorway. Within ten minutes they were at a standstill at the back of three lanes of solid, unmoving traffic that stretched far into the distance.

* * *

A parcel under his arm, Luke Cartwright threw open the front door of his house and, in his haste, almost walked straight into the postman.

"Morning, Mr Cartwright. I've got a couple of pieces here that need a signature."

Luke thanked him and made a vague squiggle on the electronic device being held under his nose. Taking the mail, he popped inside his house to double check the contents, before coming back out. He stood for a moment, as if trying to remember something, went back inside and re-emerged with his parcel.

He strode purposefully round to the side of the house and wheeled his bicycle out of the garage. Then he walked back to the front door to check that he had locked it. Then he walked back to the garage to check that door was also secure. He was about to mount the cycle, when he looked again at the front door. Had he locked it? He had only just checked and he knew he had. He knew it. But he went and tried the door again anyway.

He stuffed the parcel into a backpack, slipped the straps over his shoulders, and pedalled off up the lane to the local village, enjoying the bright sunshine and the cooling air as he sped along the road.

The trip to the village took Luke a little less than twenty minutes. He went straight into the small combined shop and Post Office, exchanged a cheery greeting with the clerk and arranged for his parcel to be sent. His main task complete, he browsed the shop, picking up a loaf of fresh, locally baked bread, some vegetables and a newspaper.

Luke then strolled over to the pub and bought himself a large cool fruit juice and ordered a ploughman's lunch. Sitting in the garden at the front of the inn, he sipped his drink and alternated between reading his paper and waving to or chatting with passing locals. After a few minutes, the landlady brought him his food and he spent the next quarter of an hour enjoying the selection of local cheeses, the crisp baguette, the sweet apple, and the home-made pickles.

A small red Ford pulled up and out got a short woman, with a round, welcoming face, and an infectious smile. She was dressed in her full clerical regalia. Luke feigned a weary expression, but with his half-smile and twinkling eyes, he was fooling no one.

"Hello, Luke. I'm glad I spotted you. I was just on my way over to yours."

"Hello, Vicar," he replied. "That sounds ominous. What would you be wanting from a simple soul such as myself?"

"You? Simple?" she teased back. "That will be the day! Look, I feel terrible asking you for this after all you've done, but we are going to have an emergency fundraiser this weekend to raise some cash for urgent repairs to the church windows. Is there anything you could donate for the raffle or auction?"

He furrowed his brow for a few moments and then said, "I think I have the very thing. Do you want to pop over and pick it up on Friday?"

"Bless you," she thanked him. "You are a star."

"You're the one doing all the work. I'm just pleased to support you."

He stood up and said, "I'd better be going. I thought I'd head over to see Margaret Hedges before I head home. Her arthritis is so bad these days that I'm not sure she is eating properly. The carers do what they can, but you know how stubborn she is."

"I do indeed. I'll look in on her later too. Bless you. See you Friday."

With that, she jumped back into her car and drove off in a cloud of dust.

* * *

"I think we are starting to move again!" exclaimed Marian. She glanced at the clock. "It's only three o'clock. Not so bad."

Susan looked confused. She fished out her phone.

"No, Mum. It is four o'clock, the clock in the car is wrong… again."

Marian looked like she was about to burst into tears.

"Damn!" she exclaimed. "We are going to be late, unless the traffic is very kind to us from here on. I hate being late, especially for Vivian."

"Mum, Aunty Viv will be fine," Susan assured her mother, "she is the most laid-back person I know. Do you want me to text her?"

"Not yet. Let's wait till we know how we are doing for time," Marian replied, glancing over at her daughter who was resting her still bare feet on the fascia of the car. "Do put your legs down now we are moving again, Susie. What if we had an accident?"

Susan moved her feet to the floor and then started to giggle.

"What's so funny?" Marian asked.

By this point Susan could barely speak from laughing so hard.

"What is so funny?" Marian demanded.

"It's not that funny," Susan managed to say. "I was just imagining what would happen if the air bag went off while I was sitting like that. You'd be saying to some policeman, 'Sorry, Officer, but my daughter is now a foot shorter than she was and has an airbag stuck up her bum'." One sideways glance at each other sent them both into giggles.

After the laughter subsided, mother and daughter just sat and smiled, both content in the company of the other. Marian finally spoke, in a soft voice.

"Thank you for this. Thank you for coming with me. It is a new start."

"What was there to stay for?" Susan replied. "There is nothing I'm going to miss about that place. It is a new start for us both. Let's put the bad behind us."

Susan half closed her eyes so that the other cars on the motorway were just colours, glinting in the sun. She saw the green of the trees and grassland, succulent and verdant, brimming with life and promise. She saw the blue of the road sign.

The blue of the road sign which read…

"Mum!" she squawked. "Mum, this is our junction. We need to come off here!"

Marian jumped. She checked her mirrors, flicked the indicator, cut across a lane of traffic and just squeezed onto the slip road before it ran out.

"Well done, Susie. My mind was miles away. Only about an hour from here. Can you text Viv and let her know, please?"

Susan said nothing, but she had one thought in her mind. It was more of an equation than anything else. Not using the restroom when she had the chance, plus one super-large cola, plus one giggling fit, plus one traffic scare, equals a strong wish to use the next facilities that presented themselves.

"Mum. If you see somewhere with a loo, please can you stop off?"

Marian was already on the lookout for herself, but just said, "Sure."

* * *

Luke was pedalling lazily home through the lanes when a movement in the hedge caught his eye. He skidded to a halt and hurried to find a small rabbit with its leg caught in a cruel wire snare. The poor little beast was writhing and tugging, tightening the noose with every convulsion.

Luke swore quietly to himself and tried to calm the tiny creature. Plucking an old pen knife from his pocket he set to work on the wire, and after a little effort, he managed cut through. In the meantime, the bunny had calmed and lay still, resigned to its fate. Carefully and gently, Luke manipulated the noose until he could slide the leg from its clutches. There was a little blood, but the damage did not appear to be as great as he feared.

He carried the now placid animal to his bike and unclipped the water bottle, pouring a little into the palm of his free hand (not easy when holding a rabbit). After an initial hesitation, there was a sniff from a twitching nose and then the water was lapped up. Luke moistened his clean handkerchief with a dash of water and tried to wipe the wound to have a better look.

Carrying the rabbit, which had now regained its spirits and was tangibly more wriggly, in one hand and wheeling his bike with the other, Luke walked back towards the village, intending to go to the vet. However, he was caught out by a particularly energetic lurch and before he could react, the creature was free. His bike fell to the road and he tried to give chase, but it was already too late. The rabbit was scampering across the field, far beyond reach. Then it stopped for a moment, absolutely still, save that it turned its head to look back at him as if to give thanks. Then it was gone.

Luke felt a profound sensation of loss, beyond his explanation. He picked up his bike, leant it against the hedgerow and sat on the bank, among the wildflowers and whispered goodbye to his friend.

How long he sat there, he did not know. Time stood still until he snapped back to the real world and glanced at his watch. He was late. He jumped back onto his bike and cycled down the lane until he came to a bridle path. The weather had been dry for some time and the earth on the path was baked solid. Cycling on it would be much bumpier than the lanes, but should knock a good bit off the time of the trip home, especially if he kept up a good pace.

* * *

"I can't believe it!" exclaimed Susan. "We've been travelling for miles and not a garage or a pub that's open or even a public loo. Could we just knock on someone's door?"

The note of desperation in her voice touched her mother deeply, not least because she was in similar discomfort herself.

"I don't think we can do that," she replied, though she did seriously consider it. "There aren't many houses around here anyway."

Just then the car hit a pothole in the road, and Susan made a noise somewhere between a groan and a scream. Every bump, every corner was becoming a torture. In her mind, her bladder was so full that she must look six months pregnant.

"How much further?" she wailed.

"Not much," her mother assured her. "A quarter of an hour at most."

"Seriously, I'm not going to make it. What am I going to do?"

Marian was decisive. She stopped the car in the entrance to a field.

"We'll have to go behind that hedge," she stated.

Susan looked appalled.

"Mum, I can't. I mean it's outdoors. Someone could see us."

"In case you hadn't noticed," Marian replied firmly, "there isn't anyone else around."

She climbed out and walked into the field.

Susan sat in the car with a look of abject horror on her face. It was at this point that she wished that she was wearing a skirt like her mother was, but finally she accepted the inevitable and gingerly went after her.

By the time she passed through the gateway into the field, Marian was already on her way back.

"Stay here, Mum. I need you to keep guard," hissed Susan.

"There is a nice hidden spot by the hedge," her mother explained. "Look, there is a little mound of earth next to it, so no one will see you when you're crouched down."

"I still need you on guard," Susan hissed again.

"OK." Marian stood patiently, waiting for her daughter.

"I can't do it if you're looking AT me! Look away, you're on guard, remember?"

Marian turned around and stood looking up the hill. There was a sound of scrabbling and muttered oaths from behind her.

"What on Earth is taking so long?" she asked.

"It's these dungarees," Susan explained, "I've pulled them down, but they're in the way."

"Well take them off then."

“What if someone sees?”

“That t-shirt you’re wearing is as long as some dresses that I’ve seen girls wearing these days. For Heaven’s sake, get a move on!” Marian told her daughter.

There was a flurry behind her, before the offending dungarees were deposited over her shoulder. Then a beeping of a horn from the road shattered the rustic peace. Marian hurried back to the gate to see a lorry trying to squeeze past the parked Citroen. She called to Susan that she had to move the car and her heart almost broke at the feeble, “Don’t leave me, Mum,” that followed after her.

After an eternity and what felt like several gallons, Susan felt an elation of relief. She started to stand up, when she heard the noise of a bicycle approaching. Peeking over the mound of earth, she saw a man freewheeling down the track at the side of the field.

Bobbing back down, panic gripped her. He would see her; he would know what she had been doing. Looking around her frantically, she spotted some flowers growing in the hedgerow. Yes, that was it! She would pretend to be looking at the flowers. She would exclaim delight at them as he passed, and he, being a country dweller, would be used to such things. She deeply wished her t-shirt was longer and she grabbed the hem and stretched it. There was a sound of tearing – the shoulder seam had come apart. More panic. And why hadn’t she put her shoes back on? They were still in the car. She could hear the cyclist was almost right behind her.

Luke was deep in his own thoughts as he coasted down the rough bridle path, dust billowing in his wake. He was almost at the gate when a young lady suddenly popped up from behind a mound of earth and exclaimed loudly, “My! What exquisite flowers!”

A combination of shock and fear of hitting her led him to jam his brakes on. The parched, crumbling soil beneath the wheels was too unforgiving and the bike gave way underneath him; he made his way to the gateway in a combination of tumbling and sliding.

Susan ran to where he was lying, asking if he was alright. Marian came running too and the ladies helped him to sit up. Once he got his breath back, he assured them that he was fine. For some reason, he felt it necessary to be even more courteous than he usually was.

“Would you mind if I asked what exactly you were doing?” he enquired. Susan looked at his gentle face and dark eyes, and found herself wishing that she had bothered to shave her legs at some point in the last month.

“I was looking at those lovely flowers,” she explained. There was an unspoken supplementary question on his part, which would have been designed to find out why such a botanical fascination would drive one to be barefoot in a field wearing only a tiny torn t-shirt dress.

But he found her smile was worth any discomfort. No harm was done. He stood up, dusted himself off and climbed back onto his bike, straightening the straps of his backpack.

“The cowslip is indeed a lovely flower,” he said with sincerity. “I do hope you will both excuse me, but I am already late for an appointment. Please don’t give any further thought to this matter; the fault was mine, as I was riding too fast.”

With that, he climbed back onto his bike and pedalled away.

Chapter 2

Marian and Susan studied the map. A frantic search through the car for Vivian's written directions to her house had been fruitless, and their respective mobile phones had taken them to two different wrong addresses for the postcode. Texts to Vivian were not replied to and phone calls to her just went straight to voicemail.

The afternoon shadows were lengthening into evening shade, but the air was still warm. It would be a rather perfect summer's eve, if you weren't hungry and humiliated in equal measure.

They had stopped the car in a small lay-by near a crossroads and they were trying to find where they were on the map, when a sturdy woman appeared, walking two large black Labradors. Marian opened her window as the lady passed.

"Please could you tell me where Hayfield Barn is?" she asked. "I don't know the name of the road it is on, so I know it is a bit of a long shot."

The lady beamed at them.

"Why yes, my lovelies, I know the very place. My Sid worked on the conversion, oh it must be getting on for fifteen years back. Take the right fork and then next right again. Follow the road for about half a mile and it will be on your left."

"Thank you so much," said Marian, while Susan did her best to smile at her.

They followed the instructions carefully, down through a small area of woodland, before turning a bend and seeing the most beautiful house they had ever seen. It was a well-proportioned Georgian building, with cream-painted rendering, white-glossed bow windows and a front garden filled with cherry trees in blossom. A sign at the end of the driveway read 'The Cherries'. The other side of an open courtyard, they saw a brick-built barn conversion, with rosewood windows and a stable-style front door, the top half of which was open. And there Vivian stood waving to them and gesturing to a bottle of wine she had in her hand.

* * *

Luke cycled straight home, locked the bike away and made his way into the kitchen, putting the kettle on as soon as he got in the door. While he waited for it to boil, he slid his backpack from his shoulders and unpacked his shopping, which was slightly squashed but still usable. There was a little blood oozing from some of the abrasions on his hands and forearms, which had absorbed much of the energy from his tumble.

Removing his shirt and wristwatch, Luke made his way to a cloakroom just off the hallway and washed his hands and arms, up past his elbows. When he'd dried off with a hand towel, he opened a small mirrored cabinet over the basin and removed a bottle of antiseptic and some cotton wool.

From the kitchen, there was the sound of a click, signalling the kettle had boiled. He hurried through, poured a strong cup of tea and sat at the table to sanitise his cuts.

He jotted some notes for himself on a small pad of paper, marking out some ideas for the donations the vicar had requested.

Luke sipped his tea, but it was still hotter than he liked it.

Wearily, he picked up the telephone and made a call, which went straight to voicemail.

"Hello, Harry, this is Luke Cartwright. Look, I was passing near Magdalen Woods earlier and I found some poor creature caught in a snare. Fortunately, it was OK once I released it. I don't know if it's one of your tenants or some locals trying a bit of poaching, but it's bloody barbaric. See what you can do about it will you? Give me a call to let me know, please? Thanks, mate. Bye."

Another tentative sip of tea was followed by a decisive gulp, washing the dust from his throat.

Suddenly, Luke realised how tired he felt and how heavy his eyelids were. He decided to let himself doze for a little while. As he slipped into sleep, his thoughts were of a young lady with dark hair and a torn dress.

He jolted awake after what felt like a few minutes, but a glance at the kitchen clock said that he'd been sleeping for far longer than intended. His upper body, still bare, was now cold, as was the half-drunk cup of tea on the table.

Aching all over, he picked up his shirt and went up the stairs to his bedroom and through into his en suite shower room. He stripped off his remaining clothes, turned on the shower and stood under the warm water, letting it wash away the dirt and sweat of the day. The memory of his strange encounter with the mystery girl once again played through his mind. Lost in his thoughts, all sense of time faded, but eventually a combination of pruning skin and a desire for some dinner wrenched him from his reverie.

Towelling himself off, Luke wandered back into his bedroom. Outside, there was the noise of a car engine. Taking care not to be seen, he edged his way to the window and looked over the cherry blossomed trees in his front garden to see an aging Citroen pull up outside his neighbour's house. Out climbed two familiar looking women, one of them wearing a torn t-shirt.

* * *

"Good grief, Susie, what's happened to you?" exclaimed Vivian as the two weary travellers climbed from their car. Susan walked towards her carrying the dungarees under her arm and nearly tripping over the undone laces of the trainers that she had slipped back on.

"Don't ask," she replied with a slight moan. "Just some humiliation, as per usual."

Vivian stared at the dishevelled teen with an expression of mild revulsion, before giving Susan the kind of hug which avoided any actual bodily contact, save for some gentle arm strumming. Marian appeared from the back of the car with a suitcase in each hand and a backpack slung over one shoulder. She put the cases down to receive a much more convincing embrace from her friend.

"Shall I get the rest of the luggage for you, babe?" asked Vivian.

"No need, this is it."

"Oh, are you having the rest of your stuff sent down separately? Very civilised."

Marian's voice seemed to break a little when she said, "Viv, this is all we have left. All we own is in these cases." She saw Susan look away and shake a little, so she lightly kissed her daughter's head.

"Look, it's getting a bit chilly to be standing out here chatting," said Vivian in an artificially upbeat voice, "come on in, you two. I've got a nice lasagne in the oven and a cracking little Bordeaux ready to go."

"Oh, lead me to it!" cried Marian, as she passed through the door, cases knocking against the door frame.

"It sounds great, Auntie Viv," Susan said, "but would you mind if I had a shower and changed first? I feel disgusting."

"On one condition," replied Vivian. "Try to stop calling me Auntie. It was cute when you were five, but now you're nearly twenty, I think you should be calling me Viv. The bathroom is upstairs on the right, sweetie, and your bedroom is the first on the left."

With a grateful smile, Susan picked up the cases and headed up the stairs. The bedroom was a fair size, with a sloping roof and a gabled window that looked over the cherry trees of the house next door. There were two beds (she would be sharing the room with her mum), a dressing table, and a wardrobe, which would provide more than enough space for their meagre selection of clothes.

She had started to look through the cases, when Viv knocked and opened the door.

"I forgot to put some towels out for you," she explained and handed a pile of soft towels to her guest. "I've got a spare nightdress and dressing gown that Jenny left when she went off to uni. They aren't your style, but may be easier than sorting your own stuff now."

"Thank you," said Susan with a smile of gratitude.

She crossed to the bathroom and turned the shower on. While she waited for the warm water to come through, she decided to make use of an actual, and (most importantly) private lavatory, before she showered and washed her hair as quickly as possible.

When she had towelled herself off, Susan brushed her hair and slipped on the nightshirt which Viv had given her. She managed to come to terms with its vivid pinkness, but when she looked at herself in the mirror, she realised it had 'Princess' written in sparkling letters across the chest. No wonder Jenny left it behind, she probably last wore it when she was fourteen! Susan snorted derisively at her own reflection, and pulled on the matching pink bathrobe. She hated to admit it, but it was magnificently comfortable and soothing to her skin.

As she entered the kitchen, she thought she spotted a conspiratorial smile and wink between the two older women. That was soon forgotten, however, when Vivian gestured to a plate of lasagne and a glass of wine which had been set for her.

As the ladies made their way onto the second bottle, Susan was persuaded to give an account of her humiliating experience of that afternoon. When she described the place where it happened, Vivian laughed and told them that it was only a few minutes' drive from the house. They realised they had been driving in circles for literally hours.

"All these country lanes look alike!" Marian asserted, to justify herself.

"If you say so," said Viv with a cheeky wink to Susan. "What did this mysterious cyclist look like, then?"

Susan gave a pretty good description of Luke and followed up with, "Still, I expect I'll never have to see him again."

Vivian said nothing and smiled to herself as she sipped her wine.

* * *

Later that evening, the three women relaxed in Vivian's living room, patio doors open onto the garden, letting in the dusky sunlight and a multitude of sweet floral scents. A bumble bee buzzed lazily in, made a complete circuit of the room and exited, as if highly unimpressed by the tasteful décor. The apian gate crasher spurred Vivian into action, as she closed the doors.

"All the bugs are going to start getting attracted by the light," she commented.

Susan was sitting on the sofa next to her mother, with her feet curled up under the soft pink fluffiness of her dressing gown, and with her head resting on her mum's shoulder.

"Thanks again for a lovely dinner," said Marian, as Vivian flopped back into a comfortable armchair and lit a cigarette.

"Do either of you want one?" she asked, holding out the packet.

Mother and daughter both declined, and the conversation turned to old times.

Marian and Vivian had known each other ever since they worked together as Saturday girls in a high-street fashion chain store. After school, Vivian had gone to university and then a career in marketing, while Marian had worked in a bank. When she had fallen pregnant with Susan, she left the bank to be a full-time mum, while a wealthy husband and a well-paid profession meant Viv would employ nannies and au pairs to look after Jenny. Both the women had married within a year of one another, each had been the other's bridesmaid, and they spent so much time together (even going on joint holidays almost every year) that their little girls grew up calling them aunts.

Sadly, Vivian's husband had died a few short years ago, affecting her so deeply that she sold her house in the city and moved to the countryside. Susan's father had walked out when she was eight years old; Marian had taken a part-time receptionist's job, but Vivian had often helped her friend with small loans and generally subsidised their vacations together.

There were many old times to talk about, and the two older women chatted like best friends do. Susan became quieter and quieter, until she started to snore. Her mother gave her a little nudge.

"Susie," she said softly, "I think maybe you'd be happier in bed."

Mumbling a half apology, half thank you, Susan made her way upstairs, summoned the energy to clean her teeth and then rolled into bed and a deep sleep.

Downstairs, the ladies chatted.

"Viv, being here means so much to me," said Marian, "I don't know what else I would have done. I'm so relieved to get Susie away from that place and all the bad memories."

"You're always welcome here, bird, you know that," Vivian responded, "but you must tell me what happened. Your phone call last week was... well, terrifying."

"Well, I've really messed up these last twelve months," Marian explained. "I, well we, moved in with Bob – did you meet him?"

"Yes, at that Christmas do we both got invited to."

"Oh, yeah. Well, that was where the problems started really. Remember how drunk Bob got? Well, it turned out that he wasn't a nice guy when on the booze. He shouted and ranted when we got home that night. Fortunately, Susie came home and that seemed to break the tension. Well, after that, he seemed to drink more and more, and then one day I thought he was going to hit me. We waited till he fell asleep and I packed some suitcases, and we went to a B&B. I left him a note saying he needed to get help for his drinking. About a week later, I got a text asking me to come over and saying he had turned over a new leaf. When I got to the house, he had piled all our stuff in the front garden – when he saw me, he chucked a match on it and the whole lot went up in flames; I guess he must have used petrol. I saw the look on his face, left and didn't look back."

Vivian sat, open mouthed.

"I did hear," continued Marian, "that he had managed to burn himself too.

His hands, I think. Look, it's over now, but after all that Susie went through before…"

She tailed off and rummaged in her bag for a tissue.

Vivian silently walked over and held her dear friend in her arms, and Marian finally gave in to the tears.

Chapter 3

Susan woke from a dream which was replaying her ambush of an innocent cyclist. She lay silently for a while, listening to her mother's heavy breathing from across the room. She hadn't heard her come to bed, so her mum had probably stayed up talking half the night. The room was already quite warm from the morning sunshine, so she slipped lightly from the bed and crept out, slipped across the passage to use the bathroom, and then tip-toed downstairs to the kitchen.

While she had a glass of apple juice and small yoghurt she found in the fridge, Susan noticed the plates from the night before had not been washed up. She filled the sink with hot water and bubbles and set to work on the glasses, crockery and cutlery, leaving them to dry on the draining board.

As she worked, Susan was gazing out of the kitchen window at the lovely cherry trees; in the distance, she could see the figure of a young man weeding one of the flower beds. However, as she finished the washing-up, he disappeared from view, behind the cream-rendered house.

She slipped off the rubber gloves she had been wearing and dabbed her moist hands on the sides of her nightdress. She wandered over to the stable door, slid the top bolts back, and swung the upper half open. As Susan basked in the sunshine, some of the cherry blossom caught on the breeze and drifted over to anoint her; she brushed the petals from her dark, wavy hair and closed her eyes, allowing her senses to revel in the moment.

"Good morning, Your Highness," said a male voice. Her eyes popped open, to see the young man she had been watching earlier, this time only a few feet away. Slightly built and only a little taller than she was, he was wearing jeans and a t-shirt, and held a garden spade and fork in each hand. He had an impish grin on his face, but his large brown eyes were gentle and friendly.

Susan was, however, confused by what he had said. Why would he call her 'Your Highness?' Her face must have betrayed her confusion, because he gestured to her nightgown and she instantly recalled the sparkling 'Princess' logo written across the front.

"Good morning, gentle knight," she said, joining in with the spirit of his joke. "Is this your house?" She gestured to The Cherries.

"No, I'm just staying here for a while."

He held out his hand.

"My name is Dominic."

Susan shook his hand.

"I'm Susan. I've come down with my mum to stay for a while."

"It will be nice to have someone younger round here. Luke, the guy who owns this place, is a great guy, he's done so much to help me, but he's a bit… old fashioned, if you know what I mean?"

Susan wasn't sure she did know what he meant, but she nodded anyway. She doubted that Dominic was more than seventeen, and those two or three years seemed like a gulf of wisdom and experience.

"So, what brought you here?" she asked, causing Dominic to look a little uncomfortable.

"Problems at school. Bullying," he replied. "You know. My family couldn't help and the school didn't do anything, so Luke offered to let me move here and tutor me for my exams. He doesn't ask for anything, so I like to help in the garden to thank him. Not that I mind, because I'm planning on going to agricultural college next year, so it's all good experience."

"That's cool," Susan enthused. "Luke sounds like a good bloke."

"He is," Dominic affirmed, nodding. "He's the only real friend I've ever had, I think. I hope you'll get to meet him soon. Normally he'd be up and about right now, but he said something about a lie-in yesterday. He was sore as hell last night. Came off his bike when he was cycling home – he said he got distracted by something and rode into the hedge."

Susan simultaneously felt her heart plunge and her throat dry up. She struggled to say something, but could not find the breath.

She was rescued by Vivian's sudden arrival in the kitchen.

"Good morning, Dominic!" the older woman said, padding to stand beside Susan at the door. "Fancy a cuppa?"

"Tempting, Viv, very tempting, but I want to get the front bed tidied before Luke gets up. I'll take you up on it soon though. Nice to meet you, Susan," said

Dominic, before walking away past the cherry trees, raising his spade in salute. "Good bye, Your Highness," he called over his shoulder.

Susan waved feebly.

"Oh God, oh God, oh my good God!" Susan exclaimed as soon as he was out of earshot. She buried her head into Vivian's shoulder and groaned, trying to escape the acute embarrassment tearing every fibre of her body apart.

"What is it, pet?" asked Vivian, who already had a pretty good idea of the cause of Susan's discomfort.

Susan looked at her with wide eyes.

"The man who owns the house next door…"

"You mean Luke?" Vivian led her.

"Yes, Luke... I think… he… he is the man I made fall off his bike."

The last half of the sentence was blurted out in such a strangled squeal that it made Vivian give a phlegmy chuckle of the type common to many heavy smokers.

"If there is a man in the world who will keep your secret, it is Luke," she reassured Susan. "Don't worry, sweetie, it's a case of least said, soonest mended. We've all done embarrassing things."

"Not like this," Susan countered.

"Yeah? How about when I thought I was making a dirty phone call from the office to my husband but had forgotten to press nine for an outside line. I'd ended up dialling the post room, and they answer on speakerphone. Of course, they let me get halfway through my sexy routine, before I heard them laughing. I had to put up with a leering smile every day when they brought the post for two years until I could change jobs. Honestly, I still wake up at nights in a cold sweat."

"Seriously, Aunty Viv? Wow!" said Susan, visibly brightening.

"Don't tell anyone. I've never spoken to anyone else about it," Vivian whispered. "Now I need a coffee and some breakfast. Ooh! You've washed up. I hope you stay for ever. Though there is a dishwasher right next to the sink…"

* * *

Dominic came in from the garden to find Luke rustling up a batch of scrambled eggs, grilled bacon and lightly fried tomatoes with mushrooms.

"That smells amazing! Let me wash the dirt off and I'll be through."

Luke piled the food on to two plates, which he placed on the kitchen table, accompanied by a rack of toast, butter, a jar of local honey and two large mugs of tea.

They munched through their meal saying very little, Dominic occasionally scrolling down the newsfeed on his smartphone and Luke revisiting the last few unsolved crossword clues on yesterday's paper.

"I met the girl that's staying with Viv when I was outside earlier. She and her mum are going to be there for a while. She seemed nice. A bit awkward, if you know what I mean, but really sweet."

Luke kept his focus on the crossword, feigning disinterest.

"Did she have a name?" he asked, as if it were a trifling detail.

"The girl? Susan," Dominic responded, and he recounted the details of their meeting.

The subject changed to the weather, and both men agreed that the fine spell they'd been having should last into the following week. Dominic discussed plans for the garden, and Luke nodded approvingly at the young man's ideas.

When they'd cleared away after breakfast, Luke picked up a pair of thick gardening gloves and secateurs and headed outside, down a path running by the back lawn to his little rose garden. He studied the bushes carefully, selecting some of the finest stems and cutting them to form a glorious bouquet, of white, pink and yellow flowers.

Returning to the kitchen, he spread the newspaper on the table and laid the roses on it. Quickly and skilfully, he worked up and down each stem, clipping the thorns away. A rummage in a kitchen unit's drawers produced a ball of coloured twine, from which he cut a length that he then used to hold the finished bunch of flowers together.

He glanced at his watch and felt confident that his neighbours would be up and dressed by that time.

Luke strode across the courtyard and, as he approached Vivian's house, he saw the upper part of her stable door was open and he could hear the voices of the three women chatting.

"Knock-knock," he called out. Vivian was sitting facing the door and gave him a smile. Marian, sitting next to her, looked up and her jaw dropped open. Susan's back was to him, but she turned to see who the caller was and immediately turned beetroot red.

"Luke! Hello!" cried Vivian. "So glad you've popped by. Girls, this is my hunky neighbour, Luke. Luke, this is my best friend in the world, Marian, and her gorgeous daughter, Susan." She paused a moment and added, "But I think you all may already know each other?"

"Welcome to our little piece of paradise," he said, holding out the flowers. The elder women looked at Susan, who knew with excruciating certainty that, as she was closest to the door, she should take the bouquet. She did so with as much grace as she could muster.

"Thank you," she said, "they are beautiful." She meant it.

"I'm pleased you like them," said Luke, with sincerity. "Dominic mentioned that a beautiful princess was staying next door, so flowers seemed appropriate."

The words sat a little awkwardly, particularly with Susan, who wrongly assumed them to be sarcastic.

"Look, I'm sure you're busy," Luke continued, "but I wondered if you three ladies would care to join Dominic and me for one of our famous picnics on Saturday. Please say yes."

"We'd love to!" said Vivian before the others could answer.

"Then it is settled," he was gratified to say. "And please don't be a stranger in the meantime. The kettle is always boiling at The Cherries! I've got to get to work now, but pop over any time. Bye."

"Bye," the three ladies chorused after him as he departed.

"There are vases in the hall cupboard," said Vivian, "I think we are going to need at least two for that bunch."

Susan trotted off to fetch them.

Marian looked at Vivian.

"Blimey, Viv, you kept him a bit quiet."

"He's a bit young for us, darlin'," retorted Vivian, with a naughty smile. "I didn't have you down as a cougar."

"I am off men for a while," Marian replied. "So how old is he?"

"Not sure. Mid-thirties at most. I know he moved down here about eighteen months before I did. The Cherries was in a terrible state, I'm told, and he spent a fortune having it refurbished and this place done up too. Then he sold it to me. Before that, I think he worked in the city, a stockbroker or something. I'm not sure what he does now, but I think it is some sort of internet business. He works from home, that much I know."

Susan was back in the room, arranging the flowers in three medium sized vases she had found.

"You should definitely have one of those vases in your room, Susie," Vivian told her, "I think he's taken a bit of a shine to you."

"Don't be silly, Auntie," Susan admonished.

"I'm good at spotting these things," Vivian insisted.

Marian jumped slightly as her phone chimed to announce the arrival of a text.

"Blast!" she exclaimed. "Somehow I've missed a call from an agency. I must have been out of signal."

"It is patchy round here," Vivian advised. "Go and call them on the landline. But look here, honey, you don't need to rush. Have a bit of a holiday first. You know you're fine here for as long as you want."

"I know, Viv, but I've always paid my own way," Marian said, the firmness in her voice betraying a deep-set desire to maintain what little pride and independence she could, now that years of managing alone had culminated in her failure and humiliation. "I'll relax when I've found something."

She hurried from the room to make her call.

After a few minutes, Susan said quietly, "Please, Auntie Viv, don't tease me. I had more than enough of that at school."

"Tease you, honey?" Vivian responded in surprise. "Sorry, I don't know what you mean."

"You and Luke," Susan whispered, "you know, calling me gorgeous and beautiful. You know it's not true. So please don't."

"Susie… you're a lovely looking girl," Vivian replied. "Please don't put yourself down."

"I'M NOT!" spat Susan, flaring up. "I'm pale and scrawny, my mouth is crooked, and my hair is wrong. It's alright for you, you always look amazing. Mum too. I'm a freak."

"You most certainly are not!" the older woman responded hotly. "Yes, you're skinny, but lots of people are. You'll be glad of those genes after a couple of decades and a kid or two. Believe me, most of my life is a battle against gravity. As to a crooked mouth, I'd call it a cute smile. Luke obviously thinks you look nice, and you don't even wear makeup!"

"He was just being sarcastic." Susan's voice was small. "I just want to be invisible." Tears started to flow down her cheeks. "Please…," she sounded strangled, "… just…"

Susan ran from the room to her bed and wept, her knees curled up to her chest, her body convulsing with the sobs.

Vivian stood to go after her, but Marian appeared in the door and stopped her.

"Leave her," she whispered, "I've tried to get through to her so many times. Leave her. It breaks my heart."

"How the hell did she get that terrible self-image?" Vivian asked, also keeping her voice low. "She was so confident when she was little."

"She was, until she was about fourteen. Then the bullying at school started. Not like it was in our day. It was constant, grinding her down. At school from the minute she got in, at home on bloody social media and email – the viciousness was terrible. I saw some of the messages. Using words that we never would. Telling her she was ugly, that she would be better dead, that no boy would ever touch her."

"Oh, poor Susie," Vivian gasped, "I never knew."

"It all came to a head in sixth form," Marian continued. "She'd been keeping up with her swimming, you know how good she was, and some girl managed to sneak a photo of her changing. It was shared around the school and on some online group they were all on and the boys were asked to rate her out of ten. They all hated her, so you don't need to guess what they said. Finally, someone printed out the photo and posted it on the school message board with SKANK scrawled over it. At least that prompted the school to take some action, but it was too little too late. The bullies won. She flunked her exams and dropped out. They broke her."

Vivian was crying. "Then we shall fix her," she resolved.

Marian said nothing, but touched her friend's shoulder and squeezed. She picked up a vase of roses and carried it upstairs to the bedroom she shared with Susan. She placed the spray of flowers on a small table under the window, where Susan would be able to see them from her bed. She then perched on the mattress next to her daughter, who was now lying curled up staring at the wall. She stroked Susan's hair and leant down to kiss a tear-dampened cheek. Marian sat holding her little girl's hand in silence, until Vivian called upstairs that lunch was ready.

Chapter 4

Dominic placed two large bowls of vegetable soup on the kitchen table, while Luke fished two cans of cola from the fridge. They sat at opposite sides of the table. Before eating, Luke paused and closed his eyes, giving silent thanks for the meal; Dominic did not pray, but did maintain a respectful silence.

Opening his eyes, the older man picked up a bread knife from the table, hacked a large wedge of bread from the farmhouse loaf sitting between them, and dunked an end of it into his soup. Dominic followed suit, and the two friends munched in silence, until Luke said,

"How is your maths assignment coming on?"

"Not bad," Dominic replied. "Complex numbers are a bit confusing at first, but I'm getting there."

"I'm sure. Want me to look over it later?"

"Please."

"No problem," Luke said. "Would you be able to give me a hand with something in the garage after lunch? I'm trying to find a set of six small oval picture frames and I can't remember where I put them. They're in good nick and would be perfect for something I have in mind that I've promised Reverend June."

"Sure," replied the younger man. "I've been meaning to ask if you'd like me to tidy up in there anyway. It has got a bit messy lately."

When they'd finished their meal, Luke and Dominic went into the garage at the side of the house and began to sort the plastic crates piled against the back wall.

"Hello, boys," called Vivian from the door, "I thought I could hear you."

"Hi, Viv," said Luke, while Dominic waved from a cloud of dust that he had managed to disturb.

"Can you spare me a few minutes, Dominic?" Vivian asked.

Luke suddenly gave a cry of triumph.

"Found them!" He fished the small frames from the depths of a blue crate.

"Looks like you can have me for as long as you like," said Dominic.

Leaving Luke inspecting his haul with a satisfied smile on his face, the woman and young man strolled out of the garage and into the back garden to sit on a small stone bench in the shade of a silver birch.

"Dominic," Vivian began, "I want to ask you a favour and it won't be easy for you."

"Go on," was the nervous reply.

"Look, we've had tons of chats, you and me, about how bad school was for you and what happened to you there. Well, I've just heard that Susie had an even worse time. That poor girl has been emotionally tortured. Can you talk to her? You may be the only one who could really understand."

Dominic looked conflicted.

"I'd like to help," he said, his pain-filled sincerity unmistakeable, "but I don't know how I'd feel about dragging that all back up."

Vivian sat silently. Since the conversation with Marian that morning, she had been going through a range of emotions. Rage at the tormenters. Pity for Susan. Frustration with herself. Exasperation with Marian that she had never said anything about it before.

Now she just felt a steely resolve to help Susan. After her husband, Tony, had passed away, Marian had been her rock and Susan had been a constant support to her and to Jenny. She remembered the beautiful picture Susan had painted for them both – Jenny had it hanging in her bedroom. That the girl could have done that when suffering at the hands of those bullies...

Rage bubbled inside Vivian again, but only for an instant. One of the many things Tony had done for her was to have a generous life insurance policy, so she was only fifty and would never have to work again, though she still did a little marketing consultancy, just for interest. Well, she was in the perfect place to help the only two people she loved, other than her own daughter. She just needed to find a way.

All this went through her head, whilst sitting silently next to Dominic.

"Sorry," he mumbled, barely audibly.

Vivian snapped back to the here and now.

"Look, Dominic," she said smartly, "it was wrong of me to ask. Please don't worry about it. Just be a friend to Susie. Please can you be a friend to her?"

"That I can do," he confidently assured her.

Vivian sniffed and realised that she had been crying subtle tears, that a teenager would not spot. She pulled a tissue from the sleeve of her blouse and dabbed below her eyes and nose.

She patted his hand twice and stood up, full of resolve.

"That's all anyone could ask, lad. Bless you."

* * *

"I've got an interview!" announced Marian as Vivian came back home. "I've just had an email from the agency. It's at a local solicitors' needing maternity cover for a receptionist. Possibility of permanent if all goes well. The agency says that they aren't interviewing anyone else, so the job should be mine."

"Well done, bird!" shouted Vivian, giving her friend a hug. Susan came charging into the room, and Marian broke her embrace with Vivian and turned to her daughter.

"Susie, I've –" begun Marian.

"I know, Mum, I heard! You're a-ma-zing." Susan flung her arms around her mother and gave her a huge squeeze. "It's going to get better, I know it is," she whispered.

"The pay is pretty good, not stellar, but I'll be able to contribute to your costs, Viv, until I get together enough for a deposit on a place for me and Susie," Marian said, pleased to feel that she could pay her way.

"And I won't take a penny of it!" was Vivian's stern response. "You two are family and your money's not good here. I'm not sure I ever want either of you to go. Please don't mention it again, bird, there's a dear. When's the interview?"

"Half four this afternoon. Look at the time! I'd better get my skates on!" Marian was halfway up the stairs by the time she'd finished the last sentence.

Susan stood looking at the space her mother had occupied just a few seconds beforehand, lost in her thoughts. Then she looked at Vivian.

"Fancy a cuppa?" the girl asked.

"You are a star, Susie."

"Got time for a cuppa before you go, Ma?" Susan called up the stairs. There was a muffled "no" from the bedroom.

"I knew she wouldn't. She'd be worried she'd need a wee halfway through the interview."

"Oh, Susie, that's a bit mean."

"No, it's true," Susan insisted. "You know she's always been like it."

"Well, maybe," Vivian said, winking.

Susan filled the kettle and got a couple of mugs from the cupboard.

"You've been so generous to mum and me."

"You're family."

For a moment, Susan wanted to press on, to make Vivian realise how much her kindness meant to them, but she realised, as her mother had done, that thanks were unnecessary, and words were often hollow to a woman who valued action over rhetoric.

"I guess I should be looking for a job too," she said instead, in a resigned voice.

"There is no rush, Susie. Rest a bit, eh?"

"We need the money," Susan thought out loud, "I think Bob got Mum into quite a bit of debt. I want to help. I'm just not qualified for anything."

"Well," Vivian said tentatively, "I know a couple that run a small holiday camp site and they are always looking for cleaners for the self-catering static caravans. Pay isn't great, but you'd be through by early afternoon and it is only about ten minutes' walk from here. Want me to give them a call?"

"Yes please!"

Vivian fished a large, tatty black leather address book from a kitchen drawer and wandered off to make the call. Susan hugged herself.

"Everything is going to be alright from now on," she whispered, "please, God."

* * *

The following day was Friday. Dominic was mowing the lawn in the front garden of The Cherries, when he noticed a hubbub of activity at the front of the neighbour's house. Vivian was showing a piece of paper to Susan, waving her arms in a variety of directions, while the girl looked increasingly perplexed. Marian was running between her car and the house, with a flustered look on her face; then she seemed to lie down on the back seat of her Citroen, feet sticking out the door, before popping back up again with a look of triumph and trotting back into the house.

Susan was now in sole possession of the piece of paper, which she stared at with incomprehension, while Vivian climbed into her middle-aged Audi cabriolet and started the engine. The roof of the car started to slide backwards and then folded neatly into the rear, just as Marian came out of the house and flopped into the passenger seat. The two old friends drove off, with waves and blown kisses to Susan and a shout of, "Good luck." Then Vivian spotted Dominic and gave her horn a toot, which she followed up with another blown kiss, just for him.

Dominic waved to the receding form of the car, before it rounded the corner of the lane with a hint of tyre squeal. He turned off the lawnmower's engine and cut across the grass to intercept Susan, who was now walking past, still gazing at the sheet of A4.

"Morning!" called Dominic, in the hope of slowing her down to make it easier to catch her. Susan paused, and looked up, smiling.

"Hiya," she said.

"Looks like there was a bit of activity going on back there," he observed. "Everything OK?"

"Yes. It's good really. Mum had an interview for a job yesterday and got offered it there and then. She starts on Monday, so she and Viv have gone into town to buy some work clothes."

"That's great news!" he enthused.

"Yeah, thanks. Well, they were about to leave when mum realised she couldn't find her phone, so she's been looking everywhere for it. She found it under the front seat of her car just before they left."

"Ha! My dad's the same with his phone." Dominic paused, thinking momentarily about his father and how he missed him. "Still, where are you off to?"

"I'm going to a place called The Cedars Holiday Park, but I don't know where it is," Susan explained, "I've got an interview for a part-time job there, but Viv's drawn a map and it doesn't make any sense. I don't suppose you know how to get there?"

"I do. Hand me the map," he said. Susan passed the paper to Dominic. After a few moments studying it, he offered, "Tell you what, the lawn can wait. Give me a moment and I'll be right with you."

He jogged back to the house and picked up his phone from the worktop and then went through to the back garden, where Luke was in a small workshop, fiddling around with the oval picture frames.

"I'm just taking Susan to show her where The Cedars is. She's got an interview there," Dominic told him, "I'll come right back."

"Don't hurry," replied Luke, not looking up from his work. "Wait for her to finish, if you like. It's harder to get back from there than it is to find it, I think."

"OK. See you in a while."

"Cheers," said Luke, but Dominic was already halfway across the garden.

He joined Susan and they walked up the lane in the morning sunshine, chatting idly about how lovely it was there and what kinds of places they had previously lived in. After a little over five minutes, they arrived at The Cedars and found a large wooden prefab hut, which had 'Site Office' written over the door. Dominic settled on a nearby hillock and fished his phone from his pocket.

"I'll wait for you here," he said, not looking up from the screen.

Susan made her way to the door and timidly pushed it open. Behind the counter was a tall, elegantly dressed black woman who was speaking to two guests who were checking out and paying their bill. Susan waited patiently for the couple to finish and leave.

"Hello – er – I've been told to ask for Tina," she said nervously.

"Well, you've found her," Tina replied, and Susan noticed her American accent for the first time.

"Hello, I'm Susan. Susan Jones. I've come about the part-time cleaning job."

Not feeling she was getting the etiquette right, she held out her hand.

"Nice to meet you, Susan, Susan Jones," Tina replied with a small wink, gently shaking the young woman's hand. "Sorry to tell you this, but I've got enough cleaners for the moment."

Susan looked crestfallen, but Tina continued,

"Don't look so worried, honey. I do still have a job going. It's only 5.30am to twelve though, Tuesday to Saturday. That's in the tourist season - there'll be less in the quiet periods."

"That would be fine. I'm grateful for any opportunity," Susan said emphatically, though inwardly cringing at having to get up so early.

"Well, here are the duties: open up in here, give it a bit of a tidy and vacuum round before me or my husband get down here at about six. Fresh coffee made, printer stocked up with paper, stuff like that. Then you'll need to print out check-in cards for the arrivals due that day. There's a small site shop selling food, groceries and stuff; you will need to stock the fridges with milk and put out the papers; both of those generally get delivered at about seven. Lastly, you'll need to walk around the site with a clipboard and make sure all the cars are accounted for – no unexpected guests and no moonlight flits without paying the bill. It's minimum wage, I'm afraid."

"Right," said a very overwhelmed Susan.

"Don't worry, you'll get properly trained and me and Jerry, he's my husband, will be here."

Tina sounded so reassuring, that Susan almost wanted to start there and then. Reaching into her handbag, Susan removed her CV, contained by a simple plastic presentation wallet, which she held out to Tina.

"Here is my CV," she said, "I have had some experience working in a supermarket."

Tina took the document and seemed to read it carefully. The truth of the matter was that she already intended to give Susan the job, as Vivian, whom she knew through Luke, had given a fulsome reference. What is more, the girl was very likeable, though the timid body language just made Tina want to mother her.

"Well, you seem to have what I'm looking for," she said with a broad smile. Susan's heart jumped.

"Come down here on Monday afternoon," continued Tina, "bring some ID, you know, passport or driving licence, and your national insurance number and we'll get you on the books and give you some initial training. Then you can start work proper on Tuesday. Sound good?"

"Amazing!" exclaimed Susan. "Thank you so much."

"You're welcome, honey."

A few seconds later, Susan was with Dominic and he was high-fiving her. The walk home seemed to fly by, but when they arrived, she realised that she had forgotten the spare key to Vivian's house.

"Don't worry about it," Dominic reassured her, "I think Luke may have one, as he keeps an eye on her place when she goes on holiday. Whatever, you are welcome to wait at The Cherries."

By this time, he had led her round to the side of the house and they entered by the kitchen door. Susan looked at the cosy room, with its oak cabinets and farmhouse table and smelt the welcoming aroma of freshly made coffee.

Seeming to read her mind, Dominic opened a cupboard and took down two mugs.

"Tea or coffee? Or we have juice," he asked.

"The coffee smells great, thanks," Susan replied.

"Good timing, young man!" Luke's voice boomed from the doorway into the hall. "Pour me one too, will you? I'd put it on for the vicar, but she's late. I expect she'll have some terrible excuse like visiting a sick parishioner." The comic irony in his voice made Susan smile, so she gave an appreciative chuckle.

Luke popped his head through the doorway.

"Hello!" he said when he spotted Susan. "I didn't realise we had a guest. Dominic, break out the custard creams!"

Dominic got a third cup from the cupboard and a packet of biscuits from another. He poured the coffee and placed the mugs on the table, with a small jug of cream and a bowl of demerara sugar.

They got their drinks to their likings, which included Susan taking three spoons of sugar for hers.

"Fancy a quick tour," Luke asked, "to see where I work?"

Susan assented and followed him into the hallway, which was a large space, with a high ceiling and a graceful curved staircase to the upper landing. Luke showed her a living room, which was furnished with two large, comfortable sofas either side of a coffee table, and a dining room, which contained an elegant long Regency mahogany dining table with eight chairs and a matching sideboard. Hanging on nearly every wall were old-fashioned paintings, etchings, maps and prints.

Then Luke opened another door.

"This is my sanctuary," he told her.

Susan walked into a long room, with a bow window at one end and patio doors at the other. All along the long wall facing her were floor to ceiling shelves, packed with all kinds of books. Some were of obvious antiquity, bound in leather of various colours, with fine gold letters glittering on their spines. Others were more modern books, a mixture of hardbacks and paperback, but all obviously loved. Bookshelves also ran on the opposite side of the room, interrupted by a marble fireplace, but these were only about half the height of the wall. Above them hung more beautiful old paintings and prints. Two high-backed wing chairs were placed either side of the fireplace, and a chaise longue was by the patio doors, near a large leather globe, showing the world as it was known in the 18th century. Close to the door where they were standing, in the bow window was a dark wood desk, with a green leather writing surface, upon which was an old-fashioned telephone, a fountain pen and ink bottle and, almost incongruously, a laptop computer.

"It's lovely," said Susan, "very you."

"I so hoped you'd think so," said Luke, walking to the far end of the room, where there was a second door, which he opened. Susan could see an artist's studio, with easels, drawing boards and various pictures in different states of completion.

"Oh! How wonderful!" she exclaimed, walking in. She picked up a small oil painting of a horse. "Did you paint this?"

"I did," he replied, "though I mainly specialise in birds."

"I like to draw and paint too, but nothing like this," said Susan.

"Then I hope you will consider this your studio too. It's all a matter of practice. What do you like to paint?"

"All sorts," she replied. "I wish I'd kept it up at school, as I've got no training."

"Then you'll have your own style. I'd love to see some of your work," Luke said, his interest clearly genuine.

"I'd be too embarrassed!" Susan objected.

"When you're ready." He did not want to pressure her.

"May I ask you a question?" said Susan to change the subject. "What do you do for a living?"

"I'm mainly a book dealer," he explained, "I co-own a specialist bookshop, but I don't go there very often, as I have a great business partner running it. Most of my business is done online though. I also sell some artwork through various galleries I deal with, including the occasional humble offering of my own."

Susan glanced at the laptop screen, which had a share trading site open.

"That looks rather complicated," she said, pointing to the computer.

"It really isn't. I used to work in the city and I still manage a small portfolio for myself."

"Were you a banker?" Susan asked.

"Not really. Just a trader in a stockbroker's. I promise I wasn't responsible for any financial Armageddon."

The doorbell rang.

"Ah!" declared Luke. "That will be the vicar."

Within a few moments, he was ushering the clergywoman in through the large black front door.

"Come in, come in!" he welcomed her. "Have you time for a coffee? We have a fresh brew in the kitchen."

Luke noticed Susan lingering, in hovering uncertainty by the study doorway.

"Let me introduce you to Susan," he said. "She and her mother are staying with my neighbour, Viv, for a while. Susan, this is Reverend June Leicester, the conscience of this rustic parish."

June shook Susan's hand.

"Lovely to meet you, Susan," she said warmly, and then, "conscience of this rustic parish? Oh, Luke, I think you're stuck in the 19th century!"

"I do hope so," he chuckled, "though that may be a bit modern for me. Now, how about that coffee?"

"Sounds lovely."

"I'm on it!" Dominic's voice drifted from the kitchen.

"Come into the study," said Luke and he followed the two ladies into the room. He picked a crisp cardboard box from the floor by the desk and laid its contents on the green leather. "What do you think?"

There were six small, gold, oval frames, each containing a delicate black and white image surrounded by an ivory mount.

"Last month, I picked some books up at auction and among them was a volume of Oliver Twist which had received quite a bit of damage," Luke told them. "It wasn't a particularly rare example and didn't warrant restoration, but the illustrations were rather fine reproductions of the Cruickshanks."

June noted that Susan looked a little confused, so she decided to spare the girl's blushes.

"What exactly is a Cruickshank?" she asked.

"Not what but who," Luke enthused. "He was a prolific illustrator and printmaker of the Victorian era. Wonderful stuff – you'll find a couple of his etchings hanging in the hallway.

"Anyway," he continued, "as I said, I thought they looked rather fine, so I removed the undamaged ones and framed them up. I thought you could auction them or raffle them, either individually, or as part of a set."

"They are great," said the vicar, "brilliant! Thank you so much!"

Susan stooped to look closer at the pictures.

"I thought so too," Luke responded to June, "I also have a decent copy of Aesop's Fables, which I thought may be nice and a sweet little volume of Pilgrims Progress, both of which you're very welcome to."

"Are you sure you can spare them?" June asked. "You've already been very generous."

"It's a good cause," he pointed out.

Luke packed the frames and books into the box. "I'll put this in the boot of your car, while you go and get that coffee," he said.

Susan and the vicar made their way into the kitchen.

"I hope you're settling in to the area," said June, "I'm quite new here myself, but most people have been very welcoming."

"Yes, thank you," replied Susan, "everyone has been very nice since we got here."

"Susan's got herself a nice little job down at The Cedars," chipped in Dominic, "lovely five-thirty starts every morning."

June grimaced and gave a little shudder. "I thought eight o'clock morning prayer was an early start. Don't worry though, Jerry and Tina are lovely people."

"Five-thirty in the morning!" exclaimed Luke, coming back in from putting the box in the car. "Totally uncivilised."

He paused to take a swig of coffee.

"June," he continued, "I've just noticed one of your tyres is looking rather deflated. I expect you've picked up a thorn or sharp stone on the road, or whacked one of those blasted potholes. Want me to give it a bit of a reflate to get you to the garage?"

"That's very kind of you," replied the vicar.

"I'm on it!" said Dominic and he bolted out the door.

"Thank you," she called after him, and then said to Luke, "he really is a great kid."

"He is," agreed Luke, gulping another mouthful of coffee, "I just wish he didn't feel he has to try so hard."

"I don't think he does," piped up Susan, causing the other two to stare at her, "I mean, I don't think he feels he has to. I think he does it because he wants to and because he likes you."

June looked at her with calm appreciation. "You're an astute young lady," she said.

The clock in the living room chimed the hour.

"Goodness!" exclaimed Luke. "I'd better organise some lunch. Would either of you care to join us?"

Susan nodded gratefully, not least because she had so few other options. June politely declined and went outside to see how Dominic was getting on with her tyre. A few minutes later, the sound of her car driving off drifted through the open door.

Dominic came back in.

"When I got a decent look at it, there was quite a bit of damage to the tyre," he told them, "I'm pretty sure she's hit a pothole and maybe damaged the rim. Anyway, I thought it easiest to swap it for the spare."

"Good plan," Luke's voice came muffled from the open refrigerator, from which he was extracting a selection of cheeses and pickles. He bolted outside for a few moments, leaving Susan alone, as Dominic had made his way through to the cloakroom to wash his hands.

Luke reappeared with freshly picked tomatoes and lettuce in his hands and a cucumber tucked under his arm.

"Ready for one of my famous cheese sandwiches?" he asked Susan while he washed the salad at the sink.

"Yes please."

"Blast!" Luke exclaimed, inspecting a large red apple he had taken from a fruit bowl. "I meant to ask Rev June to the picnic tomorrow. Dominic, drop her a text and ask her, will you?"

"What about her other half?"

"Of course, him too, but I'm pretty sure that he's working. She was telling me a while back that it's her first Saturday off in ages and he's busy the whole day."

He was now at a chopping board, slicing and dicing salad and cheese and bread, to various degrees.

"She's a great vicar, but she works too hard," he continued. "She looks after five churches in the area and is down a curate. She deserves a little break."

Soon after, Susan was presented with a plate which was supporting the largest, most elaborate and ultimately most delicious cheese sandwich and side salad she had ever experienced. Yet, she somehow found the room to force down a large slab of home-made chocolate cake as dessert.

After lunch, Dominic's phone announced a text from the vicar, accepting the invitation to join the picnic the next day. Then he left to finish the gardening that he had interrupted earlier in the morning.

Luke put two large pans on the hob and began to boil eggs.

"For the picnic," he explained.

"Can I do anything to help?" offered Susan.

"No, thank you," he replied firmly, "it is all top secret."

"Then let me wash up the lunch things," she insisted.

Luke sensed that there was little point in arguing, and thanked her. He bustled about the kitchen, while she cleaned the dishes, and they enjoyed silent companionship until he broke the silence.

"I'd love to see some of your pictures sometime."

Susan paused.

"I haven't any left," she replied uncertainly, "they're destroyed."

As she stood at the sink, she sensed Luke looking at her. Without knowing why, she suddenly started to tell him, a man she had known for less than a day, all her recent problems. Of her mother's drunken, destructive boyfriend, of failing her exams, and just a little about the school bullying (that topic was still too sore and private).

"I'm so sorry," sympathised Luke, "but I'm a great believer in new beginnings. You must have great strength to have endured all that, and you can carry that strength into your new life. I admire you and your mother hugely."

Susan had now long since finished the washing-up and turned around to face him. She was leaning back against the sink with her hands behind her. Luke saw the light from the window passing through the loose strands of dark hair on her head, crowning her with a golden halo.

"I'm glad you've come here," he said.

"I'm glad we came," she responded.

They heard the roar of an engine and looked out of the window to see Vivian and Marian pull up and get out of the car. The two women proceeded to take a large number of bags from the boot, all of which had major high street fashion brands on them.

"Thanks for having me!" Susan called to Luke, as she darted out of the door and ran to greet them.

"Good grief, Mum!" she exclaimed when she saw just how many bags they had. "How much did you buy?"

Marian waved two of the bags at her daughter.

"These are mine. The rest, Vivian got carried away with. They had some nice leggings on sale, which I picked up for you, by the way."

"Thanks, Mum," said Susan brightly, "they'll be good for work."

Susan took some of the load from her mother and Viv, and the three women entered the house, bags knocking against the doorframe.

"Oh, yes!" said Vivian. "How did the interview go?"

"I got the job," Susan told her. "Early starts, but I'm sure I'll cope. I start next week."

"Wonderful!" exclaimed her honorary aunt. "We'll pop a bottle of bubbly tonight to celebrate."

* * *

Saturday morning arrived, with warm, bright sunshine and the hint of a cooling breeze. Marian came downstairs to the kitchen. She could hear Susan in the shower upstairs. Two cigarette butts in an ashtray and an empty coffee cup by the sink told her that Vivian was up too.

Kettle on and teabag in cup, she poured some muesli into a bowl and added milk. She glanced at Vivian's packet of cigarettes and lighter, which were sitting on the kitchen counter. Temptation came over her to have a sneaky smoke and her hand reached out to the packet.

"Mum, what are you doing?" Susan interrupted her. Marian turned to see her daughter standing in the doorway, in the pink dressing gown and running a towel down her long dark hair.

"I gave up the day I knew I was pregnant with you, Susie. Twenty years ago, and I still fancy one," she replied wistfully. "Thanks for saving me from myself."

Susan trotted over to her and kissed her cheek.

"Pour me a cuppa and your secret is safe," she whispered.

"Secrets? What secrets?" Vivian asked from the doorway. Marian and Susan jumped and turned to see her waft gracefully across the kitchen to scoop up the cigarettes and lighter from the counter. She wore a cream dress, with a large but delicate floral print, and a stylish wide-brimmed hat to match. Only her shoes suggested that she was going to anywhere but Royal Ascot, as they implied an element of practicality.

"Crikey, Viv, are you going to a wedding?" asked Marian.

"No, bird, it's for the picnic. Luke always puts on a special show."

"Viv, I haven't got anything like that. You know that," Marian exclaimed, waving her hand down the front of her simple ensemble, being a pair of jeans and a pale blue t-shirt. She sensed a whimper from her daughter beside her. "Neither has Susie."

"Yes," Susan added, "I was just going to wear leggings and a long t-shirt."

Vivian looked at Marian.

"Sorry, doll, I didn't think," she apologised. "Do you want to look through my wardrobe to see if there is anything suitable?"

Marian hovered for a moment of indecision, but nodded and trotted upstairs.

"You're welcome to look through Jenny's stuff. She had some lovely outfits she didn't take with her," Vivian offered Susan.

With a face like a schoolchild being told they had an extra double maths lesson, Susan made her way upstairs to Vivian's daughter's room. There she flapped through the assortment of outfits hanging neatly in the wardrobe.

Marian entered the room, wearing a simple blue dress speckled with small gold dots. She put her arm across her daughter's shoulders and looked at the clothes.

"That one is rather nice," she said, pointing to a pastel print summer dress.

"Too pretty for me," muttered Susan.

Marian sensed the potential for a panic attack and decided to take firm action. She spied a simple yellow long thick-cotton top with a high circle neckline.

"Slip this on with your white leggings and I think you'll be fine. Very anonymous."

Susan brightened at the suggestion, and slipped off her dressing gown while Marian took the top from its hanger. Susan pulled it over her head and let it fall down her slender body; she was a few inches shorter than Jenny, so it came to her mid-thigh. She looked at her reflection in the mirror as Marian peered over her shoulder.

"Looks nice," said the mother.

Susan picked up a pair of canvas lace-up pumps from the shoe rack in the wardrobe and disappeared into her own bedroom to put on her leggings, while Marian went back downstairs to talk to Vivian.

"Bloody hell, that looks better on you than it does on me," drifted upstairs.

Within a few minutes, Susan was in the kitchen.

"I'd forgotten Jenny had that top." Vivian's voice was upbeat. "You look very presentable. I've got just the thing to finish it off."

After a brief hunting expedition, she returned with a large straw hat, with a band of yellow ribbon attached.

"Very nice," she remarked, putting it on Susan's head, no easy feat as the girl was in the process of tying her drying hair into her usual ponytail. Vivian picked her lit cigarette from its resting point in the ashtray and drew on it, inhaling deeply. After a few seconds, she exhaled, two long streams of smoke jetting from her nostrils. She saw the other women's expressions of restrained forbearance.

"Filthy habit," she muttered apologetically.

"It's fine, Aunty Viv," Susan reassured her, kissing her lightly on the cheek and inhaling her familiar scent of Chanel mixed with smoke, "thank you for the hat."

Marian looked out of the window.

"A red car is pulling up outside The Cherries," she remarked. Susan peered past her.

"That's the vicar, June," she told her mother. "She's very nice. She's coming today too."

* * *

June got out of her car and made her way to the entrance to The Cherries. She was wearing a dark patterned blouse, with a white skirt, a matching linen hat and tennis shoes. Not one inch of her looked like a vicar, which was a rare occasion for her – not so much a liberation, for she loved her dog collar as her clerical badge of office, but rather a relief, offering some time for anonymity and uniformity with everyone else.

"June!" hailed Luke, emerging from the house like a force of nature. "I'm so glad you could make it!" Then he paused to look at her. "Crikey, you scrub up alright in civvies," he said, feigning a sly wink. "Does that husband of yours let you out looking so unprofessional?"

"I am a modern, liberated woman," she replied in mock approbation. "He has no say in the matter. Besides, he's got a wedding today, so he's no idea where I am."

June's husband Peter was also a local vicar. They had met at theological college (he was in his final year, when she was in her first) and been ordained within a few years of one another. Now they had almost adjoining parishes, though his furthest church was a good forty minutes' drive from the vicarage they shared.

"His loss is our gain," said Luke.

"You look rather smart yourself," she remarked. His six-foot frame was sporting a light linen suit, with waistcoat, a white shirt, and a crimson and gold cravat. With his straight back and neatly combed dark hair, he looked like a dashing example of a 1930s film star.

"Why thank you, madam," he responded. "Would you be happy to go and fetch the ladies from next door, while I get Dominic?"

"Um... do you think I could use your loo first?" she semi-whispered to cover her typical British awkwardness.

"Of course. Let's switch jobs," he replied. As she made her way indoors, he strode across the courtyard to the barn and knocked on Vivian's kitchen door. It opened immediately and the three ladies inside joined him in the sunshine.

"Well, you all look very smart!" Luke declared, as Dominic joined them, sporting a white shirt with grey flannel trousers.

"We are going to have a short walk," Luke continued. "Would everyone be OK to carry something?"

They all nodded. Luke and Dominic then ferried into The Cherries and back out again, bringing folding camp chairs, two rolled picnic blankets and a small black backpack. Now joined by June, the women distributed these items between themselves, while Luke and Dominic vanished one last time. Soon they emerged carrying a large picnic basket between them, strapped to the top of which was a second, only very slightly smaller, one.

"Rethinking not taking a car?" wheezed Dominic as they lowered their load to enable him to lock the door to the house.

"It will be lighter on the way back," reasoned Luke, as he adjusted the strap of a leather messenger bag which was slung over his shoulder.

Dominic stared at him.

"It will also be uphill most of the way," he stated. But he said no more as they once again lifted their burden.

The party made their way down a small pathway that ran between hedgerows marking the boundaries of the fields behind their houses. Soon, it began to drop away quite steeply in front of them, and, after about five more minutes, the sound of running water became audible. Finally, the pathway broadened onto the cool tree-lined banks of a gently flowing river where two rowing boats were tethered to a mooring post.

Luke stepped into the larger boat and he and Dominic heaved the picnic baskets in after him. Then Dominic jumped into the second craft, and the women handed their various items to him. He held out his hand and helped Vivian and Marian to join him on board. Susan and June joined Luke, and they cast off.

The two men were both experienced rowers and they made good progress along the cool waterway. Susan allowed a hand to skim lightly upon the surface of the river.

"I've never been in a boat before," she volunteered.

"Didn't they have a boating pond in your local park?" asked June.

"They didn't even have a park," said Susan, more in seriousness than humour.

A shriek from the other boat caused her to add, "I don't think Mum has, either."

"Are you OK?" bellowed Luke over his shoulder.

"Fine," Dominic replied. "We just had a little wobble, that's all."

"Landlubbers," Luke said lowly to his companions, with a wink.

Soon they arrived at a low jetty, which came out into the water from the opposite riverbank. Dominic moored beside it and leapt out, rather too readily, causing the boat to rock and its two occupants to squawk. He apologised and took the chairs, blankets and backpack from the ladies before assisting them on to the jetty. By this time, Luke had moored on the opposite side, so Dominic helped his passengers to disembark. Finally, the baskets were hauled out, followed by Luke.

The walk to the chosen picnic site was a little over fifteen minutes. Passing through the trees on the riverbank, they climbed a hill, through several fields and negotiated two awkward stiles with their burdens. Finally, they reached the brow and set up camp under the shady awning of a broad oak tree.

The view was magnificent. Undulating hills rippled away into the hazy blue distance, bright patches of yellow and green were lit by the brilliant sunshine, and white dot-like sheep could be seen in sprinkled patches over the fields.

The picnic rugs were laid out and the chairs set up. Then the hampers were opened. In their lids, small leather straps held in place patterned plates, matching china cups, white handled knives, forks and spoons, and a small cruet set. From the cavernous baskets emerged plastic boxes packed with assorted sandwiches (ham, cheese, salmon, sardine, cucumber, egg and cress, and beef and tomato), salads (mixed leaf, rice and sweetcorn, potato and chive, and pasta in tomato and basil) and cakes (chocolate, coffee and walnut, Victoria sponge, and a selection of scones). There were tubs of fresh clotted cream and jams for the scones, punnets of newly-picked strawberries, three bottles of Cabernet Sauvignon in thermal coolers and a carefully packaged box of wineglasses. From the black backpack, packs of paper napkins were produced, along with four large thermos flasks, containing tea and coffee.

Susan's and Marian's eyes had grown steadily larger as the feast was laid out. Vivian was relaxing in a chair with a satisfied smile on her face, while June gave little sporadic claps as new dishes were revealed.

"Before we start, please would you bless this meal, Reverend?" said Luke.

Susan's hand was halfway to a ham sandwich and froze. She thought she caught sight of Vivian's eyes rolling at the suggestion.

Thankfully, June was as eager as the rest to tuck in, so her blessing was blissfully short.

Luke, Vivian, Marian and June settled in chairs; Dominic and Susan sat on a blanket, but Marian soon slid off her chair and joined them. Wine glasses were filled and passed around, plates were handed out and soon piled with food. The atmosphere was one of great contentment – munching sounds were interspersed with general chitchat and light laughter.

As the last of the sandwiches had gone, the cake and scones demolished, and teas and coffees poured, Luke opened the messenger bag he had brought with him. He produced three books and began to read from them.

The first was The Wind in the Willows, and he read an extract telling of Ratty and Mole's own picnic trip. Then it was The Pickwick Papers – everyone laughed as Luke brought to life the picnic that the members of the Pickwick Club enjoyed in their friend, Mr Wardle's, carriage after a disastrous military review. Susan quietly marvelled at how Luke managed to create the different voices of the characters, perfectly catching the comic timing. If anyone had told her before that day that she would be laughing at Edwardian and Dickensian literature, she would have thought them ridiculous.

Luke's final readings were poetry from The Oxford Book of English Verse. Keats, Blake, Wordsworth and others were given an airing. The guests sat in the shade of the tree, letting the warmth flow over them as they drifted on a sea of romantic verse.

When he finished reading, the group sat in silence. Without warning or prompting, Marian began to sing; it was a beautiful, ancient Irish folk song which she later told them was called 'As she moved through the fair':

"I once had a sweet-heart, I loved her so well
I loved her far better than my tongue could tell
Her parents they slight me for my want of gear
So, adieu to you, Molly, since you are not here
I dreamed last night that my true love came in
So softly she came that her feet made no din
She stepped up to me and this she did say
It will not be long, love, till our wedding day
My young love said to me, my mother won't mind
And my father won't slight you for your lack of kind
And she went away from me and this she did say:
It will not be long now till our wedding day.

She went away from me and she moved through the fair
Where hand-slapping dealers' loud shouts rent the air
The sunlight around her did sparkle and play
Saying it will not be long now till our wedding day.
When dew falls on meadow and moths fill the night
When glow of the greesagh on hearth throws half-light
I'll slip from the casement and we'll run away
And it will not be long, love till our wedding day
According to promise at midnight he rose
But all that he found was the downloaded clothes
The sheets they lay empty 'twas plain for all to see
And out of the window with another went she."

Marian's voice was so sweet, so pure, that all sat in rapt silence. Susan looked at her mother with tears glistening in her eyes.

"Mum," she said so softly that she feared it may be inaudible, but anything louder would seem harsh after the enchanting melody, "that was beautiful. I never knew."

"It was a song my grandmother used to sing with me as I sat in her kitchen shelling peas," Marian explained.

"That's it!" Vivian interjected with sudden inspiration. "There is an open mike night at The Bull, the local pub, next week. You are coming with me, no arguments, darling. If nothing else, we can rock some ABBA together!"

The spell was broken and laughter broke out once more.

As the afternoon drew on, Susan and Dominic walked a little way from the rest of the group. She sat on a five-bar gate, feet hooked behind a crossbeam. He leant against it, as they shared the view.

Finally, she asked,

"Why are you living with Luke?"

Dominic flushed slightly and a scowl crept over his features. Susan panicked that she had offended him.

"Oh, I'm so sorry, Dominic," she apologised, "I shouldn't have asked. Please forget I said anything. I have so few friends... I –"

"It's fine," he interrupted, "honestly, it's fine. It is a difficult subject. I had a very rough time at school over it. People don't understand."

"Was it… bullying?" Her mouth was dry. "I had a bad experience… ruined everything."

"Well, it was really my own fault, in a way." Dominic's initial reluctance was fading into an earnest desire to talk. “About a year ago, I was having a kick around in the park with some mates and managed to injure my knee in a stupid tackle. It wasn’t anyone’s fault, just one of those things, but I was signed off all sports by the doc for a month. Well, I’m on a couple of teams, swimming and gymnastics, and the school expects that if we can’t play for some reason we turn up for training and games to back the others, you know?”

Susan had never been on a sports team in her life, but she nodded as if it was all totally normal to her.

“Anyway,” he continued, “I went to watch the swimming trials, but it was pretty boring. It had more or less finished, but the coach was getting them to do a final relay practice, so I went to the changing rooms to wait for my mates. I was surfing the web on my phone while I was waiting for them, and I didn’t hear one of them come in the room. He snatched my phone from me, you know having a joke, I was trying to get it back off him, and then he looked at it. He saw what I was looking at…”

He tailed off, struggling to find words.

“Was it – um - porn?” Susan asked, trying to be supportive and figuring that he was a teenage boy. “I’d have thought most of the people on your team were watching it.”

Dominic’s reply seemed to be stuck in his throat. He forced the words, one by one.

“Yes. No. Well, in a way. It was a website… for… seeing if you’re… gay.”

He said the last word so quietly, that Susan took a moment to digest it.

“You’re saying that as if it is something to be embarrassed about,” she said. “I mean, it’s not a big deal these days.”

“Maybe not in some places, but a sports team in a small town?” he replied. “My so-called mate showed it to all the others when they came in, and within seconds I was outed as the school queer. People started saying they didn’t want to share a changing room with me – it was utterly humiliating.”

“How awful for you!” Susan sympathised. “Had you no friends?”

“Lots of people stuck by me as it got around the school,” Dominic explained. “Quite a few of the girls made an extra effort to be friendly, and my two best buddies didn’t drop me altogether, but everyone’s attitude changed a bit. I can’t blame them, I suppose. Anyway, someone overheard a few homophobic remarks being made to me and reported it, so now all the teachers knew too. In the end, I had to tell my parents what happened.”

“How did they take it?” she asked.

"Surprisingly well… at least they said all the right things," he told her, "but the truth is, they didn't know how to cope, because I didn't know what I needed from them. I withdrew from everyone and everything. I quit teams and clubs, tried to avoid people. Then one day, Dad suggested that I chat to Luke – we've known him for a while, as he and Dad are both into classic cars."

"Luke's not gay, is he?" asked Susan.

"No, but he is a great listener. We talked for hours, and he was the only one who understood what I'd been trying to say."

"Which was?" she asked.

"That I don't know what I am," Dominic answered. "That I think I might be gay, or as he put it same sex attracted, but I might also like girls… or maybe both… or neither. The trouble was that people were very binary – the school decided that I was gay and that's that. My mother spent all her time trying to say everything other than 'it's just a phase'. Luke realised that I needed space and privacy, or I was in danger of blowing my education. So, he asked me if I'd like to come and stay at The Cherries and he offered to help tutor me. No pressure, no opinions, no special treatment, just an honest promise that whatever I decide to do with my life, he'd be my mate."

"Wow. That was a generous offer," said Susan.

"It was. He got a lot of negative abuse too from some people. I know some at his church disapproved, and some people at the school called him a closet queer."

"I hadn't thought of that," she said.

"Well, he laughed it off," Dominic continued. "He said that people will say what they say and we should just ignore them. Viv has been great, and Reverend June. They know what's what. Everyone else round here just thinks I'm a friend visiting. Want to know a funny thing?"

"Go on," she encouraged him.

"I think the truth is that I'm just not bothered about any of it," Dominic told her. "You know, romance and love and that. Luke has made me realise that I have loads of time to decide what I want in my life. I know I have one friend, come what may."

Susan placed her small hand on his.

"Two," she said, "and thank you for sharing it with me."

Then she told him of some of her own hardships from the bullying, not so much from a need to speak of them, but rather to cement the new bond that had formed between them.

"It has been a long time since I met someone to trust," she confided.

"You've met two," Dominic told her. "Luke will take anything you tell him in confidence to his grave, I promise you."

* * *

It was a weary but content group that made its way back to the boats. The hampers were much lighter, though their stomachs were rather heavier.

They rowed gently beneath the trees, serenaded by Vivian's and Marian's renditions of various '70's and '80's hit singles, almost none of which the others knew.

Finally, they climbed the hill, through the lengthening afternoon shadows, to their houses.

"Thank you for a lovely day," said June.

"Yes, thank you," chorused the other three women.

Then Marian piped up, "Look, everyone, it is Susie's birthday on the 21st of next month. Her twentieth. Please would you all come to dinner? It would mean a lot to us. You're welcome to bring your husband, June."

"Oh, yes, please do!" enthused Susan.

Diaries and mobile phones were fished out, schedules checked and promises to be there were made, though June did say she would have to check with her husband.

The vicar gave everyone present a hug, climbed into her car and drove away. They all waved after her, until she turned the corner with a final double toot of her horn.

Luke and Dominic refused all offers to help with washing-up, and went back into The Cherries to a final chorus of thanks from their neighbours.

Marian thought she saw her daughter gazing wistfully at the receding figures of the men. She wondered if she might fancy one of them.

Back in the kitchen, Vivian looked in the fridge.

"I suppose we should start thinking about putting some dinner on," she said, without enthusiasm.

"Oh, don't talk about food, please!" groaned Susan. "I'm still stuffed from the picnic."

"Me too," Marian concurred.

"That's a relief!" Vivian exclaimed. "Let's have a bit of a rest, and then some soup and a roll in front of the telly this evening." She crumpled into a chair and lit a cigarette. "Be an angel and stick the kettle on will you, Susie?"

As Susan waited for the water to boil, she saw Luke emerge from his house and carry the rubbish from the picnic to the bins outside. As she watched him sort it between various recycling receptacles and putting the remainder in the wheelie bin, she caught herself paying more than neighbourly attention to his lean physique. He looked up and spied her through the window, giving a cheery wave. She waved back.

Suddenly, she opened the door and scampered to where he stood.

"Can I ask a favour?" she panted.

"Anything," he replied.

"That book, The Wind in the Willows."

"What of it?" Luke asked.

"Well, I was wondering if you had a copy I could borrow?" she requested. "I've never read it. I mean, I've seen it on TV but not actually read it."

"Of course. I'll drop it over to you later."

"There is no rush."

"It isn't like it's a long way," he reassured her, "and I enjoy any excuse to pop over to see you."

As she walked back to pour the kettle, she questioned the meaning of the last sentence. For a moment, she acknowledged an attraction she felt to him.

"You idiot, Susan," she reproached herself, "he's being nice. Why would he ever be interested in anyone like you?"

In his study, Luke berated himself.

"Why did you say that to her, Cartwright? You came across as a creepy old man chatting up a pretty girl. What's wrong with you, man?"

* * *

That evening, when they had finished their soup, Vivian was dozing in her armchair, while Marian and Susan were trying to watch a reality talent show; unfortunately, the snoring made it hard to appreciate the TV's offerings. Mother and daughter strove to contain their silent giggling.

There was a loud knocking at the kitchen door, causing Vivian to jump awake with a splutter, followed by a short bout of chesty coughing.

Marian went to open the door and returned to the room shortly after, with a small rectangular package in her hand.

"It was Luke," she explained, "he wanted me to give you this."

She handed her daughter the packet. Susan opened it and pulled out a slender hardback copy of The Wind in the Willows. There was a handwritten note tucked inside, which read:

'Dear Susan, Please accept this copy of one of my favourite books as a gift to thank you for your excellent company this afternoon. I hope you enjoy it.'

Susan handled the book lovingly. She treasured it. It was quite literally the only book that she owned.

* * *

That night, Susan went to bed early and sat up, supported by pillows, to read her new book. She was aware of the sound of chatter coming from downstairs, but it didn't interfere with her reading.

Page after page drew her deeper and deeper into the world of the Mole and the adventures of Toad, until she was quite startled by her mother entering the room. While Marian disappeared into the bathroom to clean her teeth, Susan rearranged her pillows and straightened her bedding. Marian returned and got into bed, turning out the light.

The two women lay in the dark, breathing quietly.

"It was a lovely day, wasn't it, Mum?" Susan asked softly.

"Yes," replied Marian, "I can't remember a happier day for a long time. We were properly pampered."

"That song you sang. I think I remember it."

"I used to sing it to you when you were a tiny baby. Fancy you remembering. I wish you'd known your great grandmother, she was such a special person. She only died a few years before you were born, you know."

"You should sing more," Susan stated emphatically.

"It's been a while since I felt like singing."

"Yeah. Things are better here."

Silence descended once again.

"Mum…?"

"Yes?" Marian answered sleepily.

"Do you believe in God?"

There was a pause.

"I think so," replied Marian, trying to rouse herself. "When you were little, I wanted you christened. I had a big fight with your dad about it, and Viv was no help. Superstitious claptrap, they called it. But it meant something to me, so I did it anyway. But now, well, so many bad things have happened, that I don't feel… anything. I guess there is more to life than this. Gosh, Susie, it's a bit late for a debate on the existence of God!"

"Sorry, Mum," Susan said with feeling. "It's just somehow, lately, I've found myself thinking about it. And then Luke asked Reverend June to bless the meal, and she thanked God for it, when Luke and Dominic had done all the work. And Luke seemed so pleased. And the words she said were so beautiful. Well, if two such nice people believe in him, there's got to be something in it."

Marian was snoring lightly. Susan suspected that Vivian and her mother may have split a bottle of wine downstairs while she was in bed reading.

"Mum?"

Marian surfaced enough to respond.

"I don't know, Susie," she sighed, "I suggest you talk to the vicar about it if you're so interested."

"Maybe. Maybe I'm just being silly. Goodnight, Mum."

"God bless," mumbled Marian drowsily.

Chapter 5

Susan and Marian both began their new jobs that week.

Marian immediately made a good impression at the solicitors', picking up her duties quickly and professionally. It was a practice of four partners, with a further six junior solicitors, supported by a team of secretaries, and she relished being in a stimulating environment.

She learnt her role so well that they soon asked her to take notes in important meetings and to assume responsibility for maintaining and ordering office supplies. However, Marian especially appreciated the occasions when she was asked to take an urgent document to a client or another solicitor – the short trips out of the office made her feel like a lucky school girl who'd been given a pass to go into town when all her peers were stuck in a French lesson.

She even decided to get the air conditioning repaired in her car. As fate would have it, this heralded a period of grey skies, low temperatures and intermittent rain; in short, a typical English summer.

Her spirits were particularly lifted by the open mike night at the pub. Vivian had almost literally dragged her and Susan to The Bull, with the promise of a top-notch bar snack. The food was indeed excellent, and after a juicy steak and onion baguette, and several gin and tonics, Marian was persuaded to sing.

The hubbub of conversation died away as she performed, and every face in the bar turned to watch her. When she finished, there was a sincere round of applause and several patrons took the time to congratulate her. As the evening wore on, Vivian dragged her back up to the stage and the two old friends rocked out several ABBA hits.

As they left, the landlord approached Marian and took her to one side.

"You were really good tonight, well when you weren't caterwauling with Viv. Would you like a regular spot to sing? I can pay you twenty quid and a free dinner."

"Blimey," she replied. "Yes, please."

The other two were waiting for her at the taxi they had booked to take them home and were delighted for her when she told them her news.

"Next stop: Wembley," exclaimed Vivian.

* * *

Susan's new job went similarly well. Her duties were exactly as Tina had described them, and she found them to be very straightforward. She was there diligently well before five-thirty every morning, though she found the schedule exhausting. Sharing a room with her mother was a little strained, as she had to go to bed early and get up two hours before her. Marian felt that it would be impolite if she went to bed when Susan did, as she would be deserting Vivian, and Susan felt guilty as, however hard she tried, she tended to wake her mother when she got up.

Susan's other frustration was walking to The Cedars in the dawn. Visibility was sometimes poor and it was a little eerie making her way there alone. The problem was solved by Dominic, who lent her a powerful torch and a fluorescent jacket from Luke's garage.

She enjoyed the company of Tina and Jerry, who were both considerate bosses, and their two sweet twin infant daughters, who would sometimes be toddling about the office. Jerry was a powerfully built African American; he must have been six-and-a-half-feet tall, and Susan felt dwarfed by him. Most days he wore chinos and a polo shirt, but on one particularly hot day, he came into the office in long shorts and Susan realised that he had a prosthetic leg. He certainly didn't let it be an impediment, and he and Tina made no mention of it, but Susan was curious.

But she was more curious as to how these two Americans came to run a camp site in rural England. One day, when she and Tina were taking a coffee break, she asked her how they came to be here.

"It's quite a story," said Tina, "but in a nutshell, it is because of your neighbour, Luke."

Susan's interest was piqued even further. Tina saw her expression and decided to elaborate.

"It may interest you to know that I am actually British. I was born in Manchester. My father was a lecturer at the university, but we moved to the States when I was about four when he was offered a professorship at Princeton.

When I went to college, I majored in Economics, which I turned out to be pretty good at. So, I did a Masters, and that went so well that I won a scholarship to read for an M.Phil at Oxford, and that's not something you turn down, so I moved back to dear old Blighty."

"And Jerry?" asked Susan.

"Jerry was a lawyer, and a damn good one. He was in corporate law and worked for a major bank, which asked him to work at their London offices. We ended up meeting at a party given by a mutual friend. Jerry also met Luke at the bank, he was a stockbroker or something, and they became close friends… until I came along to spoil their bromance. Jerry and I got married that same year back in the USA, and Luke was best man."

"So how did you end up here?"

"Well, Jerry was also an army reservist and got called up to serve. He's never told me what happened, but one day I got the call that every army wife must dread. He got off lighter than most of his unit, that much I know, but he was pretty badly hurt. He tried to go back to the bank when he recovered, but he wasn't happy, so he got in touch with Luke, who by now was living down here. Luke insisted we come stay with him at The Cherries, and, well, we fell in love with the place. So, we bought this business."

"That's quite a change," said Susan, her voice filled with admiration.

"You're telling me!" Tina exclaimed. "To be honest, it may not be forever but it is a great place to be for now. I actually do some freelance consultancy to some firms in the City - thank God for the internet, because I can work from anywhere - and Jerry occasionally does contract mediation."

"You guys are amazing," Susan admired.

"We try, honey."

* * *

One afternoon, a day or so before her birthday, Susan was sitting in the sun on Vivian's door step, when Luke came out of his house. He ambled over to speak to her.

"Are you busy?" he asked.

"Not particularly. Why?"

"I'm off to visit a lady in the village, fancy coming? I think you'd like her."

Susan felt an inexplicable pang of jealousy at the news of this mystery woman.

"Her name is Margaret Hedges," Luke told her. "Wait here and I'll get the car."

"I'll just pop in and get my bag."

Susan skipped in through the door and went to the cloakroom before collecting her handbag. When she got outside, she saw Luke's car for the first time. It was a Jaguar XJS in dark blue with a creamy leather interior – it was a later model, but nevertheless Luke had it carefully restored to better than original condition. Two doors, a long nose and sleek lines made it look sporty, but it was built to be a comfortable tourer.

Susan slipped into what was probably the most comfortable seat that she had ever sat in, inside a car or otherwise. The lustrous wood-trimmed fascia glistened in the sunlight as Luke slipped the automatic gearbox into drive and the car pulled away with a throaty roar. Once they were on their way, the car was whisper quiet.

"It's not cheap on petrol, but I don't drive much," Luke volunteered. "I fell in love with these when I was a boy and always promised myself one."

"I can see why," Susan said, running her palm over the upholstery.

"They had a bit of a poor reliability record in their day, but this one has been expertly overhauled and had a few updates."

Luke inwardly chastised himself – was he showing off?

He changed the subject, and as they drove to the village, they discussed various topics, such as Susan's job and how her mother was getting on at the solicitors'.

Before long, Luke parked outside a terrace of picturesque, sandy natural-stone cottages, with white windows and long gardens in front of them. Luke led Susan up the pathway of one, where he punched some buttons on a small key safe attached to the wall beside the front door, removed a key from a hook inside the safe, and opened the door. Before going in, he returned the key and secured the safe.

They entered a small hallway, with stairs directly in front of them, but Luke opened a door to his left and gently cooed.

"Margaret, it's Luke. I've brought a new friend to meet you. This is Susan."

The living room was quaintly old fashioned, with dark exposed wooden beams in the ceiling and a small inglenook fireplace, surrounded by well-polished horse brasses. A dark oak Welsh dresser stood in one corner, displaying blue china plates, cups and saucers, and arranged around the hearth was a simple green cottage-style suite, comprising two high-backed armchairs and a sofa, all of which were backed with a crisp, white piece of lace.

Sitting in one of the chairs was a very sweet-faced elderly lady, wearing a tweed skirt and a blue cardigan over a ruffled cream blouse, on which rested a small wooden crucifix that was hanging around her neck. On one side of her was a metal walking frame, and on the other was a small table, on which stood a radio, a framed black and white photograph of a young man in a military uniform, a carafe of water with glass on the top, and an assortment of jars holding prescription medication.

"Luke!" Margaret exclaimed. "How lovely to see you. And this is Susan, you say? How do you do, Susan?" She extended her small hands to them both and Luke held one tenderly between his own. Susan took the other lightly, observing how cruelly swollen and deformed it was, with fingers twisted like a gnarled tree.

The old woman watched her keenly from behind her thick-rimmed spectacles, and Susan's face must have betrayed some of the shock she felt at seeing nature's cruelty.

"Awful, aren't they?" moaned Margaret. "Arthritis. Don't get old, dear, stay lovely and young like you are now."

"You look radiant," boomed Luke, as he stooped to kiss her cheek, still holding her hand.

"You're a terrible liar," Margaret tutted. "But bless you for trying, dear."

Luke's foot knocked against something and looking down, he saw a tray with a plate of food on it.

"Is that your lunch?" he asked. "You've hardly touched anything."

"It was too hard to cut up, love," the old lady complained. "I had a bit of potato and the peas and carrots, but I wasn't really hungry."

"The carers are supposed to help you do stuff like that," he pointed out.

"Those girls work hard enough without chopping up an old woman's food like she's a baby," Margaret asserted, petulantly. "I had the pudding with a nice bit of custard."

"That isn't a proper meal. You have got to look after yourself." Luke sounded firm but caring.

"I was a nurse for forty-five years, and he's telling me how to look after myself," Margaret complained to Susan, with a not so subtle wink.

"I'm sure he's right," responded Susan.

"Indeed, I am," asserted Luke. "What's more, I'm going to rustle something up for you now."

He made his way out of the room, and the sounds of cupboard doors opening and closing filtered from the next-door kitchen. He returned with a frown.

"Do you know that there is almost nothing to eat in your kitchen, Margaret?"

"Oh, I know," she replied. "But the girl who does my shopping's been on holiday. She'll be back the day after tomorrow."

Luke sighed.

"I'm off to pick up some essentials to tide you over," he told her.

"Thank you, young man," Margaret said with more than a hint of gratitude. "Susan will keep me company, won't you, darling?"

Susan had little option but to say, "Of course," but she was more than content to remain. Luke shot her a look of apology before he hurried out of the front door to go to the local shop.

"He's so good to me," said the elderly lady, "he is always dropping by to see how I am."

"He seems to be good to everybody," Susan mused.

"Are you his sweetheart, then?"

Susan flushed and gave a startled, flustered response. "Goodness, no. He's my neighbour."

"Oh, I think he might like you a bit, though. I saw how he was looking at you. God has blessed me with ninety-four years on this Earth, and I've got to know a thing or two."

Susan maintained a sceptical silence.

"You know, Susan," Margaret confided, "he's mentioned you every time he's visited me since you arrived. He tells me you're a bit of a botanist."

Susan's flush was now a glowing beetroot.

"Er, well I do like flowers," she said, in desperate hope that she would not be questioned further. There was a mischievous glint in Margaret's eyes, but she saved Susan further blushes.

"He's like a son to me," was all she said, "I never had children of my own. I have a niece, but she lives in Australia and never writes. But me and my Freddy never had any of our own, well there wasn't time." She gestured to the photo next to her, "That's him. He was a navigator on the big bombers during the war, but he was killed in action in 1944."

Susan looked at the young man in the photograph, so full of life and confidence.

"I'm so sorry," she said.

"We only had three years together," Margaret told her, "but they've lasted me a lifetime. You know, when you meet the one for you, well there's no point in second best. He was the one for me."

Susan was at a loss for something to say, but the emotion of the words touched her deeply.

"No use getting maudlin over it," Margaret continued, "I've had a good life and I'll be reunited with him soon enough."

She used her stiff fingers to pluck a crumpled tissue from the sleeve of her cardigan and dabbed lightly under her nose.

"Now, scoot over a bit nearer to me so I can get a proper look at you."

Susan moved to the chair next to Margaret and endured several moments of awkwardness as her companion looked her up and down.

"You have very pretty eyes," was the verdict. Susan, for the first time accepted a compliment, even though a small voice in her head laughed at the notion.

"Thank you," she said. "So do you."

Margaret smiled broadly.

"Can you help me up, sweetheart? I need to spend a penny."

Susan jumped to her feet and supported Margaret as she rose from her chair and steadied herself on her walking frame. Then there was a slow procession out of the living room, into the hall, through the kitchen to a small bathroom annexed to the back of the house.

"Thank you, dear," Margaret said as she entered the room and closed the door behind her. Susan decided to wait in the kitchen, in case she was needed for the return trip, when she heard the front door being pushed open (Luke had left it on the latch). She went into the hallway and found Reverend June walking in.

"Susan?" she was surprised to see her. "I saw Luke's car outside and thought I'd stop off. How lovely to see you!" They embraced warmly. "Is Luke not here?"

"Margaret hadn't any food in the house, so Luke went to buy some," Susan explained.

By now the vicar had made her way to the living room threshold.

"And where is Margaret?" she asked.

Susan was still lingering by the kitchen door, so that she would hear Margaret if called.

"She's in the loo," she replied, "I don't want to leave her in case she needs help on the way back."

"Sensible. I'll wait with you," June said.

They stood in the kitchen for several minutes before the bathroom latch lifted and a walking frame passed through the door, followed by Margaret.

"Hello, Vicar," she said, "thank you for coming by. I'm having such a lot of visitors today."

Suddenly, her foot slipped from beneath her and she dropped heavily to her knee with a screech of pain. June and Susan were with her within a fraction of a second and each took a frail elbow to help her stand up.

"I'm such a foolish old lady," she moaned. She started to take a step, but as soon as she put weight onto her left leg, she once again cried out.

"Don't try to walk, let us take the weight," instructed June, her concern registering in her voice. She and Susan managed to more or less carry Margaret to her chair.

June knelt next to her elderly parishioner and examined her left knee.

"It's starting to swell," she stated.

Susan moved purposefully to the small refrigerator in the kitchen, and found the remnants of a pack of frozen peas in the ice box. She brought them to the living room and placed them gingerly on Margaret's knee.

"This should help the swelling," she said, "should we call for a paramedic?"

"Dr Salmon would be quicker, if he's at home," June decided, "I'll call and see." She fished her phone from her capacious handbag and went into the front garden to ring him.

She passed Luke on the way out and told him what had taken place, so he hurried into the living room. Susan took the shopping from him and unpacked it in the kitchen, while she also made a cup of strong, sweet tea for Margaret.

June arrived to say that the doctor would be over in about half an hour. Margaret was becoming rather agitated, getting cross with herself for the mishap. Luke spoke quietly to the other two.

"I think there may be too many people here for her to cope with," he told them quietly, "I'll stay with her until the doctor comes, and if necessary, I'll go to Casualty with her. Why don't you two slip away – Reverend, could I impose upon you to give Susan a lift home?"

"Of course, no problem at all," replied June, "I think that is a sensible plan."

She walked to Margaret and took her frail hand in hers. She spoke slowly and clearly.

"Margaret – Susan and I are going to leave now. Luke is going to be here for you until the doctor arrives."

Margaret nodded.

"Will you pray for me, Vicar?" she asked.

"Of course. Would you like to pray together now?"

"Yes please."

June softly spoke a blessing, and as she did so, Margaret grasped the wooden cross hanging from her neck as tightly as her swollen fingers would allow. Luke bowed his head in silence, so Susan, feeling slightly awkward, followed his lead.

After the women had left, Luke sat on the very edge of the settee waiting for the doctor's knock at the door.

"She's a nice girl, that Susan," said Margaret looking directly at him. "She's a real keeper."

Luke smiled awkwardly.

* * *

Luke drove home later that evening. The doctor was content that the knee injury was just a sprain, and Luke had sat with her until Joan, another friend of Margaret's, arrived. Joan, a quiet amenable woman in her late seventies, had packed a suitcase and planned to stay at the cottage until Margaret was more mobile.

When he had put the Jaguar to bed in the garage, he went for a stroll across the fields opposite The Cherries. In the early dusk, he could see a multitude of rabbit heads pop up from among the grassy tussocks, alerted by his approach.

As he neared them, they scampered away to the far side of the grassland. Except one – it stayed to let him get nearer. He was puzzled. It allowed him to stretch out his hand, and though he did not touch it, the creature sniffed the air at his fingertips.

Then it too turned and hopped away. Could a rabbit limp, or was it just a flight of fancy?

"Don't be ridiculous, Luke," he said to himself.

Then he walked back to the house, unaware that he was watched by a solitary bunny.

There was a light on in Vivian's kitchen, and Luke realised that, although he had texted June to let her know about Margaret's knee, Susan probably may be still worried. He knocked at the stable door and Marian answered. Over her shoulder, he could see Vivian sitting at the kitchen table, smoking.

"Good evening, ladies, how are you both?" he asked. Vivian picked a glass of red wine up from the table and waggled it very slightly by the stem.

"We are very well, thank you," she said. "Care to join us for a glass of vino?"

"Well, maybe just a small one, thank you."

Marian fetched a glass from a shelf and poured him a rather generous measure, as he continued to speak.

"I was wondering if Susan was here. She was present when a friend of mine had a little accident this afternoon, and I thought she may like to know that everything's OK."

"She's upstairs in the shower, but I don't expect she will be long," said Marian. "She told us about your friend, Margaret, and she was very worried about her."

On cue, the light footsteps of Susan descending the stairs could be heard, with a, "Mum!" at the halfway point.

"Susan –" called Marian, who was hoping to warn her daughter of their visitor, but there was too little time. Susan was in the room, wearing long flannel pyjama trousers and a baggy t-shirt featuring an oversized teddy bear under the motif 'I Wuv U' (it was another of Jenny's cast-offs). On her head was a lime green bath towel, wrapped around her hair like a ludicrous turban. She entered through the door from the hallway almost backwards, her head down as she was straining to look at her own backside, with the hem of the t-shirt pulled up by one hand and the waist band of her trousers tugged down to expose her buttock.

"Mum!" she said in an exasperated tone. "I think I've been bitten by something. Can you have a look? It's right on the top of my bu – oh bugger!"

The last two words came as she realised that Luke was in the room. Her bare feet slithered to a halt on the tiled floor, and she froze with a look of horror on her now bright pink face. For some inexplicable reason, she couldn't bring herself to return her clothing to its natural state, but remained, very slightly leaning forward, with her lower back and upper left buttock still exposed.

Vivian started to snigger, which turned into a chuckle. Marian's head turned several times from her daughter to Luke (whose eyes were almost out on stalks) and back before she too started to laugh. Luke was trying to maintain his composure and was struggling to know what to say. His evident discomfort drove the two older women on, and the amusement became convulsions of silent giggles, which were ultimately dispelled by Vivian developing a violent bout of coughing.

Finally, Susan found the presence of mind to move her hands and straighten her attire. Luke stood with one hand on a kitchen counter top and the other rubbing the back of his neck. Once he'd managed to stop staring at her, his eyes roamed the room, trying to find any point of interest other than Susan.

"I – er..." he began, deciding that the kitchen light fixture merited visual inspection, "I thought you might care to know that Margaret had merely suffered a – um – minor sprain and that she should be right as rain in a few days."

"Why thank you," responded Susan, in her best telephone voice, "I do appreciate you taking the time to let me know."

Vivian, dabbing tears from her eyes that were the result of laughter and coughing, snorted.

"I should go," said Luke.

Susan took an involuntary step forward.

"Oh, no please don't," she entreated, but not knowing why.

"Yes, you haven't finished your wine," Marian chipped in.

"Yes, have your wine. I'll be right back," Susan said, darting from the door. The occupants of the kitchen heard the rapid padding sound which marked her ascent of the stairs.

Susan tore the towel from her hair and perched on the edge of her bed, angrily brushing, forcing past the tangles in painful penitence for her stupidity. Again and again, she replayed the scene in her head, moaning softly to herself.

For once, she didn't tie a pony tail, but allowed her locks to fall in their natural waves. They were still a little damp, so she used Marian's hair dryer to make herself look a little more presentable.

For some reason, she wanted to give a visible signal of regaining her composure. Her pyjamas were perfectly decent, but she wanted to feel on even terms, so even slipping on the 'vile' pink fluffy dressing gown, to which she had secretly grown rather attached, seemed insufficient.

Did she dare? She walked into Jenny's bedroom and scanned the closet where there hung a dress that had caught her eye several times. Dark blue, with a subtle silver swirling pattern, it was neither ostentatious nor trashy, just stylishly anonymous, such as someone might wear to a work function.

She carried it back to her room and put on underwear and thick black tights. Then she slid the dress on. It had a high neck at the front, but the back dropped away slightly to reveal the top of her shoulder blades, and the skirt hem came to just below her knee. It looked very sophisticated, which may have accounted for Jenny leaving it behind.

She slipped on a pair of Marian's work shoes, slightly shiny with a small heel. Lastly, she hung a small gold locket around her neck, which had been a gift from her grandmother. She did not apply makeup, for she never wore it anyway.

Susan could hear that the other three had moved into the lounge. When she joined them, it was Vivian's turn to sit there open jawed. Marian too was surprised, but proud of the confident young lady that walked into the room – a month ago she would have been upstairs comforting a sobbing daughter. Luke just smiled and was his usual ebullient self, but his eyes rarely strayed from Susan.

Her initial inhibitions soon passed, helped by a glass of wine, and Susan's confidence grew. However, she told herself that this was a one-off, amongst friends and family, with whom she couldn't embarrass herself any further than she already had done.

The evening, like the claret and the conversation, flowed well, and any residual awkwardness was forgotten. Topics drifted from cars, Luke telling them that Dominic would soon be taking his driving test, to jobs, to Luke's business, to why he was interested in art; this ultimately led to Luke commenting on how disappointed he was that Susan had none of her pictures left, as he would have loved to have seen them.

"Yes you do!" exclaimed Vivian to Susan. "You did one for me, remember?" She climbed, a little unsteadily, from her chair and went upstairs to her bedroom.

"Oh, no!" Susan cringed. "I'm sure it is awful. You look at so many lovely pictures."

Vivian returned with a watercolour. It featured a large silver moon in a meridian blue sky, which was reflected on the waves of the seawater beneath it, and on the horizon there was the silhouette of a single-mast sailing vessel. It might have been the re-creation of a real memory, or a fantasy scene.

"Oh, this is rather good," Luke enthused. "No, really it is," he added when he saw Susan's sceptical expression. "You have a true talent."

His sincerity was unmistakable and Susan's heart was filled with warmth.

* * *

That night, neither Luke nor Susan found it easy to sleep. They each lay in their beds, separated by two windows and a courtyard, and their thoughts were of the other.

While Susan could not escape occasional flashbacks to exposing her backside, she dwelt more on the better events of the day – meeting Margaret, seeing a man exhibit such tenderness as she had witnessed in Luke with the old lady, and, above all, the sense of achievement that she had experienced when Luke praised her painting.

After years of being treated by some as a less than human failure and by others as a pitiable victim, she was now surrounded by people who brought only kindness and friendship. Her old life seemed so long ago – was it truly just a few weeks, if not days, past?

Her mother whimpered slightly in her sleep, kicking her leg out from under her duvet. For a moment, she seemed to be about to wake, but instead she rolled onto her side and her breathing grew deeper.

Susan could also hear muffled snoring from down the corridor. Vivian may have been closer to passing out rather than simple sleep. Susan had picked up four empty wine bottles when she had helped Marian to tidy the kitchen and living room before bed that evening, and by her reckoning, she, Luke and her mother combined barely accounted for two of them.

As Morpheus's drowsy embrace finally lulled her to sleep, Susan's last thoughts were memories of glancing at Luke's profile as they drove down country lanes, in the classic opulence of his old Jag.

Meanwhile, Luke had cracked the bedroom window open a little, and lay propped up on his bed. Wine on top of an empty stomach (he had not had dinner), meant that he had taken some antacid tablets before bed. It was a humid night, and he lay bare-chested on the bed, small droplets of perspiration forming on exposed skin, cooling him.

The events with Margaret played on his mind, but he had been struck by the friendship that she and Susan had immediately struck up and by how the younger woman had responded so well in the events following the fall in the kitchen.

He thought of the little flash of Susan's exposed skin that he had seen in Vivian's kitchen that evening, and more of the sophisticated young woman who had appeared later in the living room. Luke put those thoughts from his mind – it was almost indecent of him to think of her in that way – he was angry with himself.

And the picture she had painted. Yes, it was a little clumsy in execution, but it contained such wistful and intangible emotion that he had genuinely found it moving. He almost envied it, because with all the technical precision in his own work, he could never produce anything so… so… genuine. He knew that it was his job in life to help her nurture that talent, and he accepted that mission with all his heart.

* * *

Luke never realised he fell asleep, but came to in the bright sunshine of the new day full of determination. Showered, he bounded downstairs with great resolve for the day ahead, only to find Dominic eating scrambled eggs and studying The Highway Code.

"I left some for you in the pan," said the young man, gesturing to the hob without looking up. "And there's fresh coffee."

Luke poured a cup of black coffee, pulled a spoon from the drawer and ate the eggs straight from the saucepan, for today he was in a hurry. Dominic broke off from his reading.

"You look like you're on a mission," he remarked, with a quizzical look.

"I am," Luke concurred. "Fancy coming shopping for Susan's birthday present with me in a bit? You can drive the van."

As well as the Jaguar, Luke had a small, aged and battered Vauxhall van in the garage, which he used for lugging boxes of books and paintings. It only had a small petrol engine, so adding his young friend to the insurance as a learner had been relatively inexpensive.

Dominic's excitement at being on the road was tangible.

"Really!" he exclaimed. "You bet I would! But I thought you'd already decided on giving her chocolates and that old children's book you found?"

Luke felt a little like he was about to be caught in some minor deceit, so he blustered to prevent detection.

"Old children's book? The complete works of Lewis Carroll cannot be so lightly dismissed, my lad. I can see we are going to have to work on your grasp of English Literature."

Dominic was wholly unimpressed.

"So, can I give her the chocolates you bought?" he asked craftily. "It would save me having to cough up for something."

Luke rolled his eyes and looked up, as if seeking divine patience. He gulped the last of the eggs down.

"Come on, buddy, get the van out while I lock up and I'll stand you a burger at lunch," he said, throwing a Vauxhall-tagged keyring to Dominic, who casually caught it one handed. Luke was unimpressed by the dexterity, for he was already walking to his study to fetch his wallet and house keys.

* * *

Much earlier, Susan had jumped awake as her phone's alarm went off. She immediately wished that she had drunk a little less the previous evening and gone to bed a lot earlier. From the other side of the room, Marian swore mildly and pulled her pillow over her head.

"Sorry, Mum. Go back to sleep," she whispered loudly, as she struggled to turn off the alarm. She grabbed underwear, leggings and a sweatshirt and tiptoed out of the room and into the bathroom. There, under the unforgiving florescent light over the sink, she looked at herself in the mirror. She looked like she had had about three hours sleep, which was probably about right.

Blast, she thought. She'd left her hairbrush and her handbag in the bedroom. She didn't want to go back in and wake her mum. She was still holding her phone, so she didn't need much else in the bag, but her hair looked like an electrocuted Muppet, meaning she did need a brush. Inspiration struck when she realised that her mum's bag was almost certainly downstairs, and she always kept a spare brush in it.

Susan washed her face and dressed, and then padded lightly down the stairs, where she found her mother's handbag hanging on the back of a kitchen chair. She rummaged inside, and as she did so, her eyes took in the other items her mum carried with her. She stopped rummaging.

An idea planted itself in her mind. It was so unlike her, so daring for her, that it was almost a sensual taboo. She was alone. No one would know. Carrying her mother's bag, Susan stole back upstairs and into Jenny's bedroom.

The idea was a natural progression from the sensations she experienced the previous evening, when she had entered the room in the blue dress and for a few moments felt a thrill of imagined desirability. At some level, Susan felt that she may, just may, manage to pretend that she was a normal, attractive young woman; not that she had the confidence to believe anyone else would think that of her (years of remorseless bullying had removed any such illusion about herself), but she could at least play out her own private fantasy.

She rummaged through the chest of drawers, before selecting a small peachy pink, slightly fluffy jumper and a pair of pale skinny jeans, which Jenny would have grown out of years ago. Carrying them to the bathroom, she slipped out of her own clothes, and took a disposable razor from the cupboard to shave her lower legs, from the knee down. They looked a little red afterwards, as she had only moistened them with water from the tap, but they were silky smooth.

She pulled the jeans on – they were a very tight fit, and, as she suspected, were three-quarter length, with the legs finishing at the mid-point of her shin. She pulled the pink jumper over her head, which exposed just a little of her midriff, and brushed her long dark, wavy hair.

Then she applied a little eyeliner from her mother's bag, some foundation, a hint of eyeshadow and a light covering of lipstick. She knew that most other women would be following the same routine that morning, and probably adding a lot more makeup, but for her it was like tasting a forbidden fruit.

She looked at the finished result in the mirror. Did she look ridiculous? Probably, but no one would ever know. Downstairs, she slipped on a pair of her mother's shoes; Marian complained they hurt her feet, so Susan knew that she wouldn't spot they were missing.

She was too excited and fearful of discovery to eat breakfast, though she did make herself have a glass of apple juice. Then she quietly crept out into the dawn. In her hand was a carrier bag containing her sweatshirt and leggings, a pair of trainers and some moisture wipes. Her plan was to walk to work and then change in the office toilet and remove the makeup before Tina or Jerry showed up. She was early, so there was little likelihood of being discovered.

Susan discovered three things on her walk. Firstly, being secretly dressed like that was rather exciting. Secondly, her mother's opinion that the shoes hurt her feet was painfully correct. Thirdly, it takes a lot longer to walk a few miles in heels you're not used to wearing than it does in a pair of trainers – there were several slips and slithers, and a prolonged slide down a steep bit of road that she'd never even noticed before, grasping the grass bank to maintain balance.

No one saw her on her journey, but rather than being a quarter of an hour early, as she had planned, she was only just on time. She clacked up the wooden steps and slipped into the office, intending to go directly into the lavatory to affect a speedy transformation.

"Susan?" It was Tina's voice. Susan stopped, and turned with an almost apologetic look.

"My God, girl, let me have a look at you," Tina said, standing up from her desk and walking over, looking Susan up and down. "You look amazing, I hardly recognised you. What's brought this on?" Then a sly grin, "Is it a boy?"

"No!" squealed Susan.

"A girl?" teased Tina. "Listen, honey, I've lived in LA, so I've seen it all."

"No, nothing like that," Susan insisted.

She realised that she was trapped, and the best way forward was to confide the truth. As Tina already knew much of Susan's back story from previous chats over coffee, she could put the remaining pieces in place for herself.

"Listen, honey," she reassured Susan, "you look great. Jerry is away on a consult, that's why I'm in here early to cover for him too. Why don't you stay looking like this? It's just going to be me and a few campers who you're never going to see again. Change when you want to – now or just before you go home. It is our secret."

Susan was conflicted. She was embarrassed, grateful, still a little excited. But still the small voice in her mind was saying, "You're an ugly disgrace. They'll laugh at you." She set her jaw.

"OK," she said determinedly. "Thank you. I'll give it a try."

Tina hugged her, and then they set about their normal day of work.

During their coffee break, the two women sat and chatted, while Susan brought up the topic of her painting and Luke liking it.

"Well, he has excellent taste," commented Tina.

"He's amazing. He's just got everything in life sorted out," enthused Susan.

"Honey, no one has life sorted out, certainly not Luke."

Susan was taken aback by the remark. Tina sensed this and after a moment of reflection continued.

"Have you ever noticed that Luke almost never goes outside the village?"

"Well, I haven't known him that long and I don't keep a track of his movements!" Susan answered. "What exactly do you mean?"

"I mean that when we all lived in London, Luke started to get anxiety attacks. He hated the big city, that's partly why he jacked it all in. There was some personal stuff too. I hear he went through a tough time, but that's not our business – I think Jerry knows about it."

"Luke?" Susan repeated, the note of incredulity in her voice palpable.

"Yes, Luke," Tina insisted. "I see that he has developed coping strategies, but, if he can, he stays in his house, if he must, he goes to the village, and if he can't avoid it, he goes to somewhere larger. He copes by only ever going to places he knows. If he must go to somewhere like London, he stays in the same hotel every time, and only ever takes a taxi between there and where he has to go. Jerry went with him to some important auction or something last year; he said Luke was incredibly anxious, like a caged animal the whole time."

"Poor Luke," said Susan, with deep sympathy.

"He's open about it, so he'll tell you himself if you ask him," Tina told her. "Always says, 'Why would I want to be anywhere but here?' One thing I can tell you, if you ever hear he's driven into town for something, it has got to be something pretty special."

* * *

Luke walked down the high street of the town with Dominic. He held in his hand a piece of paper containing a strict list he had written while Dominic drove; it was an itinerary of places he wanted to go and what he wished to buy in each shop. These purchases would be used to create Susan's birthday gift.

"OK, mate," he said, "you don't want to hang around with me. I'll meet you at the burger bar at midday. Is that good for you?"

"Yup," replied Dominic. Although he felt uneasy being in town, he knew that he probably wouldn't run into anyone from his old school, as they were likely to be in lessons. Luke walked off, studying his list intently. Dominic watched his friend and mentor vanish among the throng on the high street and debated sticking with him to keep him company. However, he knew that Luke would probably rather deal with the crowds on his own.

He drew his mobile phone from his trouser pocket and messaged his mother. She was a manager in a charity shop in the town centre and should be due her morning break before too long. He asked if she was free for a quick coffee, and within half an hour they were sitting together on a wooden bench in the park sipping from disposable coffee mugs and eating Danish pastries.

"You're looking well, Dombo," she said, "he's looking after you well."

Dombo had been his nickname in the family ever since they had watched a certain cartoon film when Dominic was a small child and he had mispronounced the title character's name.

"Luke's the best, Mum," he replied, "I miss you and Dad, though."

"We miss you too, son." Her voice cracked a little. "But, hey, we have text and phone and internet stuff, and you can come and stay whenever you want."

"I know, Mum. We'll see."

"Do… do you think you're any closer to… to… knowing what you… want?" she asked nervously.

"Mum, please drop it," Dominic replied testily. "Please. I need time to get my head sorted. Please just leave it be."

"Sorry." She ruffled his short hair. "It's not easy being a mum either."

"I know," he sighed.

"Love you," she cooed.

"You too. Hey, I do have some news. We have new neighbours at The Cherries. A mum and daughter, staying with Viv."

And so their conversation changed to being one of typical family news swapping, reminiscing and updates on grandparents' health, until Dominic's mum realised the time and trotted back to work, leaving him to dispose of the detritus from their snack.

He mooched around the shopping centre until midday, when he made his way to the burger bar. It was maybe a few minutes past twelve, but Luke was standing outside with three huge paper carrier bags in his hands and an anxious expression on his face. He was relieved to see Dominic.

"Let's get in and order. The sooner we do, the sooner we can get home," said Luke.

Dominic knew the score. Luke would always try to put others ahead of his own feelings, and the burger joint would be a torture to him. But Dominic did love a burger.

"Luke, do you mind if we don't stay?" the young man asked. "I think it might be nicer to stop at The Bull for a ploughman's."

Luke's face displayed his relief, and Dominic walked with his friend back to the car park. He was also rather keen to be back behind the wheel, so it wasn't all sacrifice.

* * *

As the morning at work wore on, Susan grew more confident about her appearance. She even noticed that some of the delivery drivers spent more time than usual chatting to her.

Her last duty was to walk around the park to check the static caravans, gas supplies, electricity points and anything else the guests may require. She would continue the task down through all the mobile caravans and motorhomes that visitors brought themselves, and then onto the camp site, where tents were pitched.

Susan debated changing first, especially as the shoes were starting to hurt quite a bit, but she decided to maximise this one-off experience. She had no intention of repeating this – she would dress down from now on… well, maybe a bit of eyeliner and some lip gloss, but that's it.

She worked her way through the park, her lack of self-confidence increasing the further she got from the office. She exchanged pleasantries with various guests, made notes on her clipboard of things that needed to be attended to, but all the time she could feel herself suppressing a rising panic.

Finally, Susan reached the tents. She worked past each plot, noting the empty ones on her check sheet. Then, as she was passing a medium sized green tent, she heard the zip of the entry flap being undone from the inside and a young woman, about her own age, crawled out; she met Susan's gaze and the two recognised each other immediately. Susan would never forget those eyes, for they burned with hatred. They were the eyes of Katherine Willis, her worst tormenter at school.

A wicked leering grin came across Katherine's cruel mouth. A young man had followed her out of the tent.

"Look," she said to him, "look what we have here. It's the ugly effing skank. What a lovely surprise, ugly, ugly dog-girl."

The young man peered at Susan. He was one of those boys who had graded and degraded her photograph. If he were a stronger man, he would have apologised for the hurt he caused and have told Katherine to leave off. Instead he joined in with the taunts.

"Oh, yeah. The Skank."

Susan's heart was beating too fast, her breath was rasping, and her head was spinning with shock. Here? Katherine Willis was here of all places?

"Look at you all done up," continued Katherine. "You know you can put lipstick on a pig, don't you, runt?"

She let out a sudden roar and lurched her body at Susan, who jumped and fell backwards to the ground.

"Maybe I should give the little runt a kicking, for old time's sake," crowed the tormentor.

"No, no, please." Susan squeezed the words from her constricting chest.

Katherine made as if to lunge at her again, so Susan pulled her mother's shoes off and clasping them to her clipboard, she ran barefoot, banging into objects as she fled, with her torturer's laughter and taunts echoing after her.

She continued to run blindly. A discarded tent peg cut into her foot and she didn't notice. She ran through the camp to The Cedar's entrance and out into the road. A post office van screeched to a halt, barely missing her.

"Idiot!" shouted the woman driving the van. She drove around the traumatised girl, who was frozen to the spot in terror.

Dazed, Susan made her way to the roadside verge and vomited coffee and apple juice. Then the flight instinct returned and she sprinted back into the office, picked up her carrier bag, threw her clipboard onto the counter, and ran into the loos.

She ripped open the moisture wipes and violently smeared at the makeup on her face, trying to remove all traces.

"Ugly, stupid Susan!" she screamed at her reflection in the mirror. She tore off the pink jumper and tried to put the sweatshirt on, but the room was spinning. As she slumped to the floor and blacked out, she could hear Tina knocking and calling to her, but it sounded so very, very far away.

* * *

Tina had seen Susan rush through the office and knew instantly that something was very wrong. She leapt from behind her desk and knocked frantically at the locked toilet door. She heard her shouting something and then a muffled thud.

She scrabbled on a nearby desk for a letter opener and with trembling fingers, used it to turn the lock from the outside. The makeshift tool slid from the narrow slot several times before Tina felt the mechanism move and heard a loud click. Cautiously opening the door, she was confronted with Susan's crumpled form slumped against a wall, and a long dark smear of blood on the tiled floor. The girl's face was smeared with residual traces of black and red makeup, mixed with tears.

Tina knelt beside her.

"Susan! Susan, can you hear me?" she called.

Susan moaned quietly and opened her eyes; she stared with a glassy expression.

"Come on, Susan, come with me, honey."

Tina helped the docile girl to stand and led her to the small back office, away from view. Then she went to fetch two towels (one of which she put under warm water), and a first aid kit. She wiped Susan's face clean and dried it gently. Then she cleaned and dressed her cut foot. Finally, she cajoled Susan out of her grass-stained pale denims and helped her into the leggings and sweatshirt.

"I'll get these cleaned for you," she said, holding up the pink jumper and jeans. Susan nodded dumbly.

"Can you tell me what happened?" Tina asked.

Susan seemed to jump awake and looked around in terror, her breathing gathering pace.

"Calm down, sweetie, calm down." Tina hugged her. "Tell me."

Between coughs and gasps and sobs, Susan managed to give the details of what had happened. Tears formed in Tina's eyes and she gave a little gasp, holding her hand to her mouth, when she heard of the near miss with the post van.

"Thank you for telling me, Susan," she said calmly, though it was a thin veneer of calm. "Wait here."

She picked up the telephone next to her and dialled a three-digit number.

"Please could you ask Sharon to come up here?" she said.

Sharon was a kind, matronly woman who was responsible for running the cleaning teams on the camp site. She was as discreet as she was good-natured.

Tina sat next to the traumatised Susan and stroked her hair.

"Please don't tell Mum and Viv!" Susan abruptly cried. "Please. I don't want to worry Mum. But, oh God, now they've found me again. We must have left some clue we were coming here. I was so careful. What am I to do?"

"I won't tell your mum or Viv, honey," Tina reassured her, "and we don't know why those little scumbags are here, but I'll wager it is just coincidence."

There was a tentative knock at the door, and Sharon walked into the room.

"Ah, thank you, Sharon," said Tina, "I wonder if I might ask for your help. Susan has cut her foot rather deeply and I need you to drive to Dr Salmon to have him check it out. I think it may be wise for her to get a tetanus shot. It has been rather a shock for her, so please will you drive her home afterwards?

You may take my car if you wish, the keys are beside the phone on my desk."

"Oh, my poor darlin'," clucked Sharon, seeing Susan's condition, "I'll go and get the car and bring it to the front."

Tina helped Susan slip a trainer onto her good foot and limp to the front of the site office; shortly afterwards, Sharon arrived in her boss's silver Volkswagen Golf. Once Susan was in the passenger seat, Tina walked to the driver's window.

"Thank you for doing this, Sharon," she said, "I'd do it myself, but," her eyes turned to the camp site, "I've got some trash to take out."

* * *

Luke and Dominic had just entered The Cherries when the phone started to ring. Luke was taking his shopping to the study, so Dominic answered.

"It's Tina from The Cedars," he called. "Could you spare a minute?"

Luke reappeared and took the receiver.

"Hello, gorgeous," he said playfully, "I wondered how long your husband would be away before you called old Luke." He smiled at his little joke, the result of years of friendship.

Dominic was rather disturbed to see the change in Luke's expression as he listened to whatever Tina was saying. There was only one way to describe it. Cold rage.

"I'll be there directly," said Luke in a quiet voice, his throat tight. He replaced the receiver and marched to the door.

"What's happened?" cried Dominic.

"Nothing for you to worry about," Luke replied tersely, snatching up the keys to the Vauxhall from the hall table where Dominic had only just set them down.

A few moments later, the van squealed from the driveway and accelerated down the lane. Dominic had never seen Luke drive so quickly before and he was worried.

* * *

It felt to Tina that Luke arrived at The Cedars almost as soon as she put the phone down.

"Thanks for coming," she said, "I'd like a witness, and I'm pretty riled up.

If Jerry were here, I wouldn't trouble you. Then again, I don't like to think what Jerry would do to them."

"I wouldn't miss it for anything," Luke assured her.

They walked together through the camp site and arrived at the tent Susan had described. Katherine and her boyfriend were sitting outside, drinking lagers.

"I hear you have been harassing my staff, Miss Willis," said Tina, reading the name from the reservation card she had brought from the office. "We don't tolerate such behaviour here, so I need to ask you to leave."

"Sod off," said the boyfriend, "we've paid for the week."

"Then I will refund you your balance."

Katherine stood up and walked belligerently to Tina.

"We aren't going anywhere," she snarled, "you can't do this to us. I'll call the police."

The boyfriend also stood with a very aggressive stance. He glanced at Luke, who looked totally unperturbed by his attitude.

"Yeah, Kathy," he encouraged his girlfriend, "they've got no proof of anything." He displayed his middle finger to Tina.

"Look, son, let's have a quiet word, man-to-man," said Luke. Katherine and her partner were too foolish to notice the note of menace in his voice. "You're a big guy, you've got nothing to fear, have you?"

The young man moved a few steps away with Luke, who seemed to put a fatherly arm around his shoulder as they spoke in quiet voices.

A few moments later, he returned with a very white face.

"Maybe we should go, Kath," he said, with a slight tremor in his voice.

"What? What's got into you?" she asked, taking pleasure in belittling him.

"I just think it's better to leave, OK?"

"No, I'm not going!" Katherine insisted. "I'm not going to let one of her kind tell me what to do."

"One of what kind?" asked Tina innocently. "American?"

"You know," hissed Katherine.

Tina did know. She looked at the green hatchback parked next to the tent. It had a pink steering wheel cover and a picture of a woman in a bunny-girl costume on the rear tailgate. She made an educated guess or two.

"Is this your car, Miss Willis?" she asked, with an officious tone.

"Yes."

"Then I'm going to give my very good friend Sergeant Perry down at the local station a call, and I'm going to suggest that he comes down here and does a check for insurance and tax on every vehicle. You don't strike me as someone who would want that to happen."

Katherine was silent, with glaring, hate-filled eyes.

"OK," she said with what dignity she could muster.

"You have ten minutes to get the hell off my camp site. And don't ever come around here again, get me?" Tina told them.

Luke then added a few final words.

"Don't forget, we have your home addresses on this card. I don't think you'd want any local difficulties following you home, so let's not have any more unpleasantness happening to people we know, eh?"

Tina and Luke watched Katherine's car leave The Cedars. The driver and passenger managed to find sufficient courage to make obscene gestures as the vehicle drove down the road.

"Sergeant Perry?" asked Luke. "We don't even have a local police station."

Tina gave a satisfied smile.

* * *

Vivian had only just got up, having slept past noon, when Susan arrived home and hobbled into the kitchen, aided by Sharon.

"Bless me!" she cried. "Whatever has happened, Susie?"

"I cut my foot on something. It's no big deal."

"We've been to Doctor Salmon," explained Sharon. "He says that the cut is clean, but he gave her a tetanus shot, and Susan needs to change the dressing regularly. I'm Sharon, by the way." She held out a plump hand to Vivian, who shook it lightly. "Doctor says to stay off the foot as much as possible for a few days, but she should be fine by next week."

"Not much of a birthday for you, my poor Susie," commiserated Vivian. "We'll make it special, though."

"Thanks, Aunty Viv. I think I'll have a lie down for a bit. I'm exhausted," Susan said.

She stood up on her good foot and made her way to the door by hopping and holding the kitchen counter. Vivian moved to help, but Susan was insistent that she wanted to manage alone. She thanked Sharon for her help at the doctors before crawling up the stairs on hands and knees and rolling onto her bed, where she immediately fell into a deep sleep.

She was awoken by the sound of raindrops on the window. It was early evening and she was cold, so she curled her duvet around herself, but before long she hauled herself up and hopped to the bathroom. As she made her way back to her room, her mother appeared at the top of the stairs.

"I heard the loo flush, so I thought you might be up and about. Let's have a look at this foot. It's not like you to go wandering around outside with no shoes on."

Susan lay on her bed, and Marian gently removed the bandage. She wiped the area with an antiseptic pad she had brought with her and then applied a fresh dressing.

"Brave girl," she said, kissing her daughter's head. "You know, you're a popular girl – loads of visitors. Tina's been up to check on you, Luke and Dominic too. He brought you a box of chocolates – maybe he's a bit sweet on you."

"Mum, I can pretty confidently say that that is very unlikely."

"Oh, Susie, don't be so negative about yourself," Marian chided.

Susan smiled.

"OK, Mum."

"Susie, can I ask you a question?" Marian enquired tentatively.

Susan was filled with dread.

"When I got up," her mother continued, "I found my handbag in the bathroom with the lipstick on the side of the basin."

Susan closed her eyes - how could she have been so forgetful as to have not taken her mother's bag back downstairs that morning?

"And those shoes I hate were in a carrier bag with your mobile phone," Marian added.

Susan groaned. She had no option but to come clean, and so she related all the events of the day while her mother sat quietly listening.

"I'm proud of you, Susie," Marian said when her daughter had finished, "you took a brave step today. Don't let that little bitch get you down. You're tougher than you know. Now, why don't I help you downstairs and we can watch telly and pig out? There's fish pie keeping warm in the oven for you and Dominic's chocolates too."

"Sounds good, Mum."

Marian helped Susan change into her pyjamas and they made their way slowly to the living room. Her phone had had several text messages waiting for her. One was from Tina, and simply said 'They're both gone and they are never coming anywhere near here again. Hang in there, babe, because you have friends'.

Susan sat with her legs stretched out on the couch, while Vivian and Marian fussed over her. The events of the day receded in her mind as they watched trash TV and laughed with one another.

As she looked at her mother's eyes sparkling in the reflected light of the television, and saw Vivian sipping a gin and tonic between puffs of a cigarette, she felt a deep sense of contentment.

She realised that tomorrow she would face the bad memories resurfacing, and she needed to find a way to manage. But now she knew someone who had found coping mechanisms, and maybe he would help her find her own. He was just a short distance away across the courtyard, and he seemed even more precious a friend than ever.

* * *

Susan spent the night on the living room couch, curled up under her duvet. She had watched television into the early hours after the other two had gone to bed, before she had been able to sleep. She slept through Marian peeking in to check her before leaving for work, but she was stirred by Vivian's somewhat noisier descent of the stairs and was then fully awoken by her honorary aunt flinging the door of the room open and searching for her cigarettes.

Vivian jumped when she turned around to see Susan on the sofa.

"Oh, my! Susie, you gave me such a start! I forgot you were in here. I didn't wake you, did I, sweetie?"

"No," Susan lied.

"Well, Aunty Viv is going to spoil you rotten today."

Susan rolled off her makeshift bed and crawled to the downstairs cloakroom. It was easier to stand from her seated position on the toilet and she tried tentatively to put weight on her sore foot, but it was painful. She hopped back to the couch – there was a smell of toast wafting from the kitchen.

Vivian arrived carrying a tray loaded with two rounds of fresh toast, jars of jam, honey and marmalade, a pot of yoghurt, fruit juice and a cup of tea. She decanted some items to the coffee table beside Susan and placed the tray on her lap.

"Anything else, luv?" she asked.

"This looks amazing, thank you."

Aunty Viv kissed her head.

"Actually, there is one thing I really want," ventured Susan.

"What's that, darlin'?"

"A shower. Or a bath. But…" Susan gestured to her bandaged foot.

"I'll put my thinking cap on. Eat up."

Susan munched her toast whilst watching daytime TV. A little while after she had finished, she heard Vivian go upstairs and the sound of a bath running.

"Let's get you upstairs while the water's hot," said Vivian.

Susan found it easiest to just crawl on hands and knees to the bathroom, where she perched on the plastic rim of the steaming bath and slid out of her pyjamas. She had never undressed in front of anyone before, so was intensely aware of the other woman's presence.

"For crying out loud, Susie, I've seen you naked hundreds of times."

"Not since I was six!" protested Susan, shyly trying to conceal whatever she could.

Vivian grabbed the ankle of Susan's bad foot, almost tipping her backwards into the bathwater.

"What are you doing?" Susan squawked, arms flailing. Vivian slipped her foot into a supermarket carrier bag and started to wrap duct tape tightly around the plastic, just above the ankle.

Susan peered past, trying to see what was going on.

"Hmmm, not sure that's going to be watertight," mused Vivian. "You'll have to stick that leg out of the bath to be on the safe side."

It was the least relaxing bath imaginable. It was hard enough to get in the water with one leg resting on the rim of the bath, but every time she tried to sit back, Susan slid down and her head disappeared under the bubbles. Finally, Vivian agreed to stand behind her and grab her under the arms if she started to lose traction. With all Susan's thrashing and flailing, Vivian was almost as wet as she was.

It was a relief to be able to get out; Susan stood dripping on the bath mat, wobbling and aching all over. Vivian draped a bath towel over her and then left to change her own clothes. Susan stumbled to her bedroom and slipped on a long t-shirt and denim shorts.

After a little effort and the help of nail scissors, she freed her foot from its plastic prison and changed the dressing. There was still an open wound, and the discolouration of bruising, but there was no swelling.

She made her way down the stairs, clinging to the banister, to once again sink thankfully onto the couch. Vivian joined her.

The television was still on and there was a feature on a 'before and after' makeover. Susan knew Vivian was interested in these things, so she stayed on the channel. As the feature went on, she could feel Vivian's eyes on her.

"Your mother told me what happed yesterday, Susie," Vivian said.

"I thought she probably would."

"I think you were brave."

"I think I was pathetic, running like a scared baby and having to be rescued," Susan said, full of self-loathing.

"Not that, though I don't think you're right in how you put it," Vivian responded. "No, I meant it was brave to try new things."

She kept staring at Susan.

"I've just realised that you're my prisoner," she said with an ominous note to her voice.

"I'm your what?"

"Stay here."

"Well, I'm not in a position to do much else!"

Vivian returned within a few minutes with a large case, rather like a builder's tool box, and a number of leather bags and pouches. When the mystery box was opened, a vast array of cosmetic items was revealed, many of which Susan had no idea what they were.

"I've wanted to do this for you for so long," said a happy Vivian. Susan resigned herself to her fate.

After what felt like an eternity of eyebrow plucking (ow, ow, ow), leg waxing (ouch, ouch, ouch), and hair detangling (for the love of God, please stop), Vivian had prepared her canvas and was ready to work her art. Brushes, pencils, sponges, and a multitude of other exotic methods of makeup application took place, followed by a mini manicure and pale nail-polish.

Vivian stood back to admire her work.

"Not bad, not bad at all," she congratulated herself. "Wanna see?"

Susan nodded, reluctantly. Vivian produced a large hand mirror and held it up for her.

"Is that me?" Susan asked.

Vivian had done a better job than the TV show's makeover. Susan almost didn't recognise herself. She liked what she saw, but it also felt alien, false. She supposed it would take time to adjust.

A ring on the doorbell summoned Vivian, and she re-entered with Reverend June in tow. Susan smiled self-consciously.

"Goodness, Susan, you're looking very glamorous," the vicar declared, "and here I was, expecting to find a helpless invalid, who might like a bit of company."

"Good timing," chipped in Vivian, "I need to pop up to the shop, so I'm happier for Susan to have someone with her. She's got to stay off that foot for a couple of days."

With those words, she was out the door.

* * *

Luke was standing in the village shop, waiting in the queue for the post office to send some more of his parcels of books. The bell over the shop door tinkled as a middle-aged man with a broad chest under his check shirt came in.

"Morning, Helen," the man shouted at the similarly aged woman standing behind the shop till. The bespectacled gentleman in the post office booth visibly winced at the volume of the newcomer's voice.

The middle-aged man stood in the centre of the store, searching the shelves with his eyes.

"Where do you keep the glue, Helen?" he bellowed.

"It's here, next to the till," Helen replied with disinterest, as she stood with her weight on one leg and the other slightly bent, looking out of the window at a van trying to squeeze past a tractor parked outside. "I think you're blocking the road a bit," she pointed out.

He glanced out of the window.

"Doesn't anyone know the width of his own vehicle these days?" he complained. He exited the shop and climbed into the tractor's cab with a wave of acknowledgement to the van driver. They watched as he expertly repositioned the huge vehicle closer to the store, until Helen almost took an instinctive step back from the window as one of the giant wheels seemed about to be coming through.

The van resumed its trip and the man re-entered and approached the till to look at the range of glues. He picked up two different brands and threw them casually on the counter in front of Helen. As she scanned the items, he withdrew a wodge of tens and twenties from his trouser pocket, peeled off the topmost note and placed it into the shop assistant's outstretched hand.

While he waited for his change, he rested his large, work-worn hands on the edge of the counter, and gave a long, slow, loud exhalation, as he gazed around him. His eyes lighted on Luke.

"Ah, Cartwright!" he boomed. "I want a word with you."

"Hi, Joe," replied Luke.

"Here's your change," interrupted Helen, placing an assortment of coins onto the counter. Joe slid some, the larger valued ones, to a collection to his left on the counter and a few others to his right. He cupped his left hand and used his right to sweep the leftmost set of coins into it. He pocketed them. Then he repeated the action with the other collection, which he then distributed amongst the assorted charity collection tins by the till.

By now, Luke was at the post office counter and was having his parcels weighed. Joe sauntered over to him.

"Your field," he said to Luke.

"Which one?" Luke asked. He understood that Joe was an amiable man, but straight talking, which to some people seemed aggressive.

"That's forty-seven pounds and thirty-eight pence," stated the post office clerk.

"The one opposite your place," said Joe, "and the one beyond it too, now I think about it. I'd like to rent them from you for a couple of years. Do a bit of grazing on them. Worked well last time. Good for your fields too."

"Sheep again?" Luke enquired. Joe nodded. "I don't see why not. I'll print off a leasing contract and drop it over to you next week. I'd have thought it's getting a bit late in the year, though."

"Forty-seven pounds and thirty-eight pence."

"I need the space now," Joe explained. "Given the weather, another lambing may not be out of the question. Same price as last time?"

"No, I'd want another ten percent," Luke replied, spitting onto his hand and holding it out.

"You're a hard man, Cartwright," but Joe spat too and accepted the handshake. He went to leave but stopped to pick up a chocolate bar. He waved it to Helen and lobbed a pound coin onto the counter. "Stick the change in a tin, love."

As he left, Helen sighed the sigh of the oppressed and dragged herself past the till to retrieve another of the same chocolate bar to scan.

"Forty-seven pounds and thirty-eight pence, please!"

Luke looked up.

"Sorry, how much?" he asked the frustrated man behind the post office counter.

"Forty-seven pounds and thirty-eight pence," was the exasperated reply.

Luke slipped his business debit card into the reader and typed in his PIN.

"Helen, has the dry-cleaning delivery come in yet?" he asked as he waited for the receipt to print.

"I think so," the assistant replied with her usual level of enthusiasm.

Helen opened a door to a small storage room, beside the cigarette cabinet, and peered in.

"Yeah, it's here," she called. "Yours was the dinner jacket and shirt, wasn't it?"

"Should be some trousers as well," Luke replied, a little concerned.

"Yeah, they're there too. It's all paid for."

She brought the three garments, each sheathed in a long plastic bag on a hanger, to the till, while Luke took his receipt from the under-appreciated post office clerk. He scooped the clothes onto one arm, thanked everyone present and made his way to his van, where he opened the back doors and laid the assembled garments flat on the floor.

He walked up the narrow road to Margaret's cottage and unlatched the front gate. As he passed through, a sleek black Mercedes stopped next to him, engine purring.

"Luke," called the driver through his open window.

"Hello, David. Good to see you," Luke replied, stooping to speak through the window. "Are you still able to give us a lift this evening?"

"That's just what I was about to confirm with you," the driver answered. "Shall I pick up Linda and you at yours, say seven-thirty?"

"Perfect. Thanks, David. Send my love to Chris," Luke said, tapping the roof of the car as it started to pull away.

He made his way into Margaret's home and called out a greeting. As expected, she was in her living room, leg out on a foot stool. Joan was there too.

"I'll stick the kettle on," he said, slipping into the kitchen. He toasted some crumpets, which he'd bought for her when he went shopping, and slathered them in thick farmhouse butter.

As they ate together, he remarked,

"I'm off to a midsummer ball this evening."

"How lovely," said Margaret. "Are you taking Susan with you?"

"What?" he asked surprised. "No. No, I'm escorting Linda Winston."

"Linda Winston," Margaret pulled a face like she had tasted something sour, which Joan copied.

"Linda Winston," she echoed.

"Linda Winston is a perfectly nice lady," Luke protested. "She and I have many interests in common, and we enjoy each other's company on these occasions. Nothing more."

"That's not what I've heard. I think she's set her cap at you," Margaret insisted.

"Well, maybe that's not a bad thing," he remarked, a little nettled.

"Well, I like Susan," Margaret stated.

"Susan," echoed Joan.

"You've not even met her, Joan," said Luke, with exasperation. "Susan is a young woman, she's not wanting an old fogey like me."

"You're both but babes in arms," argued Margaret, and from her perspective, it was hard to dispute.

"Babes in arms," agreed the echo.

"Well, Susan couldn't come anyway," he explained, "she's hurt her foot and can't walk for a few days, let alone dance."

"Oh, the lamb!" cried Margaret.

"The lamb!" came the echo.

"It's her birthday tomorrow," Luke said, trying to move the conversation along.

"Her birthday? Well, goodness me! Joan, Joan darling pass me my handbag, love. Luke, in the drawer in the dresser back there are some notelets and envelopes, bring them to me, will you?"

Supplied with all she had asked for, Margaret looked about her with annoyed puzzlement.

"Where have I put my glasses," she asked, "I had them just now to look at The Radio Times?"

"They're on your head," Luke pointed out.

"On your head." Now he too had an echo.

Margaret patted her head and found her spectacles with a little mea culpa grin.

She picked up a notelet and her pen, stared thoughtfully into the distance for a few seconds, and then began writing, with the best penwomanship her gnarled fingers would permit.

Luke sat in polite silence, but felt he was neglecting Joan.

"Having a nice stay, Joan?" he asked.

"Nice stay, yes."

"Weather has been very changeable," he observed.

"Changeable, yes."

"And a little chillier at night," he tried.

"Chillier at night, yes," this time the echo was accompanied with a little mime of shivering.

Luke couldn't face the thought of trying to drag the conversation further, but thankfully Margaret finished writing her note. She slipped it into its envelope, accompanied by a five-pound note which she had taken from her purse. Lastly, she licked and sealed it with a triumphant flourish and handed it to Luke.

"Don't you forget to give it to her," Margaret instructed him.

"I won't," he promised. "Actually, I had better be going," he kissed her cheek, "I'll see you in a couple of days. You too, Joan."

He was almost out of the front door, when Margaret called him back.

"Luke, Luke!"

"Yes? What is it?" he sighed.

"I've got something else you must give Susan. Now where the blessed is it?"

"Blessed is it," came the echo.

* * *

Linda Winston sat at her dressing table, admiring her reflection. She put on a necklace, sparkling with diamonds, and matching earrings and bracelet. Her long, red hair was wound into an elegant bun at the back of her head, allowing a clear view of her graceful neck.

She stood, admiring the way her emerald green gown flowed over her slender form. She looked every inch the wealthy divorcee.

A final squirt from her perfume atomiser, before she picked up her designer clutch bag and went to her car. The large Lexus 4x4 made quick progress through the country lanes.

* * *

Luke walked into Vivian's living room, dressed for the ball. All three women said how smart he looked.

Susan was particularly impressed; she thought he looked a bit like James Bond, and said so. Luke was flattered, and coloured slightly.

"Don't you think Susie looks nice this evening? Notice anything different?" asked Vivian.

Luke frantically tried to identify what he was supposed to have noticed.

"Um, she looks very nice," he played safe.

"You've not noticed, don't pretend you have," scorned Vivian. "Typical man! She's only gone and had a makeover."

"Oh. Oh, yes. Yes, it's nice," he complimented. "Not that I'd really noticed before."

It was painfully clumsy. What his heart wanted to say was that she was already beautiful, so any cosmetics were unnecessary. That's what he thought he'd said. Susan, however, was confused as to what he meant, and was even more confused as to why she cared so much for his opinion.

Luke decided to make an escape.

"Look at the time. I must be going," he excused himself. "Oh, wait, I almost forgot. Margaret sent this for you for tomorrow."

He passed Susan the envelope which had been entrusted to him earlier.

"Oh, and there's this."

He reached into the hallway and retrieved a walking stick that he had propped against the wall in there on his way in.

"She says it's her spare and you can use it for as long as you need," he explained.

"That's kind," said Marian.

"Actually, it's a good idea," said Vivian, "why didn't any of us think of it?"

Luke said a final goodbye and took his leave.

A little later, Susan decided to try the walking stick and to answer a call of nature at the same time. It did make matters a lot easier, particularly getting up and sitting down. She practised walking around with it.

Through the window in the darkened kitchen, she saw headlights of a large car. Luke came out of The Cherries to meet it, and chivalrously opened the driver's door. A tall, graceful woman in an elegant gown disembarked and gave him a slow kiss on the cheek. As the two figures stood talking, a sleek Mercedes arrived, and Luke opened a rear door for his date, before getting into the back on the other side.

She wouldn't want to admit it, but Susan was jealous.

* * *

The midsummer ball was in full swing. Linda and Luke had several dances with each other and with other friends. Luke was not enjoying himself, however. He disliked being among so many people, and the music, though very pleasant, was rather too loud for his tastes. The only reason he went to such events was to network for his business, although he did like many of the people there on an individual basis.

He was sitting with David and Christine, discussing the antiques trade. David was lamenting the state of the market, wondering if it was time to get out. Luke was unconcerned, as this was David's general line of conversation whenever he reached his fourth glass of wine. He glanced at Chris, who as the designated driver was sipping a mineral water; she mouthed a 'tut' and rolled her eyes skywards.

Luke, scanning the dancefloor (was that Reverend June and her husband making a passable stab at a foxtrot?), sighted Linda walking towards them, holding the arm of the grey-haired man of about sixty who was accompanying her.

"Luke, darling," she cooed as they got nearer, "I've been looking all over for you. This is Hank Goldberg and he owns one of America's most prestigious private collections of antiquarian books. He and his wife are staying at the Golden Gables Hotel for a few weeks and I simply had to introduce you."

Luke stood and had a firm handshake with Mr Goldberg.

"I'm very pleased to meet you, sir," he said respectfully.

"Likewise, Mr Cartwright," came the response, with a Brooklyn accent.

"What brings you to our out-of-the-way neck of the woods?" Luke enquired.

"Well, my niece is getting married close by, so my wife and I thought we would make a bit of a trip of it. You know, see Stratford-upon-Avon and Stonehenge."

Sensing that her date was struggling not to point out that those places were nowhere near to each other, let alone to where they were staying, Linda interjected, "Luke, darling, I thought it would be rather fun for you to have them to one of your lovely soirées at The Cherries - a proper English evening party."

"Why yes," said Luke, suppressing annoyance at being presented with a fait accompli, "that would be a wonderful idea."

They compared diaries and set a date for the following week.

As Linda and Luke travelled home in the back of Chris's and David's car, she leant close to him, holding his arm.

"I told you how good I can be for business," she quietly boasted.

Luke gave a semi-nod but said nothing. He was still annoyed, but he did appreciate the significant contact that Goldberg could be. However, he resented her for inviting people to his house; it was presumptuous at the very least.

When they alighted at The Cherries, Luke walked her directly to her car, preventing any pretext of being invited inside.

"Thank you for being a wonderful companion this evening," he said, being cordial but not allowing any misinterpretation of his intent that she should leave.

Linda wore her most sophisticated smile, and gave him a semi-embrace, touching her cheek to his jacket shoulder. She allowed him to open her car door and she slid slowly onto the driver's seat.

"Call me," she purred.

Chapter 6

Susan awoke in her own bed, rather than the couch, on the morning of her birthday. Marian's alarm clock had roused them both, for, while Susan was signed off work, her mother still had to go to the office.

"Happy birthday, Susie. Try to go back to sleep, darling."

"I don't think I can," Susan replied excitedly.

"Well, try, or I shall feel guilty," Marian requested. "How does it feel to not be a teenager anymore?"

"Old!"

Marian chuckled and headed off to the shower. Susan sat up in bed, willing herself not to look out of the window. Her willpower was insufficient, however – she twisted slightly, and pulled a curtain aside, peeking out to look at The Cherries. The big 4x4 was gone. Good.

She started to prod at her sore foot, trying to establish if it was getting better. Her unscientific self-diagnosis convinced her that there was an improvement. She should leave it alone now, Susan told herself. She decided to change the dressing.

Marian returned to the room to find Susan in a neo-contortion peering at the hole in her foot.

"What on Earth are you doing?" she mothered.

"Trying to see if it's closed up," Susan told her, looking up brightly. "Do we have a magnifying glass?"

"Susan, will you give it time to heal? I know you hate sitting around, but you have to," Marian scolded.

She sat on the mattress beside her daughter, making the bed wobble briefly. She took a fresh dressing and a clean bandage and firmly covered up the wound.

"Now, I know we are saving presents for this evening, when everyone is here, but…" Marian reached under her bed and pulled out a sizable gift-wrapped parcel, "I can't resist. I thought you'd appreciate it today."

Susan squealed. The wrapping paper was shredded in seconds and she was holding up a creamy-yellow summer dress with a pattern of tiny pink flowers.

"I saw it yesterday when I was on lunch. I wanted you to have something nice of your own," Marian explained.

Susan hugged her. "Thanks, Mum, it's lovely. I shall wear it tonight."

* * *

Susan had an uneventful morning. She had a brief chat with Dominic as he passed by the kitchen, and Vivian helped her with her makeup, this time in front of a mirror, explaining to her what she was doing and why.

Tina had promised by text to drop by to say happy birthday at some point and she arrived just after lunch. She asked Susan how she was feeling and how her foot was. Tina was nervous that Susan may not want to come back to The Cedars; she was a good worker and had also become a friend in a short space of time. She had been trying to think of a way to gently determine her employee's intentions, but to her surprise, Susan spoke first.

"Tina, this isn't easy to say, but I want to apologise for what happened the other day. I behaved like a little girl, and there is no place for that at work. I don't want to lose my job."

Susan didn't go on to say, "But the idea of going back fills me with horror." She didn't need to; Tina knew and understood.

"You're golden, hun," Tina assured her. "But I don't think you should come back for a while, and maybe more of a desk role when you do? Less having to walk around the place?"

There was logic to her offer. Firstly, she recognised that Susan was a much more intelligent and able person than she had appeared at first interview, all due to low self-confidence. Secondly, Tina had come to miss doing many of the tasks she had assigned to Susan (walking the camp site, for example), whereas she found the admin rather dry. Lastly, while Susan's words were courageous, her voice betrayed her stress and anxiety, so Tina concluded that removing the requirement for Susan to deal with customers directly (at least for the time being), may help restore her confidence.

"Yes please," Susan answered. She exhaled a long breath, through narrowed lips. "That's a nice birthday present."

"It doesn't stop there," said Tina, taking two gift-wrapped boxes from her handbag, one cube-shaped and the other a small, slender oblong. Susan excitedly opened them.

The cube contained a novelty mug, with her name on it. The slender oblong had a small blue crystal pendant and matching earrings.

"Thank you, they are lovely. This day keeps getting better," said a happy Susan.

* * *

Marian was having a hectic day at work, as in addition to her normal duties, she was having to provide cover for two absent secretaries; one was on a scheduled holiday and the other had been admitted to hospital at short notice on the previous evening with suspected appendicitis. Naturally, it also fell to Marian to organise a 'Get Well Soon' card to be taken in by one of the partners, who would visit their ill colleague on her way home.

Marian's mind was even more troubled by thoughts of organising Susan's party for that evening. She had planned with Vivian to bake a cake for the occasion, but Susan's injury meant that she had been at home all the time, preventing covert preparation, and while Susan was no child, Marian wanted it to be a surprise. That morning she had decided to see what cakes the local bakery sold and to make do with that by adding some writing to the icing when she got home. The meal itself was to be a straightforward roast chicken with all the trimmings, but she hadn't yet had an opportunity to go to the supermarket. Now all her extra workload made working through lunch a distinct probability, especially if she wanted to leave at a reasonable time.

As she typed furiously, she was interrupted by a client coming in through the front door, and she looked up to see Luke waiting behind the reception counter. She moved swiftly to meet him, and after a mutually warm greeting, Luke asked for one of the partners by name. Marian scanned the diary displayed on the computer screen.

"It doesn't say he has any appointments now. Let me see if he's free," she said, picking up the phone and dialling his extension. There was a brief conversation, that Mr Cartwright was in reception and wondered if he might have a word. Putting the receiver down, she advised Luke that the partner would be down shortly, and suggested that he may care to sit in one of the comfy chairs in the foyer to wait.

"You're looking a bit stressed, Marian," he commented in a concerned voice. After she had explained how her day was going and that she was worried about getting the cake and food for the meal, he offered, "I can pick that up for you and you can call by and collect it when you get home."

"Really? That would be a huge help," she said in relief. "I guess I should have been more organised and ordered it online to be delivered, but it is probably too late now."

"Well, my picking it up is the easiest solution," he assured her, "and if I can't find a decent cake, Dominic and I can probably knock up a basic sponge in time."

"Do you need money up front?" Marian asked, slightly panicked. "I don't have much cash on me."

"No, that's fine. Pay me back when convenient."

The solicitor he had asked for arrived, so Luke broke off his conversation with Marian to speak with him.

"Thank you for seeing me at short notice," Luke said, "a local farmer wants to rent a couple of fields I own. I had a nice little lease agreement that I used with him a few years back, but when I re-read it this morning, I spotted a few things I'd like an expert eye to look at."

"Of course," said the partner. "Come on through to my office and we can go over it."

Forty-five minutes later, Luke was on his way out through reception.

"Don't worry," he called to Marian, "I have it all in hand." She opened her mouth to say something, but he was already through the door with a, "See you when you get home."

"Oh dear," she said to herself, "I didn't tell him my budget. With his tastes, I may be having to pay in instalments."

Luke strode to the bakers to examine their offerings of cakes, but was unsatisfied that any of them were worthy of the honour of being Susan's birthday cake. Aware of time ticking by, he jogged back to the van, where Dominic was waiting behind the steering wheel, itching to be back on the road.

"We need to stop off at the big supermarket on our way back," Luke announced, "and when we get home, we're going to need our chefs' hats."

* * *

That evening, Marian parked outside Hayfield Barn and walked straight across the courtyard to The Cherries. Luke was out, but Dominic let her in. She was relieved to find that Luke had shopped very conservatively, so the costs were a little under what she was expecting, despite his having bought the chicken at a farm shop instead of the supermarket.

She was even more pleased with the moist chocolate sponge, with a rich buttercream layer, that the boys had made, ready for her to ice and decorate. Dominic brought the shopping bags to Vivian's, while Marian carried the cake.

After she'd given her birthday girl a big long hug, Marian banned Susan from the kitchen. Vivian had decorated the rarely used dining room during the day, polishing the wooden table until it gleamed and festooning the walls with 'Happy Birthday' banners.

With half an hour to the time the guests were due to arrive, Marian, Susan and Vivian went upstairs to change. Susan was a bit disappointed she couldn't wear shoes because of her injured foot, but she could at least bear to slide on a pair of flesh-coloured tights.

Reverend June, her husband (Reverend Peter), Dominic and Luke met outside The Cherries and walked across the courtyard together. Soon they were sitting in the living room with Susan, savouring the smell of the roasting chicken which was drifting through the house. From the kitchen, they could hear the clatter of pots and pans, generated by Vivian's and Marian's cooking.

"Smells delicious!" June called to anyone who might be listening.

"Excellent. We're about to serve up, so if you'd care to go through…" Marian responded.

Susan stood, with moderately little difficulty, and hobbled ahead of the small procession to the dining room. Little, handwritten place cards told them where they were each to sit; the birthday girl sat at the head of the table, bubbling with excitement.

Some bottles of white wine were in a cooler on the sideboard, so Luke filled everyone's glasses while Marian and Vivian brought through the chicken, gravy, bacon, chipolatas, roast potatoes and assorted dishes of vegetables.

When everyone's plate was filled beyond capacity with food, Marian stood with her glass raised, to Susan.

"To my lovely Susie. Happy birthday, sweetheart."

Everyone else raised their glasses.

"Happy birthday," was their united and heartfelt salutation.

Susan watched Luke, by far the fastest eater at the table by habit, as he raised his first forkful of food to his mouth.

"I think as we have two vicars at the table, someone should say grace or something first," she proclaimed.

Luke, along with everyone else, froze in position and they slowly returned their cutlery to their plates. He turned his gaze to her and she popped the tip of her tongue out in a playful 'I got you back'; he smiled, knowing he was bested.

The two vicars exchanged glances, fighting a momentary, private, unspoken battle of which of them was going to bless the meal. Peter, not knowing if he had won or lost, ended up speaking.

"Benedice, Domine, nos et dona tua, quae de largitate tua sumus sumpturi, et concede, ut illis salubriter nutriti tibi debitum obsequium praestare valeamus, per Christum Dominum nostrum."

With the exception of Luke and June, the other diners looked mildly baffled. June gave her husband a kick under the table and a 'you're incorrigible' glare.

"What?" he said innocently.

"Now I remember why I like you so much, Peter!" said Luke, laughing.

"What my husband said in his medieval high Church manner, was: 'Bless, O Lord, us and your gifts, which from your bounty we are about to receive, and grant that, healthily nourished by them, we may render you due obedience, through Christ our Lord'," explained June, looking around those at the table and realising that the translation may not have been much more enlightening.

"I think he wishes he was still at Cambridge," she added, and then mouthed at her husband, "and so do I." The twinkle of love in her eyes belied those words.

"I thought it was rather pretty," remarked Susan.

"Will people just start eating!" interjected Marian.

After dinner, when the table was cleared and the dishwasher humming, Susan sat on the couch, surrounded by friends and eyeing excitedly a pile of presents and envelopes that lay before her.

She opened the first envelope, which was from her grandmother and contained a card and a twenty-pound note. Next was the notelet from Margaret, which she found very touching.

"We weren't sure what to get you," explained June, as Susan opened the thick red envelope that she and Peter had given her. As well as the anticipated greeting card, inside was a bar of Swiss chocolate and a gift token for a high street department store. Susan was most appreciative.

"Mine next," insisted Dominic, with a slight smirk. Susan eyed him with mock suspicion as she removed the paper from the oddly-shaped package. The contents were a slender, shiny booklet on the flowers of English hedgerows, and a plastic silver child's tiara with a pink cardboard inlay emblazoned with 'Princess'. Smiling, Susan lobbed a cushion across the room at him, which he caught easily and sat on. She donned her tiara, and adopted a regal pose.

Luke's present was by far the largest in size.

"That's a big package you've got there, Luke," snorted Vivian into a glass of port. Marian leant over and gave her the kind of light slap on the upper arm that a mother gives to a cheeky teenager.

"Viv! Really!" she hissed.

Everyone else had chosen to ignore the remark, though Dominic and Susan both knew that if they looked at one another, they would start laughing. The birthday girl started to tear off the wrapping paper to reveal... a large cardboard box.

She picked away at the masking tape holding the two halves of the lid together and peered inside.

"Oh, wow!" Susan breathed as she started to remove a complete set of artist supplies: sets of watercolour and acrylic paints, tins of pencils, rubbers, erasers, brushes, assorted pads of paper (sketching, watercolour, board), two small easels (one table-top and one collapsible free-standing) and some books on techniques and art history.

Last to come from the box was a birthday card which Luke had painted himself, which was a cartoon of Susan eating a giant birthday cake. She held it up to show everyone else.

"Thank you so much. It's so very generous," she said. It touched her soul that he of all people should see her creative desire as something to be encouraged. Looking at him sitting, smiling, hoping that she liked the gifts, she felt an excited tingling in her spine that seemed to radiate down her arms to her fingers and down her legs to her toes. Her throat seemed to tighten a little.

"Not really," Luke replied, "I'm going to be one of the ones who gets to see your pictures, I hope, so it is for my benefit as much as yours."

He moved over to give Susan a hug; it was a normal hug to the onlookers, but to Luke it lasted an hour. Her arms seemed to hold him joyously tight (he could feel her palms pressing through his jacket onto his shoulder blades); her soft hair brushing against the side of his face was intoxicating.

"Happy birthday," he whispered into her ear. As he rose, Susan's slender lips lightly grazed his cheek, stirring something almost primitive within him. When Luke returned to his chair, he saw her eyes were bright with life.

"Now mine!" exclaimed Vivian, breaking Susan's and Luke's momentary reverie.

The wrapping paper was excitedly torn aside to reveal a jewellery box. The outside was covered in padded material, a pale pastel mauve, with an intricate gold thread woven around the edges. Susan opened it, and a tiny clockwork ballerina popped up and pirouetted in front of a little mirror set in the top of the box, while a tune plinked from the mechanism.

"I remember you liking them when you were a little girl," said Vivian.

"Oh, I still do! Thank you, Aunty Viv, it's lovely," Susan enthused.

Inside the box were a few items of costume jewellery, rings, pendants, bracelets; nothing of great monetary value, but priceless to a young woman who had arrived with little more than the clothes she stood in. There was an envelope too, which contained the expected birthday card; however, an unexpected piece of paper fluttered onto her lap when she opened it. It was a cheque to her from Vivian for three hundred pounds.

"Oh, Auntie Viv, I can't take this!" Susan objected.

"Yes, you can!" Vivian insisted. "Don't reject my gifts. But there are two conditions."

Susan was wide-eyed, and a little overwhelmed.

"First condition," continued Vivian, "is that it is spent wholly on you. Specifically, clothes and shoes, so you can stop nicking my Jenny's stuff."

"Sorry, Aunty Viv, I thought you didn't mind," started Susan.

"I'm joking. Crikey, kids today can't get a joke."

Vivian rolled her eyes and glanced around the older adults for their agreement, but not actually caring whether or not she received it.

"What was I saying before I was interrupted?" she continued. "Oh, yes, it must be used for clothes, shoes and accessories. Second condition, you must wait three weeks before you spend it."

Susan was rather puzzled.

"Okaaaay," she said slowly.

"And you must wait three weeks, because then your very own personal shopper will be here to help you," Vivian told her mysteriously.

Susan stared at Vivian, dumbfounded.

"Who's that?" she asked.

Vivian gave a half smile.

"Who is it?" demanded Susan with almost excruciating curiosity.

"Can't you guess?" Vivian's eyes danced with delight at the sight of her honorary niece's agitation.

Realisation dawned.

"It's Jenny, isn't it?" Susan bounced up and down, giving little claps. "Jenny's coming."

She jumped up to hug Vivian, but sat down again with an "ow," holding her sore foot. Then she got up more carefully and limped round to Vivian's chair.

"Thankyou-thankyou-thankyou," she squeaked, as they embraced.

"You're welcome, darlin'," replied Vivian, her chin resting on Susan's shoulder.

When her daughter was back in her seat, Marian handed Susan a small package and two envelopes.

"Happy birthday, Susie," she almost whispered, her voice affected by the emotion of the evening.

"You've already given me my present," protested Susan, gesturing to her dress.

"There are no rules," insisted Marian.

Susan decided to open in order envelope, present, envelope. The first contained a 'Happy Birthday Daughter' card. The gift turned out to be a single small ring, white metal, incorporating the shape of a dolphin, inlaid with turquoise enamel.

"It's very pretty," enthused Susan, holding it up to her eye. She placed it in her new jewellery box.

"Open the other envelope," said Marian.

Susan obeyed, and pulled out a piece of paper. It was a voucher-receipt for a course of driving lessons and she literally screamed with excitement.

"Watch out, everyone, here I come!" she cried, miming a steering wheel. "Thanks, Mum!"

Marian was laughing with everybody else. She was ecstatic to see Susan so happy, to see how much her daughter had changed in just a few short weeks, growing in confidence. There was still a long way to go, but she began to see the girl was a woman, who someday soon could be independent of her mother. It was bittersweet, but blissfully so, and Marian slipped out of the door as the laughter and conversation grew in volume.

June spied Marian's departure, and after a minute or so, followed her to the kitchen.

"I thought you might need a hand in here," she said, startling Marian, who had her back to her. She had been crying.

"Susan seems so happy," June ventured, handing a piece of kitchen paper to Marian, who was patting around her pockets for a tissue.

"She is, and I am too," Marian assured her. "If you could know the change in her since we arrived. Well, it's a miracle."

"I do know a little of what happened to her. It must have been very hard on you."

"It was," Marian agreed emotionally. "No one can understand what it is to listen to your child cry themselves to sleep every night. To find that you ration the number of aspirin and paracetamol tablets in the cupboard, just in case. To worry if she's home late, to worry that she doesn't want to go out, to beg her to eat, to worry about everything."

June squeezed her arm.

"And now, look at her," Marian continued.

"She is blossoming," said June. "You should be proud."

"I am. She's my world, June, but God forgive me, seeing her this evening I felt… relief… I felt…"

"Yes?" encouraged the vicar.

"… free." Marian forced the word from the depths of her soul, with a single, low, convulsive sob.

June embraced her.

"Marian, I think Susan is special," said the reverend, "I think God has a plan for her and for you. I will pray for you both."

"Thank you, Vicar. That means a lot."

"I'm here if you need to talk," June assured her, "always in confidence."

"I don't like to be a burden."

"Well, it is kind of my job, you know," the clergywoman pointed out.

Marian smiled.

"Look at the time! I'd better get the coffee on," she exclaimed, opening a cupboard and lifting out cups and saucers.

A few minutes later, June carried a tray with coffee pot, cups and saucers, and side plates, napkins and cake forks.

Then Marian's hand snaked through the doorway and flicked the switch to turn off the lights. Everyone went "ooh" as she walked through the door carrying a birthday cake with candles and two sparklers pushed into its icing, their flickering light casting dancing shadows onto the walls.

"Happy birthday to you," she started to sing.

"Happy Birthday to you," the others joined in, as Marian laid the cake on the coffee table in front of her daughter, illuminating her smiling face.

"Make a wish!" shouted Vivian as Susan blew out the candles. Marian sat next to her on the sofa and gave her a huge hug.

"Speech!" cried Peter.

"Yes, speech, speech!" joined in Luke and Dominic.

Susan held her mother's hand and gazed around at the smiling faces, turned to her in expectation.

"I wish that all of you could be as happy as I am right now."

Chapter 7

The following days passed quickly. Susan's foot healed well and she was soon walking around in trainers with barely a discernible limp. She had also applied for her driving licence and, most importantly to her she was painting or drawing at any and every opportunity.

Luke was focussed on organising the soirée that Linda had bounced him into, though he did find time to go to see Joe and organise the leasing of his fields.

Dominic received news that he had been accepted into the agricultural college for that autumn, a year earlier than he had anticipated, thanks to Luke's tutoring. The college was only a short distance by car, so his great focus was on learning to drive and his father was coming over regularly to give him lessons.

Marian continued to perform at The Bull, and started to receive a bit of a following. She even received an invitation, which she accepted (after encouragement from Vivian and Susan), to sing at the much larger wine bar in the town; a date was set for the following month.

Linda was a frequent visitor to The Cherries, graciously bestowing her interior design tips and helping Luke to draw up a guest list for the get-together being organised for the Goldbergs. Luke had envisaged a simple gathering of maybe a dozen people, but Linda's influence had pushed the total to over sixty. His anxiety grew when he filled in and sent the invitations, and it accelerated when the RSVPs began to arrive.

* * *

Luke and Dominic had spent much of the morning moving furniture around and giving the house a thorough spring clean in preparation for the forthcoming soirée. Linda had been successfully diverted into town, to discuss wine lists at the vintners, which had allowed them to make good progress without her supervision.

Luke manoeuvred the van to the closest point it could get to the front door without spoiling the lawn, and he and Dominic had begun to ferry back and forth with dustbin bags, piles of cardboard and other items of household detritus, when Susan came past, still discernibly hobbling.

"Hello!" he called. "How are you?"

"I'm OK thank you," she replied, with a jaunty wave. Luke pointed to her leg.

"You're limping," he observed. "How far have you walked?"

"Just back from The Cedars."

"I thought you were supposed to be taking a little more time off?"

"I am," Susan confirmed, "but I wanted to see Tina and to chat about the duties she wants me to take over. I'll start back Monday. To be honest, I was feeling a bit stressed about going back, so I appreciated the chance to go there without having to stay too long."

"How did you feel?" Luke enquired.

"Better than I expected," she was relieved to say, "I guess it's a bit like falling off a horse – you need to get straight back on."

"Done much horse-riding, have you?"

"No, but I did like watching the DVD of Black Beauty when I was little," Susan confessed with a laugh.

Luke pointed to her foot again.

"If you ever need a lift home, just give me a call," he offered. "It is good to see you walking properly again, though." Luke's face brightened as an idea occurred to him. "Tell you what, I'm taking this junk up to the recycling centre; why don't you come with me and we can stop off to see Margaret on the way home and you can give her back her walking stick?"

"Sounds like a plan," replied Susan, "I'll just pop in and fetch it."

"While you're at it, do you want to ask Viv if there is anything she needs taken to the dump?" he called after her.

While Susan was inside, Luke went to fetch the last bags from the house, as well as his wallet and phone. He started the engine and reversed up to Hayfield Barn, so Susan wouldn't have far to walk.

"Auntie Viv says that she pays more than enough council tax to have the bin men take the rubbish away, thank you all the same," sighed Susan as she climbed into the passenger seat.

"That sounds like Viv," Luke remarked with a chuckle.

The drive to the dump was picturesque, until the last quarter of a mile, at which point the destination came into sight. Susan did make a mental note that the Jaguar was by far the more comfortable of Luke's vehicles, as she began to wonder if the van's suspension had some private vendetta against her spine.

As they joined the queue of cars waiting to get in, Susan plucked up courage to ask Luke a question that she had been phrasing and rephrasing in her mind for days.

"Luke, may I ask you something?"

"Of course you can," he replied warmly.

"It is a bit personal."

"Well, that's getting me worried," he said without meaning it.

"I know…" Susan faltered, "I know you have anxiety issues. I… I want help so that I don't go to pieces like I did the other day. When I heard that you feel like it too, well… it kind of helped."

Luke remained silent, staring straight ahead. Susan was fearful that she had offended him.

"It's not easy to talk about or to explain to other people," he said at length, "though I am flattered that you ask me. To be honest, my problems are probably a bit different to yours. I over-worry before an event about all the things that could go wrong, I find I become stressed if I'm away from familiar places, and I don't like large groups of people. I cope because I must cope, I suppose. I use breathing techniques and I'm a logical person, so I devise escape routes, or reasons why I must manage and push my way through. It plays hell with the old digestive system, though."

He paused a little longer.

"Look," he continued, "I don't want to come across like some Bible basher, but I do also use my faith. It's hard to explain, but it is a comfort and an armour. I don't think it makes me a better person, I know lots of good people of all religions and none who are way nicer than I am, but it does help me want to keep trying to be a better person… I'm not the one to speak to about this, June or Peter are much better placed."

"Maybe," said Susan looking out of the window, thoughtfully.

"Sorry," Luke apologised. "Lots of people cope with anxiety without religion. I have some books that I bought years ago that might help. The honest truth is that most of the time I don't mind my anxieties; why should I care that I don't want to go anywhere, if I live at The Cherries?" He glanced at her, "Especially when I have such nice neighbours."

"Well, of course," she joked, relieved things had taken a lighter tone.

Luke insisted that Susan did not help unload the van, as he didn't want her to risk hurting her foot on some unseen menace, so, while he moved back and forth about the recycling centre, she sauntered over to a shed that sold various reclaimed items which were still in working order.

When Luke had shut the van doors, he joined her as she was looking at a slightly old-fashioned ladies' bicycle.

"Fancy it?" he asked. "Much easier than having to walk to work."

"Yes, but…" Susan hesitated.

"But what?"

"It's embarrassing," she squirmed, "I've never owned a bike before."

"Never?" he repeated, astonished and moved.

"Well," Susan clarified, "I had one when I was little, long before Dad left. But that had training wheels. After that, we never lived anywhere where it was safe to have one, even if Mum could have afforded it."

"So, you don't know how to ride a bike?"

"No," Susan replied. "Well, Jenny had one and I used to get to have a go on hers sometimes, so I kind of got the hang of it."

"How much for the bike?" Luke asked the grey-haired man who was running the store.

"Seventy quid," was the gruff reply.

"You're having a laugh, mate. Here, I'll give you fifty."

Luke opened his wallet, pulling out three tens and a twenty before Susan could protest. The old man grudgingly took the money.

"You really shouldn't have!" Susan objected." I don't have the money to pay you back."

"I apologise," Luke responded contritely, "sometimes I act a bit rashly. Overcompensation for what we were talking about earlier. I do know how you could pay me back, if you're up for it."

Susan wondered if she was about to be asked to perform some unspeakable act in a lay-by on the way home; the thought was a little bit exciting. She was all set to be offended, when Luke continued.

"I want one of your pictures," he stated.

"What?" Susan was simultaneously baffled, shocked, touched, and subconsciously disappointed that no lay-by was suggested. "Which one?"

"I don't know yet," Luke replied, "let me see them when we get home. Your mum's been telling me you've been painting and drawing. Well, I want to be able to tell people I was the first person to buy a Susan Jones."

"You're mad!" she stated, disbelief evident in her voice.

"That's what people keep telling me," Luke agreed as he heaved the bicycle into the back of the van and slammed the doors. "Come on, let's go and see Margaret."

* * *

Margaret's knee was much improved, so Joan, who had popped to the shop, would be returning to her own home the next day. The nonagenarian positively gurgled with glee to see Susan, insisting that the young woman sit on the chair next to her and share her footstool. According to Margaret, she and Susan were "a pair of sillies" for hurting themselves for no good reason.

Susan thanked Margaret for her birthday message and for the five pounds. She was then interrogated rigorously about all the gifts she received; each item described was followed by "what a delight" or "how lovely" or "such a blessing."

"You know," said Margaret, "your jewellery box sounds like ones I used to look at through the windows of the big department store when I was a girl, back before the war. Once a month, my father would take us all into town for the market, oh it was such a thrill, and my sister, Polly, and I would have a penny for sweets. Well, we would run to the high street and up to the sweet shop and buy a ha'penny's worth of broken rock and go and suck it, looking at all the beautiful toys in the big shop window. Then my sister, she was always the brave one, would walk in through the door, just like she was a duchess and I would creep in behind her, and we would go to haberdashery to spend our other ha'penny on a pretty ribbon. We thought we were quite the big spenders, and the staff were ever so nice to us."

She sagged back into her chair.

"They're gone now," she sighed with wistful sadness which only the most exquisite nostalgia can cause. "Luke," she brightened up, "Luke, there is a blue shoebox in the bottom of the wardrobe in the spare room. Fetch it, will you?"

He bounded up the stairs and into the smaller bedroom at the back of the cottage. A large rosewood wardrobe, with an oval mirror on the door, dominated the room, and at the bottom, he found the box, as described.

Margaret clapped her hands when he returned and cried, "Good lad!" as if he were a particularly gifted golden retriever. She opened the box, pawing at the lid with her twisted fingers. Inside was a tangle of ribbons, a kaleidoscope of rich entwined colours.

"These are them," she chortled.

"Oh, they're lovely," Susan enthused, "such colours." She tentatively touched some with the tips of her fingers, "They look like new - I can't believe they have lasted all these years."

Margaret started to take individual ribbons and hold them against the side of Susan's face and hair, and the young woman made sure to sit perfectly still.

As she sorted through the contents of the shoebox, the old lady's fingers caught on a fine metallic chain, which she slowly pulled out to reveal a slender gold cross. Holding it up to the light, her free hand went to her mouth.

"Oh, my," she gasped, "this was given to me by Polly just before she and her husband left for New Zealand back in fifty-six. I remember putting it in here years ago. I felt silly wearing it; it's something for a sophisticated young woman, not an old thing like me."

Her eyes fixed on Susan.

"I want you to have it," Margaret stated.

Susan was shocked by the unexpected offer.

"No, I couldn't possibly!" she protested. "I mean, your sister gave it to you. It's too special."

Margaret leant forward and looked fixedly into Susan's eyes.

"My girl, you are the only young woman who has wanted to come and visit me here, to spend time with an old woman like me, other than my carers. They are all lovely girls, but you are my friend. We are friends, aren't we?"

"Always," Susan promised.

"Then you will take this," Margaret insisted. "If I'd had a daughter, it would be hers. I want someone to have it who knows the story. And besides, a jewellery box needs jewellery, and I like the idea of this being in a box like we used to look at in the windows."

Susan took the necklace as if it were a Nobel peace prize.

"Thank you. I will treasure it always," she assured her friend.

She fastened it around her neck, trying, with little success, to hold back tears. Then she reached into the box of ribbons, selected a velvety blue length and reached towards Margaret's hair.

"Turn your head, please," she said, voice laden with emotion. She tied the ribbon amongst the fine white locks. Margaret gave a little gasp, and Luke brought a mirror from the dresser for her to see herself.

"So many years," she whispered, stroking her locks. She picked a similar length of succulent purple, and held it to Susan. "Now you."

Susan pulled her hair back into a bunch and tied the ribbon so she had a full ponytail and turned to face away from Margaret, so she could see the results.

"Lovely," said the old lady. "I'm very tired now - I think I'd like a little nap before Joan gets back."

Susan kissed her cheek, noticing the faint dewy trace of a tear drop.

"Thank you again," she whispered.

Margaret had closed her eyes, her hand still resting in the box of ribbons. Luke went to move it, but Susan held his wrist and shook her head.

"I think she wants to dream of her sister," she whispered into his ear.

* * *

When they were back at The Cherries, Luke unloaded Susan's bicycle from the van.

"Want to give it a try?" he asked.

"I'm not sure it's a good idea today," she replied unsurely.

"Go on," Luke encouraged her, "I'll run behind holding the saddle, if you like?"

"That's not as stupid an idea as you think it is," Susan said in earnest. Nevertheless, she did climb on and allowed gravity to coast her a short distance. Then she tentatively tried pedalling a little way up the lane and freewheeled back down, all of which she achieved with minimal wobbling.

"Not too shabby," Luke congratulated her, "no training wheels required."

Susan dismounted.

"Thanks," she said with relief, "I think I'll stop now as it hurts my foot a bit to press on the pedal. I'll try again soon."

"You should get a helmet before you go too far afield," he advised her.

"Good point. I'll look online later."

"So, you're keeping the bike? In that case, madam, I believe you owe me a picture," Luke said in his most business-like voice. "You go and fetch your finest offerings and I'll put the kettle on."

Susan wheeled her bicycle into Vivian's garage, while Luke let himself into The Cherries. Dominic's disembodied voice came from the dining room.

"Did I just see Susan on a bike?" the young man called.

Luke wandered through to chat to him, so neither saw a large 4x4 park outside.

* * *

Susan went through her small portfolio of work several times before deciding that it was all equally poor quality.

"If I gave it all to him for fifty quid, he'd have paid forty-nine pounds ninety-nine pence too much," she said to herself, with a rueful smile. She squeezed the artwork under her arm, "Here goes."

She stopped short when she saw the big Lexus. Susan recognised it immediately; she'd seen it several times lately. It was the beautiful lady's. Did she have the courage to meet her? If Luke likes her, she must be nice. Twice she started to turn back and twice she pressed on.

Screwing up courage, she knocked at the door. Dominic let her in, and they entered the kitchen to find Luke and Linda sitting at the table.

"Should I come back?" asked Susan. "I can see you're busy."

"No, no, come on in," said Luke. Then, recognising anxiety in Susan's eyes, he said, "Tell you what, let's go into the study. Better light in there. Please excuse us, Linda, we shall be back directly."

Susan gratefully tailed him to the book-lined room and handed him her artwork; she writhed in discomfort as he looked through it with a critical eye.

"Susan," he said, fixing her with a stare, "have you been having me on?"

Susan sank into despair. The work was even worse than she thought. He was displeased. Maybe he wanted his money after all.

"I don't think so…" she replied, a small tremor in her voice.

"You have never had any lessons?" he pressed.

"Well, I did art at school, if that's what you mean?"

"Susan, these are good," Luke told her, "I mean bloody good."

From despair to exultation in a tenth of a second.

"Thank you!" she effused.

"No, I mean you could do this for a living, with some more practice," he stated, factually.

"Really?" Susan asked incredulously.

"I know it," he affirmed. "Now, I am torn between these two."

He held up two pictures. The first was a pencil and watercolour study of the front door of The Cherries, which she had drawn from her bedroom window. The second was a quickly drawn pencil sketch of a rabbit, which had hopped into the courtyard one evening.

"Which should I have?" Luke asked.

"You can have them both," Susan gladly offered.

"But our deal was for one."

"Then the other is a gift," she insisted.

"Thank you," he said admiring his new acquisitions. He looked up, "Let's seal the deal with a cup of tea."

Linda was tolerating her conversation with Dominic; she found him quaint, rather as an Edwardian explorer thought of a simple 'savage': useful, but beyond real civilisation or sophistication. She considered him a mild intrusion to her perceived developing relationship with Luke.

But when Susan entered the room with Luke, she sensed a genuine threat; the friendly body language between them was unmistakeable. Her eyes narrowed.

"Linda, allow me to introduce Susan, who is staying next door," said Luke. Susan held her hand out and Linda took it as if accepting a snotty tissue from an infant.

"Ah, yes. The girl with the foot," Linda said, as if remembering an anecdote. "You shouldn't run around outside with no shoes on, didn't your mother tell you that?"

Susan almost visibly shrank.

"There were extenuating circumstances," explained Luke, oblivious to Linda's undertones.

"My dear, I'm sure there were," Linda condescended to say. "Oh, I see you've got some pictures you've drawn, Susan. Would you like to show me?"

Linda moved to stand next to Susan, whose posture was now a little hunched, partly through embarrassment and partly from holding the bulky artwork. This deliberate move enabled Luke to compare Linda's own statuesque poise against the girl's ungainly stance.

Dominic spotted exactly what was going on.

"Susan, I completely forgot," he interrupted, "Vivian was looking for you earlier. You'd better pop back to check. She seemed pretty insistent."

With a look of gratitude to her young friend, Susan took her leave.

"Such a sweet little thing," said Linda looking at her receding figure, "one might almost say homely."

Luke gave her a sharp look, but said nothing.

* * *

That night, Susan was awoken by the sounds of car engines revving. Wondering what the time was, she felt around on her bedside table for her phone and turned it on. It took a few seconds for her eyes to focus, especially as the screen was bright in contrast to the ink black of the night. It was half past three in the morning.

She lay back on her pillow, with a groan. Occasionally, a bright beam of light, Susan presumed headlamps from the cars, would come through the window and arc across the room. It was ironic, Susan reflected, that she had grown up in places where traffic never seemed to stop and where nocturnal police sirens were a lullaby, that she was now so used to the relative silence of the countryside, where nature provided the background noise with screech owls and foxes, that she could be wrested from slumber by a couple of boy racers.

"Give it a rest, lads," she muttered to herself, trying to muffle the noise by burying her head under her pillow.

Then a shot rang out. And another. Susan sat up in bed. More shots. She ran to the window, trying to see what was happening.

"What's going on out there, Susie?" Marian asked in a sleepy voice.

"I can't see. They're on the field next door."

More shots. She could see spotlight beams playing over the surface of the nearby grassland. Every so often, a beam would stop at a particular spot and a shot would be fired. Susan peered harder. What was that they were shooting at?

A few seconds later, she was pulling on her clothes as quickly as she could.

"What's happening, Susie?" asked her mother, now worried.

"They're killing them, Mum!"

"What? Who?"

"The rabbits, Mum, the rabbits," Susan spluttered as she ran from the room.

The occupants of The Cherries had also been awoken by the noise, but they guessed what was afoot before the first shot was fired.

"They're mad!" exclaimed Dominic, as he and Luke met on the stairway. "I mean, they're disobeying nearly every rule of lamping. Did you know they were going to do this?"

"No! So, that's another broken rule you can add to the list," Luke replied as he picked up the phone from its charging cradle.

Dominic shouted, "Look," pointing through the window to the

unmistakeable silhouette of Susan running full pelt from Hayfield Barn towards the field.

Throwing the receiver to Dominic, Luke pulled on Wellington boots, which were kept by the front door. "Get on the phone to Joe Miller and ask him if he's got anything to do with this. He's supposed to let me know about lamping."

He picked up a torch and hared out of the entrance.

"Stop! Stop!" Susan was shouting, but in the cool night air her voice was tiny and undetectable over the engines. "Stop!" she screamed. "Please."

She slipped forwards on the moist soil. Pushing herself up from her hands and knees, she raised her head. A circle of lamp light was passing rapidly over the grass towards her. She followed its movement with her eyes, until she was dazzled by the light onto her face. Then she was struck by a force that knocked the wind out of her.

It was Luke rugby tackling her, just as a shot rang out.

"Lie still," he whispered, pinning her down with his weight.

"They are killing them!" she gasped, starting to get air back into her lungs.

"I know," he panted, "it's called lamping. Keeps pests under control. But not like this; they're not supposed to do it like this."

The sound of men's and women's laughter came from the vehicles. More shots rang out.

"I think they're drunk," Luke continued. "Keep your head down! They use the lights to dazzle animals, foxes or rabbits usually - they just stand still to get shot. Our eyes look pretty similar at that distance, so keep your head down."

Dominic in the meantime had managed to reach Joe on the phone. The farmer's voice was thick with sleep and annoyance when he answered.

"Joe, this is Dominic from The Cherries. There's two truckloads of people lamping in the field opposite – do you know anything about it?"

Joe swore.

"No, I don't, lad. Can you see who it is?"

"No, it's too dark," Dominic told him. "One of the cars may be a silver Mitsubishi Warrior, I think. Whoever it is, they're mad. They're driving around while they're shooting, breaking about every rule in the book."

"It's my bloody nephew and his crew," exclaimed Joe with an oath, "I was talking to him about it being overrun with rabbits up there."

"Luke and one of our neighbours are out there. I'm worried about them," Dominic explained.

"Right, I'm on my way."

When he'd hung up, Dominic thought hard. Calling the police was his first thought, but it would probably take them at least half an hour to get a car out to The Cherries. A plan formed in his mind.

He snatched the van keys from a hook on the kitchen wall and ran to the garage, dragging open the large wooden doors. As the Vauxhall's engine ignited, he flicked on the headlights, full beam and then drove quickly across to the field, through the gateway and onto the grass. Almost too late, he spotted Luke and Susan as they lay prostrate on the ground before him, and he stabbed his feet onto the brake and clutch pedals, stalling the car but thankfully stopping with the front bumper mere millimetres from Luke's shoulder.

Luke had only become aware of the rapidly approaching van during the last few moments of its arrival. Panic and lack of time meant that he took no evasive action; he braced himself, trying to protect Susan with his flesh and bone from any impact. Susan, too, had sensed the vehicle and she had the presence of mind to try to crawl away, but Luke's weight meant that she did little more than wriggle beneath him for a few moments.

When they realised the van had stopped, they both experienced an enormous rush of adrenalin, an ecstasy of life renewed, a moment outside time when they were one with the earth and the sky and which reached into the deepest part of their very souls. Susan felt the grass pressed against her cheek, and the cool night air felt like fire in her lungs.

After a second or two, or maybe a lifetime, the van door opened, and Dominic called out,

"Luke? Susan?"

"Crawl to the back of the van and keep low," Luke spoke into Susan's ear.

He rolled onto his side and waited for her to start before following her to shelter. He lugged open the rear door and they clambered onto the back of the van.

"Well done, Dominic," he panted thankfully. "That was bloody close though."

"I thought I'd hit you," said the relieved young man. "I didn't know what else to do. Joe's on his way over."

"You did the right thing," Luke assured him. "Can you reverse back to the house?"

The headlights flickered as the engine restarted, and Dominic reversed back towards the driveway of The Cherries, with Susan and Luke bouncing on the hard floor, trying to stay away from the still open rear door. Sadly, lack of experience on the part of the van's young driver, meant that the rear bumper impacted on the low stone wall running around the front of the property, bringing the vehicle to an abrupt halt and almost ejecting the two rear passengers.

"Sorry!" Dominic apologised, getting out to inspect the damage as best he could in the dark, while the others completed the disembarkation that inertia had started for them.

"Don't worry, mate," Luke said, patting him on the shoulder, "you're not the first to get caught out by that wall."

Unbeknownst to the trio, Marian had been watching the latter events from the doorway of Vivian's kitchen.

"Are you all OK?" she called, and then seeing that they were, added, "oh, Susie, look at the state of you."

Susan slithered from the back of the van and hugged her mother.

"You're getting mud and God knows what on my dressing gown," complained Marian, though she did nothing to break the embrace.

Joe arrived in his Land Rover. He got out and walked to them, using his hand to shield his eyes from the still full-beam headlights.

"Is that you, Cartwright?" he called. "Good. Do you want to come with me and get this sorted?"

Luke most certainly did. They made their way to Joe's vehicle, and the sure-footed 4x4 made its way across the field. Susan, boiling with rage, had started to go with them, but Dominic caught her arm.

"They won't take kindly to a stranger getting involved," he advised. Susan was still simmering, but stayed where she was.

As they watched the receding lights of the Land Rover bumping over the grass, Dominic got back into the van.

"I'm going to put this in the driveway, then I'll make us a hot drink while we wait for Luke," he told the mother and daughter.

He executed a three-point turn, and drove nose-first into the drive. They then went into The Cherries' kitchen, where Marian insisted she be allowed to make hot chocolates for everyone.

Sitting at the kitchen table, they alternately blew on and sipped the steaming contents of their mugs.

"It's so cruel!" Susan exclaimed at length, anger in her voice. "Those poor little rabbits."

"It's the countryside for you, I'm afraid," Dominic replied, matter-of-factly. "Rabbits are often just pests. Most farmers are OK with a few around their crops or livestock, but they can be devastating. And some carry diseases too."

"But shooting them?" she protested.

"Well, it's pretty humane if it's done properly, but those idiots don't seem to know a thing about it. I know Luke would never do it, which is probably why there are so many up there. He didn't care enough about the numbers getting larger, but there is a chance of myxomatosis getting into a population. That's a horrible way for a rabbit to die."

"I suppose so," Susan said slowly, digesting the information. "But I wish there was another way."

"Me too," Dominic concurred. "But don't judge people who are genuinely trying to conserve nature by confusing them with that bunch of hooligans."

He looked at the kitchen clock.

"I wonder how Luke is getting on."

When Luke and Joe arrived at the shooters' vehicles, which were stopped at the far corner of the field, the shooting had stopped for some time. In fact, the headlights of the van had made them aware of a potential problem, and the Land Rover's arrival was confirmation.

"Is that you, Uncle?" asked a young man of about nineteen, jumping from the back of one of the trucks.

Joe was not one to mince his words.

"What the bloody hell are you playing at, young Gary? Is that your father's shotgun?"

"No, they're all Bill's," said Gary, gesturing with his thumb to the driver, "we've all got licences."

"Not for much longer behaving like that," Luke interjected sharply.

Joe shone his powerful torch across the vehicles, highlighting two groups of young men and women of about Gary's age.

"Have any of you idiots been drinking?" the farmer asked sternly.

"Some of us have had a few jars, Uncle. Look, what's your problem?" Gary was recovering from his initial shock and was replacing it with an aggressive self-righteousness.

"Speak to me like that again and they'll be the last words you say from behind those teeth," Joe advised him, in a menacing voice. "You've embarrassed me, boy. I gave Cartwright here my word that we would manage his land properly, and you take it in your head to make a liar of me!"

He shone the torch on the driver's face.

"Have you been drinking?" he barked.

"No, Joe," was the frightened reply.

The beam swung to the other driver.

"How about you?"

"No!" a young man's voice squeaked. "My dad would kill me."

"Well, he may not have had the bother with these idiots on the guns," Joe remarked dryly. He turned back to his nephew, "Collect the guns and put them in the back of my truck. And make sure they're safe."

Gary complied and as he was placing the last weapon in his uncle's Land Rover, Joe turned to the remaining youths.

"I'd have thought a bunch of boys and girls like you would have better things to do with your time than nearly bloody kill yourselves and our neighbours. Do you know how close you came to shooting the lass that lives over yonder and Cartwright here? Then you'd all be facing prison! Now bugger off home! And don't think I don't know your faces, yes that means you, young Sally Perks, I'm not finished with you lot yet."

Gary was slinking off to join his friends.

"Oh, not you, my lad. I'm driving you home," menaced Joe to his nephew. Luke considered that he had heard more benign offers of a lift in gangster movies. "Now apologise to Mister Cartwright."

Luke was momentarily touched by Joe using the term 'Mister'. He allowed Gary to shake his hand.

"The person you ought to be apologising to is my neighbour, Susan, as you did almost shoot her," he told Gary. "Right now, I don't think that would be a good idea though, because there is a good chance she would do you some serious damage."

"He'll make it right, don't you worry, Cartwright," promised Joe. Then the farmer gave Luke a firm handshake. "Sorry you've had this bit of trouble, it won't happen again."

He walked to the back of the Land Rover and retrieved his own shotgun and a box of shells, which he put into his coat pocket.

"Before we go, we are going to check if there are any of these little blighters that need finishing off," he said, passing his torch to Gary.

Luke took his own torch from his pocket and made his way back to The Cherries. During his walk, he heard the occasional cry of, "There!" followed by a gunshot.

He wondered if the strange rabbit with the limp was among those killed.

When he arrived back in the kitchen, Luke gratefully drank his hot chocolate while he briefed the others on the events in the field.

"I've never heard Joe apologise for anything before," he told them, "I think he was pretty shaken up by his nephew's actions."

"Do you think we should go to the police?" asked Dominic.

"I don't know. I'm not sure what good it will do," Luke replied slowly, as he reasoned his response. "Let me talk with Joe first. They had the fright of their lives when they realised what nearly happened."

He looked at Susan.

"What do you think?" he asked her. Susan's eyes flicked to look at her mother, and then back to him.

"I think… I think that they could have their lives messed up," she answered, still angry. "When I think of what they were doing to the rabbits, I want them locked up - but that's not the illegal part, is it?"

"To be honest, I'm not sure they have broken any laws," Luke told her.

The four sat in silence, before Luke suddenly brightened up.

"I'm very glad you've come over," he said to Susan, "I have a customer complaint. The goods you sold me are incomplete."

Susan frowned with confusion.

"Come with me," he commanded and she followed him to his study. "Look," he pointed at the two pictures she had exchanged for her bicycle.

She gazed at them, nonplussed.

"You haven't signed them," Luke explained, offering a pen to her.

Susan scribbled her name at the bottom right corner of the pictures and laid the pen on the desk next to them. Luke thanked her.

"No! Thank you," she replied, "for following me into the field."

"That was my honour."

They returned to the others.

"Susan, you need a shower and then back to bed for both of us," said Marian in her most motherly way. "You head on over and I'll catch you up."

As her daughter vanished into the night, Marian gave both Luke and Dominic a gentle hug and a kiss on the cheek.

"Thank you both for what you did tonight. For looking after my Susie."

* * *

Mary Masters stood in the changing room at the gymnasium, rubbing the sweat from her arms, back, and chest after a vigorous training session. She had debated having a shower at the gym, but preferred the privacy and comfort of the bathroom at home. Her mid-brown hair was still in a tight bun on her head, so her towel sat snugly on the back of her neck while she pulled on her tracksuit bottoms.

Two friends shouted for her to get a move on.

"Go on to the café and get us a table," Mary called, "I'll be right there."

She stuffed the towel into her holdall and pulled out her tracksuit top and an aerosol deodorant. She had a lengthy spray under her arms and around her top, and sniffed to make sure that the worst excesses of her workout were suitably masked. Mary then put her tracksuit top on over the top of her leotard, pulling the zip up until it reached the bottom of her neck, and slipped her feet into a pair of navy-blue ballet pumps.

She looked at her young, symmetrical round face in the mirror and applied a very little eyeshadow and lip gloss. Throwing the sports bag over her shoulder, she hurried after her friends.

Mary Masters was sixteen years old and had four secrets, which she could never ever divulge: firstly, she did not care for her mother's macaroni cheese; secondly, she didn't actually enjoy gymnastics or want to be on the team (she missed spending Saturdays with her sister); thirdly, she had once kissed her cousin after sampling the alcoholic punch at a Christmas party; lastly, she only started doing gymnastics because she had been in love with a boy called Dominic ever since she was eleven years old, and now her heart was broken because he had gone away.

She walked along the street with purpose, hoping to catch her friends before they had finished queuing for drinks at the café. As she passed a charity shop, she almost collided with a middle-aged lady, who was standing on the pavement looking at the window display with a critical eye. She was the manageress and she was also Dominic's mum.

"Hello, Mrs Peterson," said Mary.

"Why hello, Mary," Dominic's mother responded. She knew the girl quite well, for the two families had lived on the same road, within sight of each other's houses, for about seven years. "Been to gym?"

"Yeah," replied Mary. "How is Dominic? We really miss him, you know."

"Oh, he's OK, dear, thank you for asking."

"I've sent him some texts," Mary said tentatively, "but he never replies."

"I think he's changed his number, dear."

"Oh, please could you let him have mine?" Mary asked, and she pulled a pen and a small notebook from the side pocket of her holdall. She scribbled her mobile number on the paper and handed it over.

Dominic's mother took the paper, almost as if she were being handed the forbidden fruit in the Garden of Eden. She saw the look in Mary's eyes, and the girl's fourth secret was known to her.

"Thank you, dear," she said, oozing benevolence, "I'll give it to him next time he visits."

With a sincere, "Thank you," the girl ran off to the café for a milkshake, watched by the woman with a calculating look. Mary was the kind of girl any mother would want her son to bring home.

* * *

The day of Luke's drinks party for the Goldbergs arrived, and he woke with a sense of dread. More than ever, he wished he had never gone to the Summer Ball.

He spent most of the morning tidying, organising furniture and accepting a series of deliveries, from the off-licence and from the online grocers. He also had to go into town and pick up various items from the delicatessen. By lunchtime, he was very stressed.

Dominic was tidying the garden, giving the lawn a mow, and setting out tables and chairs for the guests to use, should any of them choose to come outside, placing ashtrays on them for the smokers. He also opened the gate to a small paddock adjoining The Cherries (Luke had at one time entertained the idea of having a horse, so he had partitioned it from the sizeable gardens) and hung on the gatepost a sign saying 'parking' with an arrow underneath, pointing into the field.

Luke came out to meet him, looking flustered.

"Blasted vintners haven't sent enough glasses and we haven't ordered anything like enough fruit-juice or fizzy drinks for the drivers to have," moaned Luke. "I'm going to have to go back into town again."

"Why don't you ring Linda?" Dominic suggested. "It's easier for her to go and get them on her way over, anyway."

"Yes! Good plan," Luke concurred, scurrying away to the phone. As he did so, Susan cycled past on her way home from work.

"Hello!" she called with a cheery wave.

Luke stopped in his tracks.

"Oh, hello!" he said, with evident pleasure. "I didn't think you were around today."

"Why is that?" Susan was puzzled.

"Well, none of you accepted your invitations for this evening, so I assumed you were busy."

"What invitations?" Susan asked, bemused. "I never received one, for sure."

It was Luke's turn to be puzzled.

"How odd," he commented, "I was certain that I asked Linda to pop them through your letter box when she was leaving the other day. It was the day after that lamping business, so I was a bit groggy. Maybe I made a mistake," he tailed off, trying to remember exactly what happened. Then a realisation dawned; "That means you'll all be able to come," he added with evident delight.

"Oh, I don't know," Susan said, "Mum and Viv are going to the bar in town that's booked her to sing next month. I think they've got an appointment."

"Well, that is a shame." Luke sounded disappointed. "Maybe they could stop off on the way home. But you can still come?"

"Oh, I don't think I could," she replied quickly, "I've never been to anything like a 'sorry' before."

"A soirée?" Luke asked to be sure he had understood. "It's just a glorified name for a drinks party. Please come. It would mean so much to me."

"But I don't have anything to wear. Not posh," Susan objected.

"I'm sure you have something," Luke pressed. "It's smart casual – I'm sure you have something classical."

"I'm not good in crowds," she tried.

"Nor me," Luke said with feeling, "I could do with the support of someone who knows what I'm going through."

Susan had no further excuses.

"Ok. What time?" she asked, resigned to her fate.

"People should start arriving at about seven," he answered before glancing at his watch. "Gosh, I have to ring Linda! Must dash. Looking forward to seeing you."

* * *

Later that afternoon, miles apart, Linda and Susan looked in their respective wardrobes, but with very different emotions.

Linda unhooked an elegant Dolce & Gabbana black dress from the rail, which she had had sent to her from Harrods for the occasion, and slid a matching pair of high-heeled black-leather shoes from her shoe rack.

Susan, however, was suffering great anguish. The dress her mother had given her for her birthday didn't seem sophisticated. Some days ago, Vivian had kindly offered to adjust Jenny's old blue one with the silver swirls to fit Susan's smaller frame, as it tended to gape and ruckle at the top, and, being Vivian, she had left the job half done. In desperation, Susan picked a cream blouse that she and her mother often shared and a mid-length black pencil skirt that Marian had bought for work, but which was too small for her; as it was a sale item, it could not be returned to the shop, and so it became Susan's. She reluctantly decided to wear the shoes of torture that she had borrowed from her mother on that fateful day at The Cedars.

As Susan scoured the chest of drawers and managed to locate a clean pair of tights that didn't have a visible ladder in them, Linda had slipped a pair of fine silk stockings over her long smooth legs.

Susan brushed her hair, letting the dark waves hang loose. From her jewellery box, she removed the blue-crystal earrings and pendant set that Tina had given her. Linda wore a matching set of jewels, comprising a diamond and sapphire necklace, bracelet, earrings and hair comb, which tucked into her elegant French twist.

Finally, both women stood before a mirror in their respective ensembles. Linda felt complete satisfaction; Susan did not. Consequently, while Linda left her house, drove to the vintners, had glasses and soft drinks carried to her car, travelled to The Cherries, and assumed the role of gracious hostess, Susan sat on her bed, next to some withered flowers and a 'Sorry' card (all that remained from Gary's apology for almost shooting her), and struggled to find the courage to go downstairs and cross the courtyard; three times she started, two times she turned back and debated whether to hide at home with the lights off.

When she did start to walk the short distance to Luke's house, there were already several cars parked at the front and the paddock was beginning to fill. The front door was open and the sounds of conversation and laughter spilled into the night air.

She entered and saw groups of well-dressed people, gathered in groups, comfortably speaking with one another; she envied their easy manners and ability to mingle comfortably. Susan made her way from room to room, looking for a friendly face. In the kitchen was Dominic, who was busily opening bottles, pouring drinks and setting them on trays, which a waitress from The Bull, whom Luke had bribed to assist for the evening, was carrying to various tables in the house and garden.

Dominic flashed Susan a friendly smile, but his time was being monopolised by a softly spoken dapper man of about forty, who seemed to find the young man fascinating company. She waved and drifted back into the hallway.

Luke was in his study, which he hated being filled with people he barely knew. He was sitting on a dining room chair, next to Mr Goldberg, who was residing in one of the comfortable high-backed chairs that was normally in the room. They were looking at a rare volume of Jane Austen which Luke thought may interest his guest, and Goldberg was clearly impressed with Luke and his knowledge of book collecting.

Mrs Goldberg was sitting in the other easy chair as Linda pandered to her, while dazzling all present with her charms. The two women had established that they were mutually interested in the ballet and charity work, and regaled one another and those around them with great performances they had seen and what worthy causes they had helped.

Linda glanced at Luke and saw that, while he was carrying on his conversation, his eyes had fixed on another point in the room. She discreetly followed his gaze and saw Susan, who had entered the study and was standing in patient hope that he may rescue her from her isolation.

With a brief word of apology to Mrs Goldberg, Linda made her way to Susan, and put her arm around the girl, who welcomed the attention.

"Susan, my darling, how sweet of you to come over. Such a delight for us that you should spare your precious time. Luke did say he'd asked you to pop in," she oozed, guiding her victim from the room.

Susan was struck by Linda's use of "us" – were she and Luke now an item? She stole a glance at Luke over her shoulder, but he had returned to his discussion of books, thankful that Linda was being kind enough to make sure that Susan wasn't lonely.

The two women made their way into the dining room, where an array of drinks sat on the table. The waitress from The Bull was now walking around with a tray of assorted glasses, offering them to groups of guests.

"Susan, my lovely girl," Linda said as if confiding a secret, "I don't suppose you would give that young lady a hand with passing around some drinks, would you? I thought that silly Luke must have got his calculations wrong having just one waitress, but now I see why he asked you to come by. I'm so worried about making sure this all goes well for him, aren't you?"

Susan was humbled. How had she misunderstood? How foolish of her to think that she would have been asked as a guest. With a meek "of course," she picked up a tray and began to move silently among the guests, her eyes prickling with holding back tears of humiliation which she believed she had brought on herself.

The waitress smiled at her when their paths crossed.

"I'm so glad they got more help," she said in a friendly voice, "I was wondering how they expected me to manage on my own. I'm Tracy, by the way. Where do you work, then?"

"I'm Susan. I work at The Cedars."

"I didn't know they had waitress service there," commented Tracy, as she moved off with a fresh tray of drinks.

Susan was anonymously carrying a tray in the hallway, when a man standing inside Luke's study beckoned to her, and she moved quietly to stand before him. Luke looked up, his eye caught by the movement. The waitress looked familiar. Cold realisation came upon him, and he glanced to Linda who seemed to have a very satisfied look on her face.

Taking his leave of Mr Goldberg, Luke moved purposefully to Susan, who jumped slightly when she saw him nearing her. He took the tray from her hands and laid it on his nearby desk.

"I think there has been a misunderstanding," he stated.

"I'm sorry," said Susan, "was I doing it wrong?"

Luke shook his head gently and taking her by the arm, led her to the centre of the room.

"Ladies and gentlemen," he announced loudly to the assembled company, "I am delighted to tell you all that we are privileged to have moving amongst us this evening a very promising young artist, Miss Susan Jones."

Linda looked up sharply, flushing behind her mask of perfection.

"I have recently acquired two of her pictures," Luke continued, "which you will find hanging on the wall beside the door."

Susan was astonished to see that Luke had taken down some of his treasured old paintings and that her two pictures were hanging in their stead, beautifully framed and in a prominent position next to the door. A polite applause rippled through the room, as Luke brought Susan to meet Mr Goldberg, who took her hand and complimented her undoubted talent, for Mr Cartwright was "a very discerning expert."

Susan then became a focal point for the guests; she was constantly being spoken to, or being taken by the arm by someone or other, as she "simply must meet" someone she had never heard of. Oddly, she didn't have time to feel nervous or anxious about meeting so many people because the constant attention didn't afford her the opportunity to think. She moved about the room, her eyes flashing with excitement, and Luke watched her with great inner satisfaction and a broad smile; Linda's expression, however, was fixed.

As the evening drew to a close, Susan thanked Luke for inviting her and went home exhausted and with two invitations to go and visit the proprietors of art galleries.

After the last of the guests had left, Luke strolled through the house from room to room, thinking how much work there was going to be in the morning clearing up. Dominic, spent from his efforts in the kitchen, disposed of the phone number the dapper gentleman had given him and headed upstairs to a well-earned sleep.

"Thanks for all your help tonight, mate," Luke called up to him.

Tracy the waitress appeared, sore footed, wearing her coat. Luke paid her the agreed fee plus a very generous tip. Her eyes almost shot out on stalks when she saw the small wedge of cash he handed her, and she thanked him every few seconds until the door closed behind her.

Linda, still looking perfect, walked up to him and placed her arm around his waist.

"I thought it went very well," she exulted.

"Yes, I suppose it did. In no small part to you," replied Luke. "Thank you, Linda."

"Oh, you know little me," she cooed, "always happy to oblige. And Mr Goldberg?"

"I think we have some very good opportunities together. I should probably pay you a commission or something."

"Or something, indeed," purred Linda. She placed a single finger on his lapel and drew it down his chest. "You know, it is awfully late to drive home tonight. Maybe I could…" her eyes moved to fix his with a smouldering look, "…stay here?"

Luke returned her gaze with a piercing look that almost made her legs turn to jelly. He took her hand gently in his.

"Of course," he said, "I'll just go and make up the spare bedroom for you."

He released her hand and made for the stairs, but stopped when she spoke.

"Maybe I will head home after all. I have an early start. Good night, Luke."

"Goodbye, Linda," he said as she closed the front door behind her.

Chapter 8

Marian was late getting up for work. She hadn't stirred when Susan left for her shift at The Cedars, and her alarm clock had roused her only sufficiently to turn it off. She had jumped awake twenty minutes after she normally would have left the house and read the time with a surge of panic.

Fumbling around the room, she threw on all the clothes she had worn the previous day, fixed her hair and repaired her makeup. In the kitchen, she gulped a glass of orange juice and retrieved a granola bar from a cupboard, so that she might have a bit of breakfast on her drive in.

She glanced at her watch; if the traffic was kind to her and if she could quickly find a parking place not too far from the office, she may just make it. Balancing yoga-like on one leg and then on the other, she pushed on her shoes and was out the door and into the car.

As soon as she turned the key, her heart told her the day was about to get worse. Though the engine did start, it sounded like someone was feeding a running tractor through a waste disposal. She tried again, and this time flashing amber lights on her instrument panel confirmed her non-expert diagnosis that something was wrong with the car.

Cursing, she popped the bonnet and peered into the engine bay. She didn't know why, as, unless the problem could be solved by checking the oil level or topping up the windscreen wash, there was little she could hope to do.

"Car problems?" Luke asked, seemingly appearing from nowhere and making her jump.

"Oh, you startled me! Yes, I don't know what's wrong."

Luke stared closely at the engine, and made a "hmm" noise. He'd been mooching in the garage for some time that morning, rearranging the crates of odds and ends and debating whether the weather would hold off enough to give the Jag a wash, when he heard the Citroen's spluttering.

"Would you like me to start the engine?" asked Marian, in the hope that Luke may help get her on the road quickly.

"If you like," he replied.

She got back in and turned the key. Again, the agricultural spluttering met their ears.

"Turn it off!" he shouted.

Silence was restored, and Marian returned to his side, hugging herself, more from worry than because she was cold.

"Do you know what's wrong?" she asked with begging eyes.

"Sorry, no. It could be something as simple as a sensor, maybe. You're going to need a mechanic," Luke answered, with more than a little guilt, as his desire to help and his male ego greatly outstripped his mechanical knowhow.

"Oh, no!" Marian moaned. "I'm going to be so late for work."

Luke glanced at his watch.

"I have someone coming to see me later this morning," he told her, "but I have time to drop you in to work, if that helps? I don't know if I can get in to bring you home later, though."

"Oh, thank you!" Marian grabbed her bag from her car, "Viv will pick me up, I'm sure."

"Where is Viv anyway? Still in bed, I expect," Luke asked and answered.

"She was a bit merry last night," explained Marian, wanting to add, "she's merry most nights."

By now they were climbing into Luke's Jaguar.

"This is lovely," she enthused, running her hand over the wooden dashboard, "it must have been ever so expensive."

"To buy, no," he replied, firing up the engine to a throaty roar, "however, the running costs are a different story."

Luke made good progress through the leafy lanes, and knew several shortcuts that were new to Marian, who tried to make a mental note of where they were. They made such good time, that she started to grow hopeful that she might not be late at all.

"I'm glad I have you by yourself," said Luke, "I want to discuss something with you. It is about Susan."

"Go on," Marian responded with trepidation in her voice. Was Susan in trouble in some way? Was she going back to her old ways of self-degradation? Had Marian been a bad mother, and missed something?

"Nothing to worry about. Quite the opposite," Luke reassured her. "Marian, her artwork is exceptional. Did you know that two galleries are interested in trying her work?"

"Susan had said something about it," Marian replied, "but I think she wants to just paint for herself for the time being."

"I'm glad," Luke said, relieved. "She has a natural gift, but she could be even better. She could make a good living from it one day. I'm pleased that she has agreed to come and use my studio from time to time, so that she can experiment and make a mess without causing disruption to Viv."

"That's kind of you," Marian said, bursting with pride.

"It is my pleasure. But here is what I wanted to ask you: how did she do in her exams at school?"

"Her GCSEs were fine," Marian told him. "She was never going to be a professor, but mainly B's and C's. An A in art. Her AS's were poor and her A-levels were a disaster. You know what happened to her at school? Well, with GCSEs, I could give her a hand. But when the bullying got worse, she struggled more, and the A-level work was beyond me to be able to help her. In the end, she got a C in Environmental Science and an E in Spanish."

"What if I told you that I think that those results and her portfolio of work could be enough to get her onto a degree in Fine Art? Would you think that would be the right thing for her?" Luke asked.

"If you'd asked me a few months ago I'd say no," replied Marian, "but now I think it would depend on where it was."

"It was suggested to me by someone who met her at the evening party I held a few weeks back," Luke told her. "He works at a university about an hour and a half from here, but importantly he says she could do the first two years locally, as they have a deal with the Sixth Form college. People do a two-year foundation degree there and the last year at the uni, if they want a BA."

Marian was elated; she had always wanted Susan to 'better herself', but she was also concerned that her daughter may not be ready for it.

"I'm not sure that she might not find it too big a step," she cautioned.

"You know her best. I will defer to your judgement. I won't say anything to her, but would you sound her out? If she wanted to go this autumn, it may not be too late, but we'd have to get a move on."

"Thank you, Luke, you are a good friend to her."

"She deserves it," he stated, "both for her talent and herself."

As they pulled up outside the solicitors' offices, Luke continued speaking. "Do you want me to get someone from the village garage to look at your car?"

"Oh, would you? Thank you!" Marian said gratefully and passed him her car key. "I owe you big time!" she said, climbing from the Jaguar.

Luke gave a wave as she closed the door and he pulled into the traffic. Glancing at her watch, Marian sighed with relief. She was bang on time.

* * *

Mary sat at the kitchen table in Dominic's parents' house, sipping from a mug of tea and wondering why she was there. It had made her feel rather grown up to receive a text message inviting her over, and she initially hoped it meant that Dominic would be there too, but it seemed that Mrs Peterson just wanted to be friendly.

"So how is Dominic?" Mary asked.

"Oh, he's doing very well," replied his mother, "he's been accepted to the agricultural college a year early, you know."

"Oh, that's amazing," Mary enthused. "He does love all that countryside and conservation stuff."

"And what about you?" asked Mrs Peterson. "What are you studying?"

"Biology, Chemistry, Maths, and German."

"Oh, my, that is very clever," the older woman enthused. "What do you want to do with that?"

"Biomedical Sciences. Dad's a bit disappointed. I think he wanted me to be a barrister. Only because he watches all those courtroom dramas on TV."

"And do you have a nice boyfriend?" the older woman probed.

"No," Mary replied, slightly embarrassed, "Mum and Dad think I'm still a bit too young to be worrying about it, and I expect they're right. I don't much like parties and stuff. I get tiddly if I have a glass of sherry at my nan's. I do like boys though, but you know what they're like – they just want to get drunk and mess about with you for an evening."

"Not all boys are like that. Dominic isn't," Mrs Peterson said, sounding offended.

"Yes, but… you know… Dominic is… Dominic."

"Yes?" Mrs Peterson wanted to know what Mary meant.

"Well, at school, everyone says he… you know... doesn't like girls."

"Well everyone at school is wrong, then," Dominic's mother said emphatically.

Mary was thoroughly confused.

"But –" she began.

"But nothing!" interrupted the older woman. "Sometimes boys go through these phases. They just need a pretty girl to make them realise what they are missing."

"I see," Mary said, filled with an impossible emotional mixture of scepticism, hope and excitement. With every fibre of her being, she wanted to see Dominic. Her young face once again betrayed her thoughts.

"You are a very pretty girl," cooed Mrs Paterson, placing a subtle emphasis on the 'you', as she lightly patted Mary's hand. "Oh, my dear, just look at the time. I must be getting on now, but please come over again soon. Maybe for some dinner? Dominic's father and I do so miss having company at the dinner table."

Mary was ushered out of the house, her cup of tea left unfinished on the kitchen table.

* * *

Susan was now a confident cyclist. She not only used the bike to get to and from The Cedars, but also to travel into the village. This newfound freedom allowed her to take her sketchbook further afield; she developed a liking for finding gnarled old trees and making studies of their bark, branches, exposed roots and of the ivy sometimes growing on their aged trunks.

She also made sure to drop by and visit Margaret on every occasion that she could, showing her friend her latest pictures. However, that afternoon she found Margaret in the kitchen, with a smashed cup on the floor, having been trying to make a cup of tea for herself.

"Oh, it's all so difficult," the elderly woman sobbed, "this silly old body of mine. Oh, Susan, I used to be able to do so much, and now… I'm a useless old woman."

When she'd settled Margaret, Susan cleared up the broken cup and made a pot of tea which she brought into the living room and set on the coffee table.

The elderly lady pawed the old leather bible from the table top next to her and flapped through the pages, searching keenly. She peered at a page and then threw her head back against the back of her chair in frustration.

"Susan, my love, I can't see properly. I think I need new glasses, but what's the point at my age? I have a magnifying glass somewhere…" she moaned, as she searched amongst the paraphernalia on her little table.

“Let me read it for you,” offered Susan, picking the book from her companion’s lap.

“Would you, oh you’re a dear. Is it at John 16?”

“I think so,” Susan replied.

“Start at verse twenty, would you?”

Susan hadn’t ever properly looked at a bible before, so the numbering seemed confusing, but she assumed Margaret was referring to the sentence with a small number twenty written to its left. She started to read aloud, stumbling from time to time over the unfamiliar language:

“Verily, verily, I say unto you, that ye shall weep and lament, but the world shall rejoice: and ye shall be sorrowful, but your sorrow shall be turned into joy. A woman when she is in travail hath sorrow, because her hour is come: but as soon as she is delivered of the child, she remembereth no more the anguish, for joy that a man is born into the world. And ye now therefore have sorrow: but I will see you again, and your heart shall rejoice, and your joy no man taketh from you. And in that day ye shall ask me nothing. Verily, verily, I say unto you, whatsoever ye shall ask the Father in my name, he will give it you. Hitherto have ye asked nothing in my name: ask, and ye shall receive, that your joy may be full. These things have I spoken unto you in proverbs: but the time cometh, when I shall no more speak unto you in proverbs, but I shall shew you plainly of the Father. At that day ye shall ask in my name: and I say not unto you, that I will pray the Father for you: for the Father himself loveth you, because ye have loved me, and have believed that I came out from God.”

“Stop there, please, my darling,” Margaret muttered sleepily. She held out her gnarled hand, which Susan held to her cheek and kissed lightly.

When Margaret was drowsy, Susan plucked out her phone and sent a message to Luke.

‘M needs eye test. R U OK to set up? Ta’

She slipped out of the front door and was just about to push off on her bike, when a reply from Luke arrived.

‘Thank you for letting me know about Margaret’s requirement for an eye test. You are very considerate. I will organise something as soon as possible. I hope all is well with you and your mother. Yours, Luke.’

Susan could not help but smile. Only Luke could produce such a verbose and overly formal text message.

Her cycle route took her past the church, where she encountered June exiting through the small gabled gate at the entrance to the graveyard. Susan stopped and, after exchanging greetings, she told her about Luke's long, punctuated text messages. The vicar laughed, and said that Peter's were even worse.

"I'm sorry to hear Margaret's eyes aren't so good, though," added June.

"It's so sad," Susan agreed. Then she added, "Reverend, I don't understand why someone like Margaret believes in God when she has had so much bad happen to her that she doesn't deserve. Her husband dies in a war. She works for forty years as a nurse and ends up with crippling arthritis. How does God figure in that?"

"You like to ask the tough ones, don't you?" said the rector.

"Sorry."

"No, don't apologise," June said. "Look, to understand why there is suffering goes to the very heart of faith. Why would a benevolent, all powerful God allow suffering? Well, I don't think anyone can understand it, but I do know this: I have seen people undergo the worst pain and heartbreak, and through it all, God is their comforter. I believe that God was made flesh and suffered beside us as we do, so that we can know Him."

"I can kind of see that, I guess," Susan said, thoughtfully. "Margaret seemed to be much happier after I read her a piece from her bible. I can't say I really understood it, though."

"She is a bit of a traditionalist, is Margaret," June replied. "There are much easier to read versions, which," she looked around as if fearful of being overheard by some imaginary spy, and whispered, "I prefer. Please don't tell my husband."

Susan gave a polite laugh.

"If you're interested, I run a short course," June continued. "A few friends gather together for a meal and we watch a film and discuss it. It explains the basics of Christianity, but no pressure. Some people come to one or two sessions and decide it's not for them, some come to all ten and come to the same conclusion, and some find faith."

Susan looked uneasy.

"Oh, I'm sorry," apologised June, "I've made you uncomfortable. I promise I'm not trying to recruit you into a cult. I will say no more."

"No, it's not that," said Susan, "I am interested. I mean, I think there is something more, something bigger. God, I suppose. It's just, I don't think I want to do a course."

"I can understand that," said the vicar. "Look, come back into the church with me a moment."

Susan followed her in. She had never been inside the building before, and she was struck by its peaceful serenity, the smell of must and old wood, the colours on the stone floor and oak pews cast by the stained-glass windows, the high arches overhead, and the rich gold of the altar cross, glinting in the light.

"It's very pretty," commented Susan, looking around her. "Would it be OK if I sketched in here sometimes?"

"Oh, please do!" came June's voice, drifting from a small side room she had entered. There was a sound of drawers being opened and closed. She returned with a small book of New Testament and Psalms.

"This is for you," explained the vicar. "Keep it, don't keep it, read it, don't read it, it's yours without strings attached or any pressure. If you have anything you want to ask me, then I'm here. Or you can talk to Peter if you want a much longer answer, but I promise not to say anything more about the subject unless you ask me."

"Thank you very much," said Susan, "I can't promise anything."

They walked outside together, and June waved Susan off as she pedalled home.

* * *

As Susan coasted past The Cherries, she noticed a small, light blue Nissan hatchback parked in the driveway. However, her attention was then taken by a large van from the local garage parked next to her mother's car, which had its bonnet open. A slightly balding man of about fifty, clad in blue overalls, was working on the Citroen, and he looked up as he heard the wheels of her bicycle scrunching on the gravel drive.

"Alright?" he greeted her, with a courteous nod.

"Hello," answered Susan, brightly. "Is something wrong with Mum's car?"

"It's your mum's, is it? Well, I can't be sure here. It'll have to come back to the workshop. These aren't normally too bad to fix, but this one has got a fair few miles on it."

Vivian poked her head through the stable door of her kitchen.

"Want a cuppa, Frank?" she asked the mechanic.

"Milk, two sugars please," he replied. "Not a moment too soon, I'm gasping."

Susan wheeled her bike into the garage, as Frank closed the bonnet of her mother's car and then started to prepare the tow hitch on his van. Her bike secured and her helmet off, she walked back to the front of the house, rubbing her fingers in her hair to undo any ill effects of the headwear on her appearance.

Vivian and Frank were standing together, and the woman was speaking.

"Do what you can to help her, Frank. Marian hasn't got much money and she needs it for work."

Susan was grateful for Vivian's kindness to her mother, but her pride was stung and she took a little umbrage that Vivian should speak so freely of her mother's situation. She knew that her mum would probably say the same thing herself, but that was her business.

"I'll try to do what I can. I can get parts for these Citroens cheapish at the scrap yard. Thanks for the tea," the mechanic replied.

He passed his empty cup back to Vivian, leaving an oily black thumbprint smeared on its side, and proceeded to hitch Marian's car to the tow hitch on the van. He grunted as he worked.

Susan, standing in the shadow of his van, watched him manipulate the apparatus with an artist's eye. The hands were powerful and calloused, yet dexterous; she wished it were possible to whip out her sketchbook from her backpack and draw them.

"Will it take long to fix?" she asked, uncomfortably aware that she was staring.

"Probably a couple of days at least," he replied.

He stood and brushed his hands on the trousers of his overalls., eyeing her closely.

"I've seen you up The Bull, haven't I?" Frank burred.

"Possibly. I've been there a couple of times when Mum's singing."

"That's your mum singing, is it?" he said, as if solving a riddle. "Well, she's got a lovely voice. Very handsome woman, too." He climbed into the cab of his van and fired up the engine, "Very handsome indeed."

As the van drew away, Susan's view of The Cherries was restored, and she saw Luke, who had his back to her, standing beside the blue hatchback she had seen earlier. He was speaking with a slender, pale skinned woman, with long flowing blonde hair which was blowing in the gentle breeze. With delicate facial features and large blue eyes, Susan thought she looked a bit like a fairy-tale princess. The woman reached up to stroke Luke's face with a gentle caress, and then tiptoed to give him a goodbye kiss. He stood, watching her drive up the road, before returning to The Cherries, not knowing that Susan was watching him.

Susan was lost in thought, when Vivian's voice intruded.

"I've got to pick your mother up at five. Do you fancy coming into town for the afternoon?"

"Sounds good," Susan replied.

* * *

Marian was delighted to see Susan as well as Vivian when she left work. She noted that, while Vivian was carrying several carriers marked with fashion labels, Susan was carrying a single large shopping bag bearing the logo of the local art shop.

"Susan, you're never going to have any money if you just go and spend all your earnings on paint and stuff," she chided, only partly in jest.

"I don't spend all of it!" was her daughter's indignant response.

"Well, if it makes you happy, then what the hell? It's only money!" interjected Vivian.

"Whose side are you on?" Marian laughed. She turned to Susan, "Susie, you really love this art stuff, don't you?"

By now, they were at Vivian's car and putting bags in the boot.

"I love it, Mum," Susan enthused, "I know it must seem like a terrible waste, though. I won't buy any more. I've got enough put by if you need help paying for the car, though."

"You keep your money, sweetie," Marian said, moving the front passenger seat forward to allow her daughter to get into the back of the two-door Audi, before sliding it back into position and getting in herself. "I just have something I need to discuss with you."

"Sounds scary, Mum!"

Marian proceeded to tell Susan of the conversation she had had with Luke, about a degree and university and opportunity.

"It's a second chance!" Vivian exclaimed when Marian finished speaking. "I loved uni and so did Jenny – she has never looked back. It can open doors for people, having a degree."

Susan sat quietly, deep in thought.

"What do you think, Susie?" asked her mother.

Susan wanted to say, "I wish I was tall and blonde and pretty."

"What about my job?" she asked instead. "We need the money."

"We'd find a way, darling," her mother replied.

"And you say I would start at the local college?"

"Yes, honey."

"It might be a bit too much like school," Susan worried, "I couldn't go through that again."

"And it might not be like it at all," Vivian broke in. "Why not have a look and see?"

Susan was already looking up the details on her phone.

"It says here that the fine arts degree is taught in a special building, together with an arts foundation course. So not part of the main college," she announced. "That doesn't sound so bad. I'm not sure about going away to uni and deserting you though, Mum."

"That's ages away, sweetie, and you don't absolutely have to go. You can just do the foundation degree," Marian pointed out.

"I am a bit tempted," Susan said, trying to suppress her growing excitement, "but it's scary."

"You don't have to decide now. Why not have a think about it, darling?" was the motherly advice.

"All this academic talk is doing my head in," Vivian butted in, sensing that the others needed a diversion, "I need to get home and get a glass of Pinot Noir down my gullet. Just for medicinal purposes," she cackled.

When they got home, Marian put pizzas in the oven, Susan prepared a large bowl of salad, and Vivian opened the wine.

"None for me now, thanks," said Susan to stop Vivian pouring her a glass, "I think I'll wait for dinner before I have any."

"Suit yourself, darlin'," Vivian responded with a little snort before turning to Marian. "How about you, bird?"

"Just a small one, thanks, Viv."

The telephone rang, and Susan answered.

"It's for you, Mum. Frank from the garage."

Marian brushed her hands together, more from habit than the presence of any pizza flour, and took the receiver.

"Hello? Yes, this is Marian. Yes. Tomorrow afternoon? Wonderful! How much? Well, that's not too bad, thank you. What's that? Yes, I do sing at The Bull and soon at the wine bar in town. Um. Can you hang on a moment, please?"

She placed a hand over the mouthpiece.

"Which one is Frank, Viv?" she whispered. "Is he the one I met before?"

"Yeah. Well-set bloke," Vivian replied. "Nice brown eyes, but maybe a bit short in the hair department. He's quite often up at The Bull."

Marian took her hand from covering the microphone.

"Frank? Yes, well that sounds nice. Yes. OK. About seven? OK. Thank you, Frank."

She hung up the phone and stared at Susan and Vivian dumbfounded.

"Well, blow me down!" she said to the others, who were bursting with curiosity. "You send your car in to be fixed and you end up being asked on a date!"

* * *

Jenny's arrival at Hayfield Barn was heralded by a beep-beep from the horn of her little red car. Vivian was outside before her daughter had even got out of the hatchback. The two women held each other in an extended, tight embrace, making up for their long separation. Vivian stepped back.

"Let me look at you, girl. You are a sight for sore eyes, darlin'."

They walked into the kitchen, and Vivian started to make tea.

"I'm just going to the loo, Mum," announced Jenny, "I'm bursting. Didn't stop once all the way down."

Just as she left the room, Susan arrived back from work.

"Is that Jenny's car?" she asked, with a note of thrill.

"Yes. She's in the loo," responded Vivian. Then an idea came to her. "Quick, hide in the tall cupboard and we'll surprise her."

She propelled Susan backwards into the confined space, which she had to share with a vacuum cleaner, and a red plastic mop and bucket, and closed the door. As the back of the cupboard was lined with shelves, stacked with cleaning materials, packs of kitchen paper, boxes of tissues, shoe polish, lightbulbs, and various other items for the smooth functioning of a household, Susan was forced to stand hunched forwards. She could hear their muffled voices when Jenny returned.

"Jenny darling, get a packet of jammy dodgers from the big tall cupboard, will you?"

"When did you start keeping them in there? Seems a funny place."

"I don't know. Seemed like a good idea at the time. Get them for me, will you?"

"I'm not that hungry, Mum."

"But they're your favourite."

"Yeah, but I had chocolate on the way down, and I'm all bloated."

"Well, get some for me, then."

"But you don't even like jammy dodgers!"

"I do now. They make me think of you. Now please, get them, will you?"

"Oh, alright!"

Jenny pulled the door open and did a double take when she saw Susan.

"Surprise?" said Susan, almost as a query.

Jenny screamed. Susan screamed. They hugged like they did when they were little girls.

"Oh, Susie, Susie! I've missed you, bird!" declared Jenny.

"I bet I missed you more!"

"Impossible."

They finally stopped hugging and stepped back from one another, though Jenny still held Susan's hand tightly.

"You look amazing, Jenny!" said Susan.

"You've brushed up alright yourself!"

They stood in happy silence for a few seconds, with Vivian smiling on.

"You!" asserted Jenny, pointing her manicured finger at Susan. "You are going to sleep in my room while I'm here. It will be like old times!"

"Jenny, I have to be at work for five-thirty in the morning," Susan explained cautiously, "I don't think you'd appreciate being woken up then."

"I'll sleep through anything. Not going to miss a moment with you, bestie."

"That's good, because I was testing you," Susan laughed, "I've got the next few days off."

"You sly tart! Having me on like that."

"Jenny," barked Vivian, "that's a horrid thing to call her!"

"I've been called worse things," Susan reassured them.

"And I'm the one that's called her them!" Jenny claimed, with a big wink at her mother. "Now, I believe someone said something about jammy dodgers."

* * *

Dominic got out of the passenger side of the driving school car. Before shutting the door, he shouted inside, "Thanks for everything!"

He sprinted up the driveway of The Cherries, in through the kitchen door, through the hall and into Luke's study, where he found the occupant reading at his desk.

"I passed!" shouted Dominic, waving a piece of paper.

"You passed? First time? You're a jammy so-and-so!" cried Luke, jumping to his feet and shaking the young man's hand vigorously. "This calls for a celebration!"

"We're out tonight, remember?" Dominic reminded him. "Marian's singing at the wine bar."

"Oh, yes," Luke said with a sinking heart. The idea of spending the evening so far from home in a place full of people was not to his liking; but he would not let Dominic, or Marian or Susan down.

"I'm going across to tell them!" shouted Dominic as he left the room at the same velocity as he had entered.

Outside, he spotted Susan and another girl unloading suitcases and bags from the back of a red Peugeot hatchback.

"Susan!" he shouted. "Susan! I've passed my driving test!"

Susan screamed a congratulation and ran to embrace him warmly.

"Well done, well done!" she exclaimed. "Come and tell Aunty Viv!"

Dominic went inside and Susan went back to Jenny and her luggage retrieval duties.

"How much stuff have you brought for four days?" Susan asked.

"A girl's gotta have her essentials, babe."

Once all the luggage was upstairs, they joined Dominic and Vivian in the lounge.

"Dominic's been telling me his news," said Vivian. "He's a clever lad. Oh, Dominic, this is my daughter Jenny. She's come down to stay for a few days."

"Only four," remarked Jenny with a slightly apologetic tone. "I'd wanted to stay for longer, but you know, w-o-r-k."

"What I want to know," Vivian said to Dominic, "is how you passed your test so quickly. I thought you'd only just started."

"Well," he explained, "I had had some driving lessons when I first turned seventeen. Then Luke started to teach me in the van and Dad came over in his car too. But when we realised I could start at agricultural college this year, Mum and Dad paid for me to do an intensive course. So here I am."

"Congratulations," said Jenny.

"Thanks!" Dominic replied excitedly. "I've got a little money in savings and

Dad says he'll add to it and take me to buy a car. Shoot, I haven't rung Mum and Dad to tell them! I'd better dash."

He sprinted from the room, and the house seemed to shake when he slammed the back door behind him.

"Ah, youth," said Jenny.

* * *

As they got ready to go out that evening, the two old friends sat in Jenny's room, catching up on each other's lives. They remained casually dressed, Susan in leggings and a long, smart t-shirt, Jenny in jeans and crop top, with a light cardigan. Susan admired Jenny's hairstyle, a long, layered bob, with the natural honey colour enhanced by subtle highlights and lowlights. She looked at her own, naturally wavy dark tresses and worried that she looked very boring next to her glamorous friend.

When it came to makeup application, the girls sat side by side at the dressing table, chatting and laughing while they got ready. Jenny glanced at Susan's reflection.

"Blimey, Susie, we're supposed to be going to a wine bar, not a Playboy shoot!" she exclaimed.

"What do you mean?" said Susan, taken aback.

"Well, darlin' you've got it layered on a bit heavy, haven't you? Who told you to do it like that? I bet it was those tarts in the department store on the high street."

"Well, no it was, er…" Susan said, struggling to know how to tell her friend who her instructor was.

"Oh, Lord, it was Mum, wasn't it?" Jenny realised without assistance.

Susan nodded.

"But she's so sophisticated," she exclaimed. "Have I been going around looking like an idiot?"

"Mum might have been sophisticated in nineteen-eighty-bloody-seven, but not now," Jenny told her. "And no, you don't look like an idiot, Mum isn't that stupid. Let me do it. Turn around and face me."

She grabbed cleansing wipes and removed much of what her companion had put on her face. Susan had to fight the giggles, as, every time Jenny wanted her to purse her lips or close an eye or raise an eyebrow, she pulled the exact same expression.

"Will you stop laughing, babe!"

Finally, Jenny was satisfied with the job she had done, and allowed Susan to see herself in the mirror.

"Not too bad," Jenny said. "Less is more. Well, with your look, anyway."

"What look is that?" Susan asked nervously.

"Nice. Good girl," Jenny replied, a little mischievously.

"What are you, then?"

"Naughty," snorted Jenny.

"Well, I think you look fab," Susan told her friend, "I've always wished I could look more like you, but nowadays you look even more amazing."

Jenny looked serious for a moment.

"Susie, I'm the kind of girl loads of guys want to sleep with, but you're the kind of girl a nice guy will fall in love with," she said with a hint of sadness.

* * *

That night, a small convoy comprised of two vehicles drove up the lane outside The Cherries. In the Audi were Marian and Vivian. In the Jaguar, were Luke, Dominic, Jenny and Susan.

"Susan seems to want to go in that Jag every chance she gets," Vivian complained to her passenger.

"I know, but can you blame her? Have you been in it?" replied Marian.

"That's not the point," Vivian sulked, "Jenny wanted to go in it, too!"

"I expect they'll come with us on the way back."

In Luke's car, the conversation was much more boisterous.

"This is so retro!" exclaimed Jenny to Susan beside her in the back seat, as she looked around the Jaguar's interior.

"It's old, like I am," laughed Luke.

"Is the music that old, too?" she demanded to know.

"Older," Luke answered with false solemnity. Dominic sighed in agreement.

"What, like The Beatles?" Jenny enquired.

"Way older," Luke replied.

"How old?"

"Well, the current disc of choice features a little number by a man who died a little over two-hundred-and-fifty years ago."

"Play some then," Jenny instructed.

Dominic fiddled with the controls.

“You asked for it,” he said.

As the opening bars of Bach’s St Matthew’s Passion circulated through the car, Jenny made an announcement.

“It will completely do my head in if we have to listen to this all the way in.”

“I quite like it, actually,” said Susan.

“You’re not being a square tonight, Miss Jones,” Jenny scolded her. “Now, gentlemen, turn this off and find me some decent music by someone who isn’t dead or very likely to be in the near future, or my friend and I here will be forced to sing.”

“Have you been drinking already?” Susan whispered, slightly in awe.

“I’m not driving, am I? I may have sampled a couple of G&T’s from Mum’s secret stash. You don’t expect me to survive four days with my mother, sober, do you?”

Dominic successfully found a radio station that was playing Taylor Swift.

“Yay,” the girls chorused and joined in with the song.

Luke leant towards Dominic.

“I have no idea what they’re singing about,” he half shouted to his young housemate. A glance to his left, however, told him that he was defeated, for Dominic was singing, too.

* * *

Luke wouldn’t have believed that being in a wine bar with a live band playing could seem like peaceful relief from being in his car. The group had a table for five reserved, but at present only he and Susan were sitting at it. Dominic had spotted an acquaintance and was having a quiet word with him, Marian was backstage getting ready, Vivian was at the bar, and Jenny was in the foyer engaged in a telephone conversation.

Susan took the opportunity to speak with Luke alone.

“Mum told me about your degree idea,” she said, leaning towards him to make herself heard over the noise of the bar, “I’m a bit apprehensive, but I would like to look into it.”

“That’s great news that you would even consider it! I’ll see if I can arrange something with the college for next week – you can have a look around and a chat with a course tutor,” Luke replied.

“Thanks,” Susan reached out and placed her hand on his.

"They'll bring the drinks over," Vivian proclaimed, as she arrived at the table, taking her seat with an elaborate cocktail in hand.

"Aren't you driving this evening, Viv?" Luke enquired.

"Don't worry, Marian's going to drive back. So, tonight I shall be imbibing," Vivian cackled.

Jenny came to the table.

"Right, bird," she said to Susan, "I've got things all planned out. Tomorrow, we are shopping. The next day, we are shopping and then going to a fancy-dress party!"

"Oh, I don't think that I'd like a big party," Susan muttered in a worried voice.

"Look, darlin', don't worry," Jenny reassured her. "When I started at uni, my mate dated a third-year bloke from around these parts, by the name of Todd. Well, I got to know his kid sister, Lucy when she came up to visit him, and we really hit it off. She's about a year younger than me. Anyway, she's just rung and told me that her brother is having a small do with a superhero theme - blokes and their sci-fi! Anyway, turns out that she isn't a big fan of that sort of thing and wants a mate or two to make the evening more bearable – how can we say no? What's more Todd is a bit tasty, and I hear that he's back on the market."

"Still," said Susan, knowing she would lose any argument, "I don't have a costume."

"Leave that to me," Jenny told her. "Promise you'll come? Promise, promise, promise?"

Susan promised.

In the far corner of the room, Dominic's conversation with his friend was interrupted by his phone buzzing. The call was from his father, so he found a quiet spot and answered it.

"Hi, Dad! Did you get my message?"

"Yes, Son. Well done. Passed first time, like a true Peterson. Proud of you."

"Thanks, Dad."

"As I recall, I promised to take you car hunting. How does the day after tomorrow sound? We can make a day of it."

"Really? Thanks, Pops."

"Hang on a minute, Son, your mum's saying something to me... OK... Dominic, your mum wants to know if you'd like to come for dinner afterwards, to have a proper celebration."

“That would be nice. I think Luke and his friend Jerry are going to something in town, so they should be able to give me a lift ho- back to The Cherries.”

“OK,” said Dominic’s father, trying to overlook his son almost referring to Luke’s house as home; but it cut deep. “Can you get into town in the morning?”

“Yeah, I can ask our neighbour Marian for a ride when she goes to work.”

“Looking forward to seeing you, Son.”

“You too, Dad.”

* * *

Dominic’s father stabbed at his phone’s touch screen for a few moments after he’d finished speaking to his son. He looked at his wife, who had been hovering anxiously in the room while he made the call.

“He’s coming,” Mr Peterson stated simply, causing his wife to sigh with relief, “I’m going to watch the football.”

She watched him leave the kitchen where they had been standing and waited until the television was turned on, before stalking along the hallway and silently closing the living room door. Then she marched back to the kitchen and picked up her own phone, dialling a number. A familiar girl’s voice answered.

“Mary? Hello, Mary darling, it’s Mrs Peterson. Look, Mary, we’ve had some wonderful news, Dominic has passed his driving test! Yes! Look, we are going to have a little family celebration dinner the day after tomorrow, and I thought it might be rather fun for Dominic to have a friend there, so he isn’t just stuck with his fuddy-duddy parents. Would you care to join us? Yes? Wonderful! Shall we say six-thirty?”

* * *

Marian’s turn on stage at the wine bar was such a success that she was persuaded to perform two extra songs. Susan, Jenny, Dominic, Luke and Vivian weren’t even her loudest admirers, though they did their best.

Finally, she joined their table, flushed with praise and exhilaration.

“You were great, Mum!” shouted Susan over the music and the congratulations of their friends, as she stood to give her mother a hug.

"It did seem to go well, didn't it?" Marian said to those at the table. "I need a drink!"

"Already organised," Vivian announced. "It's being brought over in a moment."

"I thought you were very good," Luke remarked to Marian, "even better than that Taylor Sparrow girl that these young ladies introduced me to on the way over."

"Taylor Swift!" shouted Susan and Jenny in unison, and there was much laughter at the table.

Two waiters arrived, one with an ice bucket containing two bottles of champagne, and the other with a tray of glasses, which he set before them.

"Surprise!" crowed Vivian. "Two celebrations. Young Dominic passing his driving test and your triumphant performance, bird."

Marian hugged her.

"You're amazing, doll, but I think you've forgotten something," she said to Vivian, pointing to Luke, who was nursing a pineapple juice. "Him and me. We've both got to drive home. And I've got to go to work in the morning." She gestured to the waiter, who was standing ready to pour the contents of a champagne bottle into the glasses he had brought. "Just a mouthful of that for me, dear, and could you bring me an orange juice?"

Vivian guffawed.

"All the more for me!" she cackled.

* * *

Shopping with Jenny was like experiencing a force of nature.

Both girls had woken rather the worse for wear after the night before. Not only had they had more champagne than Susan would have wanted, mainly to prevent Vivian from getting too carried away, but they had then sat in Jenny's room, talking until the early hours. They had finally both fallen asleep without even getting around to changing into pyjamas; sprawled on the king size bed, they were awoken by Jenny slipping off the mattress and landing on the floor with a thud.

After having showered and changed, they drank two cups of black coffee each, before deciding to catch the bus into town, as there was a strong probability that Jenny was still over the limit. They planned to hitch a lift home with Marian after she finished work.

Susan was amazed by her friend's shopping skills. With the money from Vivian, June and Peter's gift card, and a little cash Susan had put by, Jenny helped her to buy a good assortment of clothes, shoes and accessories. From a discount fashion-label shop, they got the obligatory little black dress, with matching shoes and handbag, and an elegant long burgundy coat. From budget stores, they got cheaper dresses, trousers, skirts, blouses, crop tops, hair slides, gloves and scarves.

Susan felt that she had got undressed and redressed more times in that day than she had in her previous life to date. When they were together in what she was hoping was the last dressing room of the day, she became aware that Jenny was eyeing her critically as she was putting her clothes back on.

"Haven't you got any nicer undies than that?" Jenny demanded to know.

"It's all pretty much the same as this," replied Susan, somewhat embarrassed.

"Come on," Jenny instructed, grabbing Susan by the arm and dragging her in tow.

"Jenny, stop! At least let me put my top and shoes on!"

"What? Oh, yeah, sorry," Jenny chuckled.

She tapped her foot impatiently, while Susan hastened to finish dressing. They collected their vast array of shopping bags and navigated their way through their fellow shoppers.

"I saw a nice-looking lingerie place back up a way," said Jenny, walking briskly along the street. Susan started to follow, but then decided to go on strike; she stopped walking.

"Jenny!" she shouted after her friend, who turned around. "No more. Please, no more. Not today. I'm so tired. My feet hurt. I'm starving hungry. I just want to find a café and have a cup of tea and something to eat."

Jenny looked at her blank faced, before she broke into a smile.

"Oh, thank God! Me too!" she exclaimed.

They found a café, with a table for four, so that their shopping could join them, ordered teas, two chicken Caesar salads, and giant slabs of cake: coffee and walnut for Jenny, triple chocolate for Susan.

"How come we always act like a couple of kids when we are together?" asked Susan.

"Because sometimes you need to forget that you're grown up. We haven't seen each other for years, so we've got some teenage kicks to get out of our systems. But I do know what you mean – we were both rather childish last night," Jenny responded. She leant forward across the table, her eyes locked with Susan's, "And you loved it!"

* * *

That evening, Susan and Marian went to The Bull for a bar snack, to give Jenny and Vivian some private time together. Marian had asked Frank to join them, but when he popped to the bar for a top up, Marian took advantage of his absence to speak to Susan alone.

"I can't believe how many clothes you bought today," she said, loading a scoop of fish pie onto her fork. "How are we going to manage between us with that little wardrobe?"

"I hadn't thought of that," replied Susan.

"We'll figure something out. I'll chat to Viv."

Susan looked at the mechanic standing at the bar.

"How are things going with Frank?" she asked.

"He's a good guy," Marian replied looking at her admirer, "but I don't think I'm ready for any kind of relationship. I've told him as much, and he's happy for us to just see each other occasionally. It's nice to have someone interested in me though, and he is very sweet."

* * *

That evening, Susan showed Jenny her growing art portfolio.

"Susie, you are so talented!" Jenny exclaimed. "Who knew? That Luke guy has done you a real favour, getting you to do all this."

"He's been a real friend to me and to Mum," Susan agreed. "He's a really good artist himself."

"It must be wonderful to have such a talent for creative things," Jenny said enviously. "I was never bothered when I was at school - well you must remember what I used to be like. Just wanted to mess about and watch a bit of telly, if I wasn't doing school work."

"I remember your poems," Susan pointed out, "they were sweet."

"Oh, yeah. I'd forgotten them."

"Something about a goddess and a unicorn, wasn't it?" Susan reminded her, with an innocent expression.

"Don't remind me!" groaned Jenny. "Seriously, Susie, you have a real talent, and I think you should take this chance you've got for uni. You'll get to do what you love. I enjoyed doing my degree, but Business and Marketing? I'm earning a good living now, but I'm not doing anything special."

"That's because you're already special," Susan told her with real affection.

"This is true," Jenny laughed. "I'm seriously knackered though. Let's turn in."

Jenny switched off the light, and the friends fell asleep on the bed, just as they had done through their childhood.

Chapter 9

Dominic awoke early, with a rush of excitement; today was car hunting day, and he would be spending it with his dad. He jumped from his bed, showered and dressed in smart jeans, a long shirt, which he left untucked, and put on a pair of stylish black leather ankle boots. He wanted to look mature when he visited the garages, and, moreover, he was having dinner with his mum and he knew she would appreciate the effort.

Downstairs, he put bread in the toaster and made himself a bowl of cereal. There was already fresh coffee in the pot, so he reasoned that his housemate must be up and about somewhere. The young man was thickly spreading marmalade on the toast when Luke entered the room.

"Morning," Dominic greeted him. "You doing anything much today?"

"Bits and pieces. I've got a couple of orders to despatch and there's a picture I want to finish off. Of course, it's the big day. Buying your first car!"

"Yup!" said Dominic with eager anticipation. "I've got to dash as I don't want to keep Marian waiting. Are you still OK to give me a lift home tonight?"

"Sure," replied Luke, "Jerry and I should be through by about ten. Shall we be at yours for ten-thirty?"

"You're a star! Thanks, mate."

And with those words, Dominic was out of the door.

* * *

Mary awoke with a knot of excitement in her tummy. She listened to her sister stirring in the bunk above her.

"Are you awake?" she hissed. There was no reply.

"Are you awake, Lily?" she hissed louder. This time there was a groan in response.

"Sod off," came a sleepy voice from above.

Mary debated kicking the frame of the bed but thought better of it. A light snoring from her sister told her that she would not be getting any conversation for some time. She slid her phone from under her pillow and scrolled down her friends list to see who was online. A dot was next to the name she was looking for.

'R U awake?' she messaged. There was a delay, but a reply was forthcoming.

'Yes. Wish I wasn't. Cat was sick on my bed. Mum told me to sort it. Yuck.'

Mary sent a sad face emoticon followed by a green one, which looked like it was vomiting. Then she typed a further message.

'Can I still come over for the stuff U said I can borrow?'

'Yes. Come after lunch.'

'Thnx xxx'

'Go back to sleep! X'

* * *

Dominic discovered Susan and Jenny waiting with Marian in the kitchen of Hayfield Barn, drinking tea.

"I'm not late, am I?" he asked in a worried voice.

"No, we are early," replied Marian. "These two seem raring to get going, but they'll have to be patient, because I need to get petrol in the village and the garage isn't open yet. Want some tea?"

"No thanks, I've just had a coffee. Isn't the village garage a bit pricey?"

"I think she has an ulterior motive," Jenny said in a very cheeky voice before coughing while saying, "Frank."

"Jenny!" said Marian, flushing. "You are awful. No, it is simply a case of supporting local business."

"So, what are you girls going into town for?" Dominic asked.

"My feminist instinct shall overlook you referring to us ladies as girls, and simply say to you 'knickers'," replied Jenny.

"What?" Dominic was caught off guard.

"Knickers!" she said louder, as if he were slightly deaf, with a deadpan expression on her face. "We are going to buy knickers. Susan doesn't have any."

Susan spluttered into her tea cup.

"No! I do!" she looked imploringly at Dominic and turned bright red. "Really, I do!"

Marian and Jenny were in convulsions of silent laughter. There was no option but for the other two to join in.

"Jenny, you're awful!" said Marian, tears running from her eyes.

Jenny gave an evil cackle.

* * *

Susan spent more time looking at underwear that day than she had in the sum-total of her previous life. Hitherto, she had bought briefs in rolls of six from the supermarket and the occasional bra from a department store. She hadn't been measured for a bra since her mother had last dragged her to a shop when she was seventeen.

Now she had been prodded by several slightly officious women, forced to look at endless streams of underwear, and spent money she would much rather have spent on art materials. She had tried to point out that she already had matching sets of undies, but Jenny simply explained that just because they are white doesn't mean they match and that most of her smalls were now grey from age and washing.

Susan was now the bemused owner of several matching sets of lingerie items. She had black, white, and floral sets of bra and knickers, a red basque with suspender straps, two garter belts and several pairs of stockings in varying colours. Of course, she would also have denied vigorously that it was, maybe, perhaps, just possibly, a little bit exciting.

One mercy was that the items purchased were not bulky, so she carried everything in the anonymous supermarket carrier which she kept in her handbag.

Jenny suggested that they stop for lunch as she wasn't sure what food there would be at the party that evening, so they had a burger and fries and watched the passers-by. Then, it was back to pounding the pavements, but this time it was more a case of window shopping.

As they passed the museum and art gallery, Susan looked wistfully inside. Seeing this, Jenny asked if Susan would like to go in and look around while she went to pick up their fancy-dress costumes. She gratefully accepted, and they arranged that they would meet in the gallery in twenty minutes.

Jenny had an unexpectedly pleasant hour or so when she re-joined Susan, as her enthusiasm for the art on display was very infectious.

* * *

As arranged, Mary arrived at her friend Katie's flat just after lunch, and they went directly into her bedroom, which had a strong smell of bleach mingled with the faint, yet unmistakeable aroma of cat vomit.

"Here's the stuff you wanted," said Katie, holding out a jute bag.

"Thanks," Mary said, an excited smile playing at the sides of her mouth, "I can't tell you how much I appreciate this. You know what my dad's like; he wouldn't let me have stuff like this."

"Yeah, he is a bit strict," Katie agreed, "but at least he's there, and you don't just get to see him every other Saturday for a burger in the café."

"Sorry. I don't think sometimes."

"No worries. So, what are you getting all dressed up for? Is it a boy?"

"Maybe," Mary replied, coyly.

"OMG, who is it?" Katie demanded to know excitedly.

"Dominic Peterson," Mary whispered confidentially.

"Um, Mary, I'm pretty sure he's gay or something. It was all over the school; that's why he left."

"No, apparently it was all a mistake or something."

"Are you sure?" Katie asked, her voice laden with doubt. "That doesn't sound right to me."

"His mum said so," insisted Mary. "She's really nice and wouldn't lie about something like that. Oh, Katie, I'm so excited – I like him so, so much."

Katie looked at her friend with concern, but accepted that Mary knew more of the situation than she did.

"Just be careful. Don't get your hopes up, OK?"

* * *

"Right," said Jenny, looking at the time on her phone. "Let's go to The Feathers. We can have a quick drinkie or two in there and get changed in the loos – they're pretty clean, I'm told. I'll organise a taxi to pick us up outside at six-fifteen, OK?"

Susan nodded, and they crossed the road and walked to the pub, while Jenny telephoned to book the cab.

"Having to telephone for a taxi instead of booking online?" she commented in an appalled voice. "It's like going back a hundred years, visiting this town."

At the bar, the landlord asked what they would like to drink.

"A white wine spritzer, please," said Susan.

"Belay that order!" bellowed Jenny. "White wine spritzer? You'll have no such thing, young lady! Two vodka and oranges, please handsome."

The pub was almost empty; there were two men in their mid-twenties at the bar arguing over who was going to win a rugby international, and a slim, sallow youth who was feeding money into a slot machine. Susan and Jenny took their drinks to a booth with long green benches on each side of a table, and sat facing each other.

The two men at the bar finished their rugby debate. Barry, about six-foot tall and quite athletic, nudged his shorter friend, Mike, subtly nodding his head in the direction of Susan and Jenny.

"She's a bit tasty," he said.

"Which one?" asked Mike, discreetly peering towards them.

"The one with lighter hair," Barry told him.

"I think they're both alright, but out of your league, mate."

"They all love Bazza in the end. Now, I'm going to take a leak," Barry announced and headed off to the gents.

Jenny was interrupted mid-sentence by her phone ringing. It was the taxi company, so she answered.

"Hello? Yes, this is her. OK. No, that's the wrong way around – to pick up from The Feathers and take us to Ten, Bartlett Drive. No, that's OK, glad you checked. Yup. Thanks."

She put her phone away and rolled her eyes at Susan.

"How could they get something that simple wrong?" she complained. "Anyway, pleased with your purchases?"

"They are very nice, but a waste of money. I think I've already got buyer's remorse," Susan replied.

"No way! You are going to look so hot for some lucky guy in that outfit."

Susan felt shocked, but also that she was unreasonable for doing so.

"I wouldn't know," she mumbled.

"Well, you know the boys like a bit of lingerie in the bedroom?"

"Not really," Susan admitted, cringing with embarrassment.

"What, you mean you never…? You know." Jenny was astonished.

"Yes, never."

Jenny seemed to freeze frame in front of Susan to process this information.

"Just to get this straight, you do mean S-E –"

"Please don't spell it out," Susan interrupted angrily. "Yes, I've never been with a boy."

Then she almost crumpled.

"In fact, I've never even been kissed."

Jenny stared at her, wide-eyed.

"What… why?" she stammered. "I mean, you're lovely."

"Well, no one has ever offered," Susan replied with a sigh. "I'm starting to wonder if I'll never know."

Jenny sat in thought. Then she leant forward conspiratorially towards Susan.

"Come closer," she whispered, looking around to make sure no one would hear her cunning plan.

Susan bent towards her friend. Quick as a flash, Jenny clapped her hands to the back of Susan's head and held it firmly, while she planted a long kiss on her lips. Susan's eyes bulged with shock, and she made a squeaking noise through her nose in protestation. After what felt to Susan to be an eternity, Jenny released her and sat back in the bench.

"That's one thing off your bucket list," Jenny said, with great self-satisfaction.

This time it was Susan who was frozen in position. Finally, she looked around the bar to see if anyone had been watching, but the three other patrons were otherwise engaged.

"What the hell was that?" she hissed at Jenny.

"You said you'd never been kissed. I thought I'd help you get it out of the way. You know, get the monkey off your back so to speak. Now you can say you have been kissed."

"It wasn't exactly what I had in mind!" Susan objected.

"That was one of my best kisses," Jenny told her. "You're a lucky girl. Never had a complaint."

"I really don't know what to make of you sometimes, Jenny, but you do make my life interesting."

Unfortunately, Susan had scanned the room for voyeurs a little too late; Barry and Mike had witnessed the whole thing.

"I think I'm in heaven!" was Barry's comment. He gestured for the barman to come over and asked, "Those two birds over there. What did they have to drink?"

"Vodka and orange."

"Two more, please, mate. And top up our pints."

Barry and Mike each carried two drinks to Susan and Jenny's booth and sat down uninvited, one beside each woman, effectively trapping them in.

"Hello, ladies," oiled Barry, "me and my friend here thought you two looked a bit lonely and wanting some company."

"Well, sorry to disappoint you but you're both wrong," Jenny retorted indignantly.

"Oh, come on. We bought you drinks," he pressed on.

"We don't take drinks from blokes we don't know in bars. Please take your drinks and go!" Jenny said forcefully.

"That's not being very nice, is it?" Barry was unrelenting.

"Look, just go away before we call the landlord over and have you chucked out for harassing us," Susan interjected, with a force that startled everyone at the table including her.

Barry's face momentarily became a picture of malevolence, but his oily composure returned.

"Calm down, ladies. You only needed to ask nicely. Come on, Mike, let's leave them in peace."

He stood up and moved out of the booth to stand at the end of the table.

"I should have known better than to waste good money on a couple of dykes like you," he suddenly spat venomously, and with a sweep of his hand he knocked the two vodka and oranges over on the table, the liquid spilling onto Susan's lap.

"Oh!" she screamed, jumping up.

"What the hell's wrong with you?" shouted Jenny.

"Right you two!" the barman shouted at Barry and Mike, halfway across the room. "Get out and bugger off!"

"Chill, mate. We were going anyway," Barry said with incongruous calm, given what had just happened, and he stalked away.

Mike lingered for a few seconds. "I'm… sorry," he faltered, "Barry… he's..."

"A nutter," Jenny finished his sentence for him. He nodded slightly and left the room.

"Come on, babe," said Jenny to Susan, "let's get you out of those wet things. We were going to change about now anyway."

Outside the bar, Mike remonstrated with Barry.

"What were you doing, mate? You blew any chance we had acting like that."

"I haven't given up yet," Barry replied in a determined voice.

"What do you mean?" Mike asked, confused.

"I heard the blonde one talking about a party tonight at Ten, Bartlett Drive. Her name is Jenny, but I didn't get the other girl's. I think you and me should saunter over there after our shift finishes. They should be nicely loosened up by then."

"So why get so angry, why spill the drinks?" Mike wanted to know. "I mean, you were like a psycho."

"I wasn't angry. I just wanted to be sure that no one could check what was in those drinks," said Barry, with a leer and a wink.

"You don't mean you put something in them?"

Barry stared Mike in the eyes for a few moments, reading his associate's reaction.

"Nah," he lied, "I'm having you on."

Mike was relieved.

* * *

Dominic was ecstatic. He and his dad had found a six-year-old Ford Fiesta with low mileage in mint condition. They had crawled all over it and under it, and given it a thorough test drive.

Bargaining had been tough, but his father was a good negotiator and they got the price to just within Dominic's budget. They paid the deposit and arranged collection the following week, by which time it would have been serviced and have a new MOT.

"Thanks again, Dad, it's great," Dominic said when they were back in his father's car.

"You deserve it, Son. You've done well. Getting into college and passing your test."

Mr Peterson looked at the clock in the car dashboard.

"You know," he ventured, "your mum's not got dinner set for another two hours. How do you fancy us stopping off for a frame or two of snooker?"

"Sounds good."

They parked the classic Rover and were soon breaking off a game of snooker in the club adjoining the car park.

"Want to hear a funny story?" Dominic asked.

"I could do with a laugh," his father replied.

"Well, I got a lift in with Luke's neighbours," Dominic told him. "The girl who lives there, Susan and Viv's daughter Jenny are going to a party tonight. Guess where?"

"Go on."

"Bartlett Drive, literally just around the corner from our place, what are the odds of that?"

Dominic's father smiled as he walked around the table, lining up his next shot. "Are you having a good time at Luke's?" he asked.

"Yeah, Dad. I miss you and Mum though."

"I miss you too, lad," the older man replied, stooping to take his shot. "No chance you feel ready to come home?"

Dominic's face betrayed his inner conflict.

"That wasn't fair of me to ask," said his father.

"No, it was perfectly fair. But no, no I'm not. It's not you so much, Dad, though I think I've made you sad, but Mum… Mum can't let it go."

"I'm only sad because I have to watch the footy without you, Son. What do you say we go to a match soon?"

"Try and stop me."

* * *

Susan looked in horror at the costume Jenny handed to her – or at what little there seemed to be of it.

"Just what kind of place did you get these from?" she demanded to know.

"It seemed legit," Jenny replied, "though now I think of it there were quite a few blokes in there giving me a funny look."

"Batgirl never wore anything like this in anything I ever saw!" complained Susan. "And what the hell is yours?"

"It's supposed to be Cat Woman. Come on, it's probably not as bad as we think."

Susan reluctantly changed into her costume. There was a solid bodice in black and pale blue, which left her shoulders exposed, and had straps for stockings hanging underneath a barely mid-thigh length black miniskirt.

"I'll keep my tights on," she said.

"You can't, they're soaked with orange juice, remember?"

"I could rinse them under the tap and dry them with the hand drier," Susan suggested, exasperated.

"Bird, be sensible."

Susan reluctantly pulled on the supplied pale blue stockings, while Jenny knelt, shortening the suspender straps by an ingenious method, meaning the hosiery would stretch further above the hem of the skirt. Susan donned a pair of knee-length high-heeled boots, tied a cape with the bat symbol on it around her neck, and slipped her hands into matching elbow-length gloves, to which the ends of the cape were attached. Finally, she slipped on an eye mask and looked at herself in the mirror.

"Blimey!" exclaimed Jenny.

While Susan brushed her hair and applied lipstick, Jenny put her own costume on. It was a tight black Lycra cat suit, which left little to be imagined, with a long tail attached to the lower back, tall matching boots, a collar, an eye mask, and a pair of ears on a headband.

When they were both ready, they studied themselves in the mirror.

"We can't go out like this," whined Susan, "what if someone sees us?"

"Um, you're going to a party," Jenny assured her, "of course people will see you. Don't worry, you're wearing a mask."

"Ha bloody ha."

Someone knocked on the door of the Ladies. "Taxi here for you."

"Can't back out now!" Jenny declared. "Grab your bags and let's go."

Susan followed, much more willingly than she expected.

* * *

Mary stood in the bedroom she shared with her sister, looking at her reflection in the mirror. She had put on the outfit which she had borrowed from Katie, which was a figure hugging blue mini dress, and matching high heels. Her sister Lily watched as she inexpertly applied the last of her makeup.

"What do you think?" Mary asked.

"I think Dad won't let you out of this room looking like that," Lily answered as if her sister was a moron.

"I meant what do you think of the look?" Mary clarified testily.

"A bit heavy on the eyeshadow."

Mary grabbed some tissues and dabbed at her eyelids.

"Better?"

"What do I know?" Lily answered in exasperation.

"Well, you were an expert just now!"

"I'm just not used to seeing you like this," Lily told Mary. "I've never known you go against Mum and Dad like this," but seeing the look in her sister's eyes, she added, "but you do look nice though."

"Thanks, Lily. Now, this is where I need your help."

"Oh, hell, you need a diversion don't you and you need me to do it?"

"Pretty-please," begged Mary.

"OK," Lily said, giving in with a sigh, but also feeling the buzz of excitement. "Good luck, Sis. Hide in the bathroom until the coast is clear. Mum's not back yet, so we only need to distract Dad."

Mary stole across the landing and hid in the bathroom, the door slightly ajar. She signed a thumbs-up to Lily, who then stood in their bedroom and screamed at the top of her voice.

"Dad! Dad!"

There was a thud of footsteps in the hallway and then up the stairs.

"What is it, Lily, what's wrong?"

"Dad, there's a massive spider in my room. Please, please, please come and get it!"

Her father sighed and finished the trip to the top of the stairs.

"Where is it?" he asked in a world-weary voice.

"Under the bed," Lily replied in a little girl voice.

"I can't see it."

"It must be there," insisted Lily, gently pushing the bedroom door shut. On cue, Mary slipped from the bathroom, down the stairs, out the front door, and across the road to the house of the awaiting Mrs Peterson.

"Very nice, dear," she said when she saw Mary.

* * *

The taxi pulled up outside Ten, Bartlett Drive, and Jenny and Susan got out rather unsteadily, as neither of them had often worn such high heels before. They paid the driver, made their way to the front door, carrying their bags, and rang the bell.

It was hard to judge who was most shocked when a boy of about thirteen, wearing a Superman costume, opened the door, but the way his chin dropped led Susan to assume it was the young man.

"Um. We're here for the party," said Jenny, "Lucy invited us."

Without saying a word, Superman stepped back and allowed them to enter. In the hallway, an equally youthful trio of Spiderman, Hulk, and Batman froze in surprise. There was an awkward silence for some time, broken only when a pair of legs wearing jeans appeared on the stairs, to gradually reveal Lucy, whose contribution to fancy dress was an Iron Man t-shirt. She stopped short at the bottom step when she saw her guests.

"Jenny?" she asked, incredulously as she completed her descent. "What the hell are you wearing?"

"Hi," said Jenny. "This is Susan," Susan waved awkwardly, "and we are very, very confused."

"I'm not sure how," said Lucy through gritted teeth.

"You asked us to come to a party?" Jenny asked.

"Yes."

"Fancy dress?"

"Yes."

"For your brother?" Jenny enquired in a small voice.

"Yes."

"Todd?"

"No," replied Lucy in frustration, "my younger brother, Jason. Mum and Dad are away and they asked me to watch over the kids rather than cancel the party."

"Oops!" Jenny said innocently.

"And now you and your friend have turned up looking like every adolescent boy's fantasy!" accused Lucy.

"Sorry!" a contrite Susan and Jenny spoke in unison.

"Now I think about it, I may have just said 'brother' to you on the phone, but – I mean, Todd hasn't lived at home for years!" said Lucy.

"Oi, you! Paws off!" growled Jenny to an adventurous fourteen-year-old. By now, the guests in the living room, playing an assortment of video games, were also watching them, their entertainment on pause.

"Oh, what the hell," Lucy sighed, "you may as well stay now, if you want."

A huge cheer ripped through the house, and Jenny and Susan were led into the living room and begged to play video games.

Superman lingered in the hallway and then hugged his elder sibling.

"You're the best sister ever!" he said squeezing Lucy with great affection.

* * *

Neither Dominic nor his father were pleased to see Mary when they got home, though both could see the hand of Mrs Peterson at play. The Machiavellian lady in question emerged from the kitchen, and addressed her husband.

"Come and lend me a hand, will you, darling? Dominic, why don't you take Mary into the living room? Isn't it a lovely surprise to see her?"

"Yes," replied Dominic politely. "We are old mates, aren't we, Mary?"

"I hope so," said Mary, shaking with nerves.

Dominic led her into the living room, where he motioned for her to sit on the sofa and he sat on a chair nearby. He was fond of Mary, and was wary of hurting her feelings, so he made general chitchat about schoolwork, the gymnastics team, and mutual friends.

Finally, they were called through to dinner.

"Would you like wine with yours, Mary?" asked Dominic's mother.

Mary had only ever had alcohol twice before: the sherry at her nan's last Christmas, which she did not enjoy, and the alcoholic punch at a family get-together that she had liked even less. Nevertheless, she said, "Yes please," as she felt rather mature to be asked and she wanted to steady her nerves. The slight burning sensation when she sipped it made her eyes water a little, and she had to stifle a small cough.

"There's cola, if you prefer," offered Dominic, but she shook her head and politely declined.

After the meal, the youngsters offered to help clear the table, but Mrs Peterson wouldn't hear of it. Dominic made a silent plea to his father not to be left alone with the girl, so the three of them went into the living room, much to his mother's irritation.

His father's conversation mainly ran to football and classic cars, which turned out to be rather one sided from Mary's perspective. Even Mrs Peterson was sensitive enough not to push matters further when she came to the living room, so the four of them passed the time quite pleasantly and everyone began to relax.

About half an hour before Luke and Jerry were due to collect him,

Dominic's mother suggested that he might like to walk Mary home and he felt it was the polite thing to do.

* * *

The party long since over, Cat Woman and Batgirl, both now unmasked, sat with Lucy, sipping wine and eating leftovers from the birthday bash. The sound of the washer-drier in operation hummed from the utility room; Lucy had been kind enough to wash Susan's day clothes, which had been soaked in orange juice.

"I still feel pretty stupid," said Jenny.

"You still look pretty stupid!" replied Lucy, with a giggle.

"The taxi is booked to pick us up at midnight, so I guess I'd better ring and ask them to come earlier," mused Jenny.

She was about to call, when the doorbell rang. Lucy went to answer it, and Susan and Jenny looked at each other with astonishment when they recognised Barry's voice.

"Hello, darlin', we're here for the party."

"I think you're in the wrong place," Lucy replied cordially but coolly.

"No, we are in the right place, I think. Look, we've brought booze." Barry and Mike each held up a small glass bottle of cider. "Come on, Jenny asked us here."

Lucy caught Jenny's negative gesticulations in her peripheral visions.

"I don't know a Jenny," Lucy stated firmly. "Now, unless you want me to call my father downstairs, I suggest you leave."

Barry made to push his way in, but Mike grabbed his arm.

"Leave it, mate, you must have got the address wrong."

"No, I didn't, this little cow is lying!" Barry snarled. "Are we not good enough for you? Maybe I should come back some time when you're on your own, sweetheart, would you like that?"

Lucy pulled her phone out and snapped a picture of Barry and Mike.

"Tell you what," she said, "I'm going to put this picture up on all my social media sites and I'm going to say that if anything bad happens to me that they should look for you two."

Barry was momentarily taken aback but regained his composure.

"Darlin', you won't know anything bad has happened to you," he promised.

He blew Lucy a kiss and left, a confused Mike following in tow.

Lucy slammed and bolted the front door, shaking from head to toe. Susan and Jenny tried to comfort her.

"Did you tell them to come here?" Lucy demanded to know.

"No, I promise you!" said Jenny, while Susan shook her head vigorously. "I don't know how they knew. They must have overheard us in the bar somehow. They tried it on with us and when we told them to sod off - they're the ones that threw a drink over Susan."

Lucy accepted the facts, but was still badly shaken.

"Guys, my parents won't be back until the morning. Would you mind staying over?"

Jenny called and cancelled the taxi.

* * *

Dominic escorted Mary to her garden gate.

"Thanks for coming over," he said, "it was nice to see you."

"Was it? Do you miss me?" she asked hopefully.

"Of course. I miss lots of the gymnastics team," he replied noncommittally.

Mary's mind was a little muffled by the wine, or she would have detected Dominic's response for what it was.

"But you missed me?" she pressed.

"Of course."

"Don't you want to kiss me goodnight?" she asked in an attempt at a sultry voice.

Dominic wasn't sure of the right thing to do. Maybe a kiss on the cheek? He made a half-hearted movement, and was met by Mary with a quick kiss on the lips.

"I really like you, Dominic."

"I like you, too," he replied cagily.

"Really?" Mary said, elated. "I mean I really like you. I always have."

She took a step forward and he stepped back.

She stopped.

"I'm sorry," he pleaded, "I really am. I don't feel that way about you, about any girl, about anyone! I'm sorry."

The glass was shattered, and Mary beheld herself for what she most feared and loathed. She was foolish, stupid, undesirable.

"Go away!" she said, tears starting to flow.

"I don't want to leave you like this. Please," he too was on the point of losing his composure. "I do care about you, but I can't be what you want."

"I… I... I'm so stupid. Just leave me alone," Mary cried, and she turned and ran up the road, stumbling in her unfamiliar shoes. Dominic looked on in wretched uncertainty, as she turned the corner into Bartlett Drive.

Mary ran, crying, head down and then she bumped into someone.

"I'm sorry," she muttered.

"That's alright, honey," replied Barry. "What's the matter, gorgeous?"

The cheap compliment mixed with wine in her system appealed to the young woman, and she smiled slightly and looked up at him. She thought he looked quite nice.

"What's your name, cutie?" he asked.

"Mary."

"Tell you what, Mary, have a little sip of this cider, it will help clear your head. It's not very strong," Barry offered soothingly. It seemed that he broke the seal on the bottle when he opened it and handed it to her, so Mary reasoned that a little sip couldn't hurt.

"There's a nice bench in the park over there, let's have a sit down and a chat, eh? You can tell me all about it."

Mary was feeling more confused. Sitting down seemed like a good idea.

As they entered the park, Mike grabbed Barry's arm.

"Stop this, mate, she's just a kid," Mike insisted.

"You're not a kid are you, Mary?" asked Barry.

"No, I'm sixteen," she answered vacantly.

"There you go, mate, she's sixteen."

"It's not right. Not a girl of her age," Mike reasoned.

"Then, sod off and mind your own business, or I'll kick your sorry arse."

Mike backed away, and Barry and Mary continued into the park and sat on the bench.

"I don't feel so good," she whispered.

"Then have another sip of cider, darlin'," he coaxed, holding the bottle to her lips.

"I'm a bit dizzy," Mary mumbled, "I don't drink very much. I'm sorry, I think I need to go home."

"No hurry," Barry reassured her. "Let's walk along the path. We can go and see the bandstand."

"OK."

He led her to the small wooden structure, in a quiet corner of the park. The combination of a late summer sunset and nearby street lamp meant it was better lit than Barry would have liked, but he was having to think fast to maximise his opportunity. He pointed to the slatted steps of the bandstand.

"Sit here, Mary. Have a sip more cider."

He started to nuzzle her neck.

"Is that nice?" he asked.

"Yes. Where's my mum?"

"She's at home." He kissed her neck and began to stroke her thigh; she responded to his touch.

"My dad will be wondering where I am," she whimpered.

"He knows you're here with me, Mary. I'll look after you. Why don't we have a little kiss?"

* * *

Dominic raced along Bartlett Drive as fast as his legs would carry him. He was getting very worried about Mary. He had waited for a few minutes, expecting her to come back home, and when she didn't, he started to try to track her.

He spied a man at the far end of the road, pacing back and forth, wringing his hands.

"Have you seen a young girl in a blue dress?" Dominic panted.

"Yes, oh thank God," said a panicking Mike, who was in paroxysms of indecision. "She's in the park with a bloke called Barry. I think he's given her something. Should I call the police?"

"Probably, but they'll take too long," Dominic replied anxiously. "We'll have to sort this ourselves."

Realising they would need help to search, Dominic tried to ring his dad, but the call would not connect. With a curse of frustration, he instead gave Mike his address and told him to fetch his father. Then, he ran into the park while Mike raced in the opposite direction.

When Barry slid his hand further up Mary's leg, he also tried to push his tongue into her mouth; this was a miscalculation, as the bitter taste of smoked tobacco gave her a moment of clarity. She turned her face away and pushed at his head, driving her nails in to his skin as deeply as she could.

"Help! Please help!" she screamed.

“Shut up you little slut!” Barry menaced her, putting a hand over her mouth and nose, so that she couldn’t breathe. Her gymnastic training made her strong and flexible, so Barry was briefly unable to control her, but his greater strength and weight, combined with the returning influence of the drugs, and oxygen starvation from his hand restricting her airways, meant that he soon had her subdued.

“Leave her alone!” Dominic said.

Barry slowly turned his head and saw the young man standing, phone pointing at him.

“I’ve got this on video,” Dominic continued. “Let her go and we can forget all about this.”

Barry left Mary, now almost unconscious, and walked towards Dominic. Suddenly, his arm flashed out and knocked the phone to the path; he brought his heel down and crushed the handset beneath it.

Dominic assessed the situation. This man was bigger than him, and looked in good shape, but there was little option but to try and face him down.

Barry peered closer at the young man.

“Hey, I know you,” he announced, “you’re that little faggot from my brother’s school. I hate poofs like you.”

The first punch caught Dominic unawares, and he stumbled backwards, his eye stinging. He evaded the second strike and came in with a pretty good punch to his assailant’s lip.

“Why you little sod,” snarled Barry, and he launched an assault that Dominic could only try to absorb.

Mike had found Dominic’s house and spoken to his father. The two men were about to leave, when Luke and Jerry arrived in Jerry’s people carrier. After a brief explanation of the situation, all four men went in the vehicle to the park.

“Spread out,” ordered Jerry, “holler if you find them. I may not be as fast as the rest of you, but I’ll get there.”

Dominic was having trouble seeing. One eye was swollen shut, but he kept coming back for more and still managed to land the occasional punch on target. Mary had regained some of her senses, and when she saw what was happening, despite being disorientated, she jumped on Barry’s back and clawed and kicked at him, screaming for help.

Barry threw her to the ground so hard, that she thought for a moment that he had broken her ribs. She started to get up, when a voice shouted.

“That’s enough!” Luke hollered. “Leave them alone.”

Barry decided to run, but met the formidable figure of Jerry, advancing menacingly. He backed to the bandstand and felt around for the cider. Holding it by the neck, he smashed the base of the glass bottle against a rock beside the steps of the wooden structure, which had the double benefit of arming himself, while also disposing of the spiked drink.

Barry decided to go on the attack. If he had known of the prosthetic leg, he might have realised that Jerry may have been more unstable if rushed than Luke. As it was, he tried to get past the smaller of the two men, who brought him crashing to his face. He attempted to jab the bottle at Luke, who grappled it while struggling to hold him in place. Jerry decided to sit on the prostrate Barry, and that ended the fight.

Mike and Mr Peterson arrived. The latter had called Mary’s parents on his mobile, and they were soon there to comfort her. In the meantime, Jerry dialled for the police.

“You’ve got nothing on me!” shouted Barry. “Just because I brought some little tart here, and her faggot friend tried to get all noble. We had a fight and he came off worse.”

Dominic, supported by his father, made his way to where Barry was lying.

“Video,” he said.

“Oh, dear,” mocked Barry, “the little fairy forgot his phone got broken in the fight.”

Dominic got even closer to him.

“Cloud,” he croaked.

“What?”

“What he means,” explained Jerry, “is that his phone is on the cloud. That video was uploaded automatically. Is that right, Dominic?”

Dominic nodded.

* * *

Lucy, Susan and Jenny were watching an entirely forgettable movie on television, when Susan’s phone buzzed with a text message. When she read it, she visibly blanched.

“What’s wrong?” Jenny asked.

“It’s from Luke. He says Dominic’s been beaten up! Hang on, I’m going to call him back.”

She walked into the hall with the phone pressed to her ear.

"Who's Dominic?" Lucy asked.

"A young guy who's staying with my mum's neighbour," Jenny answered. "Seems a nice bloke. Very sweet; not the type to get into a fight."

Susan came back into the room.

"They're at Dominic's parents' house, which Luke says is just around the corner," Susan explained. "Would you mind if I went over there? Luke says he can drop me home."

"Of course not!" the others responded.

"I think you'd better change first," suggested Lucy. "Your stuff should be dry by now, I'll get it for you."

Susan was changed in five minutes, warmed by the residual heat from the tumble-dryer. Lucy explained to her how to get to Dominic's home.

"Do you want me to leave my costume so you can return it tomorrow?" she asked Jenny.

"No, it's yours to keep. Muggins here bought them. I didn't fancy wearing an outfit some other person had on their sweaty bod," Jenny sulked.

"That must have cost you a fortune!" scolded Susan. "Well, thank you. I'm not sure when I'll have cause to wear it again, but thank you."

"Are you sure you're OK walking there on your own, it's pretty late?" asked Lucy.

"I'll be fine, thank you. You should see some of the places my mum and I had to live!" Susan replied with gratitude.

She hugged Jenny, gave Lucy a polite air-kiss goodbye and headed out of the door to see Dominic.

Lucy topped up Jenny's wine as they sat back down.

"Your friend Susan is a sweet girl. It was so funny when you were telling me about her reaction to you kissing her. She's very… innocent," she observed.

"Other worldly, Mum says," replied Jenny. "Yeah, she's a good girl."

"Not like us!" Lucy said in a naughty voice.

"Definitely. I hope Susan finds someone who will treat her right."

"Well, she's obviously totally in love with this Luke bloke."

Jenny goggled at Lucy, as the truth of the words hit home.

"I mean, she talks about him all the time," continued Lucy. "Nice bloke, is he?"

"Yeah," answered Jenny, thinking about it. "Old, but nice… maybe not all that old, I suppose."

"Did you like kissing her, Jenny?" Lucy asked. "I mean, I know it was a joke, but what was it like?"

"I don't know. It was just a crazy kiss. It was softer, I suppose, but just a kiss. Mind you, Susan wasn't exactly enthusiastic."

"She wouldn't be," Lucy observed. "She's not the type. Enthusiasm is always important."

They sipped their wine. Jenny felt intensely aware of the presence of Lucy, of her movements, of her still eyes that seemed to see everything. Had the kiss with Susan felt different? Yes. Not better than kissing her boyfriends, but not strange, as she might have expected.

"How's the love life?" Lucy enquired. "Still lots of boyfriends, or are you settled down now?"

"I got fed up of the dating scene," Jenny said a little sadly. "And I was never one for swiping left or right on my smartphone to find a bloke. No, I've been trying to concentrate on work. That's why I was sort of feeling hopeful about that party tonight, but that was a washout. I don't know, maybe I'm destined to be alone."

"No one in their right mind would think that," said Lucy earnestly. She yawned, "I think it's been a long day, shall we hit the hay?"

Lucy began to clear the table, taking empty glasses and dishes through to the kitchen. Jenny helped, her costume's tail swaying behind her as she walked. Then Lucy checked the doors and windows were locked shut, while Jenny stacked the dishwasher.

"Come on, I've got a nightie that should fit you, and a spare toothbrush," said Lucy.

A little later, Jenny was back in the living room, unrolling a sleeping bag on the sofa, wearing a white cotton nightdress. Lucy walked into the room, her bare feet silent on the carpet, carrying two small liqueur glasses.

"Nightcap," she explained. She looked at the sofa. "That doesn't look very comfy, does it?"

"I'll manage," Jenny replied softly.

"If my brother comes in here in the morning, just hit him with something."

"He'll be fine. He's a good boy."

Lucy placed her hand on Jenny's shoulder.

"I should warn you that I'm not always a good girl," she said in her naughty-schoolgirl voice. Then she added nervously, "I'm not very good at these things... but... this evening doesn't have to be a wash out."

Lucy made her way to the doorway, and looked back.

"That couch does look very uncomfortable," she reiterated, "not at all like my nice soft bed."

Jenny watched Lucy walk away and swallowed. She was trembling as she turned out the living room light and followed her hostess up the stairs.

* * *

Susan reached Dominic's parents' house in double-quick time. Luke, Mike and Jerry were waiting in the living room, Dominic and his parents were in the kitchen with two police officers.

When she saw Mike, Susan was shocked and stepped back. Mike was similarly surprised.

"What is he doing here?" she demanded to know, pointing at him. "He and his friend scared the hell out of us earlier." She told Luke and Jerry what happened at the bar and then later at Lucy's house.

"I'm so, so sorry," Mike apologised with excruciating sincerity. "I didn't know what Barry was like – I've only known him a while from work. We go to rugby matches together. I truly am so, so sorry. I just didn't know how to handle him."

"He did the right thing this evening," Jerry interjected. "If it wasn't for Mike here, we wouldn't have been able to help Dominic or Mary."

Susan shrank for a moment, but then found inner strength. She held out her hand to Mike.

"Then, I guess I should be thanking you," she said matter-of-factly. He gratefully accepted the handshake.

"How is Dominic?" she asked them.

"He's OK, thank goodness," Luke replied. "A black eye, swollen lip, bruises. The police called an ambulance for Mary and the paramedics also gave him a quick once over. Provided he doesn't start showing signs of concussion, we've no need to worry. He's as lucky as he is brave."

"Barry's a scary guy," remarked Mike, "I hadn't realised how afraid I was of him until this evening. I should have done more to help the girl."

"Each according to his several abilities," quoted Luke. Realising he was being cryptic, he explained, "I mean, you did what you could. You got help. If you'd tried to take Barry on by yourself, you might be unconscious and Mary in an even worse condition."

"How is Mary?" asked Susan. "How old did you say she was? Sixteen?" She shuddered.

"I don't know how she is. How can you when someone has been through what she has?" Jerry said. "I think physically she is OK. Well, maybe some cracked ribs. Whatever he gave her was more than a drink, though, because she kept falling asleep and waking up every few minutes."

"And Barry?" Susan almost growled his name.

"Well, young Dominic gave a pretty good account of himself," Jerry explained. "His face ain't too pretty either. And he may have a bit of trouble walking for a while, too. I'm not saying Mary's papa did give him a huge kick in the nuts while we held him down, and I'm not saying he didn't. I didn't see a thing. Did you, Luke?"

"Well, it was getting dark and it is hard to tell," Luke replied with an expression of innocence.

"He's lucky to have something to be kicked," Jerry added. "My friend Mr Cartwright here seemed to be thinking of using the broken bottle that Barry threatened him with to make the man sing soprano for the rest of his years."

Susan looked at Luke half shocked, half fascinated by this hidden side of him.

"What happened to turn the other cheek?" she asked.

"For myself, yes," he replied, "but more difficult when it is innocent third parties. I wasn't serious though."

"Barry sure as hell thought you were!" laughed Jerry. "I think he may have had a bladder malfunction."

The kitchen door opened, and the police officers came out, followed by Dominic and his parents. Susan told the officers of her earlier encounters with Barry, and they said they would be in touch if they thought the information would be of material use.

When the police left, Dominic's father brought everyone up to date with what they had said, and it wasn't good news. Firstly, the video that Dominic had shot of Barry's attempted assault of Mary was too dark to make any identification or to establish exactly the facts of the events of that evening; unless Mary was to press charges and be prepared to testify, the police were pessimistic of it reaching court let alone getting a conviction, even with Mike's background statement. As to Dominic, because his injuries did not require hospital treatment, the assault may not be classed as severe; however, the homophobic language Barry used classified it as a hate crime, provided firstly that Mary could corroborate that he used the words and, secondly, that Dominic would attest to them, which he was not prepared to do.

There was a pause when he finished speaking, while everyone digested the import.

"But if he drugged Mary, surely that must mean something?" Luke asked.

"Firstly, they would have to show that she had been drugged," Mr Peterson explained, "which isn't easy as a lot of these things can leave the blood system quickly or be virtually undetectable. He smashed the bottle, remember?"

"We both bought a bottle of cider at the same time," Mike added. "I didn't see him doing anything to it, but we got them before going back to work, so he could have done something to his when I wasn't with him."

"Quite!" agreed Dominic's father. "And they would have to prove that he gave her the drug and that she hadn't taken it somewhere else. It didn't help when we told them that Mary had had alcohol when she was here. The police did say that our friend Barry was already known to them, but I've got to say I think he's going to get off with a fine and a slap on the wrist for a minor affray."

"One thing is for certain though," Susan said after digesting the import of the conversation. "Dominic is one of the bravest people I have ever met."

"Too right," Jerry concurred. "He's the kind of man you'd want by your side in a fire fight."

Dominic tried to smile and winced. He motioned to Luke that he would like a private word with him, so the two men stepped into the hall.

"I think I'm going to stay here tonight. I'm still a bit angry with Mum for trying to set me up with Mary, but she couldn't have known what was going to happen. She's beating herself up. I think it would help her and, to be honest, I think I need to be with my mum and dad," he explained.

"I think it is the wise decision," Luke reassured him.

"And I can pop over to see Mary in the morning," Dominic added.

* * *

Mary arrived home from the hospital in the early hours of the morning. She was tired of questions, tired of being examined, tired of her mother fussing over her, tired of knowing how angry with her that her parents were trying not to be. She also felt utterly humiliated; less than human.

Despite the late hour, she wanted a shower, and stood under a stream of steaming water until it started to run cold, and even then, she stood beneath the flow and shivered. Finally, she climbed into her bed, and listened to the soothing sound of Lily's breathing.

She must have slept, because she woke up, aware that she was crying out and kicking her legs. Someone was stroking her head, and she jerked away in terror.

"Shh, shh, it's me, Mary, it's Lily," whispered her sister.

"Oh, you scared me!"

"Sorry, but you were crying out. I didn't know what to do." Lily sat beside Mary on her bed and put her arm around her, kissing her forehead gently. Mary's panic subsided. "Want me to sleep down here with you tonight?"

In the darkness, Lily saw her sister's head nod. The two sisters lay together for hours in the inky black of the night, believing the other to be asleep, and thinking of what so very nearly happened.

* * *

The following morning, Lucy walked with Jenny to the bus stop and they got there just a few moments before the vehicle arrived. Neither sure how to say goodbye, they hugged; Jenny savoured the scent of Lucy's shampoo in her auburn hair.

"Promise you'll come and stay soon?" Jenny murmured into her ear.

"I'll book train tickets today," was the breathless promise.

Jenny climbed onto the coach and Lucy stood at the kerbside waving until it disappeared into the traffic. Barely two minutes passed before she received a text.

'Missing U already. Can't wait to C U again. Wear the cat suit ;-) L xxx'

She messaged an emoticon with hearts for eyes. Leaning her head against the window, Jenny watched the urban roads turn into leafy lanes. As the bus stopped at a junction, she reflected that she had reached a fork in her own road and, for the first time in her adult life, she realised she didn't know where she was headed.

As she completed the final leg of her journey on foot, walking towards her mother's house, she recognised Luke's Jaguar driving down the narrow lane towards her. It slowed as it drew near, and the passenger window slid down to reveal Susan.

"Hi, Jenny! We are just heading over to see Dominic. I've been messaging you to ask if you want a lift home."

"Have you?"

Startled by this news, Jenny looked at her phone and saw that she had indeed missed several messages.

"Sorry, Susie. My head is in the wrong place today! I'll see you later."

The car purred away and Jenny continued her walk to the house.

* * *

When Susan and Luke arrived, Dominic was looking glum. It seemed that after he had gone to bed the previous night, he could hear his mother and father having an argument. When he had come downstairs, he found his dad had slept in his armchair. Both parents put on a display of business as usual when he was around, but Dominic sensed an iciness between them.

"They were arguing about me," he said.

"You don't know that," Luke replied, "a lot has happened. Tempers fray when people are tired and upset."

"Maybe," Dominic was uncertain, "but none of this would have happened if it wasn't for me."

"If it wasn't for you, Mary could have been raped," corrected Susan. "You're a hero, whether you like it or not. It's not your fault you don't fancy someone, whether you're gay or straight."

"Yeah, I've been turned down by loads of women, and I don't think any of them was a lesbian," Luke added.

"Really?" Susan blurted in astonishment. "Who would turn you down?"

Luke was enormously flattered. "Anyone with half a brain cell," he chuckled. "Now you on the other hand, would be impossible for any man to turn down, eh, Dominic?"

"If you two could stop this nauseating spectacle of mutual admiration, it would undoubtedly aid my speedy recovery," was all the young man had to say, amused by their antics. "Anyway, I know who you really are, Susan."

"What?" said Susan, worried for a moment.

"I know your secret identity is… Batgirl!" Dominic announced.

"Oh, no!" Susan moaned. "Who told you?"

"Jenny told Viv when she got home this morning, and Viv texted me," Dominic exulted.

"I have absolutely no idea what you two are talking about," commented a perplexed Luke.

"You'll have to get Susan to model the outfit for you," Dominic suggested.

"No!" squawked Susan. "It will never see the light of day again!"

"I am still none the wiser," complained Luke.

"You'll have to be in suspense until the next dynamic episode," joked Dominic. "But in the meantime, go and do what I know you're itching to and talk to Dad about some archaic Morris car you're both in love with."

Luke took his cue, and left in search of vehicular conversation.

"Susan, can I ask a favour?" Dominic asked when they were alone.

"Anything."

"I'd like to talk to Mary, to see how she is, but I feel really awkward. She might not want to see me. I know that if I involved any of our parents, things will get twisted one way or another. I wanted to write a letter, or text her, but it seems cowardly and may mean I don't get to see her and talk to her."

"I can see why you'd think that."

"Will you go and ask her for me? You are a girl, and you're nice and not at all intimidating," Dominic asked, feeling guilty, as he could see her wavering; he nevertheless pressed on. "Please. It would really help me."

Susan reluctantly agreed and made her way along the road to Mary's house. She rang the doorbell and a young lady answered it.

"Hello, I'm Susan. I'm a friend of Dominic Peterson. Are you Mary?"

"No, I'm her sister Lily."

"OK. Would it be possible for me to speak to Mary, please?"

Lily looked at Susan.

"Wait here," she said and closed the door.

Susan waited. The door reopened and Lily invited her into the living room, where Mary was sitting on the couch.

"Hi, Mary, I'm Susan."

"Hello," replied Mary softly, "I've heard of you. Dominic says you're nice."

"Well, that's kind of him," said Susan. "Mary, I wanted to ask if you feel up to seeing Dominic. He would like to see for himself that you are OK. He cares about you. Would you be willing for him to come over and see you?"

"I don't think that is a good idea," Mary replied in a cold voice.

"OK, Mary. Thank you for seeing me," Susan said, not wanting to press the issue with the girl, who was beginning to struggle to maintain her composure. "I can see myself out. I am glad to have met you both."

As she reached the doorway, Mary spoke with a low croak.

"Five minutes at our front gate."

"I beg your pardon?" said Susan.

"Tell Dominic that I will meet him at our front gate in five minutes," Mary repeated.

"Thank you, Mary," Susan said gently and left.

Dominic asked Susan to accompany him for the meeting, and she reluctantly assented. They made their way to the gate and stood waiting. The front door opened and Mary, wearing a large baggy jumper and tracksuit bottoms, walked to them, accompanied by Lily.

"Hello, Dominic."

"Hello, Mary."

"How is your face?" she asked.

"A bit sore. How are you?"

"I'm OK," Mary replied flatly. "Look, Dominic, I want to say thank you for coming after me and for stopping that man."

"It's what friends do."

"Friends!" Mary laughed the word as if it were bitter in her mouth. "Yes, I suppose friends do."

The four figures stood in silence.

"They want me to press charges and stand up in court," she told them.

"I see," Dominic said quietly.

"I can't!" she spat. "I won't! I just want it gone and forgotten."

"I can understand that."

"Can you? I don't think anyone can. My parents certainly can't."

Lily was standing a little behind Mary, and she started to stroke her sister's arm, trying to soothe her.

"Sorry," mumbled Dominic.

"Sorry? For what? Humiliating me and then rescuing me so that I have to feel grateful?" Mary shouted.

"I didn't mean to humiliate you. I'm sorry!" Dominic reacted, almost on the point of crying. In an instant, he had been inwardly torn between genuine regret and a sense of injustice, for he believed that he had done very little wrong. He had no idea what he expected of the conversation when it started, but he didn't anticipate such personal vitriol to be directed towards him; now he was beginning to understand the sense of guilt that he felt, justified or otherwise, was to be a permanent scar.

Mary calmed a little.

"I know. I'm sorry, Dominic, that wasn't fair. None of this is fair, but I can't see you anymore. It is too difficult for me."

Tears were trickling down her cheeks, and Lily too was visibly upset.

"Goodbye, Dominic," she said huskily turning and walking briskly back to the house, accompanied by her sister, who put a comforting arm around her.

Susan squeezed Dominic's arm.

"Goodbye, Mary," he whispered, too quietly for the girl to hear.

* * *

Much to his mother's disappointment, Dominic was reinstalled at The Cherries that afternoon. Jerry came up to visit him, as did the Reverend June.

Susan headed back to Vivian's house for Jenny's last evening before travelling back. She was also resolved to book her first driving lesson, and as it was only a little before five in the afternoon, she telephoned and made the appointment before finding the other occupants of Hayfield Barn.

Vivian and Jenny were in the sitting room. The mother was looking sad, steeling herself for her daughter's departure the next day by drinking a large gin and tonic between puffs on her cigarette. Jenny was distracted and distant, but not unfriendly.

Susan updated them on the events of the previous night and some of what had passed that morning. They were both pleased to hear that Dominic was back at The Cherries.

"That poor girl though," said Jenny. She shuddered. "It could have been us, Susie."

Everyone nodded soberly.

Vivian creakingly started to stand. "I'd better get tea started. Jenny's last day home, so I want her to have a proper meal."

"I'll cook it," offered Susan. "You two should spend as much time as possible together. Please let me."

Vivian sank back into her chair.

"You're an angel sent from above, Susie," she sighed.

Susan headed into the kitchen, put the oven on to preheat and removed a large duck from the fridge. As she set about peeling potatoes, Marian arrived home.

"You cooking, Susie? Let me wash up and I'll give you a hand."

Mother and daughter chatted happily while they prepared dinner. By contrast, in the living room Vivian and Jenny were sitting in silence. Jenny was so preoccupied with something that she was monosyllabic in her short responses to any of Vivian's attempts at conversation.

Finally, Vivian snapped.

"Jenny, what has got into you today? You're not talking. Are you feeling OK, love?"

Jenny was startled from her reverie.

"Sorry, Mum," she said with a conscious effort to sound affectionate, "I've got a lot on my mind. Thinking about all the work I'll have on my desk when I get back."

"Are you sure? Not boy trouble?" asked her mother.

"No, Mum, definitely not boy trouble," replied Jenny. "No, I guess I'm a bit tired, that's all."

"OK, darlin'. So long as you're happy."

"Mum, I think I'm happier than I have been for some time."

After dinner, Susan and Jenny loaded the dishwasher, while Marian and Vivian drowsed in the living room.

"Susie, would you mind sleeping in your own room tonight? I'm knackered and I've got a long drive tomorrow," said Jenny.

"Sure," Susan replied, hiding her disappointment, for she had enjoyed their girly sleepovers. "Are you OK, Jenny?"

"Yes, I'm fine thanks."

Everyone went to bed quite early that evening.

Jenny lay awake, listening to the others settle down for the night. She couldn't sleep for thinking of an auburn-haired girl she had come to see in a whole new light.

She plugged headphones into her mobile and listened to some relaxing music. Then her screen flashed with the announcement of an incoming video-call from Lucy and Jenny smiled.

Chapter 10

Susan had enjoyed looking around the college campus. The art department, situated in a stand-alone red-brick Victorian building that had once been a primary school, had high ceilings and large windows, meaning that the lighting was perfect, and there was an array of studios for painting, printing, sculpture, pottery, metalwork, and several crafts that she had never heard of.

Her meeting with Luke's contact went so well that she was told on the spot that she would be accepted if she applied, but that it was urgent for her to get the application submitted. He was very impressed with the examples of her work which Susan had brought with her and with the knowledge that she had accumulated through conversations with Luke, reading books, and visiting galleries.

She wasn't entirely sure that she wasn't floating on air when she eventually joined Luke at his car.

"How did it go?" he asked, almost as excited as she was.

"They want me! Can you believe it?"

"Very easily," he told her. "Now, we need to move mountains to get your application in before the deadline."

"It is starting to seem very real," said Susan in her frightened voice.

"It is real."

"Maybe I shouldn't. I'm probably not good enough."

"That is patently untrue," he insisted.

"But what about The Cedars?" she worried.

"They'll cope. And anyway, you'll still be able to help in the holidays if you want to."

"You have an answer for everything!"

Luke gave a little grin as he watched the road ahead. Susan felt overwhelming gratitude to him for his support and encouragement.

"I have you to thank for this," she told him.

"No," he contradicted, "this is your achievement. I just gave you a little push."

Susan smiled at him, and put her hand on his, as it rested on the gearstick.

"Will you drop me off at The Cedars, please?" she requested. "I wouldn't feel right about not letting them know my plans straight away and in person."

Luke nodded. They travelled the rest of the way in contented silence. Susan texted both Jenny and June with her news, and respectively received responses of 'You go girl!' and 'Congratulations. Well done'.

At the entrance to The Cedars, she gave Luke a wave goodbye, and scampered into the office. As Susan entered the cabin, Tina looked up with a serious expression on her face.

"Is everything alright?" Susan asked, concern evident in her voice.

"There is something I need to discuss with you," Tina replied ominously, "but first tell me how it went at the college."

"They want me," Susan nervously informed her, "I start in the autumn. But I'm worried about letting you down."

"Praise the Lord!" Tina yelled, and she laughed with evident relief. "Oh, Susan, I had been dreading this conversation if you had come back and told me it went badly."

"Why, what have I done?" Susan asked in a worried voice.

"Nothing, honey," Tina reassured her, "Jerry's mamma back in the States passed away last night."

"Oh, I'm so sorry. It must have been a shock."

"It was. She had a weak heart, but we thought she had a bit more time left in her. Poor Jerry's taken it bad. He's flying out there tomorrow. Look, honey, Jerry and I have been thinking about moving back out there for some time to be closer to family and now he wants to look after his papa, who isn't too well on account of his diabetes. We've had someone interested in buying The Cedars for a long time, but they're a big company and don't want any of the management here, which is Jerry and me and you."

"I see," said Susan, "so I'm out of a job?"

"Not until we sell, but yes, hon. So, your college offer is just the best news I could have had on such a sad day."

Susan suddenly started to cry.

"What's the matter, darlin'?" asked Tina, concerned. "I mean, you couldn't have done the job and gone to college."

"It's not that," sniffed Susan, "I just realised how much I'm going to miss you and Jerry."

"Now you've got me started." Tina embraced Susan and the emotion of the day swept over her.

* * *

Barry had been asked to go to see Maureen Jenkins, his company's Human Resources manager. He sat in the small corner office, facing the smartly dressed woman; also present was his line manager, Simon.

"Thank you for coming to see me this morning," Maureen began. "As I outlined in the letter I sent to you dated last week, there are a series of disciplinary matters that I wish to discuss with you relating to your employment at Wilkins-Dobson. Do you have any questions at this juncture?"

"No, Maureen," replied Barry.

"And I also note that you have not exercised your right to have a personal third-party representative present at this meeting. Is that correct?"

"Yes, Maureen."

"Now, Barry, I note from your record that you already have a verbal and a written warning for previous misdemeanours relating to your conduct with several of your female colleagues. As outlined in your letter, you now have several further allegations, each of which you will have an opportunity to address in the course of this meeting. There is also a report that you are in the court system for an assault on a young man in the local park, and that you have admitted to that assault."

"It was a minor scuffle. A disagreement about a girl. He didn't like it that she preferred me. He came off the worst, that's all," Barry explained.

"Nevertheless, you have admitted to a criminal offence, and under the terms of your contract, that is sufficient for us to find gross misconduct and consider immediate termination of your employment. It is the purpose of this meeting to find the facts of the matter to enable us to reach a conclusion. Your company handbook outlines the appeal procedure, should you disagree with the findings."

Maureen took a piece of paper from the folder on her desk.

"Now," she continued, "if I could ask you to look at the first grievance stated in the letter I sent to you, we can –"

"Don't bother," interrupted Barry, "it's all a fix. You want me out? That's fine. I quit."

"Barry, am I to understand that you –"

"You can understand what you like. Sod the lot of you!" snarled Barry, and he strode from the room, slamming the door behind him.

"Good riddance to bad rubbish!" Maureen remarked, with evident satisfaction. "Simon, please would you make sure he clears his desk, hands in his pass-card, and is escorted from the building?"

"It will be a pleasure," replied Simon, already opening the door.

Fifteen minutes later, Barry was walking down the pavement smoking a roll-up. He wasn't upset to be out of a job, as the writing was on the wall, and the meeting had gone as he expected. Indeed, he had intended to resign long before the meeting; he was only annoyed with himself that he had stayed at the firm long enough to get a written warning, as such records can follow you from job to job.

He took his phone from his pocket and dialled a contact.

"Hello, Kevin? Yes, it's Barry. Yeah, it's happened again. You got anything going? Yeah, pretty much anything to earn a few quid. Yeah, that sounds good. See you Monday, mate."

Excellent. A new job already and no need for references from that cow Maureen.

He was tapped on the shoulder. A young man in a grey hoodie was walking beside him.

"Hey, Baz, you got anything mellow?" asked the youth.

"Not on me. You think I take that sort of stuff to the office? Meet me in The Vine at six. I'll have something for you then," Barry replied in a low voice. "And bring money this time. No more credit, understood? And don't let that little tart girlfriend of yours offer one of her trades, she ain't got the goods."

The young man nodded and vanished up a side street. Barry made his way home to change and head to the gym.

* * *

That evening, Susan sat with Marian, filling out the online application form for the degree.

"Are you sure you can afford me not earning, Mum? I could find another job."

"Don't you ever ask about that again, Susie! It was my dream that you'd go to university and have opportunities that I never had. I'm so proud that you feel you can make this step. So, don't you ever worry about me needing money. Anyway, I'm earning good extra cash now from my gigs at The Bull and the wine bar."

"Thanks, Mum. I want to get something nice for Luke to thank him, but I can't think of anything. I think he has all he wants."

"Maybe something for his car?" Marian suggested.

"Ooh, good idea! I'll have a think."

* * *

Mary was sitting cross-legged on her bottom bunk, trying to concentrate on some holiday revision. She had always found that her schoolwork soothed her, so she was starting to put what she called 'the events in the park' behind her.

Her sister came into the room looking anxious, and Mary was worried by her expression.

"Are you OK, Lily?"

"Mary, have you been online today?"

"Not since breakfast, no. Why?"

Mary picked up her phone and saw that she had thirty-seven updates from social media. Curious, she opened one. She froze. She read another, and another. They were from a mixture of people, some she knew, some she didn't, and some she even thought of as friends. All of them used the same word to describe her – 'slut'. Two more notifications appeared as she read them.

"I don't understand," she said, numb and confused. She looked at her sister, "Why?"

"Because they're scum," Lily told her emphatically.

"But Tracy Millard is on the gym team with me. She's my friend. We always have cake together after practice. I don't understand. And who are half these people? What do they know about me?"

"Ignore them, Mary."

Another notification.

"They keep coming!" Mary screeched.

Lily grabbed the phone and turned it off.

"Let's go and have tea," she instructed her sister.

* * *

On a rainy late summer's evening, about a week after her meeting at the college, Susan was in the kitchen, making a cup of hot chocolate before going to bed, when there was a knock at the door. Luke was on the doorstep, holding a newspaper over his head.

"I have a favour to ask," he said.

"Ask away," Susan replied.

"I'm taking Margaret for her eye test tomorrow. I was going to ask Dominic to lend me a hand, but he's meeting his father about something. Would you be able to come with us so I can stop outside the entrance to the opticians and you can help Margaret into the shop?"

"Of course, I'd be happy to," Susan said with a smile. "With this weather, I haven't been able to get over to Margaret's. It will be nice to see her."

"Great," Luke responded with great relief. "Tina is lending me The Cedars' minivan, as the Jag is only a two door. It is Jerry's car, but he still isn't back from the US, so it's available."

"Good idea," Susan commented. "It's a shame Tina can't get over for his mother's funeral. Still, at least they can live-stream it."

"Have you seen Dominic's new car?" Luke asked.

"I have, and he has already made me go for two rides in it," she replied with a little skyward glance. "He's a good driver."

"He is," Luke agreed. "And did I see a driving school car outside yesterday afternoon?"

"You did. I don't know who was more scared, me or my instructor."

"Everyone feels like that at first. Anyway, thanks for saying you'll help tomorrow. I'll pick you up around two."

* * *

Dominic sat in the living room of his parents' house, trying to come to terms with the news his father was giving him. His parents had decided to separate. The house was on the market and already had a firm offer on it.

He felt numb.

"Your mum's staying with your nan until we sell this place. We should get enough for both of us to buy a nice little flat or something. Though I reckon your mum may well stay at your nan's; they are so close," his father said.

"But why? After so long? Was it the business with Mary?" Dominic demanded to know.

"No, nothing like that. We've been having problems for a while, it is a mutual thing. We've been getting on better since the decision was made."

"So, you haven't got another woman?"

"One at a time for me, Son. And before you ask, no, your mum doesn't have another man, either. Mind you, I think that business with young Mary over the road is what pushed your mother to move. She felt so guilty every time she passed the house."

"Maybe she deserved to," remarked Dominic, with a trace of venom.

"Maybe you're right, Son."

* * *

Mary was arguing with her parents again. For sixteen years, she had never spoken a harsh word to them, and now she couldn't seem to stop.

"I don't care, Dad, I am not going back to that school!" she shouted.

"But, Mary, your A-levels," he pleaded. "You've got such a bright future."

"Have you seen what they're saying about me, Dad? Have you seen the vile, horrid lies? About me. Your little girl. And you want me to go back there?"

"Ok, darling," he said in a placating voice, "you're right. I'm sorry. I could talk to the school, have them do something about it. Isn't there a law against this sort of thing online?"

"Dad, they'll still be thinking it!" she cried. "They'll still be saying it behind my back. I can't, I won't go back."

"But your gymnastics," interjected her mother.

"I am never wearing a leotard again. Ever, Mum!" Mary insisted. "I'm not letting a bunch of pervs ogle me."

"So, what are you going to do?" asked her father, reasonably. "Some kind of apprenticeship?"

"No, Dad. I don't want to give up my A-levels, just going to the school. I went to the college today and they said it's late in the day, but I can transfer there if you give your permission."

"Of course, Mary, of course," her father agreed with relief. "What do I need to do?"

"Can you come in with me tomorrow?"

"Yes, yes," he said, "I'll let the office know I won't be in."

"OK then… thanks, Dad," Mary sadly apologised, almost deflated by the ease with which she had achieved her objective. "Sorry I got angry. Sorry, Mum."

She left the room, and her parents exchanged anxious looks.

"I wish she would talk to someone, a counsellor or something, if she won't talk to us," said her mother.

* * *

Margaret treated her trip to the opticians as if she were going on a grand tour. She looked at every passing tree, car, signpost, cow, and pedestrian as if it were a rare and exciting artefact.

"Oh, such a treat to go into the town," she would declare at regular intervals.

When they arrived outside the opticians, Luke stopped on the double yellow lines and activated the hazard lights. He retrieved Margaret's walker from the back of the minivan, as Susan helped her down from the passenger seat. He then drove off to find a place to park and the ladies went into the shop; by the time he reached reception, Margaret was already in the consulting room and Susan was sitting in a comfy chair flicking through a magazine. When Luke had arrived, Susan had put down the magazine so that they could chat, but he almost immediately received a call from Dominic, which he went outside to take, so she picked up her phone and flicked through her messages and emails.

Luke returned, saying, "That was Dominic. He seems a bit upset – it looks like his parents are getting a divorce."

"Poor Dominic," Susan sympathised. She hesitated before going on to say in an excited voice, "I've just had an email. Formal confirmation of my place at college. I feel a bit bad about saying anything after Dominic's news, but I had to tell you."

"I'm glad you did. Congratulations," he replied warmly.

"Thank you so much!" she said, giving Luke a big hug.

"Ah, that's a lovely sight," Margaret declared as she emerged at a snail's pace from the consulting rooms.

Susan and Luke let go of each other and turned to their elderly friend.

"I need new glasses!" Margaret continued. "And I have to pick out the frames I want. Such a palaver compared to the old days."

She started to peer at the selection of spectacles on the walls, and Susan and Luke patiently helped her select two designs, one for reading and the other for distance. Frames chosen and paid for, they were advised that they should return in a week for the completed glasses to be ready.

"Another trip out! How exciting!" exclaimed the old lady.

"Do you want to sit here while I fetch the car?" asked Luke.

"Could we have a cup of tea somewhere before we leave?" implored Margaret.

There was a pleasant coffee shop in the nearby department store and they decided to go there. As they walked through the huge foyer, Margaret was fascinated by the perfumes, so they stopped for her to try some samples and she insisted that Susan help pick her favourite. She bought a small bottle of scent, paying for it by counting out her cash with trembling hands.

Then she stopped at a selection of scarves.

"These look nice and warm for winter," she stated.

"I think they are men's scarves," Susan explained. "The ladies' winter wear is over there."

"Silly flimsy things," Margaret dismissed them without looking.

She selected a fine woollen scarf, and again paid for it herself. Then, at long last, they took the lift to the café, where Margaret enjoyed a pot of tea and devoured a buttered tea cake, while Susan sipped a milkshake and Luke had a latte. The elderly lady insisted she pay for all their drinks.

When they were ready to go, Luke went ahead to fetch the car and was waiting with the hazard lights flashing by the time Susan and Margaret were on the pavement.

On the drive home, the conversation turned to how much the town had changed over the years, and by the time they reached her little cottage, Margaret was exhausted from the trip.

Susan helped her to the bathroom and then settled her in her chair, while Luke prepared a light supper and a fresh pot of tea for his old friend.

They were about to leave, when she asked them to stop. She fished the scent bottle and scarf from her bag and gave the former to Susan and the latter to Luke. They were both surprised and moved, particularly when Margaret said, "I can't remember the last time I was able to buy a gift for someone myself. Today has been a wonderful, happy treat and I thank you both."

They each kissed her and then left, a final "thankyou" being called to them as they pulled the front door shut behind them.

"Let's walk up to the church," suggested Susan.

They wandered up to the grey stoned building and walked among the ancient pews.

"I think I'd like to get married here," said Susan, almost surprising herself.

"I think you'd be a beautiful bride," Luke replied.

Susan looked at the little rough cloth-covered hassocks sitting on the wooden benches.

"You kneel on these when you pray, don't you?" she asked.

"Some people use the hassocks, yes. Others just sit and bow their heads."

"Do you use one?" she asked.

"I do," he replied.

"Luke… how do you pray?"

"Do you know The Lord's Prayer?" he enquired.

"Yes, I'm not that ignorant," Susan feigned outrage.

"That's a good place to start," Luke told her.

"Yes, but there's more to it, isn't there?"

"Hard to explain," he replied. "Think of it as a conversation, opening your heart and listening. Different people pray in different ways."

"Show me," she requested hoarsely. "I want to thank God for bringing me here and for giving me a new life."

"That's all you need to say. Say it out loud or say it in your head."

Susan moved a hassock onto the floor in front of a pew and knelt on it.

"Thank you, God for bringing me here and for everything that has happened. I am so happy, I don't deserve it," she whispered, eyes screwed shut. Then she felt guilty. "God, please give Dominic and Mary the same happiness, oh and Jenny, and Vivian, and Mum, and especially Luke."

She sensed Luke moving a second hassock to the floor and kneeling next to her. "Thank you for bringing Susan here, Lord. Help me to be her good friend. Bless her, Lord," was his earnest silent entreaty to his God.

* * *

When she finished at work, Marian found a voicemail on her mobile phone from the owner of the wine bar asking her to call back or drop in for a word. It was only a short walk from her offices, so she went there and found the proprietor supervising arrangements for a party in the private function room.

"Hello, Marian!" he exclaimed on seeing her. "I almost didn't recognise you in your work clothes."

"Hi, Jim," she replied. "You asked me to come by?"

"Oh, yes! I'd almost forgotten. Well, it seems you have a fan. Come to my office."

Jim led the way to a cluttered cupboard with a desk and chair wedged in. He rummaged through a mess of papers on the desk, and produced a business card, which he handed to Marian.

"This lady runs a talent agency, or something," he explained. "She's got a holiday home somewhere near here and she's become a regular when she's down."

"Thanks, Jim," Marian said as she took the card. "See you Saturday night."

When she was back in the car, she looked at the business card. The name on it was Emma Woodcock. Curiosity got the better of her, and Marian dialled the number printed on it. She reached Emma's personal assistant, who she was surprised to discover was expecting her call. Would Marian be available for a telephone conversation at seven o'clock on Monday evening?

Marian drove home, burning with curiosity and excited for her mysterious phone call.

* * *

On Saturday, Dominic sat with Luke, trying to work through his emotions on learning of his parents' separation.

"Maybe if I had stayed home?"

"You'd have to have left sometime," Luke assured him. "It happens. Maybe separation will help them change their minds, but you shouldn't hold out too much hope."

"I know," Dominic sounded glum. "Luke, I have something to say to you and it isn't easy. You're like my best, maybe my only mate."

"I think I know, my friend," Luke told him. "If your dad ends up living on his own, you want to go and stay with him? Your mum can cope, but you think he will struggle."

Dominic was grateful not to have had to say it himself.

"Pretty much. Sorry, Luke."

"Sorry for what? I think it is a splendid idea. I'll miss you, though, mate."

"Me too!" said Dominic, his voice catching slightly.

* * *

Susan had been thinking about Jenny. Having been so excited to have her old friend back in her life, Susan was disappointed that she hadn't heard much from her since she returned home. Any messages had been vague or general in tone, and Susan was beginning to worry that she had somehow upset her.

During a long and tortuous videocall, Jenny had finally told her about Lucy, and that she was worried that people wouldn't understand. Susan was surprised, but only because Jenny had always been so adamant about boys being gorgeous. She assured her she was happy that she had found someone as nice as Lucy.

Jenny had then confessed that she was worried that, in this new light, Susan might have misread the kiss she gave her in the bar. Susan assured her that she hadn't even given it a second thought; she knew that it was a joke and nothing more.

It turned out that Lucy was staying at Jenny's flat, so the final part of the call was with the two of them. Susan thought Jenny looked more relaxed than she had seen her in a long time, and was over the moon when they both promised to message her lots.

* * *

Monday arrived, and Marian was abuzz with excitement all day. When she got home after work, she kept checking her phone to make sure it was turned on. Almost on the dot of seven, it rang and she hurried outside to sit in her car and answer it.

"I have a call for Marian Jones from Emma Woodcock," said an efficient voice.

"That's me."

"Putting you through."

"Hello, is that Marian?"

"Yes."

"Marian, this is Emma Woodcock, I am a huge fan, darling, huge."

"Why, thank you."

"Listen, Marian, I have a little opportunity I would like to discuss with you."

A quarter of an hour later, Marian walked into the living room, where Vivian and Susan were watching telly.

"I've just had the weirdest job offer," she announced.

Vivian muted the television and looked at Marian with keen interest. Susan too was agog to hear the news.

"I've been offered a job as a singer on cruise liners. Great pay and loads of perks, including free travel."

"Amazing, Mum," and, "Good on you, bird," were the responses.

"I'll turn it down, of course," stated Marian.

"Why?" asked Susan.

"I'd be away from home for months. I don't want to desert you, sweetie."

"That's silly!" Susan told her mother. "I've got Aunty Viv, and all our friends here. I'm twenty, for heaven's sake!"

"I don't know. I mean, I have a good job here, friends, Frank."

"Look," interjected Vivian, "just have a sleep on it. Then take the job."

Marian was elated, and just a little disappointed that Susan didn't seem to need her any more.

"OK," she said, "I'll sleep on it."

Everyone there knew she would say yes.

* * *

Margaret was excited to be going to get her new glasses. She checked the clock, Luke would not be there to pick her up for an hour. She settled back in her chair, and picked up her bible and magnifying glass, and started to search for a piece that she thought Joan would like to be reminded of.

She struggled to make out the characters even more than she usually did; she certainly needed her new glasses. She stared harder, but she felt her eyelids getting heavy. Maybe a little nap before Luke arrived? Yes, a little nap.

She let the sleep embrace her, warm and soothing. Then she fancied she heard someone come into the room. It couldn't be Luke yet, that would be too early. Who was it? Oh, she was so sleepy. Oh, yes, that's who it must be.

"Is that you, Polly?" she asked.

About fifty minutes later, Luke arrived and let himself in. Dominic was outside in his new Fiesta, eager to drive it on any pretext.

Luke pushed open the living room door, and spied Margaret in her chair, bible open on her lap. She seemed to be sleeping, but something about the colour of her skin suggested otherwise.

He reached over and held the old lady's cooling hand.

"Oh, my dear, dear friend," he said softly. "Good night and God bless you."

Shaking with suppressed emotion, he called Doctor Salmon and then went outside to tell Dominic.

* * *

Susan had wept for hours when she heard that Margaret had passed away. Now she was standing next to Luke in church at her funeral service. The coffin at the front of the congregation looked pitifully small, but the pews were packed with people paying their final respects. Inside the casket, Margaret was dressed in her best dress and was holding her wooden crucifix; lying over her heart was the photograph of her late husband which had sat beside her chair for over seventy years.

The reverends June and Peter performed the service jointly, and Susan found the words and the music and the spirit of the service deeply moving; she could almost sense Margaret with them.

Susan was wearing her gold cross, and had dabbed the scent on her wrists and neck; her hair was tied back with the ribbon. The trinity of gifts to her from her departed friend. Luke was wearing his scarf, and seemed to be struggling as much with the emotion of the occasion as she was.

As they walked out to her committal in the churchyard, Joan became distraught and needed Susan and June to comfort her; it was a relief to be looking after someone else, because Susan was on the very boundary of breaking down, too.

At the wake in the village hall, the atmosphere lightened and many happy stories were told of Margaret. Some of the mourners were even people whose lives she had saved when she was a nurse and with whom she had maintained a correspondence. They showed photographs of their families and children, some of whom had grown up to become doctors, teachers, or fire officers, and none of whom would have been born had it not been for Margaret.

As they walked to the cars to drive home, Susan suddenly asked a question.

"Luke, please may I come to church with you on Sunday?"

And so, Susan came to faith. Not with a thunderbolt, but gently, like an incoming tide, it gradually covered her. She felt that she had finally acknowledged something that she had always known to be true. Her faith was simple but deep, certain but innocent, burning but gentle. She opened her heart and became content.

* * *

Joan, Reverend June and Luke were sorting through Margaret's house, organising items into three groups: those to go to charity, those to share among her friends, and those to be thrown away.

June came into the living room from the kitchen.

"I can't believe how much stuff in there was years past its sell-by date," she exclaimed, "I've had to throw a lot of it away. But there's some boxes of unopened things that the foodbank will be grateful for."

Luke was sitting in Margaret's chair, reading through the familiar black bible that had sat so often on the old lady's lap.

"There are dozens of pieces of paper in here that she's written verse numbers and people's names on," he told the vicar. "You're there, so is Joan and I get a few ones, mainly hinting that a man should marry. But she had a real thing for Susan, loads of little notes and prayers for her; beautiful, really beautiful."

"I think we should ask Susan if she wants the bible," June suggested, "I sense Margaret would have wanted that."

"I think you're right," Luke agreed.

"It was such a pleasure to see her in the congregation last Sunday," June remarked. "We have so few younger people in the church these days."

"Sadly true," he concurred.

"So," June said, looking around the room, "have you recovered from the shock?"

"That Margaret left this house to me in her will? No, not entirely."

"What do you intend to do with it?" she asked.

"Well, there's probate and stuff still to do, and I need to arrange for her cash savings to be distributed as per her wishes. As for this house, I don't know. I don't think she'd want me to sell it; maybe she knew I wouldn't want to. I think I'll rent it, subsidise it for a local family or something. I did wonder about offering it to Marian and Susan, but…"

"But you like having them live next door?" asked the clergywoman with a touch of mischief.

"No!" he replied a little too quickly. "No, I just think Viv really likes having them there. She got a bit lonely before. Now, why don't I make us some tea to cut the dust while you see how Joan is getting on in the bedrooms?"

He hurried to the kitchen.

"The gentleman doth protest too much, methinks," June said to herself. "Some people can't see what's under their own noses."

* * *

Dominic and his father decided to go on holiday together. They both felt a need to get away from everything that had gone on for the past few weeks, and one of Mr Peterson's dreams had been to drive America's Route 66. A fellow classic car enthusiast knew a firm that hired out iconic US muscle cars, and one of the options was a Ford Mustang GT.

Their plan was to go for three weeks and do the road trip together, returning two days before the start of term at the agricultural college and in time for completion of the house sale.

Dominic drove into town to buy himself some luggage for the trip, and was crouching to look at some suitcases that were on special offer, when he was interrupted by a familiar voice.

"Hi, Dominic."

He turned to see a young man called Patrick, who had been at school with him; they had both been in the swimming team for about a year when they were about fifteen.

"Hi, Pat!" said Dominic, pleased to see one of the few people from school that he was happy to run into. Though they weren't close friends, Patrick, a much more studious pupil, always had a good word for Dominic and had never participated in the bullying.

"You going somewhere nice?" asked Pat, gesturing to the luggage.

"I hope so. Me and Dad are planning on going to the States. We're going to drive Route 66."

"Cool," Pat commented. "How are you doing, mate? We missed you at school."

"Not many did, I'd reckon," Dominic replied dryly.

"Yeah, you may be right. You'd be OK now though. You're a hero for what you did to save Mary Masters."

"I don't deserve it," Dominic objected. "Honestly, it makes no sense; I win awards for gym and swimming, but I'm a hero for losing a fight that I was partly responsible for. Sissy boy to tough guy in one easy step. Ironic, that."

"Well, from what I hear, you're being hard on yourself… I hope you know that I was never part of what they said about you at school?" Pat nervously ventured.

"Yeah, I know."

"I tried texting you and you disappeared online."

"Yeah, I changed my number and dropped off the grid. Just wanted to be left alone. But I'm glad you came to say hi, though. Would you like my new number?"

They exchanged details.

"Do you want to meet up for coffee when you're back?" Patrick asked.

"I think I'd like that."

* * *

"It's a six-month contract, Viv, all food and accommodation thrown in. Half as much again as I'm currently on, too. Of course, I've told them that I couldn't start until after Christmas. I can't miss being with my Susie at Christmas," Marian said to her friend over lunch in the wine bar.

"So, you're decided then?" asked Vivian before slurping a spoonful of vegetable soup.

"I think so. I've always wanted to travel, and here I have the chance to get paid for it. There was a bit of a snag when they asked about my dancing."

"Oh, Lord!" Vivian snorted. "I love you, bird, and you have the voice of an angel, but you dance like a hippo."

"Charming!" laughed Marian. "Don't worry, I'm on as a lounge singer, not part of their main productions. Though I may have to do the occasional big number on the main stage."

"Have you said anything to your current firm?" enquired Vivian.

"Yeah," Marian replied a little sadly. "I was only doing maternity cover anyway, so there was nothing certain there. They are a bit disappointed, but they accept my reasons. Chance of a lifetime and all that. They've asked me to stay on and train a replacement and they won't start looking until mid-autumn."

"You've got it sorted, I'm proud of you," said Vivian, and then added quietly, "but I'll miss you, bird."

"I don't know what I've done to deserve a friend like you," Marian responded.

"Something pretty bad, I'd reckon," cackled Vivian.

* * *

Dominic burst in through the study door and found Luke sitting at his desk.

“Luke, I need to ask a really big favour.”

Luke sat back in his chair, rubbing his eyes after looking at the laptop screen for so long.

“What is it?” he asked.

“Dad’s mate has let us down. Can you give us a lift to the airport tomorrow?”

“Which one?”

“Gatwick.”

Luke maintained a veneer of composure, but internally his body convulsed in a sudden paroxysm of stress. He felt his chest tighten and his stomach release enough acid to dissolve several large dinners simultaneously; he was hot and convinced his perspiration must be noticeable.

This was far beyond his comfort zone. Luke’s coping strategy was to have zones. Zone zero was home, which was The Cherries, its gardens and the fields immediately in sight. Zone one was walking distance, which included the village and The Cedars. Zone two was the local town and some other places, such as stately homes in the area. Zone three was anywhere outside zone two that he had been to before and knew the route and destination. Zone four was all other locations, which most certainly included Gatwick airport.

The most frustrating thing for him was that his reactions would differ from day to day. Most of the time he could go to the village without a second thought, but sometimes it would feel like climbing Everest. Anything in zone two or above would need a conscious effort of will to make travel possible, but the degree of effort would randomly vary. What for most people would be a much-anticipated and exciting trip, say to London to see a show, would be torture for Luke, but he could quite possibly feel he could do it on the spur of the moment. Sometimes, he could be almost literally crippled with anxiety, and others he could fly like a bird. There was no telling when it would strike.

Now he was faced with letting a friend down, or making himself ill with stress by having to cope with several hours of driving.

He swallowed and cleared his throat to speak.

“Should be fine, mate. What time do we have to leave?”

“Sorry, is six-thirty alright?” Dominic replied apologetically.

Luke sighed, smiled and nodded.

Dominic looked out of the window at the garden lawn.

“Blast, Luke!” he exclaimed. “You’ve got rabbits in the garden. They’ll play havoc with your borders!”

* * *

Reverend June knocked on the door of Hayfield Barn. There was no reply, but she could hear a clattering from the garage, so she went to investigate, and found Susan fixing a puncture on her bicycle. The young woman looked up.

"Hello, Reverend!" she called. "Are you here to see me?"

"Yes, but if you're busy, I can come back."

"No, it's fine. I'm pretty much finished here anyway," Susan assured her. She stood up from her repairs and wiped her nose with the back of her hand, leaving a black streak of chain grease on her nostril as she asked, "Would you like some tea?"

"Um," June looked at her watch, "I think I may have time, so yes please."

They went into the house and Susan washed her hands (and nose after looking in the mirror), before she put the kettle on. She opened a packet of chocolate chip biscuits and offered one to June.

"I'd better not," said the vicar, "I have to struggle to keep myself from bursting out of my cassock on a Sunday."

"You have a lovely figure!" Susan protested.

"Not like yours, dear. You must have to work hard to be so petite."

The sound of Susan scrunching into two chocolate chip cookies simultaneously disabused June of that notion.

The kettle boiled, so Susan brushed biscuit crumbs from her fingers and poured two mugs of tea, placing them on the kitchen table. She reached for a third biscuit, which broke June's willpower.

"Maybe just one," the reverend said, plucking a cookie from the packet. "Are you enjoying church?"

"Yes, thank you."

"I'm glad. Now I have a couple of things for you," June said, rummaging in a fabric shopping bag she had brought with her, "firstly this."

She pulled out Margaret's old black bible and placed it onto the table in front of Susan.

"Everyone thinks she would want you to have it."

"Oh, thank you!" said Susan, very moved, "I will treasure it. I've been reading the little one you gave me. It's a bit different to the stuff they taught us at primary school."

"Challenging?"

"That's an understatement, but in a good way, I think. I shall persevere."

"That's a good way of looking at it. Now! I also have this," announced June and she extracted Margaret's box of ribbons, "Luke told me the story about them, so we thought you should have them. Open the lid though."

Susan complied and, nestled amongst the colourful strips of material, she found a small figurine of a young woman with long wavy dark hair wearing a flowing crimson ballgown.

"Oh, she's so elegant!" exclaimed Susan holding it up and peering closely at it. She noticed the perfect porcelain shoulders and the delicate hands holding a tiny posy.

"It was on Margaret's dresser," said the vicar, "Joan and I thought she looked like you."

"Oh, no. She's much too pretty," said Susan, distantly, as she seemed captivated by the sunlight glinting on the figure. She placed it carefully on the table, "Thank you. Margaret gave me so much in so little time."

"I don't think you know what you gave her," replied June. "How many girls of your age would spend time with a woman of hers? To make her feel that the life she lived was worth something to someone who has yet to live theirs? You gave her your time and you listened, and that is a rare gift today."

"You've made me miss my nan," Susan remarked, a little choked, "I think I'll suggest to Mum that we go up and see her."

"You should. You won't be sorry that you did when you look back."

June glanced at her watch.

"Goodness, I must be going!" she announced. "I have a choir meeting at the house in twenty minutes, and if Peter gets hold of them, he'll have them doing harvest festival in Gregorian chant."

As she left, Dominic arrived.

"Glad I found you," he said to Susan. "Are you working tomorrow?"

"No," she replied, "they've got accountants in at The Cedars doing something called due diligence, whatever that is. Anyway, I'm more hindrance than help, so Tina asked me not to come in. They're still paying me though, so it's a mega win from my point of view."

"Fancy a trip out tomorrow?"

"Maybe, what do you have in mind? If it's another trip like the last one, I think I'll pass. I've seen more tractors now than I ever wanted to," Susan said in mock indignation, referring to an agricultural machinery expo that Dominic had persuaded her to attend with him.

"No, it's even more boring, I'm sorry to say."

"Oh, it's not lawnmowers or something, is it?"

"No, nothing like that," he laughed. "You know Dad and me are going on holiday tomorrow? Well, we've been let down on a lift to Gatwick, so I asked Luke and he said he'd take us. I can tell he's really stressed about it; he tried to hide his reaction, but I could tell."

"He will put himself through the grinder," Susan sympathised.

"I was wondering if you'd come too?" Dominic requested. "Then at least he's got company for the trip home."

"I don't see why not. I've never been to Gatwick; it might be fun."

"It won't be," he said to assure her, "you'll just drop us off at the entrance to the terminal. Luke might be talked into stopping for a cuppa at the M4 services."

"Well, now you've talked me into it!" she laughed. "What time do we leave?"

"Six-thirty. Sorry."

"Six-thirty is a lie-in for me!"

* * *

Mary and Lily were looking at a display of tablet computers in the local computer shop. Lily was providing her technical expertise, as she prided herself on being the family IT nerd.

"Good memory, good processor, good price. I'm telling you, Sis, this is the one for you."

"It's a bit of a boring colour," Mary remarked in a disappointed tone.

"You're going to put it in a case anyway. Look, there's one with a monkey on it, that should suit you." She stuck her tongue out.

They queued up and bought the tablet and a case that was plain green.

"That's not an exciting colour either," commented Lily.

"It's on sale and I don't care," replied Mary.

"You're so good at looking after your money," said Lily, envious of her sister's financial prudence, "I've got about five pounds in my account and you must have about three hundred, even after paying for this."

"More like five hundred," Mary boasted.

"Five hundred?" Lily exclaimed. "You are a miser! Scrooge!"

"Bah humbug."

They completed their purchase and started to walk home. As they crossed at a pelican crossing, a white delivery van stopped at the red light. Mary glanced up at the driver as she passed and stopped still. The driver was Barry.

"What is it?" asked Lily.

Barry blew them a kiss.

Mary started walking, this time at double-quick pace. Barry wound down the passenger window of the van as they passed by on the pavement.

"Lovely to see you, girls," he called, "let's get together soon!"

"Sod off!" Mary screamed at him. "Sod off and die, Barry!"

The lights changed, and Barry drove away laughing.

"Oh my God!" said Lily. "Was that him? If I'd have known I'd –"

"If you'd have known, you'd have been as scared as I was," interrupted Mary, harshly dismissing her sister's sentiment as a patently empty threat, and immediately feeling cruel for doing so. How could anyone else ever appreciate the toxic mixture of anger and fear that would swell in her chest at the very mention of his name; seeing his face only intensified those emotions.

She stomped along for a few minutes and then stopped outside a hairdressing salon with a 'no appointment necessary' sign in the window.

"Time for a new look," she declared.

* * *

The Jaguar purred through the leafy lanes, onto the A-roads and then the motorway network, passing from the cool thin sunshine of dawn into the burning heat of summer. As time passed, so the traffic grew heavier, but they made good time and arrived at the airport well before lunch.

Dominic and his father climbed out, had a brief panic that they couldn't find their passports, unloaded their luggage and made their way into the terminal, after having profusely thanked Luke for the lift.

On the drive home, Susan and Luke stopped at a motorway services to use the facilities and eat some sandwiches that Luke had prepared. Susan could sense his unease.

"Do you find travel very hard?" she enquired.

"Yes," he answered simply, "I cannot explain why. When most people talk about going somewhere for a holiday or a day trip, they think only of the fun they're going to have. For me, it is the nightmare of the journey. I expect it sounds silly to you?"

"No," Susan said after consideration, "hard to understand maybe, but not silly."

"Look," Luke explained, warming to his subject, "Dominic and his dad are going to have travelled for hours in the car, then eight hours in the plane and then however long it takes to get from the airport to the hotel. Most people don't enjoy it, but once they get there, they forget it and have a good time. I on the other hand would be thinking about the return trip the whole time, dreading it. My holiday wouldn't start until I was home."

"Have you always been like that?"

"Maybe. Not really. I started being aware of it when I was living in London. Some bad things happened in my life, and I think that that may have aggravated it. At some level, I think I always had the problem, but didn't know it until it got bad. I cope, though."

Susan squeezed Luke's hand.

"I think you cope brilliantly," she assured him, as they resumed their long trip back to the sanctuary of The Cherries.

As they got closer to home, the sky overhead darkened. By the time they were on the A-roads, it was raining heavily, and once on the leafy lanes, headlights were essential, while the windscreen wipers could barely cope with the deluge of water from above. Lightning flashed overhead, charging the air around them and the shattering roar of thunder followed milliseconds behind.

"This is intense!" shouted Susan, both thrilled and terrified by the force of nature.

Gradually, the thunderstorm abated, but the sky remained dark and the rain heavy. Luke muttered a mild curse and pulled his car into a field entrance to allow a van to pass.

"Idiot," he said. "That driver can't have much better vision than we do. He had left himself no stopping distance, so it was safer to let him pass."

Now behind the van, they watched it disappear before them.

"I'll remember that for when I'm on the road," said Susan.

"How are the lessons going?" Luke asked.

"Quite well, I think. I still stall quite a bit."

"Who doesn't? That's why I like an automatic. So much easier than – HELL!"

"Oh, my Lord!" cried Susan as the Jaguar slid to an abrupt halt.

In the road in front of them lay the prostrate form of a horse rider, a little further up the road, a pony was rearing and running skittishly, and embedded into the roadside bank and hedgerow was the van.

Susan and Luke both jumped from the car and ran to the rider. It was a girl of maybe fourteen years old, and she was struggling to get to her knees.

"Where does it hurt?" shouted Luke over the raging weather.

"My chest, my chest, oh, it really hurts."

"Call an ambulance!" Luke shouted to Susan. She looked at her phone.

"I've got no reception here!" she yelled. "Check yours."

Luke checked, and saw the dreaded 'No Service' message. He tried 999 anyway, as he'd heard that some phones boosted their output for emergency services, but to no avail.

"Can you run up to the top of that field?" Luke pointed up a steep incline to the right of the road that climbed steadily to a prominent ridge above. "You should be able to get reception up there."

Susan ran immediately, up the muddy embankment, through streaming rivulets of rainwater, tripping, sliding, pushing ever upwards. Every so often, she would stop and wipe rain from her eyes with muddy hands to check her phone.

Luke meanwhile, decided to see if the rider could be moved to the side of the road. Even with his Jaguar blocking much of it from one direction, he was still worried that she was vulnerable. She managed to stagger to the grass and sat there, moaning.

"I have to check the van driver," he cried. She nodded, face twisted with pain.

"And Pansy, you must get Pansy," she insisted.

For a moment, he was confused.

"Your pony? Yes, OK. Stay still, help is coming."

He ran to the van and stopped short with shock. The front of the vehicle was twisted and crumpled and pushed back well past the point of maintaining crash-structure integrity. Parts of the hedgerow had smashed through the windscreen, strong lengths of branch deep within the cabin. The door window was broken, but Luke tugged desperately at the deformed door, though it would not budge. The pallid driver was breathing ragged gasps, eyes half open, speckles of blood on his face, a face Luke recognised.

The driver was Barry.

"Hang on!" cried Luke. "Hang on, Barry. Help is coming."

Was that a low moan from Barry? He couldn't tell over the drumming of the rain. There was a clap of thunder, and the pony became more startled. Luke was forced to make a decision.

"Hold on, Barry!" he shouted. "I've got to get the horse under control or there might be another accident. I'll be right back."

He ran almost blind through the stinging raindrops and tried to catch hold of the bridle, but the pony twisted and the leather slipped from his fingers. Luke felt a heavy blow to his arm and was knocked to the ground. He staggered to his feet and this time was successful. He was not very familiar with horses, but somehow he managed to soothe the creature enough to lead it to a sturdy fence, close to the injured rider so that she could see it, and tether it by its reins. The girl tried to get up to go to her pony.

"Stay there! Pansy is fine!" he told her.

Meanwhile, Susan had found signal and called 999.

"What service do you require?" said a voice.

"All of them!" she shouted. She had to answer what felt like interminable questions, but were in fact efficient and exact. There was a problem when she realised that she didn't know where they were, but the operator expertly helped her narrow it down.

She sped back down the muddy slope, slipping and tumbling but getting up and running. She passed the tethered pony and headed towards Luke, who was back at the van. He looked up.

"Look after the girl!" he shouted, pointing to the rider. "There's a blanket in the boot of the car. Put it around her."

"Should I put her in the car?" Susan asked.

"No," he replied after a moment's consideration, "better not move her any more unless we must. I think she fell face down, but you can't be sure there isn't a spinal injury. Keep her where she is."

Luke turned back to Barry.

"Can you hear me, Barry?" he shouted. Barry nodded slightly.

Luke ran to the passenger side of the van, which was a little less crumpled. He managed to heave the door open but couldn't sit in it because of the intruding branches. He wriggled in on his stomach until he could get closer to Barry. Luke could see the deformed metal biting into the man's legs.

"The ambulance is on its way, Barry," he reassured the injured man, "stay strong. You're a big guy, stay strong."

Barry suddenly opened his eyes.

"Do I know you?" he asked, confused.

"Not really. You ran into me a while back."

"Oh, I see."

Luke held Barry's hand.

"Am I going to die?" Barry moaned.

"No."

"How do you know? Are you a doctor?"

"No, Barry," Luke said honestly, "I wish for all the world that I was, but no."

"How do you know? How do you know I'm not going to die?" Barry's voice was faint.

Luke realised that he had to be straightforward.

"I don't, Barry. Sorry," he said, "but you're alive right now, so there is hope."

"I'm going to die."

"Don't talk like that!"

"I've done so many bad things," Barry moaned.

"You'll have a chance to put them right."

"Hey, I do know you… tell the girl I'm sorry. Tell Mary I'm sorry."

"You can tell her yourself.".

"Tell them all I'm sorry." The voice was fainter.

"I will."

"Will I go to hell?" Barry whispered.

"If you are truly sorry, then I believe that God forgives all."

"There is a lot to forgive."

"Then live and make things right!"

Barry revived a little and nodded.

"Do you want me to pray with you?" Luke asked.

Again, Barry nodded.

"Our Father, who art in heaven, hallowed be thy name," blue flashing lights were starting to illuminate the inside of the van, "thy kingdom come, thy will be done, on earth as in heaven."

Luke sensed a strong hand patting his back. He slithered out, and turned to see a policeman.

"Are you Luke Cartwright?" asked the copper. "Your friend Susan, over there, told us who you were. Come to the patrol car, let's let the paramedics do their job."

Luke nodded.

"You've done a great job, mate," said the policeman, putting a silver thermal blanket over Luke's head to help keep the rain off.

* * *

Susan and Luke arrived back at The Cherries in the early evening. Vivian and Marian were out at one of Marian's gigs at The Bull, so they both headed into Luke's house. They had dried out a little in the car, but their clothes still clung to them. Luke slipped off his jacket.

"Oh, you're bleeding," exclaimed Susan pointing to his arm.

"I did it when I was trying to catch the pony, but I'd forgotten about it. I think it's just cosmetic," he said. "I'd offer you a shower, but we don't have any women's clothes in the house."

"I forgot my key, so I'll have to find something here or be soggy until Viv and Mum get home."

Susan rummaged through Luke's airing cupboard and found one of his thick, fleecy shirts that she figured would be fine as a dress. She climbed into the warm stream of water under the shower and washed the day away.

She kept replaying the events, the firemen cutting Barry from the wreckage, the ambulance rushing him to where a helicopter could land and airlift him to hospital. The worried look on the girl's father's face when he had arrived and the sight of them getting into a second ambulance. The helpful groom from Pansy's stables coming to collect the pony.

She dried herself on a large soft towel and slipped the shirt on. It reached down to her mid-thigh, which made her realise just how large Luke was – somehow his gentleness made him seem less intimidating. A high point was discovering that the bathroom had an adjoining dressing room which was equipped with a hair drier.

As she emerged from the bathroom suite, rolling up the sleeves of the shirt, it occurred to her that she had never been upstairs in The Cherries. She wondered which was Luke's room, but she was too polite to nose around.

Luke had showered and changed in his own bathroom, and was downstairs, dressed in fresh trousers, shirt and light jumper. He had made two cups of hot chocolate and had lit a fire in the living room.

"A fire in late summer. Welcome to England!" he laughed. "I was just so cold."

Susan sat on the floor, with her legs curled under her, beside the fire and watched it flicker and spit while she sipped her warming drink.

"You were pretty wonderful today," she said, staring at the flames.

"So were you," he muttered, looking at the halo the illumination from the fire made in her hair.

"The paramedic said that the girl, Sally, probably has some cracked ribs and a broken collar bone, but he wasn't too worried. They need X-rays to be sure."

"That's good," Luke murmured.

"Do you think Barry will die?" Susan asked.

"It looked pretty bad. Not something I want to remember seeing," he replied with a tired voice.

She turned to look up at him, her face close to his knee.

"I'm sorry. How thoughtless of me," she apologised.

"You have nothing to apologise for. You are the most considerate, loving person I have ever known," he stated, leaning forward.

"Am I?" she whispered.

"Don't look at me like that," he almost implored her.

"Why?"

"You are too beautiful."

"I'm not beautiful," she said shyly.

"I'm the artist, remember? I know what's beautiful," he told her.

"OK," she nodded obediently.

"Please don't look at me like that."

"Why?" she knelt a little higher, her face closer to his.

"Because it makes me want to kiss you."

Susan knelt a little higher, her lips almost brushing his.

"Why is that a bad thing?" she whispered.

"Because –"

And then their lips were together and electricity flowed through every part of their beings. They kissed deep into one another's souls.

He reached down, scooped her into his arms and lifted her as he reclined back in his chair. She placed her hands behind his head, as she sat curled on his lap and they kissed until they had no breath.

"I love you," Luke whispered, "I am so in love with you. Isn't this wrong? Am I not too old for you?"

"You are my very soul mate," Susan answered, "I realise I have loved you for so long. Age is nothing."

He kissed her forehead and her nose and then looked at her.

They stared into one another's eyes for an age. Then they kissed again and basked in the warmth of the flames.

Chapter 11

Barry's mind was in a thick, sickly soup, caused by drugs and pain. He could see and hear the doctors and nurses moving around him, even understanding fragments of conversation. Words and phrases would break through his fug with crystal clarity, some easy to understand, some like an alien language: "legs," "circulation loss," "pneumothorax," "stabilise," "morphine," "procedure," "prep," "amputate" "subdural hematoma."

Every so often, a voice would address him. "Barry, can you feel this?" He shook his head. "Barry, we are going to have to put a little tube in your chest, do you understand?" He nodded and groaned.

Sometimes faces would loom in and out of his vision, looking compassionately at him, reassuring him. The doctor was beautiful, he thought, a long dark face set with large brown eyes; maybe Indian?

"Am I dying?" he asked, so quietly that no one heard.

Finally, the hubbub died down and he was alone in a room, with the regular beep of the heart monitor and the occasional hissing and squeezing of the blood pressure machine.

Every ten minutes, a nurse would come in to check his progress. She was a plump, pleasant faced woman, with multiple piercings up the sides of her ears.

She saw his eyes looking at her and gave him a reassuring smile, squeezing his hand.

"You're in good hands, Barry. We'll look after you."

* * *

The fire was fading to embers when the telephone rang. Still in Luke's shirt, Susan was cuddled up to him on the down-filled cushions of the long sofa, her head resting on his chest, listening to his steady heartbeat.

Luke started to move to answer the telephone, so Susan sat up to let him pass. She remained seated for a few moments, listening to his voice as he answered the call, before she lightly hopped to her feet and padded barefoot over the soft carpet to the chair where her handbag sat.

Scooping her mobile from the bag's depths, she texted a simple message to Jenny.

'Just been kissing Luke! He says he loves me. OMG!!!'

Jenny must have been using her phone anyway, because there was an almost instant reply.

'OMG!!! Nooo way! About time too! I want juicy details'.

Susan smiled and replied.

'He's a way better kisser than U!'

Luke re-entered the living room.

"That was the girl, Sally's, father," he told her. "She's home from hospital and resting, but the family wondered if we would like to visit them tomorrow as they'd like to say a proper thank you. I said it wasn't necessary, but he seemed very insistent, so I agreed. I said about two o'clock, because I didn't know if you had work in the morning. I've got their number if you'd prefer another time?"

"No, that's perfect," said Susan, slipping her phone into the top pocket of the shirt and walking purposefully towards Luke. She tiptoed, reaching behind his head and pulling him into a long kiss. Then she whispered, "You're perfect."

Luke gazed at her, unable to believe that the woman of his dreams was in his arms.

"You know what? I'm famished. I've got a quiche in the fridge. Let's celebrate with that and a nice claret," he suggested.

As they bustled in the kitchen together, Luke spoke.

"I'm still worried about how much older than you I am."

"I'm not. It's not that big an age gap."

"Thirteen years," he pointed out. "Your mum might not like it."

"I think she'll be pleased for me. Did you mean it when you said you loved me?"

"With every fibre of my being and more."

"Then that is enough for me. Please let it drop."

They sat in the kitchen and talked about what their relationship was, what it meant, and how they should organise their lives. Susan also talked about her own trust issues, about how she had felt abandoned by her father and how she was frightened of having her heart broken; she felt she had to lay bare her fears, for him to understand the momentousness of her surrendering to him, so that he may understand the almost primeval passion that burned in her heart for him. Luke said that since he had known Susan other women were almost invisible in comparison to her and that she had the most beautiful face and beautiful soul that he had ever known.

There was also quite a lot of kissing, flavoured with fermented grape.

Marian's car passed the window and stopped outside Hayfield Barn. She got out and went to the passenger door, where she seemed to be struggling to get Vivian from the front seat.

"I'd better go and help," Susan decided, slipping on her dry mud-encrusted trainers over her petite bare feet, "I'll pop back for my bag and stuff later."

"I can bring them and help, if you like?" Luke offered.

"No thanks. I think Viv may need her privacy."

She started to leave, but turned and scampered back to Luke for one final succulent kiss, leaving a trail of dried mud on the floor.

"Oh, dear! Look at the mess I've made," she apologised. "I should clean it."

"Don't you dare!" he told her with mock severity. "Just go. I hope to have the privilege of clearing up after you from now on to the end of my days."

That deserved one last kiss.

As Susan reached the car, Marian had managed to get Vivian into a standing position. She was trying to support her friend to get to the house, when she heard the scrunch of Susan's footsteps on the gravel.

"Oh, good, Susie. Take my keys and unlock the door, then give me a hand getting her in."

Susan complied. As she was aiding in walking Vivian to the door, Marian seemed to notice that she was attired in a man's shirt and not a lot else.

"What are you wearing, Susie?" she asked, with a concerned note in her voice.

"I'll explain later. Let's just get Aunty Viv in, shall we?" Susan responded, panting slightly.

After much effort, they got Vivian up the stairs and onto her bed. Marian removed her friend's shoes and slacks, while Susan helped her out of her jacket and removed some bulkier items of jewellery. Vivian's eyes had a glassy look to them, when they were open. However, as they lay her on the bed in her blouse and tights and covered her with her duvet, she fell into a deep sleep.

Mother and daughter went downstairs and Susan made them a fresh brew of coffee while she related the events relating to the accident with the pony rider, the crashed van, and the pouring rain. Marian gasped when she heard of the extent of Barry's injuries, but when she learnt who he was she commented that he might have got his just desserts.

"I don't think anyone deserves what I saw today," Susan said.

Then there was a thud from upstairs, the banging of running feet and then the sound of retching coming from Vivian's bathroom.

"She's getting worse," Susan commented. Marian stared at her as if she had started to spout ancient Greek.

"What do you mean, 'getting worse'?" she asked, confused.

"Drinking, Mum."

"Viv has always liked a tipple, but who doesn't?" Marian said in defence of her best friend.

"Haven't you noticed how much she has compared to us?" Susan asked. "If we have a bottle of wine, we get a glass each and she finishes it and another one and several G&T's. I worry about her, Mum."

"I think you're worrying about nothing, Susie. She's been like it for as long as I've known her. Not so much when Tony was alive though, but it's just her way of loosening up. She just went a bit too far this evening."

"You know best, Mum," said Susan, trying to conceal her doubt.

* * *

Luke watched out of the window long after Susan and Marian had taken Vivian into the house. Sometimes, he would catch a glimpse of Susan at the kitchen window and his heart would jump, but finally he decided he had better go and check his computer to see if he had any orders for that day. Walking to his study, he sang to himself an extract of 'On the street where you live'.

A little later he heard the back door open and Susan call his name. He hurried to meet her and they kissed before the door had swung shut.

"I've just come to get my bag and things," she explained, walking to the living room to get her handbag. Luke hared upstairs to collect her dirty clothes from the bathroom.

"I should have put these in the wash for you!" he berated himself.

"But something happened to take your mind off it?" Susan asked coyly.

"Some events could distract me from an earthquake," he declared as he stooped to kiss her. “And some things could cause an earthquake,” he added when the kiss broke.

* * *

It was not until they were going to bed that Susan plucked up the courage to speak to her mother about some of the other events of the day. She was sitting up in bed reading when Marian come back from the bathroom; as her mother slipped off her dressing gown, Susan made her announcement.

“Mum, I need to tell you something. Something wonderful. I… I kissed Luke today. He told me he has been in love with me for a long time.”

Marian gave a half smile.

“I’ve seen how he looks at you and how you look at him,” she told her daughter. “He is a good man, but have you thought about the age gap? What is he, thirty-five?”

“Thirty-three,” Susan corrected indignantly. “Yes, I have thought about it. Luke was worried too, but surely if I don’t mind, why should anyone else?”

“It’s more a case of you being only twenty.”

“How old were you when you married Dad?” accused Susan.

“Exactly, Susie. Don’t make the same mistakes as me,” Marian counselled.

Susan smiled.

“Luke thinks it may be a problem, so we made an agreement,” she advised her mother. “I’m to finish my degree, including a year at proper uni, and if I’m willing, he’d like to marry me then. I’d be twenty-three by then.”

Marian was relieved, and said she thought they were wise to take their time. She was pleased that her daughter had found a man who would honour and treasure her, and maybe at some level Marian was a little jealous that nobody had ever treated her with such respect. Luke had been the perfect gentleman with Susan that afternoon, and she was confident he would continue to be.

Luke had assured Susan that he was content for them to take the physical side of their relationship slowly. Both had a belief that the ideal outcome would be to wait until they were married to have a full sexual relationship, though Susan reasoned that, as a handsome man in his thirties, Luke was bound to have had such relationships in his past. Both her nascent religious faith and his established belief underpinned their decision. Susan decided not to tell her mother, however, partly because it was private between herself and Luke, and partly because it would be difficult to explain.

Before settling to sleep, she pulled the curtain to one side and gazed over the dark courtyard to Luke's window. A warm yellow glow lightened and framed the curtains, meaning he too was in his bedroom. She picked up her phone and sent a text to Luke.

'Good night. Luv U xx'

She lay back on her bed. How could the events of the day be so different? How could she be so happy, so full of joy just a few hours after seeing the human devastation of the traffic accident?

Her phone buzzed.

'Thank you for your message, my love. Have sweet dreams my dearest Susan. I love you too, so very much xx'

* * *

Mary scowled into her breakfast bowl as she reluctantly spooned a mound of soggy cereal into her mouth. She had lost track of how long she had been sitting there, but she sensed her mother's stare burning into her.

"All I'm saying, Mary, is that if you wanted a new hairdo, it would have been nice to pick one together. Your poor father was rather shocked when he saw it yesterday, so please don't be too cross with him. It is just such a... transformation."

"You mean you don't like it," muttered Mary. If she could have acknowledged the truth, she would have been forced to admit that she hated it too.

"No, no, darling. It is just going to take some getting used to."

Mary was growing frustrated. At some inner level, she had wanted her parents to shout at her. Her full-bodied shoulder length brown hair had been hacked away to a rough bob, bleached blonde with a striking pink flash. She wanted rage, she wanted to be a little girl again and sent to her room to think about what she had done; instead she was met with a suffocating forced understanding which felt like condescension.

She knew that she shouldn't have gone to a cheap hairdresser, she knew she looked ridiculous, and she knew that her family were exchanging worried looks behind her back.

"Just get off my case, will you?" Mary screamed and stormed to her bedroom. She wanted to go downstairs and hug her mummy and beg for forgiveness, but she had so much deep raw pain that she couldn't communicate.

Throwing herself into schoolwork might help. She reached into her pencil case, looking for a pen and instead drew out the compass she used for mathematics. Mary examined the point closely, squinting her eyes so that she could see the very end, so exquisite in its perfection.

She placed the sharp tip of the instrument against the fleshy mass beneath the thumb on her free hand and applied pressure, watching with detached scientific curiosity as the discomfort grew and the skin coned inwards. Then, oh so quickly, the point penetrated and Mary jumped. It had gone in mere millimetres, but she managed to make its withdrawal last an age until the tip was clear and a spherical globule of bright red blood balanced momentarily on her hand, before trickling down to her wrist.

Mary jumped out of her trance, and held the tiny wound to her lips, sucking it clean. For those seconds (or minutes, or hours?) she had focussed solely on the control she had on her body and all other thoughts and pain were temporarily forgotten.

She went downstairs to apologise to her mother.

* * *

Susan sat in the little office at The Cedars with Tina, who was explaining that the sale of the business was imminent and that she and Jerry were planning their repatriation to the USA.

"So, honey, there really isn't anything more you can do for us here. Jerry and I agree that it is best to give you your notice now, but not ask you to work it. That's four weeks free pay. You'll be at college by then. Have you got your student finance all sorted?"

"Yes, I have. Of course, it's all loans. I hate being in debt. Mum owes so much; I can see her getting weighed down with it sometimes."

"Some debt is good, some is bad," Tina explained. "This is your education."

"I know. Thanks. So, this is my last day here? Oh, I am going to miss you."

"Me too, babe. Come by and see us any time until we go."

There were more than a few tears shed for the next few minutes.

"Now," Tina looked at Susan through narrowed eyes, "I sense gossip!"

"Well," Susan hesitated, "Luke and I are together. You know, boyfriend and girlfriend."

"Well about time, sugar! You go, girl! It's as plain as the nose on your face that you two are made for each other."

Cycling home from The Cedars, Susan heard her phone chime. It was a message from Jenny.

'Going to call mum at 5 and tell her about me and Lucy. Can U or yr mum be around in case she is v upset?'

Susan responded in the affirmative and finished her trip home. Luke was outside.

"Fancy a bite to eat?" he asked. "I am just making sandwiches, and I keep forgetting Dominic isn't here, so I made too many."

She coasted her bike to where he was standing.

"First a kiss, then I will put my bike away, then another kiss, then I shall have a shower, then I shall come for another kiss, and then, and only then, may we have sandwiches," she instructed.

"Yes, miss," he said obediently. "Pucker up!"

* * *

After lunch they drove to visit Sally, taking the girl some chocolates that Luke had bought that morning and a spray of flowers from the garden. The girl's parents were effusive in their thanks and their daughter was in good spirits, despite her discomfort; indeed, her primary concern was for the welfare of Pansy.

During the drive home Susan told Luke about Jenny's new relationship with Lucy and that Jenny was going to tell Vivian that afternoon.

"I'm sorry, I don't know how long I'm going to be needed," she told him, "I'd much rather be with you, but duty calls."

"Yes, I can see that," Luke said thoughtfully. "Do you know, I have absolutely no idea how Viv will take it? She seems so laid back, but she's much more… let's call it 'traditional', than she lets on."

"I know what you mean," replied Susan. "What I don't get is: why the hurry? I mean, most people don't tell their parents about a relationship until they see them face to face."

"I was wondering about that, too. Why today, why now?" mused Luke. "My guess is that Viv either knows or has acquaintances in common with Lucy's parents and that they've found out somehow, so Jenny feels she needs to pre-empt something."

Susan was worried about how the conversation could affect Vivian, whose fondness for her daughter was much deeper than she allowed those around her to know. When Jenny had been visiting, Susan had overheard a conversation between the two of them, where Jenny was suggesting that Susan could use her bedroom after she had left. "After all, Mum, I've got my own flat, and I'm not home that much," Jenny had said. Vivian's reaction was volcanic. "No! That is your room and that's that!"

Luke's theory was fairly accurate. Lucy's parents had been surprised by her repeated, prolonged trips to visit Jenny, and after pressure from them to explain why, Lucy had decided that honesty was the best policy. Luke was also correct that Vivian had several friends in common with Lucy's family and that one of them had seen the girls together.

Consequently, at just before five o'clock, Susan was sitting on tenterhooks, waiting for the phone to ring. She was careful to time a gin and tonic to be ready and placed within reach of Vivian's chair.

As she had been working in the morning and spent much of the afternoon with Luke, Susan had seen little of her honorary aunt that day, but on the occasions when they had been together, Vivian was unusually ill tempered. Susan had put her behaviour down, at least in part, to a hangover from the previous night's drinking binge, but she now noticed that the older woman had the tell-tale wobble of the head and glassiness of the eyes that suggested she was once again inebriated.

In a moment of inspiration, Susan realised that Luke's prediction was almost certainly right, and that there was a cause of Vivian's binging. She took her mobile phone and desperately typed a message to Jenny.

'I think your mum knows. She is drunk. Be careful.'

She pressed send, praying that Jenny would get the message before telephoning, but Susan's heart sank as the ringing started before the text could possibly have been read.

As she heard her mother's voice say hello, Jenny's mobile buzzed against the side of her head, but she could not read the text.

"Hi, Mum! Nice to hear your voice," she said, striving to sound cheery.

"Is it?" Vivian's cold response shocked Jenny.

"Yes, of course. How are you?"

Her phone buzzed against her head again, and she looked at the screen in irritation. Susan's message, which she had sent twice to try to get Jenny's attention, made her blood run cold. She returned the phone to her ear and listened in dread to her mother's voice.

"How am I?" Vivian was saying. "I'll tell you; I'm humiliated. How do you think it feels to go for a nice little drink in the wine bar and to have some smart arse from the golf club think it very funny to tell me that my daughter is a lesbian? Oh, no I said, not my Jenny. Well, he put me in my place, didn't he?"

"Mum, I'm not doing anything wrong," Jenny expounded, "I've just fallen in love. Don't you want me to be happy?"

"With a boy, yes. How am I going to have grandchildren now?"

"Mum, being a lesbian doesn't mean they take away your uterus, I can still have kids."

The gin and tonic Susan had put out for Vivian was downed in one gulp.

"How?" Vivian asked with a sneer. "Does your girlfriend produce sperm?"

"What?" Jenny was blindsided. "No, of course not. But there are banks and donors and stuff like that. Bloody hell, Mum, I've only been in a relationship for a few weeks, and you're trying to tie me down with a family."

Susan saw that Vivian was crying and moved and put her arm around her shoulders, but was angrily shrugged away.

"Mum, please," Jenny continued, "please, I need you so much. I need you to be happy for me. Please, Mum."

"Oh, Jenny, how could you? I don't want you to throw away your life. When did you become gay?"

"I don't know. Look, I've just fallen in love with someone who happens to be a girl."

Vivian sat silently. Jenny waited and waited. Still there was silence.

"Mum?" she asked. "Mum, are you there?"

"If you love her, then you'd better bring her with you when you come home for Christmas," Vivian said simply and hung up.

* * *

Susan adored her degree course, revelling in new techniques, experimenting with new materials and enjoying the camaraderie of the small group of fellow course members.

When she wasn't at the college, she spent most of her days and evenings at The Cherries. She and Luke would spend much of their time painting together in his studio, listening to his collection of classical music, or sometimes he would read poetry or biographies of the great artists while she worked. In the evenings, they would cuddle on the sofa and read the great classics to each other, works by the Brontë sisters, Jane Austen, Anthony Trollope, and, Luke's favourite, Charles Dickens. Susan would become enthralled by the wonderful, complex stories and she had to be consoled for some time after hearing Nell's plight in The Old Curiosity Shop; she also felt an affinity for Little Dorrit.

Most days when she was in college, Susan would get a lift to and from town with her mother on her commute to work. As the bus service was not reliable enough to get her to and from lectures on a regular basis, she realised that, with Marian leaving for her new job in the New Year, she would need to get there under her own steam. Consequently, she focussed hard on her driving lessons, and was ecstatic to pass on her second attempt in late October.

Luke worked on his book business with a renewed vigour, although Dominic's moving away to live with his father made The Cherries feel very empty after Susan had gone home to Hayfield Barn in the evenings. However, Dominic did still visit regularly, often spending the weekend.

One evening, Luke teased Susan with a mystery envelope, and pushed her into an ecstasy of curiosity. When he finally did allow her to see the contents, it was two tickets for the Christmas Ball, to be held in late December; he had been planning on surprising Susan with the tickets, but knew that she would need to organise a dress.

However, the surprise presented Susan with a problem: she had no idea how to ballroom dance. She confided her dilemma in Reverend June, and the vicar came up with a solution. Twice a week, Susan would pop over to the vicarage for an alleged bible study session, when Reverend Peter would sweep her around the living room in waltzes and quicksteps, while June provided musical accompaniment on their aged piano and shouted advice or criticism as necessary.

* * *

Dominic was in a lecture when a text arrived from Patrick asking him if he would like to meet that evening for a drink. They had already had a few coffees together shortly after Dominic's return from his trip down Route 66, and had got on well with each other, so he replied 'yes'.

When he arrived at the pub, he found Pat waiting for him and it looked like he had been drinking, which was surprising, as the bar in question should have ID checked him. Dominic was driving, so he had an orange juice, but when he sat at the table, Pat offered to add some vodka to it from a bottle he had hidden on him.

"No thanks, mate," Dominic responded, "and you should go easy on it."

Patrick was fidgety, looking around as if fearful of being discovered.

"It's busy here," he said to Dominic, "why don't we go back to my house? Everyone else is out for a couple of hours."

"Let's finish these drinks first," Dominic replied, a little uncomfortable with Pat's behaviour.

"No, if we go now, they'll be out," he said more emphatically and put his hand on Dominic's knee.

Dominic reacted as if he had been pinched, snatching his leg away.

"What are you doing, Pat?" he hissed, looking around the room. "OK, let's go outside, we can't talk in here."

Once in the car park, Pat assumed they were going to his house.

"This way. We'd better be quick, it's too risky here," he gabbled, nerves evident in his voice.

"Too risky for what?" Dominic asked, before realisation struck. "Pat, are you coming on to me?"

"Yes. Why, am I doing it wrong?"

"I honestly have no idea. Look, mate, I'm sorry, but you've got the wrong end of the stick. I'm not gay. I didn't know you were either."

"I think so," Pat said in pained desperation. "Look, mate, it's taken a lot of courage to ask you. If I'm messing it up, it's because… well... I've never, well, done anything like it before."

"I am so sorry, Pat. I must have given the wrong impression. I'm not gay," Dominic explained.

"But that business with Mary Masters? You turned her down, and quite a few blokes fancied her."

"Yeah, well, I'm not straight either," Dominic sounded confused.

"You mean you're bi? So, what's the problem? Is it me?"

"No, honestly. The truth is I'm not sexual at all. I don't have… desires. I'm sorry... but that's how it is."

Patrick was distraught.

"Oh, hell! I feel so humiliated!" he said, voice shaking.

"I didn't mean to. Look, I'm just weird. Asexual if you like. Apparently, it happens. I want to be your friend."

Pat seemed to be calmed by Dominic's words. With a huge effort of self - control and empathy for his companion's evident distress, he repressed the emotional sting of his rejection.

"Sorry, mate," he said. "Yeah, I'd like to be friends too, but… I think I'd just like to go home now. Sorry to waste your time."

"You didn't," Dominic assured him, "I'm just so sorry. Look, I've got my car here. Why don't I give you a lift?"

"No. I think I'll walk. Bye."

Dominic's heart broke as he watched Patrick leave. For a moment, he thought of running after him – maybe there were things they could do together? No, it would be a lie, a desperate act on his own part to cling onto one of his few remaining friends.

Instead, he drove home for supper with his dad.

* * *

Mary was not enjoying life at the college. Yes, she liked the freedom that it offered over her old school, but the overworked staff were too busy to give her the same level of support that she had previously enjoyed and she felt like a tiny speck in a sea of students, compared to the compact sixth-form she had foregone.

In her bedroom one morning, she stuffed a lever-arch file into her shoulder bag, slung the bag over her shoulder and hurried downstairs. The rumble of her feet on the staircase brought her mother into the hallway.

"Have some breakfast before you go, Mary."

"No time, Mum, I'll miss the bus," she replied, pulling on her shoes.

"What's that cut on your arm?" asked her mother.

"Oh," Mary said, as if only just noticing it. "Yeah, I caught it on something yesterday."

"It looks rather deep. Did you wash it?"

"Mum, stop fussing."

She ran to the bus stop as if she truly was late and she was therefore obliged to spend ten minutes waiting for it to arrive, pacing back and forth on the pavement, wishing she wore a thicker jacket. Rather than take the double decker all the way to college, however, she alighted in the town centre, which was a little over five minutes' brisk walk from the campus.

Most of the shops were not yet open, but a mini-supermarket was, so Mary browsed in its aisles, relieved to be in the warm. She picked up an energy drink and some chewing gum, and then, her mother's words at some level appealing to the pragmatic scientist she wanted to be, she walked to the small area of shelving devoted to pharmacy items and selected a packet of antiseptic wipes.

Sitting on the steps of the town hall, in a sliver of morning sunshine, Mary drank the caffeinated drink and waited for opening time. She knew that she was going to miss at least the start of the first lesson of the day, but as it was laboratory work, she was unconcerned.

At nine o'clock she was the first customer into the clothes shop and bought two plain black jumpers and three thick cotton dark grey t-shirts; all these purchases had long sleeves that, when fully unfurled, would extend their coverage to her knuckles.

Satisfied that her shopping had achieved her objectives, Mary half jogged to the college, where she made her apologies to the Chemistry teacher and settled into her work.

The following lesson dragged. Mary had chosen German because she was told that she should select a fourth subject for her A-levels and she had found the GCSE undemanding. The A-level was proving very different, however, and she was already debating changing to something else, or dropping to three subjects, but her father had impressed on her that she needed four good results to get into a top university and that a language would always be marketable on her CV.

She hadn't made any friends to speak of at the college and she was beginning to feel she had missed the opportunity of bonding with anyone, exacerbating her isolation. However, as she stood up at the end of the lesson and gathered her pens and notepad, she was approached by two girls who were also in the class.

One was medium height, had long blonde hair with faint streaks of green which appeared to be airbrushed in, freckles, blue-rimmed glasses covering bright blue eyeshadow and several artistic tattoos. She wore a floral maxi-skirt and a ruffled cream top, over which hung several strings of brightly coloured beads.

The other girl was tiny (perhaps five feet tall), with long dark hair, reaching down past the waistband of her trousers, and her delicate Malaysian features were covered with thick eyeliner and dark red lipstick. She was clad in black and wore military-style boots, which must have taken several hours to lace up.

"You're Mary, aren't you?" enquired the blonde.

"Yes. It's Hannah, isn't it?" said Mary, and she turned to the shorter girl. "You're Siti, aren't you?"

"That's us," replied Hannah. "I really like your hair."

"Wow. Thanks," Mary responded, unused to a genuine compliment for her new style. "Yours is cool, too."

"We've been wanting to come and chat to you for ages, Mary, but you always rush off," Siti scolded her.

"Well, that's pretty stupid of me, because I really don't have anywhere worth going," Mary told them, a little overcome by shyness. By now, the three of them were walking along the corridor.

"I'm really hungry. Want to get some lunch?" asked Hannah.

Mary realised how hungry she was. When had she last eaten? Not for at least eighteen hours, unless you count chewing gum.

"Sure," she said, following her companions to the canteen, where she purchased a pasta salad in a clear plastic pot with a little fork fixed to the lid, and an orange juice. She started to look for a table to sit at, but Hannah had other ideas.

"Let's go over to the monument to eat, shall we?" she suggested.

The monument was well known to most residents of the town. First erected after World War One and then added to after The Second World War, it was a grey stone memorial to the fallen men of the town. It was situated in a pleasant corner close to the college, with an area of grass, flower beds, trees and benches. Mary's grandmother often used to take her and Lily there for ice cream when they were little.

A gangly lad with spiked black hair (which would be receding before he was thirty), joined them; Gareth was similarly sombre in dress to his girlfriend Siti. Mary was struck by their disparity in size; as she walked down the hill behind them with Hannah, she rather fancied that, with Siti's arm around his hips and Gareth's hand barely resting on her shoulder, they looked a little like a mobile crotchet.

Within a few minutes, they were at the monument and they sat on the stone steps taking in the rays of the midday sun, while eating their lunches. The three young women dominated the conversation, discussing how awful German A-level was, although Gareth did join in when the subject turned to music.

A young couple walked into the area, wheeling a battered pushchair that carried an unusually placid toddler. The woman, wearing a red top and tight black jeans, sat on a bench, turned the pushchair to face her, and proceeded to fuss the infant. Mary thought she would be rather pretty, if she were not so thin and her unwashed hair scraped tightly back in a vicious pony tail. The man, in tracksuit bottoms and a grey hoodie, sat on the back of the bench, his feet on the seat, and lit a roll-up cigarette, which he would hold out intermittently for the woman to drag on.

Gareth and Siti walked over to where the man was sitting and seemed to engage in an important conversation with him, which finished with a rather peculiar and incongruous handshake.

"I don't like him much," whispered Hannah, "I hear he hits her and makes her turn tricks. I don't know why those two have anything to do with him, but I guess there are only so many people in this town, so you don't want to make enemies."

"Is he a... a… drug dealer?" Mary asked, having to know if her suspicions were correct.

"That's a bit of a grand term for that low life," Hannah replied, "but yes, he's been selling low-end stuff to the college kids for ages. From what I hear, he smokes most of the profits and more. If you want to feel good or you want to be mellow, he's generally got something. Mind you, he's moved up in the kind of gear he sells in the last few weeks, from what Gareth's told me."

"Have you ever done drugs?" Mary enquired carefully. "Sorry, if I'm being too nosey."

"No. Well, a bit of weed, but who hasn't? It's nice to be able to make all my worries drift away sometimes, but I can take it or leave it. I worry about Siti though, I think she and Gareth light up way too much. He's more willing to be adventurous, too."

The other two returned and Mary spent the next few minutes using her phone to add her new companions on social media.

* * *

Dominic stood in the kitchen of The Cherries, mug of tea in hand, telling Susan and Luke of the events with Patrick.

"I don't understand it," he moaned, "I've managed to alienate and humiliate two people who I had thought of as mates. I haven't got so many friends that I can afford to lose any."

"Well, don't worry, buddy," Luke reassured him, "neither of us fancy you."

He winked at his girlfriend and she blew him a kiss in reply.

"Well, that's something," Dominic said, his voice heavy with sarcasm. "But, being serious, do you think there is something wrong with me?"

"No, not at all," Luke declared. "How you feel may be unusual, but not unheard of. Look, if just one tenth of one percent of the adult population of this country feel like you do, that's still close-on fifty-thousand people."

"I suppose so," said the dispirited younger man.

"You could become a Catholic priest," suggested Luke with a mischievous tone. "I hear they have a bit of a shortage and celibacy is a cinch for you."

"You'd love that, wouldn't you?" retorted Dominic, chuckling. "Maybe it's not such a bad idea!"

"Of course, you believing in God might be a handy addition to the CV," Luke pointed out.

"Hang around with you for long enough, and some of it rubs off," Dominic replied.

"Yes, but I'm Church of England," Luke clarified. "Clergy may marry, but you're condemned to hell if you suggest a hymn that was written in the last seventy years, or put out the wrong biscuits at a coffee morning."

"What is it that you feel, Dominic?" Susan asked, trying to bring the conversation back to topic.

"I'm scared of being alone," he answered sadly, "I like the idea of having someone. I enjoy the idea of romance, I suppose – going for dinners with a special person, or having someone there when you come home in the evening. I think people look nice when they're dressed up to go out, but I'm not attracted to them; I just don't have any urge to be physical. I'm a mess."

"No, you're not!" she declared. "You are who you are and we love you for it. Look at all you've achieved!"

"Thanks," said Dominic, grateful but still melancholy. "I am lucky to have you two, at least."

* * *

For the umpteenth time that day, Mike was texted by Barry. He deleted the message without reading it, but did send a reply: 'Leave me alone'.

He was in a supermarket, on his way home from work, wandering the aisles and trying to decide what to have for tea. He had intended to buy fresh, healthy ingredients, but thus far the contents of his basket comprised: shepherd's pie for one, a packet of hobnobs and two cans of bitter. He wondered if a strawberry cheesecake could count as one of his 'five a day', though he was uncertain what the other four would be.

His phone started to ring, and in frustration he answered it.

"Look, Barry, I don't know what part of 'leave me alone' it is that you don't understand… What? You what? Well, I am sorry to hear that. Were you injured? Oh, that's bad. Sorry. When will you be transferred to the local hospital? OK. Sure, I will come and see you. OK. Yes, I'll see you then."

* * *

After Dominic had gone home to the flat he shared with his father, Susan and Luke fixed themselves a late supper and settled down to watch a film. Susan had insisted on instigating movie night, ostensibly to encourage Luke to engage more in modern culture, but mainly because a constant diet of classic literature and music was starting to fry her brain.

"What did you say this film is about again?" he asked warily.

"She is an FBI agent who has to go undercover at a beauty pageant."

"And we are watching this because…?"

"It is the last DVD in Aunty Viv's cabinet. If you'd get an online film service, we'd have thousands to pick from."

The disc slid into the DVD player and the machine whirred and buzzed for a few seconds. Then, Luke's phone started to ring. As he answered the call, Susan padded out into the kitchen to make coffee and dessert, returning with two cups and two bowls of ice cream balanced on a tray.

"That was Mike," Luke said, and then, seeing her trying to recall the name, he added, "you know, from that business in the park with Dominic?"

"Oh, yeah," Susan said as she put a face to the name. "That's nice. What did he want?"

"It seems he has heard from Barry," Luke told her. "I feel rather bad that I never followed up with how he was, once I heard that he had survived his injuries from the crash. Well, it seems Barry isn't so good: both legs amputated above the knee, some brain damage, and several other things that I can't recall."

"Oh, that's horrible," Susan exclaimed. "He wasn't a nice man, but still…"

"Yes," Luke continued. "Well, it seems that Barry's asked to see Mike and me too, if I am willing. He's being transferred to the local hospital in a few days. Do you mind if I go?"

"You wouldn't be you if you didn't."

Susan pressed play on the DVD remote, but rather than watching the TV screen, she turned on the sofa to face Luke and gave him a long, luxuriant kiss.

"But the ice cream is melting," he murmured.

"I like it runny."

"But you can't see the film."

"I've seen it before."

"But I won't know what happens."

"Don't worry. You wouldn't like it."

"I'm getting to like movie night."

* * *

Lily was lolling on her top bunk, half reading Of Mice and Men and half wondering why all her English Literature texts had to be so depressing. She had snaffled a cheese scone from the kitchen, which she started to nibble, dropping crumbs on her duvet; kneeling up, she started to brush off the offending particles, noticing with sisterly satisfaction that some of them were falling into Mary's bed below.

The door opened and Mary tramped into the room. Lily immediately attempted to adopt an innocent pose, but her sister was oblivious and plonked herself on the bed, making the frame shudder.

"You smell like a bonfire," Lily complained. "Where have you been?"

"Some of my mates smoke, so what?"

"So what? You hate smoking."

"Stop being such a pain," complained Mary. "They're my mates. It's not my fault."

Digesting these words, Lily hung, vulture like, over the side of her bunk and looked at the top of her sister's head.

"I have two things to tell you," she reported.

"Which are?" Mary asked, feigning weary disinterest.

"Mum and Dad want to talk to you. The college called and said you've not been in German lessons for two days and you missed a test and a deadline."

"I hate German," Mary stated, "I think I'm going to drop it."

"Dad won't like that," Lily warned her sister.

"Dad can suck it."

Lily rolled back onto her bed with a silent, "Wow!"

"What was the other thing you had to tell me?" Mary enquired.

Lily popped her head back over the side, craning to see her sister's face.

"Your roots are starting to show."

* * *

Luke found a space in the hospital car park and turned to Susan, who was sitting in the passenger seat of the Jaguar.

"Are you sure you don't mind waiting here while I go in to see Barry? I feel like I'm deserting you."

She waved a copy of Little Women at him.

"I'm expanding my mind, Mr Cartwright, don't you try to stop me! I'm really enjoying this; I mean, Mum and me – sorry, Mum and I - were always hard up, but can you imagine having to sell your hair? But all the sisters are so nice. I particularly like Beth, I do so hope nice things happen for her."

Luke shuffled slightly awkwardly in his seat.

"Do you have any change for the meter, please?" he asked. Susan rummaged in her purse and extracted a handful of coins.

A few minutes later, Luke walked into the foyer of the hospital, where Mike was waiting for him. They shook hands and made their way through the labyrinth to find the ward that Barry was on.

Even though they knew what had happened to him, it was a shock to see Barry. His hair was cropped short, his skin scarred and pallid, his eyes still and sunken, and he had a strange rasp to his breathing. The shapes formed by hospital blankets suggested the prematurely shortened lower limbs, which both visitors were privately relieved that they could not see.

A woman in her mid-fifties wearing her best coat was seated on a plastic bucket seat beside the bed, her arms folded over a stiff leather handbag on her lap. She looked up as Luke and Mike approached the bed and smiled gratefully to them. Rising, she kissed her son on his pale forehead.

"Look, Barry. Your friends are here. Why don't I nip to the café for a bit while you chat to them?"

Barry's eyes followed her departure and then snapped to the two men standing awkwardly at the foot of his bed.

"Thanks for coming," he said flatly.

"Yeah, well, I can't stop long. I've got a thing," Mike told him, planning in his mind to depart as soon as he could. He was experiencing a mixture of pity, residual burning anger, revulsion, and fear at the sight of his former friend.

"Sure, mate, I understand," Barry sighed. "All I wanted to say was sorry."

"Sorry for what?" Mike asked, a note of suspicious hostility in his voice.

"For how I behaved. For how I treated you… before," Barry spluttered in unmistakable sincerity.

To his surprise, Mike felt a prickle of tears form in his eyes.

"That's OK, mate," he replied, "water under the bridge. When you're better, we'll try and organise that trip to Twickenham, yeah?"

"Yeah," Barry replied, knowing that it would never happen, "I'd like that. Look, mate, you should go now - you've got things to do. Thanks for coming – I don't get many visitors other than Mum and Dad."

"I'll come and see you again soon," Mike promised, feeling as if he'd got a 'Get Out of Jail Free' card and he almost bolted to the door.

"I won't be going anywhere," Barry commented after him.

As Mike left, Luke, who had followed the conversation with interest, moved to sit on the plastic chair beside the bed. It seemed to take Barry several seconds to remember that he was there.

"How are you feeling?" Luke enquired, feeling ridiculous, but at a loss for anything else to say. Barry snorted.

"Never better, mate," was the irony laden reply.

Luke murmured a "sorry" and reached out to touch a bandaged hand.

"In the van, it was you there, wasn't it? I didn't dream it?" Barry asked.

"It was," Luke reassured him. "I didn't know if you would remember me being there."

Barry nodded, closing his eyes, seemingly building the courage or the will to speak.

"I was sure I was going to die back there. What you said in the van just kept playing around and around in my head, even ages afterwards. Did you just say it because you thought I would die?"

"No," Luke assured him.

"Maybe I should have died. Look at me now, my life is going to be crap. Mum and Dad have let my flat go, and there will be occupational therapists visiting their bungalow next week to have it specially adapted for me. I'll be back at home, suffocating with no future."

"It doesn't have to be like that," Luke tried to tell him. "You know Jerry, the guy who was with me when … well, you know? He was caught in an explosion when he was in the military; lost one leg and a big chunk of the other."

Barry digested the information for a while with detached impartiality, as if weighing it against his own misfortune to decide if it merited comparison. After this introspection, he spoke.

"I meant what I said back there."

"What?" Luke enquired.

"When I said I was sorry. About the girl, about your friend, about everything."

"I believe you."

"I wish now that I had died," Barry sighed, "I guess this is my punishment for all that I've done wrong."

"Sorry, but I don't think it works like that," Luke said directly. "What makes you so special that you deserve divine retribution over all the murderers and sadists who have died of old age, peacefully in their beds, having never suffered a trauma in their lives? What did the kids on the paediatric ward do wrong?"

"I don't know. Why then?" Barry asked in a pained voice.

"Why not? Look, we live in an imperfect world where things happen. And, sometimes our own actions can have drastic unforeseen consequences. I can't begin to understand what you are going through, but I can say that you have a choice to look at this as a curse or a chance to live and to put right anything you wish you could undo."

Barry did seem to brighten a little at these words, so Luke pressed on.

"There was a guy called Paul and he wrote of having a thorn in his side that he was thankful for. I don't know what it was, an ulcer or something, but the point is that he had a constant reminder of his mortality. He had done terrible things, but changed. Could you look at what you have as a daily reminder that you are no longer the person you were? No longer the person who I sense you regret having been?"

"What, like try to undo what I've done?" Barry's mind played a list of faces to himself; frightened, confused, angry, desperate people into whose lives he had dripped poison.

"I don't know if that would be possible," Luke counselled, "but you may be able to give some people a little peace."

"Are you saying I should tell the police what I've done?" Barry asked, wanting to be told what he must do.

"If that is what is right, you should. But you could create a positive life, one that could help others."

As Luke spoke, he was texting.

"Barry, maybe if you were to meet some of the people you've been referring to, you might feel you can see a way forward."

Barry looked unconvinced. He played Luke's thesis in his head again and again, and Luke sat in patient silence, reading a message that had arrived on his phone.

"I don't know if I could. I have never felt shame before in my life and now I can't seem to stop," Barry finally said.

"Maybe if you met someone to whom you don't have too much to apologise for?" Luke suggested.

As if on cue, Susan walked in through the door and came to the bedside.

"Hello," she said, rather stiffly, "I'm sorry about your accident."

Barry gazed at her for a few moments, trying to recognise her. Then the penny dropped.

"The bar," he stated, "you were the one I poured the drinks over. Yeah, I'm sorry about that."

"You also scared me and my friends when you came to the house later," she told him. "What you said to Lucy was horrible. She was so scared that she didn't want to be left alone."

"So you were there," Barry said, as if being told the secret of a magic trick, "I thought your friend was lying, the sly minx. Good for her." He looked Susan in the eyes. "I am sorry for that, too."

Susan reached out and took his hand in hers.

"Thank you, Barry," she said, "apology accepted. But I think there are other people who have much more to forgive. My friend Dominic for one."

Barry nodded slowly.

"Would you like to meet him, too?" Luke asked. "I can see if he would be willing."

"Yes, but not for a while," Barry replied with a sigh. He was visibly beginning to fade. "This has been a bit too much for me. I am getting tired."

Barry's mother was walking back across the ward, so Luke and Susan made their goodbyes.

After a few paces, Susan turned back.

"Would you like me to come and visit you sometimes? When I have some free time at college?" she offered.

"Why?" Barry asked.

"Why not?" Susan responded.

Barry had no argument against the suggestion, and he was deeply touched by her generosity of spirit.

"Yes please," he said. His mother smiled too, just a little.

* * *

Dominic did agree to go and see Barry, and he found the experience shocking and cathartic. However, when Luke had first approached him with the idea, he had reacted angrily.

"Good!" he exclaimed when Luke told him of the extent of Barry's injuries. "Karma. One more perv off the streets."

"True," Luke said, slowly, weighing the import of his friend's words. "From a perspective of natural justice, it is understandable to want Barry to suffer. You have much more reason to want to see him punished than I do, and more than Susan does too."

Dominic was satisfied, until Luke continued.

"Presuming Karma works proportionally, what had you done wrong to warrant being beaten up? And what had poor Mary done, other than have a crush on a boy who could not reciprocate?"

"I still think he deserves it," Dominic insisted defiantly.

"I'm sure he does. But if he's had his just punishment, why punish him further? Is losing both legs and having brain damage not sufficient retribution for your black eye?"

"What about what he did to Mary, and Susan, and Jenny, and Jenny's friend, and who knows who else?" demanded Dominic.

"You can't forgive him for that, only they can," Luke pointed out. "But, my friend, you are in the position to help a man who is on the verge of a moral epiphany to edge just a little more into the light; for him to become a better person and to maybe even seek to make retribution to those very people about whom you are so concerned."

"Wait a minute, how am I suddenly the bad guy?" Dominic protested.

"You're not," Luke assured him, "that's why I knew I could ask you, and that's why I believe you will go. You have a strong sense of what is right; it is something I have always admired about you, Dominic."

The young man thrashed in his mind for further arguments, but he couldn't find any. So, he went to see Barry, and was glad he did.

* * *

Marian's birthday was approaching and Luke and Vivian hatched a

Machiavellian scheme in The Bull over steak and kidney pies followed by sticky-toffee pudding. They clinked their glasses together to seal their pact.

Two days before the celebrations of Marian's birth, Vivian was sitting in her kitchen bright and early, sipping coffee. Marian was astonished to come downstairs and find her best friend was up before her.

"I've got to go up to see Lawrence," Vivian announced. Marian was confused.

"Who is Lawrence?" she enquired.

"My solicitor. In London. For heaven's sake, bird, I've talked about him often enough!" Vivian sounded exasperated. "Anyway, I'm going to drive up today and stay over. I'm going to do a little bit of shopping, see Lawrence, meet up with some old friends and take in a show. I'll stay that night too and drive home the day after."

"You mean you won't be around in the morning for my birthday? It's Saturday, I thought we might spend the day together," exclaimed Marian, a little upset.

"Is it your birthday? Oh, bird, I thought it was next week! Well, I can't cancel things now. You're a big girl, you don't mind, do you? I'll be home for dinner and a celebration drinkie."

"Sure, Viv, that's fine."

Vivian did indeed drive to London and she did meet her solicitor, but she left directly after seeing him to go about her secret mission.

On the eve of Marian's birthday, twenty-four hours before she or Susan were expecting her, Vivian coasted her Audi to a stop outside The Cherries. A few minutes later, she walked into the kitchen of Hayfield Barn, much to Marian's and Susan's surprise.

She told them that her friends had to cancel, so she had decided to skip the show and come home instead, so that she could be there for all of Marian's birthday.

A little later, Luke knocked on the door.

"Sorry to trouble you," he said, "but I wonder if I could ask you all to come over and help me figure out what to do with something in my house."

"Sure," replied Susan, "we'll pop over after dinner."

"If you could all come now, it would be very helpful," he entreated.

The three women trailed across the courtyard, through Luke's kitchen and hallway, and entered the living room. Marian and Susan both yelped in shock.

"Mum!"

"Nan!"

There, sitting on Luke's couch sipping tea, was Marian's mother, Rose; the best birthday surprise she had ever had. After many tears and hugs among the three generations, Susan's nan explained that she would be down for the weekend and that Vivian had promised to take her back on Monday.

Luke came into the room, carrying a tray with six tall-stemmed glasses of champagne, and announced that dinner was organised and would be served shortly. It was a very happy party that sat at the elegant regency table, to share a side of baked salmon, with buttered potatoes, peas and green beans, and cauliflower cheese. Rose seemed rather taken with Luke's quaint custom of saying grace before a meal. For dessert, there was a succulent chocolate gateau.

"You are going to make me fat!" Susan scolded Luke, spooning a small mountain of gateau and thick clotted cream into her mouth.

"The plan is to make you so huge that you can't get out of the front door and you have to stay here with me," he revealed.

"Then I'd better have seconds," she reasoned.

* * *

Marian, Rose and Vivian were sampling a rather nice dessert wine in the living room, while Susan and Luke made coffees and stacked the dirty plates in the dishwasher.

"Thank you for the wonderful surprise," Susan said, rinsing the thick residue from the bottom of the sauce boat under the tap.

"Don't thank me, Viv did all the hard work," he answered. "And it was Reverend June who suggested that we try to organise getting you all together."

"Mum and I had planned on going up for a weekend, but it never happened," Susan explained.

He moved behind her as she stood at the sink and, placing his arms around her, began to kiss her neck.

"Stop it," she said, not meaning it. He moved to kissing the other side. "I said stop it," she said, meaning it even less, "the coffee is ready." The caress of his hands over her cotton shirt was too exquisite.

She turned her head back, allowing him access to her soft lips and sensitive tongue.

"Mmm," she said, turning the rest of her body to face him. After they stopped kissing, they maintained their embrace and lived in the moment.

"Three years is a very long time to wait," she whispered.

"You're worth it," he said, while his mind was agreeing wholeheartedly.

As they brought the drinks through to the living room, Marian was asking what the sleeping arrangements were for her mother.

"Luke has kindly said I can stay here," was Rose's reply.

Marian's response was one of disappointment. She keenly felt torn at living so far from her mother and her guilt was multiplied tenfold by her own forthcoming departure overseas, which was now almost a matter of weeks away.

"Why doesn't Nan sleep in my bed? That way she can be with you when you wake up," suggested Susan. She glanced at Vivian in the hope that she may offer Jenny's room to her, but her honorary aunt was making sure the bottle of dessert wine had been thoroughly exhausted. "I can sleep on the sofa."

Rose was clearly a little overwhelmed by the relative grandeur of The Cherries, and she leapt at the opportunity to stay with her daughter. However, she also rather liked Luke, and was very pleased that her granddaughter had such excellent prospects of marriage. Consequently, she made her own suggestion.

"Oh, lovely idea, Susie. But you don't want to sleep on the sofa - why don't you stay here? Luke's already made up the spare bedroom, and I'm sure he wouldn't mind a change of guests."

There was a tangible twinkle in the old lady's eye. Susan and Luke exchanged a glance – a slight mixture of excitement and horror, rather the equivalent to Augustus Gloop receiving the news that he had won the key to the chocolate factory at the same time as being diagnosed with chronic diabetes.

"Well, yes, of course," Luke said, a little too casually.

When Rose was getting sleepy and Vivian was tired and emotional, the women went over to Hayfield Barn, with Susan lugging her grandmother's suitcases. A few minutes later, she was back in The Cherries, washbag and nightshirt in hand.

Luke showed her, with unnatural courtesy, to the spare bedroom.

"This is the bathroom," he said, pointing to a small en suite, "this is the dressing table, the wardrobe and the er…"

His mouth seemed to dry up.

"The bed?" Susan asked, coyly.

"Yes, the – ah – bed."

Luke stared at the item of furniture that he had seen a hundred times before as if it were an unexpected addition to the room.

"Would you care for some cocoa before bed?" he asked, attempting to defuse the tension with banality. Susan shook her head and he wondered why her hair had to brush on her shoulders quite so beautifully.

"Then I think I'll turn in," he added, kissing her cheek in a manner usually reserved for a slightly inebriated great-aunt.

He departed to his room, performed his ablutions and slipped under the bedclothes. Lying in the dark, he tried to turn his mind to important matters of daily life and not the beautiful young woman just a few feet away.

Luke must have slept, because he was woken by the opening of his bedroom door and the light padding of Susan's bare feet on the carpet. She slid into bed beside him.

"What are you doing?" he asked.

"Shh. I trust you," Susan whispered back.

For the first time, they slept in one another's arms.

Chapter 12

Bonfire Night was approaching, and Susan had a bad cold, which she had picked up at Tina's and Jerry's goodbye party. The parting had been an emotional one, and Susan had given them a small picture she had painted of the view from The Cedars as a farewell present.

She was painting in one of the studios at the college, working on a piece that was simply going wrong. Her head was full of catarrh and her limbs ached, but she tried to persevere with her work. Susan's lecturer, an elegant Syrian woman called Mercedes, approached and stood considering the artwork.

"How do you think it is going, Susan?" she enquired in a manner akin to a psychotherapist opening a counselling session.

"I think I've messed it up and should probably start again," Susan replied before holding a tissue to her mouth and succumbing to a bout of coughing.

"Oh, dear," Mercedes remarked, taking an involuntary step backwards, "that cough sounds nasty. The work isn't a lost cause, but I think you need to take a break."

Susan took the advice and decided to walk up to the main college to get a camomile tea and maybe some soup.

* * *

Mary was awake long before her sister, and she lay on her side staring blankly at the wall. Her life was much changed from the one she had just a few months before, and it seemed difficult to find a chink of light in her own grey, oppressive world; she sometimes felt as if she were in a long tunnel, trying to reach the end, but only ever finding staging points from which she must move on.

Many of her problems stemmed from anger towards herself for being like she was; she detested weak submissive perpetual victims, and yet that is what she believed herself to be. Mary could see her parents treading on eggshells whenever they spoke to her and she could sense her sister's increasing irritation and exasperation with her; she ached to be close to them again, but instead she built her wall higher and thicker and isolated herself.

Except, she wasn't alone. She had the friendship of Hannah and Siti (which carried the obligatory companionship of Gareth), but it was a friendship she merely accepted, much as a man parched with thirst does not question the quality of water he is offered to drink, or the motives of the well-keeper.

Hannah was enigmatic and capricious. She was always pleasant towards Mary, but would often disappear for periods of time, or take up with another group of friends. During these times, Mary would feel abandoned, but then Hannah would suddenly insist that they should spend all their time together and must never be parted, that Mary was her dearest friend; however, a week or so later, Mary would catch sight of her laughing and joking with people to whom she did not even bother to introduce her.

Siti was a more consistent friend, but her constant carbuncle, Gareth, made it difficult for Mary to bond closely with her. Much of their conversational relationship was conducted by messaging late at night.

Mary had the sense of being a scientist, sent to observe alien humanoids. Able to blend in, yet not quite fitting in. She would sit amongst the group, often with other people whom she barely knew, and listen to them talking, see them smoking dope (or occasionally more), hear the music that they played, and constantly wanting to be a part of their world and not quite daring.

If a joint or a tablet had been offered to her, normally by Gareth, she had declined, although she had had the occasional puff, so as not to seem too square. She turned them down, not because of fear or any moral judgement, but maybe because, somewhere in her mind, she could still hear her father's voice – there was still some level at which she wanted to give him no further disappointment.

Her scientific mind led her to observe that her friends were very different under the effects of substances; Siti was giggly, Hannah was mellow, and Gareth relaxed (however, Mary thought that he was a rather aggressive, unpleasant person when he wasn't high).

However, while Mary had not yet indulged in drugs, she was still suffering from their ill effects. Desperation for friendship, and skilful manipulation from her friends, meant she constantly took money from her savings account and gave it to them, hoping for firm acceptance into the circle.

She had now accepted that she was being a wuss and it was time to bite the bullet. Today she would buy something from the guy in the hoodie and share it with the others. It would be her final initiation.

The alarm clock went off and Lily moaned.

"You awake, Mary?" she asked. Mary remained silent.

A skinny leg descended from on high, and a foot flailed in her direction. A second leg joined the first and contact with Mary was achieved.

"Quit it!" Mary snapped.

"Unless you're giving up another subject, you need to get up," Lily advised her in a sharp tone. "Do you want the shower first?"

Mary sniffed herself.

"I'll keep another day," she replied.

"Yuck!" said her sister, who completed her descent and started to rummage for her towel and clothes.

"Lily, can you lend me some money?" Mary asked cagily.

"What, moneybags wants to borrow from me?" Lily said. She looked at her sister's earnest expression and her heart melted. "There's a twenty in my phone case."

* * *

Susan was deeply involved with feeling ill, as she made her way up to the main college campus. She was miserably looking at the pavement in front of her as she plodded up the hill, when movement caught her eye.

She was quite close to the monument, and the movement she saw was a group of teenagers standing up to walk back towards the campus. But it was a figure who remained seated on the steps when the others left that caught her attention, initially because Susan thought the young woman made an attractive composition for a picture. Her next thought was that it must be cold sitting on the stone steps. Her final thought was one of possible recognition; the hair was different, but it was the unmistakeable figure and face of a petite gymnast she had met some months ago.

"Mary?" she croaked as she approached; the teenager had a look of semi-recognition on her face. "It's Susan, do you remember we met a while back?"

"Oh, yes. Hello, Susan," Mary replied cordially.

“You’ve had quite a transformation, I almost didn’t recognise you!” Susan told her, scanning the young woman and noting old familiarities in aspects of her dress sense.

“Yeah, well I wanted a change,” Mary explained dismissively.

Susan shivered.

“It’s getting chilly,” she commented, looking around, “proper Guy Fawkes weather. Very sensible to wear a nice jumper with those long sleeves.”

Mary said nothing, but nodded.

“I didn’t realise you went to the college, I thought you went to the school sixth form,” Susan continued, in a chatty voice. “This is nice. Maybe we could meet for a coffee sometimes? I don’t know many people here, so it would be nice for me to see a friendly face.”

“I’m not being rude, but we aren’t exactly friends, are we?” was Mary’s cutting response. But her politer side drove her to add, “But perhaps,” accompanied by a small shrug.

Susan decided not to push the matter, but some secret voice spoke to her and told her not to leave Mary. She was struggling to find something further to say, when a young man in a grey hoodie wandered up and sat on the park bench, looking casual. Susan regarded him with an experienced eye; she had seen many like him in some of the places she grew up, and she knew him for what he was.

She could also see Mary’s eyes darting to and from him, and the girl’s demeanour was one of agitation as she kept moving about on the step.

“Well, it’s been nice to see you again,” Mary spoke rapidly, “but I am very busy and I have to get on.”

Susan fought herself not to budge from the step.

“Don’t let me keep you,” she said, casually, “I thought I’d rest here a bit.”

Mary was tortured. Why wouldn’t this woman just go, so that she could do what she came here to?

“I don’t like the looks of that bloke over there,” Susan remarked, nodding to the hoodie man, “I’ve seen his type before. I think he’s watching us and it’s a bit creepy. Mary, please will you walk up to campus with me now? I don’t think either of us should be around him alone.”

Mary relented and stood up with Susan; she stole one glance over her shoulder as they walked away, and the hooded man was looking at her. When they had climbed the steep hill to the college, Mary stopped outside the science block.

"This is me," she explained, "I've got a biology class."

Susan looked at her companion's eyes, which glanced every so often at the path they had just walked. She took the girl's arm and led her to a quiet corner.

"Mary, I'd like to be your friend, if you will let me. I do understand how you feel," she said.

Mary was insulted.

"How dare you? You think you understand what I've been through? To have a man drug you to try to… to…," Mary heaved, "… and to then be called a slut and humiliated?"

"You're right," Susan responded, "I don't know. I mean, I have been spat at, beaten up, laughed at, and had photographs of me naked shared around the school and posted online. I have been to the lowest point of humiliation. So, no, I don't know what you're going through, but let me see if I can guess. Would you like to roll up your sleeves, Mary?"

Mary stared at her, in shock, astonishment, fear and anger.

"No," she muttered.

"What do you use? Nice clean razor blades?" Susan's directness sounded angry.

"No!" Mary gurgled, looking around desperately. "No."

Susan gazed straight at Mary with an inner force willing her on to break through the wall. But the wall was strong and the two women faced each other, both feeling pity for the other despite their own vulnerability being exposed.

"Mary, I can help you," Susan said softly, "I can be your friend. There is a path out of where you are now, and it doesn't lead to, or start with, that man at the monument. Things can never go back to how they were, but they can be better than they are now. I will wait for you right here for lunch tomorrow. I'll understand if you don't want to meet me, but I pray that you will."

Mary nodded. Susan left to go to the canteen and Mary walked to the science block, she placed her hand on the thick handle and paused. Her head turned to the direction of the monument, and she wavered first one way then the other. Finally, she turned her head to the direction that Susan had taken and then she pushed open the door of the science block.

* * *

Luke stood in the empty living room of Margaret's cottage, still sensing the presence of his old friend. Probate concluded, he had distributed the estate as

Margaret's will had instructed, with bequests to her niece and to the church restoration fund.

Reverend June was with him as they walked around, their footsteps echoing off the bare floorboards.

"Susan and I have decided what to call it," he told June, "this cottage, I mean."

"Oh, yes? What's that?" she asked.

"Blossom Cottage."

"Well, I'm sure it is more original than number one, Glebe View, and I guess it makes sense with the rose bushes in the front garden."

"That's not the only reason. I'm told that the name Margaret comes from a word that originally meant pearl."

"Yes, I think I had heard that somewhere, though I can't for the life of me think where. Peter probably told me, he loves etymology."

"Well, it seems the Sanskrit word, mañjarī, also means a cluster of blossoms."

"Well, that is a lovely thing," June tried to enthuse while feeling that Luke's name choice was unnecessarily complicated and painfully tenuous. "So what changes are you planning to make to the place?"

Luke unrolled a long folio he had been carrying in his hand, revealing some architect's plans.

"Not much on the downstairs," he explained. "I'm going to turn the bathroom into a utility room with a cloakroom; it's a later addition to the property, so there is no danger of losing the character. We will put new cottage-style units in the kitchen and make an area where you could have a small breakfast table. The upstairs bedrooms are a good size, so we are going to take a little off the master bedroom, extend the passageway and have an upstairs bathroom. Then, we are going to split the second bedroom into two, giving us a three-bedroom cottage, with upstairs bathroom and downstairs utility and WC."

"Clever boy," applauded June.

"Fingers crossed, it should all be done and dusted by February and we can start looking for tenants."

* * *

Mary stood in the shadows, looking out of the corridor window at Susan, who was standing patiently as promised in the agreed place. The waiting figure looked up and Mary stepped further back to avoid being seen.

She descended the stairs to meet Susan, much as she would to visit the dentist, dreading it but knowing she had little option. However, in the foyer, she met Hannah who threw her arms around her effusively.

"Mary, my sweet!" Hannah cried in delight. "I've been looking for you everywhere. Come on, let's go find Siti and we'll have lunch, just the three of us. Gareth is on some field trip somewhere, so it will be a treat."

Mary was torn.

"I'd love to, but I'm supposed to be seeing someone," she replied.

Hannah stopped still.

"Who?" she demanded to know.

"Her," Mary replied, pointing out of the window. Hannah stared at Susan.

"Well, she doesn't look much fun," she declared. "Come on, make an excuse and come with us."

Mary deliberated for a moment.

"OK. Come on!" she said urgently, grabbing Hannah's hand and leading her to the back door of the building.

"Have you got any money with you?" Hannah asked. "I've forgotten to bring any with me and I'm famished. I'm such an airhead sometimes."

Mary thought of the solitary twenty in her purse.

Susan stood, cold and sniffing for forty-five minutes before she gave up waiting. Coffee in hand, she walked back to the art faculty, and saw three female figures at the memorial, one of whom she recognised. She quickened her pace and made sure not to appear to be looking at them.

Susan's mind churned through her options. How best to help Mary? Tell her parents? Tell the college? Tell them what – 'suspicions'? She could destroy what little trust Mary had in her, while not achieving anything. Yet, the girl's parents surely had a right to know. Susan decided to try one more thing.

She walked to the bus stop and rode to a pleasant suburban area on the edge of the town. Using the maps on her phone to guide her, she navigated the estate on foot, finally arriving at a small bungalow set a little back from the road.

Barry's mother opened the door and showed Susan into the living room, where her eldest son was sitting. Susan enquired after his health and therapeutic progress, and they made general small talk. Then she found the courage to tell Barry about Mary and the devastating effect his actions had had on the girl. His contrition was genuine, so Susan asked him to write a sincere letter to Mary that she could give to her on his behalf.

Barry complied. Later that afternoon, Susan was taking the bus into town to get a lift home with her mother and, in her handbag, she had an envelope addressed to Mary containing his emotional confession and apology. Barry had one condition: that Susan must honestly tell him about the girl's reaction.

Susan had also spoken to him about the man in the hoodie, and Barry had said that he knew who he was. It seemed that one of Barry's minor customers had moved up onto his patch. Susan now realised a final twisting irony – that the drugs Mary was sampling may well have been originally supplied by Barry, the root source of her agony, and that he had very probably also unwittingly groomed the man in the grey hoodie to be his successor.

* * *

The following morning, Susan scoured the science block for signs of Mary, and finally spotted her hair in a Chemistry class. She waited a little way up the corridor until the students emerged, following discreetly behind the throng as it thinned out, and then dispersed until finally Mary was alone and, as Susan predicted, walking to the monument. Susan broke into a jog and caught up with her quarry about halfway down the hill.

"Mary!" she called, causing the girl to stop and turn around. "I missed you yesterday."

"Yeah, I'm sorry. Something came up," Mary justified herself, with an uncomfortable expression on her face.

"No problem, I know how busy you must be," Susan soothed her. "Look, Mary, there is something I need to tell you. Please give me a few minutes and I promise you won't have to see me again."

"OK," Mary replied, after a pause to consider, "what?"

"Could we go somewhere and chat?"

"No. Tell me now."

"OK," Susan began slowly, "there is no easy way to tell you this. Barry was in a very serious motor accident some months back. He almost died and has life changing injuries – he's lost both legs and has brain damage."

Mary stared at her.

"What do you expect me to say to that?" she demanded to know. But then she broke down in tears and Susan comforted her for several minutes. Mary's reaction was mainly relief and pleasure. However, the thought that the strong, physical man, whom she had initially quite fancied, was now a broken husk was tragic. Even worse, he was now a figure of sympathy rather than an object of hate.

"I have a letter from him, would you like to read it?" Susan asked.

Mary held out her hand and took the envelope, tearing it open and scanning it with darting eyes.

"Very nice," she said in a cold voice.

"I do believe he is sorry," Susan ventured, unable to read Mary's reactions.

Mary nodded, tight-lipped.

"Is there any message you would like to send him?" ventured Susan.

Mary's eyes were alive with flame.

"You can tell him to rot in hell!" she stormed. "Tell him that he deserves all that's happened to him and more. He wants forgiveness? If I could, I'd hack off his disgusting hands and pluck out his evil eyes. He wants forgiveness because something bad happens to him and he's seen the bloody light? There is no hell deep enough, no pit foul enough for him to fester in. That's what you can tell your friend Barry!"

"OK, I'm sorry. I've got this all wrong," cried Susan, desperately trying to get back onto an even keel after the outburst, "I want to put it right. I want to help you."

"No one can help me, Susan," Mary hissed, "all thanks to your friends Dominic and Barry. No one can save me, Susan, least of all you! You promised to leave me alone. Now keep your promise."

Susan walked away, despairing at her failure. Mary watched after her and continued her own journey down the hill.

* * *

Susan strode along the grey flagstones of the pavement with urgent purpose. She had failed Mary, but she had one last card to play. She caught a bus and then walked to Mary's house, knocking loudly on the front door. The girl's mother answered.

"Hello, Mrs Masters, my name is Susan Jones. I am glad to find you home. I need to speak to you about your daughter, Mary. It is a very urgent matter."

Mary's mother invited Susan in. She stayed for a little over half an hour before emerging and making a phone call.

Barry received the call on his mobile phone. He listened seriously to what Susan had to say.

"OK," he said at length. "Thank you for telling me this, Susan. I can't blame Mary. I'm going to be a man of my word and do what I promised you. You're a good person, Susan, you've done the right thing."

Barry terminated the call and dialled another number.

"Hello, police?"

He knew the almost certain repercussions of making the call, but prison held no fear for him – he was already serving life.

* * *

Mary sat with Hannah and Siti at the monument; Gareth was bargaining with the man in the hoodie. A familiar car squealed to a halt and, to Mary's chagrin and shock, her father climbed out.

"You're coming with me right now, Mary," he said so forcefully that she complied without thinking. He led her by the elbow to the waiting Ford and pushed her into the passenger seat.

"Dad, you can't do this!" she screamed, but it was too late.

The remaining people at the memorial went back to their conversations. However, they were soon interrupted by the arrival of several police officers, eager to speak with the hooded man and his associates.

* * *

Susan and Luke sat together holding hands on the back seat of Reverend Peter's middle-aged Subaru estate, travelling to a November the fifth fireworks display in the town. June was in the front passenger seat, debating with her husband about the best place to park.

When Peter had lost the argument, a quiet lull fell in the car and Susan recognised it as an opportunity to tell the others what had happened with Mary earlier in the day. They listened in respectful silence until she had finished speaking.

"I've managed to mess things up again," Susan stated, in self-rebuke, "I knew how she was feeling and yet I still managed to say and do all the wrong things."

"I'm not sure there is ever a right solution," Luke tried to reassure her. "It is impossible to judge how someone will react to a situation like that."

"At the end of the day, her family will be there for her," June pointed out, "which is more than many of the children that I come across have. Do you know, I was at a school the other day, where it came to light that one of the eight-year-olds was being given drugs by his stepmother, as she thought it was funny to see how he reacted?"

"I was less worried about the drugs than the self-harm," Susan explained. "Lots of people smoke a bit of pot, and more, without any ill effects."

"That's very true," Luke agreed. "When I was in the City, I lost count of the number of people I worked with who were snorting or smoking or popping something, and the great majority of them led completely normal lives. That said I was never tempted to try anything."

The other occupants of the car said much the same thing.

"Tell me, Susan, why did you think Mary is self-harming?" Peter probed.

"That's a bit of a painful subject, I'm afraid," she replied uncomfortably. "Body language and how she dressed, I suppose. I've seen it before, when I was at school. I suppose I could be wrong, which would make my betrayal even worse, but I don't think I am."

"I'm sure you are right," June assured her.

"But I did so much wrong," Susan lamented.

"Dickens once wrote: 'Every failure teaches a man something, if he will learn'," Peter remarked, "and you are too sensible a woman not to learn from this failure, Susan."

"So, you do think I failed?" she asked the reverend.

"No, but you do," Peter replied.

"I suspect there isn't a human soul on this Earth that could have done any better, even if they had all the training in the world," Luke observed. "Sometimes, whatever you say or do is wrong, because the person you want to help puts themselves beyond your reach, but at the end of the day, you have hopefully placed her where she may be in reach of someone else, or at the very least prevented from harming herself physically."

"I just think the whole situation is tragic," June remarked. "Don't reproach yourself, Susan, at least you didn't walk by on the other side."

"Maybe Mary would be happier if I had done," Susan reflected.

* * *

The fireworks arched high into the night sky and the bonfire crackled and sparked in the darkness. Susan and Luke stood arm in arm, admiring the spectacle and joining in with the "oohs" and "ahs."

Susan scanned the crowd which had gathered to enjoy the spectacle, and saw Lily. She was standing a little distance from her father and mother and an angry young woman who was closely sandwiched between her parents.

That was the last time that Susan ever saw Mary, standing guarded near the spluttering flames, but she kept the girl in her prayers and hoped that Mary may one day come to forgive her.

Chapter 13

In early December, Marian finished her placement at the solicitors' offices and decided not to work for the few weeks remaining before she left for her new job, as she wanted to spend as much time as possible with Susan and Vivian. Christmas was on the horizon and she wanted to make it a special occasion for everyone.

However, her diary was still full with singing engagements and her range of venues had broadened well beyond The Bull and the wine bar. Some of the work came through Emma Woodcock's agency, and these engagements were often for corporate functions; one such opportunity had arisen at a venue close to Basingstoke, which would require an overnight stay (to be paid for by the client).

She left early for the trip with a packed lunch prepared for her by Susan and Luke in a bag nestled in the passenger footwell of the car; the meal transpired to be of such lavish proportions that she believed that she wouldn't need to eat again for a week. Marian had allowed plenty of time for the journey and chose to avoid the busy main roads whenever it was practical to do so; she partook of her feast sitting in her aged Citroen at a picnic spot, which had toilet facilities and a small hut selling takeaway hot food and drinks.

She arrived at the venue, which was a hotel and conference centre, in plenty of time and parked in a space among a sea of shiny BMWs and Audis. Once checked in at the hotel, Marian headed straight to her room to freshen up, but within a few minutes, she heard a knock on the door. It was the event organiser, a woman in her mid-thirties dressed in an immaculate trouser suit, and her PA intern, whose youthful, bespectacled face and business-like dress was offset by impractical high heels, which made her walk like a baby giraffe.

Marian was escorted to her dressing room. Professionalism meant that she tried to hide her excitement at this unexpected turn of events, because she had never before had a dressing room.

"I'm very sorry, but you'll be sharing with one of the other performers," the organiser told her.

"That's fine," replied Marian. "May I ask how many acts there are?"

"Five, including you," piped up the intern. "Plus the compere, of course. Would you be available to do a sound test now?"

Feeling rather like a fraud, Marian followed them out onto a modern stage at the front of a huge hall, where teams of young men and women were scurrying around setting out tables and chairs. She tried to total-up the number of tables, but lost count at fifty.

"How many people will be here?" she enquired.

"Well, the conference is about eight hundred people, and some of them will have brought their spouses or partners," the intern explained.

Marian felt very small on the stage, but told herself to buck up and that there was no backing out. The doubts started to subside once the sound test started; with the music playing and technicians running back and forth, the experience felt smoothly engineered.

Back in the dressing room, she met the young woman who she would be sharing with – a young Croatian, with long black hair and long black eyelashes, who was also a singer. They bonded well in the manner of two nice people forced into a shared experience, both of whom knowing well that they will never see one another again, despite earnest promises to keep in touch. They helped one another with makeup and hair, and Marian averted disaster by getting a stain off her temporary friend's skirt.

They were interrupted by a knock on the door. The PA tottered in and asked them to follow her to meet the compere. He was a cordial man, a minor comedian that Marian had seen a few times on telly, but found his jokes too crude to be funny. They ran through the running order of the show, but his disinterest in them, or indeed anything other than his fee, was tangible.

Marian was one of the earlier acts to perform, and she nervously walked onto the stage, wishing the audience would have had more time to sample their wine. Past the glare of the lights, she could see countless faces turned to look at her, spectacles and jewellery glinting in the dark.

She need not have been nervous, because her singing was met with warm applause, and she grew in confidence with each number performed. The compere even stopped her on her way off-stage to give her a show-biz air-kiss, as if she were his oldest friend, and he held her hand in the air and persuaded her to take a bow.

Buzzing with adrenalin, she sat in the dressing room, removing some of the makeup that was caked onto her face. Her room-mate was on stage, and Marian could hear the applause rippling through the backstage corridors; she allowed herself the luxury of believing her own audience reaction was better.

A knock at the door disturbed her self-congratulation, and she moved to open it expecting to find the intern, but she was met with a very different face. It was a man's face. A face she knew of old.

"Hello, Marian," said Susan's father.

* * *

It was board game night at The Cherries. Susan and Luke had been joined by the Reverends Peter and June, and by a rather bored Vivian. Cluedo was the game of choice, and Susan was being hugely competitive, much to the surprise of the others (save her honorary aunt, who knew her well), and would regularly check the rules looking for loopholes.

Peter was shaking with silent mirth as she brandished the instructions.

"Yes, I can use the secret passage!" she crowed and then prodded Luke in the ribs.

"I stand corrected," he conceded, as he slowly stood up from where he was seated on the floor next to Susan. "Before I am further assaulted about my person, I am going to make some drinks."

"You can't, it's your turn!" Susan and June protested. Peter nodded his agreement and Vivian maintained an air of mild disinterest (she was only present because she didn't fancy spending the evening alone), though she had plucked up some enthusiasm at Luke's mention of drinks.

"Oh really? In that case I accuse Mrs White in the Billiard Room with the revolver," Luke said casually. "Who wants tea, coffee, or something stronger?"

Susan pulled the three cards from the envelope in the centre of the board. Her boyfriend was indeed annoyingly correct in his prediction.

"How did you do that?" she demanded to know.

"I knew three turns ago, but you were having such fun," Luke replied, knowing he was infuriating his girlfriend. "Now who wants what to drink?"

Orders given, he left the room.

"He has a very sexy brain," Susan said, and then realised that she had spoken what she had intended to just think. She decided that she had been wise to opt for coffee rather than another liqueur.

"In that case, I'm George Clooney!" declared Peter.

"That's just in your own opinion," June responded in mock approbation. Her husband looked rather crestfallen, so she whispered into his ear, "And mine."

Susan wandered into the kitchen to help Luke.

"Are you staying here tonight?" he asked as he poured the drinks.

"I'd like to, but I'm worried about Aunty Viv. She seems very lonely at the minute. I don't think she's really over the Jenny business," she replied in a disappointed tone.

"Didn't you say she was coming down at Christmas with Lucy? Maybe that will help Vivian," he remarked.

"How so? Oh, you mean by seeing them together as a happy couple. Let's hope so," Susan said, asking and then answering her own question.

Back in the living room, Luke laid the drinks on the table. Vivian had a coughing fit and gulped some of her gin and tonic to try to stop it.

"Still not shifted that cough?" asked Luke.

"No, it's still hanging on from that cold Susan brought back from college last month," Vivian complained.

"Yes, half the church came down with it," added June.

"Well, I'm sorry!" Susan declared in false indignation, as she packed away the Cluedo pieces. A mischievous glint came into her eyes. "Let's play Pictionary. Luke and I will be a team."

"That's hardly fair, you're both artists!" protested Peter.

"You're both vicars, so you can have divine help," Susan retorted.

"Well, none of it is being very fair on Viv," Luke pointed out.

The company looked to Vivian, who had fallen into a contented sleep.

* * *

Marian looked across the table in the lounge bar at the eyes she knew so well. The face was gaunter, sallower, than she remembered; the hair was greyer, the body thinner, the hand less steady as it lifted the cup.

"You look well," her ex-husband said. "Still beautiful."

"Nigel, I don't want your compliments, and I don't think you came here to flatter me," she responded coolly. "Actually, I'd like to know how you did find me. Were you a delegate at this conference?"

"No. No, you're becoming quite well known. I saw a picture of you online on a local newspaper site," Nigel explained. "I did an internet search and up it popped."

"Why would you look for me?" she demanded to know.

He looked at the carpet and licked his lips.

"I'll explain that later," he said, wiping the back of his hand against his mouth. "How is the child?"

"The child!" Marian's tone could not have been more incredulous or indignant. "Do you mean your daughter, Susan? Is that what you're asking?"

"Yes," he replied.

"She went through hell. When you left, she was crushed. Some of the places we had to live because you left us with nothing were like a war zone. At school, she was bullied, and yet, somehow, somehow, she has become a wonderful, beautiful young woman, whose heart is full of love and compassion."

"I'm glad," he stated, "I always felt bad about it, I'm sorry."

"Did you miss us?"

Nigel struggled to formulate a reply.

"OK," said Marian, realising she wasn't going to get an answer. "So what happened with your life?"

"I moved to Andover and became a carpet salesman," Nigel responded, choosing to ignore Marian's slight snigger. "I never married again, but…"

"But what?"

"Well, I do have a girlfriend. We have three children together. Boys. How about you?"

"I was left looking after our daughter, remember? Not a great way of attracting good husband material – not that I was ever much good at that."

Nigel seemed to jerk into life.

"I probably deserved that. I came here to tell you something," he said.

"I'm all ears," she replied dryly.

"I'm dying, Marian," he told her. "It's the big C. No hope."

The words cut into her like a burning spear to her gut.

"I'm sorry to hear that, Nigel," she said softly.

They sat in silence for a few moments.

"I just wanted to know you were OK," Nigel explained, causing Marian to nod in acknowledgement. "I'm going to have one last Christmas with my family."

That cut Marian even deeper. "Family," she repeated quietly, the word bitter on her tongue.

"Did you want to meet Susan?" she asked.

"I think it would be too… complicated," he replied, avoiding her gaze. "I'll leave it up to you to decide whether or what to tell her."

"Don't you want to see her? Or I have pictures on my phone, if you're interested." Marian was almost desperate for him to show some interest in their daughter.

"I'm sorry, but no," Nigel said firmly. "No. I let her down too badly. Lost all rights. I think it would hurt too much."

He looked at Marian's face.

"You always said I was selfish," he said and stood to go, handing her a piece of paper. "Here is my email address. Send me your contact details and I'll get someone to let you know when… I'm gone."

She nodded staring at her cup on the table.

"Goodbye, Marian," Nigel said as he walked away. She did not look up until she heard the door swing shut behind him.

* * *

Susan had been stressed for days about finding a dress for the Christmas Ball, which was now less than a week away. She constantly scanned internet sites, looking for something within her price bracket (which was very modest), but having no idea what would be right.

"Some of the boutiques in town have some lovely ball gowns," Vivian told her as Susan sat at the kitchen table staring glumly at her laptop screen. "You're struggling to find something because you don't know what suits you. Why don't you and your mum come with me into town tomorrow and we can look at some together? We can make a day of it; have lunch somewhere."

Susan was very agreeable, so she drove Vivian and Marian into town the next day in her mother's aged Citroen.

They circulated among the boutiques and clothes stores, Susan parading in front of the others in what felt like an endless stream of dresses. Finally, they decided to stop for lunch and to discuss the gowns they had seen so far.

"There can't be many more places left to visit," said Marian as they waited for their food to arrive. "What do you make of what you've seen so far, Susie?"

"Well, there was that nice red dress," replied Susan, "but I don't know if it fitted quite right under my arms. Maybe I could make some alterations, but I'm scared of messing it up."

"That's cos you're so skinny, love," Vivian remarked, sipping her Chardonnay. "Enjoy it while you can."

"It's very frustrating," Susan exclaimed, "I don't want to let Luke down after he's gone to so much trouble. He says he's organised a special lift to the ball."

"Darling, I've seen how he looks at you. You could wear a bin bag and Luke would still think he was the luckiest man in the room," Marian told her daughter, hiding a tinge of envy.

Vivian yawned slightly and looked in the direction of the restaurant's kitchens. She stood up and pulled her coat back on.

"The food's taking an age. I'm going to nip out and have a quick smoke. Come and get me if it turns up," she announced. "Don't give up hope, Susie, I've got one more place I want to take you."

"Don't forget that I'm a poor starving student artist," Susan warned as Viv passed by on her way to her nicotine nirvana.

After lunch, Vivian took the other two to a small boutique, tucked away just off the high street, where she marched to a small rack of gowns and began assessing them with an expert eye. A sales assistant emerged from a back room, summoned by an electronic beeping which had been triggered by the opening of the shop door; Susan noticed that the assistant knew Vivian by name.

The honorary aunt started to hold gowns up against Susan, cocking her head on one side as she did so as a visual sign of her evaluation process.

"This is perfect, Susan," she finally announced.

"Yes, that is nice," agreed Marian.

Susan was prodded into the changing room, where she frantically looked for a price label on the dress Vivian had given her, but the search was in vain. Afraid to try it on lest she fell in love with it, Susan reluctantly changed into the gown and felt its smooth fabric caress her body as it slid down. She slid the zip up the arch of her spine and stepped out of the changing room.

"Oh, yes!" exclaimed her two companions and the sales assistant in unison.

Susan gazed at her reflection. The gown was a dark blue V-neck maxi dress, which hugged her slender form before flaring out at the skirt, making it ideal for dancing. She tiptoed through a 180-degree turn, keeping her eyes on the mirror so that she could see how she looked from behind.

The assistant retrieved a velvet choker with a sparkling crystal inset from the hanger in the changing room, which matched the colour of the dress, and fastened it around Susan's slender neck.

"The shoes I bought with Jenny when she was down should match," Susan commented, before telling herself not to get carried away.

"Perfect!" declared Vivian. She turned to the shop assistant, "Got a bag to go with it?"

The sales assistant scuttled away.

"Please don't, Aunty Viv, you're wasting her time. I love it, but I'm sure it is going to be far too expensive for me," Susan said plaintively.

"Oh, this place often costs much less than you think," replied Vivian. "Go and get changed back into your civvies and we'll ask how much it is when she gets back."

Susan complied. When she emerged from the changing room, she walked to the till, where the assistant was now standing and holding a matching clutch bag and evening shawl.

"How much is this please?" she enquired, preparing for the worst.

"No charge," replied the assistant with a smile.

"What?" Susan asked, confused.

"Early Christmas present from your mum and me," announced Vivian triumphantly, but when she saw the look on Susan's face, she feared the emotion may get the better of her. "You can pay for the bag and the shawl yourself though," she added with a cackle.

* * *

The evening of the Christmas Ball arrived, and it was agreed that it was easiest for Susan to get ready at The Cherries. She and her mother had crossed the courtyard through a light flurry of snow, which was leaving a powdery deposit on the ground, and they now sat before the dressing table in one of the spare bedrooms, fixing makeup and hair. While undergoing her preparations, Susan wore a robe over the underwear and stockings which she had purchased on her shopping trip with Jenny. Finally, she slipped into her ballgown and shoes, and Vivian made the finishing touches to her hair and helped to fasten her choker.

From Luke's room a certain amount of thumping could be heard, followed by a series of mild curses directed at a bow tie.

"Are you sure you'll be warm enough?" Marian checked and Susan nodded.

Vivian had been kind enough to lend Susan diamond earrings and a matching bracelet that she rarely used (they were far too delicate for her tastes) and they completed her ensemble. The sound of Luke's footsteps on the stairs reminded them that the hour of departure was nigh.

As Susan walked down the stairs Luke was waiting in the hallway, wearing a dinner suit and a bow tie on a crisp white shirt; his shoes were brightly polished black leather. As he heard her footsteps on the stairway, he looked up to see her and was captivated.

"How does my girl look?" Marian asked.

Luke smiled and recited from Shakespeare.

"Did my heart love till now?
Forswear it sight,
For I ne'er saw true beauty
till this night."

He handed Susan a posy of small pastel pink and white flowers, surrounding a pale blue carnation, which she brought to her nose and inhaled appreciatively. Luke opened the front door and peered into the night; the snow flurry had passed and the moonlight was bright, illuminating the sparkling white ground and trees.

"Excellent," he proclaimed.

The faintest purr of an engine and a rumble of tyres reached their ears as a beautifully preserved Rolls Royce whispered to a halt outside the front of The Cherries. Luke took Susan's hand and led her to the car, where the chauffeur was now standing to let them in. They were watched by Vivian, who had come to her back door, and Marian, who pulled the front door of The Cherries closed behind her and walked across the courtyard to join her friend.

The engine gave a little throaty roar and Luke and Susan were whisked away to the dance, watched by the two older women until the lights were out of sight.

"Are you going to tell her about Nigel?" asked Vivian.

"Not tonight, that's for sure," replied Marian. "Maybe in the New Year, maybe never."

* * *

The unnatural silence of the Rolls was a new experience to Susan, and she gazed at the fairy-tale landscape sweeping by the windows with heightened senses. Luke slipped his arm around her.

"Warm enough?" he checked.

"Well, maybe if you hold me tight enough," she replied.

He looked at her eyes, shining with excitement in the darkness of the cabin and felt compelled to say:

"She walks in beauty,

Like the night of cloudless climes and starry skies;

And all that's best of dark and bright

Meet in her aspect and her eyes."

"That was very romantic," Susan whispered.

"Well, Byron was a romantic chap," he replied and went to kiss her.

"Mind my lipstick!" she cautioned, so he changed course and gently kissed her forehead.

* * *

The history of the Christmas Ball went back to the late eighteenth century, when the great house was built near the village. In those times, it was the preserve of the nobility and local gentry, but with the ascension of Queen Victoria, a second dance was introduced, running concurrently in the grand summer house, for local tradespersons and higher-ranked domestics from other households. By the turn of the twentieth century, the owning family had established a third event in the almost equally grand stables, which took place on the following night for people such as farm hands and parlour maids. To be a servant asked to work on the occasion of the great ball was no terrible thing, however, as they would be paid double for the night and had their own dance a few days later.

The great tradition carried on through the First World War and the great recession of the 1930s, but the house was closed during World War Two; however, the locals continued to mark the memory by holding a dance in the summer house. Sadly, the conflict prematurely ended the lineage of inheritance, and after the war, death taxes and financial hardship meant the house remained an empty shell. A prep school acquired the building in the mid-fifties, which ran for a little under twenty years, before it too was sold and an international school took over, offering residential courses for adults wishing to learn English. All through these times, local pressure and nostalgia of living memory, meant that the tradition of a Christmas dance was maintained in some way or another.

It was the late 1980s that saw a change in the fortunes of the great house. A leisure conglomerate bought the building, created a golf course and tennis courts, transformed the summer house into a swimming pool and spa, and had the stables turned into a riding school. The owners of this exclusive country club heard of the history of the building and decided to reintroduce a Christmas Ball and add a midsummer one. Nowadays, celebrities of stage and screen, politicians, renowned artists and poets, and some local people (such as mayors or clergy) were on the invitation list, while additional tickets were available for sale, with some at a subsidised price for those from the village.

* * *

They disembarked at the entrance to the grand country club, a large country house with baroque pretentions, as Luke described it. The golden light from indoors spilled onto the moonlit driveway and the sound of music reached their ears. As they climbed the steps, Susan's arm slipped through Luke's. Passing through the security detail, she began to fear she would be spotted as a fraud.

It was an evening of laughter and friendships, old and new, and of wonderful food and fine wine. Most importantly, there was dancing; Luke swept Susan around the dancefloor at every opportunity, and he was astonished that she knew how to dance so well.

From time to time, the decidedly off-duty Reverends Peter and June would glide past them on the dancefloor and shout encouragement. Indeed, Peter was the only man able to prise Susan from Luke's arms and steal a few dances with her himself, while Luke whirled June around.

At the end of the night, or, rather, the beginning of the morning, footsore but elated, Luke took Susan's arm in his and escorted her to the door.

On the driveway sat the beautiful Rolls Royce. The chauffeur opened the door for Susan, while Luke walked to the far side of the car to get in and joined her on the back seat. Waiting for them was mulled wine and hand-made chocolate truffles.

"How did you manage all this?" Susan wanted to know.

"Well, I know a guy with a wedding car business," he said casually. She laughed.

"You make me feel like Julia Roberts in Pretty Woman," she told him.

Susan sensed his confusion.

"Well, that's the next movie night sorted!" she exclaimed. "OK, you make me feel like Eliza Doolittle."

"My Fair Lady or Pygmalion?" Luke asked for clarification.

"I didn't realise there was a choice," she replied, with mild exasperation.

"Big difference in outcome," he explained.

"Well, I know something that you definitely don't know," Susan whispered.

"What?"

"I'm not worried about my lipstick now."

* * *

Christmas was fast approaching, and Susan was becoming increasingly worried about what to get Luke for a gift. She scoured shops, searched the internet, and asked mutual friends; everyone agreed that her boyfriend was almost impossible to buy presents for. Finally, a set of cufflinks in the shape of books was settled on.

Dominic was invited to The Cherries for Christmas dinner, but declined as he was going to stay with his mother and grandmother for the festive season; Mr Peterson was visiting his younger sister and her family, to enjoy time with his nephews and nieces.

Also asked, and this time gratefully accepting, were June and Peter, for whom Christmas was a hectic time of church commitments. Consequently, it was decided that there would be a combined dinner at The Cherries, hosted by Susan and Luke for their guests, plus Marian, Vivian, Jenny and Lucy.

Whilst making these arrangements, Susan realised that Luke had no family to invite for himself. He had never spoken of his relatives and was evasive when the subject came up. She decided to confront the issue.

"You never talk about your family," she commented, as the two of them sat in front of the crackling fire one evening. "Don't you have anyone you want to ask for Christmas?"

"My parents both died when I was about your age," he replied factually. "My mother had ovarian cancer and I truly believe my father died of a broken heart a few months afterwards, though the official explanation was cardiac arrest. I had a wonderful childhood though; Dad was a TV repairman and Mum had been a secretary, but she gave up when she was pregnant with me. Both of them loved art and books and music, so I was surrounded with culture. Mum used to take me to the theatre, and the ballet and the opera. Of course, Dad, being a technical man, made sure I got my fair share of the sciences, and at one point I even considered becoming a mathematician. They just wanted me to better myself, so

I worked hard at school and got into a good university. Mum and Dad had both died by the time I graduated, but I hope they would have been pleased with what I did with my life. They would have both loved you, I know that much."

"Were you an only child?" Susan asked.

"Yes. Mum was almost forty-three when I was born. I do have some cousins somewhere, but we all lost touch years ago," Luke told her, gazing thoughtfully into the flames. "Maybe that's why I'm so … you know… old fashioned."

Susan kissed him lightly on the cheek.

"I think she'd have to have been a hundred and forty-three to explain you, my love."

* * *

Jenny and Lucy were to drive down early on Christmas Eve to stay until the New Year. The day before their arrival, Vivian gave Jenny's room a thorough dusting and cleaning and placed fresh linen on the bed. Marian had offered to help, but Viv seemed set on making the preparations herself.

Susan was in her room, when she heard a strange sound from down the corridor. Walking softly, she peeped into Jenny's room and then silently withdrew to find her mother, who was in the kitchen.

"Mum," she said softly, "Viv's upstairs crying."

Marian and Susan both went to comfort their friend, as she sat at the foot of her daughter's bed, sobbing into a crumpled, mascara-stained tissue.

"I'm trying to be alright with all this business with Lucy," she said at length, "I want to be alright with it, but the thought of encouraging them by letting them share a bed a few feet from where I sleep … well, it is too much."

"Would it trouble you if she was bringing home a boy?" Susan asked.

Vivian stopped crying and thought deeply about the question.

"Do you know, it has never come up? Jenny has never brought a boy home to stay. I mean, she's had lots of boyfriends, I know, but she always kept them at a distance. I don't want to seem like a prude, but I don't think I'd be happy with her having a boy in here either."

The three sat in silence.

"Maybe," Susan ventured, "the fact that she wants to bring Lucy should be a sign that this is the first relationship that she has felt important enough to bring home."

Vivian nodded. "But still," she said, gesturing to the bed.

Susan glanced at Marian, who nodded, somehow silently understanding her daughter's unspoken thoughts.

"I think Mum and I should stay at The Cherries, then Lucy can have our room and it doesn't look too weird," Susan suggested.

Vivian brightened up.

"Really?" she said. "Would you mind, Marian? Yes, that could work."

So Susan and her mother gathered their meagre possessions and moved them to The Cherries, much to the delight of Luke, who had found himself rattling about the place since Dominic had left. Vivian set about cleaning their room and making it look nice for Lucy, while Marian and Susan helped Luke decorate his house and put up the Christmas tree.

Christmas Eve was a bustle of activity. Luke was out from early morning, picking up food, and going to the wine merchants. Susan had stayed home, as she wanted to greet Jenny and Lucy when they arrived just before lunch; she passed the time by tidying the downstairs and polishing the large mahogany dining table until it had a rich sheen. During the afternoon, she drove Luke around the locality, taking cards and gifts to local friends, and visiting some of the lonelier, housebound people of the village.

In the evening, Susan and Luke drove to Midnight Mass, a magical celebration in music and song of light coming into the world. As the bell tolled midnight, "Christ is with us" echoed through the ancient vaulted church.

On Christmas morning, Susan and Marian both awoke to an unfamiliar weight at the bottom of their bed. In their respective rooms, Susan squealed with excitement, while her mother exclaimed "Blimey," as they discovered the stockings that had been surreptitiously placed at their feet while they slept. The contents were not expensive (a magazine, some hand cream, a selection of chocolates, a little puzzle book, some pens, and a clockwork toy), but that made the surprise even more special.

"You are naughty," Susan said to Luke, kissing his cheek as he lay in the bed next to her.

"Nothing to do with me, thank Santa," he replied sleepily. "He comes to all the good girls and boys."

"Then why don't you have a stocking?" she reasoned.

"Because I am a very naughty boy," he replied, rolling over and nibbling her neck.

"I think I'd better get up before I'm tempted to be a naughty girl," she said a little breathlessly, and she hopped from the bed and into the bathroom.

By the time Marian got downstairs, Luke was in the kitchen rustling up a full English breakfast. The smell of eggs, bacon, sausage, black pudding, fried tomato, and toast permeated the house and Marian found she was hungry. With a cry of "Merry Christmas," Luke piled her plate with food and placed it before her at the kitchen table, in the centre of which was a large pot of tea and a jug of orange juice.

"Thank you for my stocking, Santa," she said, piercing a rasher of bacon and thrusting it into an unsuspecting egg. Luke responded with a little "Ho-Ho-Ho."

Marian looked at the young man as he worked, scuttling here and there across the kitchen. Less than a year ago, she would have feared leaving Susan for more than a few minutes, so great was her daughter's vulnerability. Now she was about to leave her little girl and fly to the other side of the world, and she could do so knowing that Susan was in safe hands; however, it was more than that, for she recognised that Luke was not controlling or stifling her daughter with over protection, but rather he was encouraging her to be free, independent and creative. She was leaving Susan with a man who truly and unconditionally loved her, and she again felt a little envy as well as gratitude; maybe one day she would find such companionship for herself, but to trust someone again as Susan and Luke trusted one another was something she did not know if she could do.

After the breakfast had been cleared away, a smartly dressed Luke escorted an elegantly dressed Susan to the Jaguar. As they were getting in, a figure emerged from Vivian's house and hurried over to them. It was Lucy.

"Are you going to the church service?" she asked. "May I come, too?"

Susan climbed out to allow Lucy to get into the back of the car. Once underway, they all travelled in silence for a few minutes.

"I love Christmas Eucharist," Lucy told them wistfully. "I wasn't sure if I would be welcome though."

"Why on Earth not?" asked Luke.

"Well, you know. Me and Jenny," Lucy faltered.

"I wouldn't go to a church that didn't welcome you," Luke stated and Susan agreed.

Lucy nodded absently in acknowledgement, lost in her thoughts. On Boxing Day, she and Jenny would be visiting her own family, which promised to be an awkward occasion.

After the service, Reverend June stood at the door of the church, wishing each of the congregation a Happy Christmas. She had to conduct three such services that morning, this being the second. After the third, in an outlying village, she would be driving back to the Vicarage to meet Peter, who had a similarly onerous schedule in his own parish, where they would exchange gifts before heading to Luke's house for dinner.

Luke, Susan and Lucy arrived at The Cherries to find Marian, Vivian and Jenny in the kitchen, peeling sprouts and potatoes, making stuffing, and wrapping chipolatas in bacon rashers. Luke was banished from his own kitchen with the words, "This is a revolution and we are making this dinner, young man." Beaten, he and Susan went into the living room, where he placed a vinyl record on the turntable of the stereo; soon the rich choral sound of Handel's Messiah was echoing through the rooms.

Susan returned to the kitchen and warmed some mince pies which Luke had made previously, while he brought a tray of sherries to the hard-working chef-elves.

At a convenient moment, everyone gathered together to exchange the gifts which had been placed under the tree. Luke was delighted with his cufflinks, and his gift to Susan was a delicate hand-painted antique brooch and a collection of romantic poetry.

When dinner was almost prepared, Luke and Susan laid the table with his best cutlery and lead crystal glasses, linen napkins, and Christmas crackers. A ring on the doorbell heralded the arrival of June and Peter and another round of gift exchanging took place.

The dinner, turkey and a goose, was delicious, the wines complementing the flavours; dessert was a choice between flaming Christmas pudding or chocolate Yule log (although Peter seemed to find room to sample both).

When Luke produced a selection of cheeses, accompanied by celery, grapes and a decanter of port wine, June whimpered.

"I'm glad our curates both agreed to do evening prayer," she moaned, "I'm never going to make it to the living room, let alone home."

"Well, that's good," said Luke, "because Peter and I have hatched a plot, and there is a suitcase in the boot of your car and a spare room made up for you upstairs. You are my prisoners."

"I'd hug you but I might burst. Suffice to say you are blessed, my boy," she replied, leaning back in her chair with exhaustion and waving her hand.

"I certainly am," he agreed, looking at Susan who was sitting smiling at the far end of the table.

Late in the evening, Jenny and Lucy helped Vivian back to her house and into bed; within minutes, she was snoring. In the corridor, Jenny took Lucy's hand.

"Coming into my room?" she asked softly.

"I don't know... what about your mum?" Lucy replied, torn.

"The amount she's had, she'll be sleeping until noon," Jenny told her, taking her lover by the hand and tugging her through the threshold.

In Luke's living room, the celebrants lay in various states of exhaustion.

"I'm so full," Susan announced with a moan when Luke offered her a chocolate, which she nevertheless took.

"Let's go for a nice long walk tomorrow and burn it off," Luke suggested. He took the groans from the assembled party as agreement.

"Thanks for a wonderful day," Susan added, "I've felt like a little girl."

"For it is good to be children sometimes, and never better than at Christmas, when its mighty Founder was a child himself," Luke quoted.

"Ah, Dickens," stated Peter. "Try this for size:

'Christmas Eve, and twelve of the clock.

"Now they are all on their knees",

An elder said as we sat in a flock

By the embers in hearthside ease'."

Luke frowned. "Don't try to quote Hardy at me, Vicar," he said in a warlike voice. "Let battle commence!"

"NO! Please no," interrupted June, grabbing Peter's hand, "I am going to bed, and my husband is coming with me as I may not have the energy to get there alone. Say goodnight, Peter."

"Good night everyone, Happy Christmas," he said obediently.

* * *

The New Year was a time of very mixed emotions for Susan and Marian. As they celebrated with everyone in The Bull, isolated among the partying, laughing and dancing, they both felt their impending separation deeply.

At midnight, they hugged, clinging to one another. As Auld Lang Syne was sung, they were in the chain of revellers with tears trickling down their cheeks, and when the fireworks started, they held hands as they had done when Susan was a five-year-old wanting to stand at the edge of the pond to feed the ducks.

Vivian took Marian to the airport, as Susan wanted to say a simple goodbye at home, as if her mother was just going to work like any other day.

Chapter 14

The months to Susan's birthday passed quickly. Winter turned to spring and the cherry trees once again burst into resplendent bloom. Susan continued to sleep most nights at Hayfield Barn because she correctly assessed that Vivian needed the company.

Her course was going well, and she had started to make friends, particularly with two young women who also planned to do the final third year at the university.

The first was Abigail, or Abi, who was about six-foot-tall, with a broad frame, giving the unfair impression that she was overweight. Abi was enormous fun to be around and seemed to have a joke for every occasion, and her artwork matched her personality with bold colours in large abstract works. She was slightly older than Susan, in her mid-twenties, and had decided to do the course after an unpleasant divorce.

The second woman, Bonita, was from Indonesia. She was nineteen years old and had travelled to the UK with her family when her father, a civil engineer, was recruited to manage a large development project. Bonita brought her own cultural style to her work, and she specialised in textiles, using Batik to produce exquisite patterns and motifs. She also designed colourful, delicate hijabs which she gave or sold to family and friends.

The three friends would often work with one another in the same studio, but nevertheless made a point to meet every day for lunch.

Luke had persuaded Susan to exhibit some of her work at a local gallery, and she had been very surprised that the pictures sold. She now regularly supplied pieces to the shop, which allowed her to supplement her college costs and enabled her to buy a small car of her own, rather than using her mother's Citroen, which was on its last legs.

It was by pure accident that Luke had come across the car. When he was visiting an elderly resident in the village, she told him that she was going to move in with her son and his family and that she would be giving up driving. Luke was amazed by this news, as he had never seen her in a car, but it transpired that she had a thirteen-year-old Nissan Micra in her garage (it almost preposterously had just four-thousand miles on the clock), for which she wanted very little money. Susan had fallen in love with the car at first sight, and she named it Buttercup after its creamy colour.

* * *

For her birthday, Luke took Susan to London and Paris, to visit the galleries and museums. Staying at a small hotel in Piccadilly that Luke knew well, they walked to most places, and took a taxi to further destinations, such as the V&A; Susan did not question why they did not take the Underground, as she knew Luke would hate it. They also visited so many bookshops that Susan realised that her boyfriend's mental map of London was probably designed around them.

She also noticed that Luke was becoming stressed by the number of people around them, and one evening when leaving the theatre in Covent Garden, he became very disorientated by the crowds. It was she who hailed the taxi and got them to the hotel.

The trip across to Paris was even harder for him. When Luke thought she was in the shower on the morning before departure, she had returned to the room to get her hairbrush and observed him in an anxious state, rocking himself slowly in a small chair in the bedroom with his eyes tightly closed; though Susan could not know it, Luke at that moment was desperately praying for the strength to take her on the trip.

In Paris itself, they did manage to see the Louvre and some tourist attractions like the Eiffel Tower, but he became increasingly unwell. In their room that evening, she feared he would have a heart attack, as his breathing was very heavy and he clearly had chest pains. Luke persevered though, apologising constantly for spoiling the trip, but the episode burnt itself into Susan's memory.

When they were back at home in the peace of The Cherries, she asked him about his anxiety attacks. Had he sought help? Would he consider medication? He answered honestly that he had tried the former and considered the latter, but at the end of the day, it was who he was. The fear of changing and all that that entailed was almost suffocating, he had explained; the very conversation itself was visibly having an ill effect on Luke, so she let the matter drop.

However, Susan had to reconcile herself to a harsh truth, that if she married this man, her world might become smaller. But his was the world of literature and poetry, of art and history, of discovery and science, of faith and reason; his world was limited only by what he could not imagine. She loved him absolutely and unconditionally, and if they never travelled, she did not mind; she also knew that he would never stand in the way of her going somewhere without him, but she could not bear the thought of their parting.

She felt very torn about the notion of going away for her final year of university, but Luke insisted that she should. He argued that Susan needed to exist for a while on her own, away from her mother and away from him, to be sure that the life he offered her was the right one for her. The university was not so far away that she couldn't return for weekends, and there would be the long holidays; indeed, he pointed out, the entire academic year was closer to nine months, as it ran from late-September to June.

Nevertheless, Susan looked at the man that she loved and saw that his mental state had not recovered from the Paris trip, and she worried about leaving him.

* * *

Before Marian returned from the cruise, she messaged Susan to say that she had been offered another contract, which would start three weeks after she came back. She was obviously enjoying her life and Susan assured her that she should take the offer.

However, she did return for two lovely weeks, looking well and tanned. She and Susan, who was now on vacation from college, pottered about the countryside in Buttercup and on occasions Luke or Vivian would accompany them. On one afternoon, mother and daughter went to a castle ruin about thirty miles from their home and lazed on the grass while Susan sketched the crumbled walls. As they basked in the summer warmth, Marian decided to sound Susan out about something that was troubling her.

"Susie, do you ever think about your dad?" she ventured tentatively.

Susan's reaction was brisk, as if the mention of him was spoiling the afternoon, which it was.

"No," came the curt response. "Why would I? I don't suppose he has ever thought about me."

Marian nodded and picked some daisies from the grass next to her.

"Do you ever wonder what has happened to him?" she tried.

"Look," Susan responded in a matter of fact voice, "I don't blame him for not loving me, you can't control that, but walking away from his responsibilities, that's something else."

"What made you think he didn't love you?" Marian asked, shocked by the notion.

"Even at six, it was obvious, Mum," Susan told her mother. "But if you really must know, he told me."

Marian's world stopped turning; it was a moment of breathless astonishment and anguish.

"What do you mean, he told you?" she asked.

"He thought I was asleep," Susan replied. "It wasn't long before he left us, I suppose. He came into my room and I could feel him watching me. I thought I was in trouble for still being awake, so I lay perfectly still. And he said, 'Oh, little Susie why can't I feel anything when I look at you? Poor little Susan, why should you should have a father like me?'... I'm sorry I didn't tell you before, Mum, but what is there to say? How could I tell you that it was my fault?"

Susan's sketch was being dotted by teardrops.

* * *

Marian's mind repeatedly churned over the conversation with Susan, who had bounced back remarkably quickly from dredging up the painful memories. At an opportune moment, she told Luke and Vivian what had happened, and they both were distressed by the story.

"What is worse," Marian added, "is that I got a message from his... girlfriend... to say that he died last month. What do I do? Should I tell Susie?"

"I think you have to," Luke said after consideration, "I think she should know. Surely she has a right to know?"

Vivian agreed, so the next day the two women sat down with Susan to break the news.

Susan sat there coldly, numb from shock for some time. At first, it was a bit like hearing the news of a casual acquaintance or a celebrity: it was a fact, it was sad, life goes on. But deep down, the little girl was still expecting her daddy to come home, to tell her it was all a mistake, that he loved her and her mother and that they would be a family again. And another part of her, her adult self, wanted him to see her history, to see the places that they had had to live, to hear the police sirens at night, to have to walk to school being careful not to step on discarded needles, to be scared that another nasty boyfriend was going to hurt Mum, to be alone and undefended against an army of bullies.

Susan thanked her mother for telling her the news and walked outside into the sunshine. She wandered past the front of The Cherries, through the side gate and into the back garden to sit on the bench under the silver birch tree. The world seemed extra-real, with colours brighter, sounds of bees and birds purer, scents of blossom so strong as to be intoxicating. Then she wept, alone on the bench, fourteen years of agony bursting forth. Eventually, she wiped her eyes to see that she was not alone, for she had been observed by a solitary rabbit; it hopped very close to her, with a curious little limp in its gait, and explored the grass with its twitching nose.

Susan made her way into the house and found Luke so she could bury herself into his arms.

* * *

Once the autumn college semester started, marking the beginning of her second year of study, Susan, Abi and Bonita travelled to the main university to have a look around and to assess the accommodation situation; they had been advised to get a place to live arranged as early as possible.

They looked at the university flats, which they liked for their convenience, and were advised that they would have priority applications, given that they were not in a position to easily find alternatives in the private rented sector. Each flat was comprised of six bedrooms with their own bathroom, and a large shared kitchen with seating and a television.

The positives were that they would be on campus and so able to experience university life, the rent was quite reasonable, the facilities were modern, and Bonita's family would be happier with her being in a safe environment. The negatives were that they would be sharing with three strangers and that parking permits were in limited supply. It seemed that the balance was clearly tilted in favour of the university flats, so they made their joint application that day.

Susan was a little surprised that Abi stated so vehemently that she would prefer not to have men sharing the accommodation; Bonita had the same requirement, but Susan had anticipated that. In Susan's opinion, Abi had an unfairly low opinion of men in general, which bordered on hostile.

The workload was increasing, and Susan had little time for anything other than her studies, but Luke was happy to support her, so she had few domestic demands on her time. They agreed to have a quiet Christmas – Marian would not be home from her latest contract, and Vivian was going to stay with Jenny and Lucy.

* * *

New Year's Day at Jenny's flat was becoming a trying time. The apartment had only one bedroom, so the girls had given it to Vivian and were sleeping on thin, air mattresses on the living room floor. The awkwardness with her mother regarding her lifestyle had eased, but Jenny, as well as Lucy, was frustrated that Vivian would smoke in the flat, because she found it too cold outside on the small balcony.

Vivian's inability to get up at a reasonable hour was also annoying her daughter.

"It's only one more night," Lucy said, trying to soothe Jenny as they sat on the sofa in their dressing gowns.

"It's half past eleven in the morning and I can't get dressed because all my clean underwear is in the drawer in our room," Jenny replied through clenched teeth. "I go back to work tomorrow; I'd like to spend the day doing something fun with you, and instead we're stuck here."

A bout of coughing erupted in the bedroom, and they heard the unmistakeable sound of a lighter being flicked into action. Lucy saw the look on Jenny's face.

"See, she'll be up in a minute," she said brightly.

"We are going to have to air that room for days. Everything is going to stink of fags," Jenny complained.

"I know, babe," Lucy sympathised. The truth was that Lucy couldn't wait to see the back of Vivian, but given her frosty reception from her own family, she didn't want to push away Jenny's mother, too.

At length, Vivian burst from the bedroom, straight into the bathroom, locking the door with a loud click. Jenny ran to fetch fresh clothes. While they dressed, Lucy made a suggestion.

"Why don't I fix us some omelettes? Your mum can have one for breakfast and you and I can call it an early lunch, and we can all go out somewhere this afternoon."

This seemed a wise plan, so Lucy started to beat eggs into a bowl. Vivian stumbled back into the bedroom briefly before joining them at the breakfast bar.

"I think I hit the sauce a little too heavy last night," she moaned.

"Yes, you did, Mum," Jenny replied rather too directly. "We couldn't get you away from the bar. You're a bloody embarrassment sometimes."

She immediately felt dreadful, because shock, hurt and tears appeared in her mother's eyes. Vivian put her hand to her mouth and shook her head.

"Sorry, Mum, I didn't mean it. I'm not sleeping too well on the floor," Jenny apologised.

Her mother nodded, and sipped the coffee that Lucy had placed in front of her.

"I'm sho shorry… darling," said Vivian, "they... shouldn't shell… d…"

"Have you been drinking already?" Jenny asked in an irritated tone. "You're slurring all over the place… Mum?"

Vivian was staring at her in confusion and fear, her mouth making odd shapes; strange noises were coming out, but no speech.

Lucy pulled the omelette pan from the cooker and rushed over, crouching in front of Vivian.

"Can you hear me, Viv?" she asked loudly.

The woman's face was beginning to droop alarmingly on one side, and she almost toppled from the stool she was perched on. Lucy took her weight on her shoulder.

"Call an ambulance, I'm pretty sure she's having a stroke," she instructed.

Jenny looked in disbelief.

"She can't be, I mean she's only fifty-four!" she protested.

"Well, she is, so call the bloody ambulance, babe!" shouted Lucy.

* * *

When Jenny's phone call from the hospital came, Susan immediately offered to go up to be with her and to see Vivian. However, at her friend's request she didn't go for several days; when she did go, she stayed at a small bed and breakfast so as not to be an inconvenience.

Lucy's quick actions had made a big difference, but Vivian's stroke was severe and the damage to her speech and motor skills would take time and therapy to heal; the longer-term prognosis was good, however.

Careful communication with an expert solicitor allowed Jenny to have Power of Attorney over her mother's affairs. Vivian indicated that she wished to spend her days close to her daughter, and Susan returned home to Luke with the sad news that Hayfield Barn was to be put on the market so that Jenny could buy a bungalow for her mother close to her own flat.

In such an idyllic location and priced to get a quick sale, Vivian's house was an attractive proposition and it was soon under new ownership. However, the occupants of The Cherries were most disappointed that Hayfield Barn had been bought as a holiday home, which meant that it was unoccupied for most of the time.

Although Luke did much of the packing on Vivian's behalf, as Susan was snowed under with coursework, Jenny came down to supervise the final move.

When she and Susan stood watching the removal lorry disappear up the leafy lane, it was a deeply emotional moment. The two old friends held each other closely and said that they would keep in frequent touch, and come and visit one another regularly. The truth was that they soon lapsed into an occasional message and the odd call, but that didn't detract from the life-long sisterly bond that existed between them.

Marian had flown back in to see Vivian and stayed in a hotel for several days to keep her old friend company. However, her latest contract demanded that she return to her duties and she flew out again without seeing Susan, who was still slogging away at her university work.

* * *

At the end of the academic year, the burden of studying over until the autumn, Susan and Luke spent a wonderful, lazy summer together, though it was a much rainier one than in previous years.

Luke took Susan down to a remote hotel that he knew on the Cornish coast, an early twentieth century villa perched at the top of the cliffs. The view of the sea from their room was spectacular, and the period furnishings gave the place the feel of an Agatha Christie story, especially when a spectacular summer storm came in, with driving rain and bright lightning.

When the weather cleared and the bright summer sunshine had dried the ground, they climbed to the top of a nearby hill via a long sequence of steps hewn into the earth.

Susan stood at the crest. To the south was the sea, but all other directions offered a glorious view over the verdant Cornish landscape.

"I love it here!" she exclaimed spreading her arms out wide. "This is perfect."

Behind her, Luke got down on one knee, removed a small blue velvet-covered box and held it out in front of him. Still holding her arms out Susan closed her eyes and whirled around feeling the sea breeze on her face and striking something with the back of her hand.

She opened her eyes in surprise to see Luke running back down the steep incline after a small dark object which was tumbling away in front of him.

"What on Earth were you doing?" she asked when he returned flushed and panting heavily.

"Just exercising, my love," he gasped breathlessly.

That evening they dined in their room, seated at a table set up next to the large sash windows, which afforded a view of the setting sun glinting on the waves below. Luke had ordered champagne with their meal.

"What is that for?" Susan asked. "Are we celebrating something?"

"That depends on what you say to this," he replied, holding out the box and slipping from his chair onto bended knee.

This time it was Susan's turn to be breathless.

Chapter 15

It was the week before Susan's departure for university; she was in the kitchen of The Cherries having a coffee with the vicar. The Reverend June had popped over to see her with a good luck card, and Susan was grateful for the company, as Luke had gone to town for a meeting and she was having one of her many bouts of second thoughts about going.

June was reassuring, pointing out that a year from hence it would all be over and they would be planning a wedding. She took the time to admire Susan's engagement ring once more, appreciating the delicate pale sapphire set between two small glittering diamonds.

As the vicar gave her a hug goodbye, Susan's phone received a text message from Abi asking her to meet for lunch.

Bonita sat with Abi and Susan at a table next to the café's window and they finalised their plans for travelling up to university. Bonita's parents would be driving her, so Susan, who had managed to get a university parking permit, offered to take Abi in her car.

Susan's acquisition of Buttercup had turned out to be very fortuitous, as Marian's aged Citroen had failed its MOT so comprehensively that the repair estimate had been astronomical. Frank had kindly arranged for it to be scrapped; Marian had been rather vague when Susan enquired what her mother intended to do for transportation when she was home.

Nibbling lightly on her salad, Susan looked idly out of the window, and saw Luke laden with bags from the art shop, walking down the pavement with the same tall blonde woman she had seen outside The Cherries more than two years beforehand. They stopped beside a small blue hatchback and kissed cheeks before she climbed into the car and drove away; the kiss was a strange one, certainly not romantic, but closer than friends tend to, it was almost like brother and sister. As she watched him wander off, Susan made a mental note to ask Luke who the woman was, but the question was almost immediately forgotten when Bonita showed her a headscarf which she had recently designed.

* * *

Jenny returned home from visiting her mother, who was now comfortably settled in her new bungalow, deep in thought. Lucy was in the flat when she arrived, but Jenny was almost too distracted to acknowledge her.

Having given her a little time to be alone with her thoughts, Lucy ventured a question. "Is everything OK, sweetie?" she cooed.

"Huh?" Jenny said, startled from her thoughts. "Yeah, sorry, babe. I was just thinking about Mum and me and life. You know, time just seems to fly by and seeing her looking old, feeling my own mortality, it's making me think."

Lucy stroked Jenny's arm.

"What about?" she asked, gently.

Jenny gazed at her directly, her eyes full of resolve.

"Lucy," she said, "I want a baby. I've looked into it, there's lots of ways we can do it. I want a baby for me, for us, and I want a grandkid for Mum while she can still enjoy it."

Lucy's reaction was primarily shock, as the idea came as a bolt from the blue. She was angry at some level, but could not explain why; she wanted to be calm and reasonable, but they ended up arguing about babies, mothers, families, that they were too young, that it wasn't fair to bring a child into their relationship, and ultimately, where their relationship was headed.

At length, Lucy decided that she wanted to go home to her family for a few days, to clear her head. Crying, she packed a bag, kissed an equally tearful Jenny goodbye and headed to the train station.

* * *

Susan still had very few physical possessions, she had travelled light all her life, and so was finding no problem whatsoever in fitting nearly all her worldly goods into two modest suitcases and a large tote bag. A few of her dresses, including her ballgown, still hung in the wardrobe in Luke's room, and a selection of her artwork and some of her bulkier painting equipment were in the corner of the studio.

She was shaking with emotion as Luke kissed her goodbye.

"I don't want to leave you. Let me stay," she begged.

"It's what you need to do, my love. I'm not going anywhere. Come on, get in the car. Abi is expecting you," he insisted, pushing his emotions down.

Susan complied and miserably climbed into Buttercup.

"Drive," he told her. "Don't look back until you're around the corner."

By the time Susan reached Abi's parents' house (where she had been living since her divorce), her tears had subsided, though she was still miserable. She also discovered her friend had a very strong attachment to physical possessions; even with the back seats flat down and the front seats pushed uncomfortably forward, there was little hope of fitting all of Abi's luggage in. At length, and with visible exasperation on his part, Abi's father agreed to drive up the next day with the bulk of his daughter's belongings.

Susan cheered up with having company in the car, and excitement built in the two women as they neared the campus. It was almost impossible to believe that she was going to be a student at this beautiful place of learning, and she almost felt a fraud when she parked at the flats and they went to get their keys from the admin office.

Susan unpacked her belongings in less than fifteen minutes and then drove to a nearby supermarket to buy food and groceries. When she returned, Bonita had arrived and was unloading a modern Volvo estate with the aid of her father; Susan popped her shopping into the flat and gave them a hand ferrying various items to Bonita's room.

Their other flatmates turned up in quick succession. Mia and Tessa were third-year Maths undergraduates, best friends who wanted to live together on campus for their final year. Last to arrive was Sandra, who was new to the university, reading for a Masters in Environmental Sciences.

After unpacking, Bonita and her father decided to explore the campus together and Susan joined them. They walked along the tree-lined pathways between the imposing buildings, finding the student union, the library, the bookshop, and all the other venues that they thought they should know.

When they returned to the block of flats, Susan took her leave of Bonita and her father at the entrance, to allow them privacy for their goodbyes.

"You have picked your friend, Susan, wisely," Bonita's father said once they were alone. "She is a good, respectful person and will be a good friend to you. I feel easier leaving knowing that you have such a friend."

The flatmates all decided to order in pizzas and have dinner together as a way of getting to know one another. Abi had a bottle of wine with her, though only Susan and Sandra joined her in drinking it, and everyone seemed to have a nice time.

At a little after seven o'clock, Mia noticed the time and she and Tessa hurried from the room, returning a few minutes later clutching bibles; they were on their way to a Christian Union meeting.

"We are going to a CU meeting. Anyone want to come?" Tessa asked. She was medium height, of Jamaican descent, stylishly dressed in a dark red patterned top with a long black skirt and soft boots laced to knee height. Mia was shorter and very slim, olive-skinned, with a long face, large brown eyes and slightly hooked nose; her dress sense was a little more dated, a black roll-neck jumper and a khaki corduroy A-line skirt, giving her the appearance of a woman ten years older, which may have been her intention.

"That sounds good," replied Susan, hurrying to her room for a jacket and her bible.

"Anyone else?" asked Mia. "Abi?"

Abi snorted derisively and said that she had an eight o-clock voodoo session with the tooth fairy.

"Sandra?" Mia continued, but Sandra politely declined. "Bonita? – Oh, sorry, of course not."

"Don't be sorry," Bonita replied brightly, "thank you for asking me. We like Jesus, too, you know!"

The Christian Union meeting was full of people and full of life; Susan suddenly found that she had thirty new friends to add to her phone, and five new appointments for various activities to add to her diary.

The atmosphere was energetic as the president of the union introduced himself to the group. His name was Tom, he was a PhD student in Physics, tall and muscular, with a mop of curly blond hair and designer stubble. His talk was one of welcome and encouragement.

Susan returned to her room abuzz with enthusiasm, and she immediately called Luke to tell him about her day. She explained that the CU had arranged for them to try different churches over the next three Sundays, so she might not be home for a few weeks. Luke masked his disappointment well.

* * *

Lucy's stay with her parents was going better than she anticipated. She spent quite a bit of time with her younger brother, who seemed to have grown up a great deal while she was away; when they were laughing in his bedroom or watching a cheesy movie together, many of her worries seemed to fade.

Her parents were both very welcoming, and made a point of asking after Jenny and Vivian. They had been secretly overjoyed that she had come to stay, as they feared they may have damaged their relationship with their daughter beyond repair, but time had healed any rift. Lucy and her mother spent a good deal of time baking cakes together, and she played some rounds of golf with her father.

However, Lucy could feel their inner struggle, as they were constantly trying (with some success) not to say the wrong thing. She wondered to herself if they had hoped she was going to announce a change of mind and come home with a boy, and in some respects, she wished she could.

Her elder brother, Todd, now training as a barrister, even came for a day visit, bringing his fiancée in tow. They all had a wonderful family time together, enjoying a pub lunch, and Lucy found herself looking at them with slightly envious eyes.

On the day after Todd's visit, she asked to borrow her mother's car and she travelled out into the countryside and pulled up outside The Cherries.

Luke was very surprised to see Lucy standing on his doorstep, but he ushered her in and she was soon sitting at his kitchen table, being offered scones and jam with her cup of tea.

"I hope you don't mind me calling unannounced," she said cautiously, "but I think you are one of the few people who may understand me. What you said when you drove me to church that Christmas has really stuck with me."

"Go on," Luke encouraged her, desperately trying to remember what it was that he had said.

"I'm struggling, caught between two worlds that I love," she explained. "I've tried not to think about it, but I can't help thinking about God and what I'm doing… how I live. I keep feeling one half of me wants me to ignore, to suppress my feelings about the other. Am I facing hell now or hell when I die?"

"Well, it seems to me that the fundamental tenet of our lives in Christ is to love one another and love God, and you seem to be a very good and loving person to me," Luke responded.

"Yes, but am I condemning myself to a life of sin? How can loving someone be so wrong? Is it a sin?" she asked, almost bargaining with him.

"Honestly, I can't see why it should be," he answered cautiously, "I think some things change with time. I'm not a huge Old Testament guy, to be honest, but I think in periods of limited population and infant mortality, as it was in the time of the Hebrews, well maybe all men and women were expected to do their procreative duty… but now? In the age of test tube babies and contraception? Well, the choices are less stark."

Luke could tell that his answer was unsatisfactory.

"Jenny says it's all hocus pocus," Lucy said gloomily. "The worst bit is, I'm the one who made the advances to her, and I'm the one now having these… doubts. I hear people on the street corner shouting about Sodom and Gomorrah, and my heart breaks."

"Do you know why God said he destroyed Sodom?" he asked.

From the look on her face, he could tell that she wanted a reason other than the one she feared. He hurried from the room, and returned with a bible.

"In Ezekiel," he continued, "God is giving Jerusalem a real ear-bashing, a divine kick up the backside, so to speak, to the whole city; and he said to them: 'Behold, this was the iniquity of thy sister Sodom: pride, fullness of bread, and abundance of idleness was in her and in her daughters, neither did she strengthen the hand of the poor and needy'. So, you see, Lucy, Sodom wasn't destroyed because of homosexuality, but because of the unworthy treatment of the poor and hungry by proud and greedy people. You are none of those things, Lucy. In the Gospels, Christ only says not to commit immoral acts of sex, and that seems pretty subjective to me."

Luke sat back in his chair and looked thoughtfully at her.

"I don't think it is a sin, Lucy," he continued, "but if I am wrong and it is, and there are many good people who may tell you it is, if it is, I reckon it is way down in the pecking order as far as God is concerned."

Her face did look a little less conflicted.

"Don't harshly judge those who tell you it is a sin," Luke advised her. "They are often good people with the best of intentions, who visit the sick, or look after the destitute, and who just have a different opinion to ours. Be your own testimony and change their minds. Love God, love your neighbour, live a good life and love Jenny, if that is your destiny. I for one will stand by you and I know that Susan will, too. If someone treats you badly, walk away and shake the dust from your feet."

They sat silently for a few moments.

"Have you read Jane Eyre?" he asked.

This question was so unexpected, that Lucy took several seconds to answer.

"Yes," she replied. "It is one of my favourite books."

"Excellent," Luke commented. "Well, I expect you'll like the character Helen Burns as much as I do. Well, she is a fount of wisdom, and one of my favourite quotes from her is: 'If all the world hated you and believed you wicked, while your own conscience approved you, and absolved you from guilt, you would not be without friends'. Well, Lucy, you are not without friends."

"Thank you," she replied. "I'm going to have a good excuse to read it again, aren't I?"

Luke smiled warmly and took Lucy's hand.

"God loves you and you give him much cause to. Ask him; pray and, if it is your destiny, live your life with Jenny."

"Thank you, Luke," Lucy said softly, "I think that has helped."

"Would you like to pray now?" he asked.

She nodded and closed her eyes.

* * *

Susan had found her experiences at the three churches' services very different. The first was a very traditional Church of England communion at the university chapel, familiar to her in style and tone. The second was informal, with a band playing the music and worship songs projected onto a screen rather than hymns and hymn books; the up-beat tempo was infectious, and she soon found herself dancing alongside many of the others. The third was extremely serious (although the music was more upbeat than the traditional service), with a long fire-and-brimstone sermon, apparently designed to terrify the attendees.

She discussed the options with Luke when she went back to visit him, and she decided that she would like to try the second church for a while, though she sensed that it was something he found alien in concept.

Susan also told him all about her friendships, her course and the lecturers. She spoke at length about Christian Union, or 'CU' as they referred to it, and about Mia, Tessa and the others there, and rather more about Tom than Luke would have liked. He was not jealous as such, he trusted Susan too much, but it exacerbated his sense of separation from her; he gave himself a mental ticking-off for being selfish and resolved to concentrate on enjoying his time with his fiancée.

* * *

When Lucy had returned from visiting her parents, Jenny had been terrified that she would walk in the door and call the whole thing off. While those worst fears were not realised, Lucy was more distant than usual, a little more solitary in her habits and less tactile. She was clearly going through a period of deep introspection, and Jenny thought it best to give her time and space.

One crisp sunny autumnal morning, Lucy went for a walk. She passed through the park, over the bridge and along the canal bank, watching the joggers and cyclists whizzing by. Finally, she came to a willow tree and she walked beneath its arching boughs until she felt almost invisible behind the shield of leaves, which were slowly getting ready to be shed.

There she stood and prayed, to the God of this world and the next, to the God that lives in the moment, and through the moment and outside of the moment. She prayed for forgiveness, and strength and direction. A breeze picked up and rustled the leaves, awakening her from the emotional sleep she had been in since coming back from her parents.

When she returned, Lucy entered the flat and stood, smelling of fresh air, before Jenny, who looked up nervously from her seated position.

"I'm sorry," Lucy told her, "I'm sorry that I have been so distant lately."

"That's OK, babe. I dropped a bombshell on you about the baby. It was wrong of me," Jenny replied.

"No, it was fair of you. But I've been trying to understand how I can balance my worlds," Lucy explained. "I love you, and I'm happy as we are, but I can't imagine bringing up a child out of wedlock."

"So, what are you saying?" Jenny asked nervously, fearing she was being asked to choose between Lucy and having a baby.

"I'm saying I think we should get married," Lucy replied, gazing into her love's eyes.

Jenny burst into tears of happiness and relief and jumped to her feet to hug Lucy, who also wept. They held one another so tightly they could barely breathe.

"Oh," Lucy added, "by the way. You're not the only one who gets to have babies, OK?"

* * *

Susan was sitting in the kitchen with all her flatmates when the message from Lucy and Jenny arrived. She squealed with delight when she saw their news.

"I'll be going to a wedding in March next year!" she exclaimed. "Two dear friends of mine."

"Some poor woman throwing herself away on a worthless bloke," Abi commented bitterly. Then she spied Susan's glittering engagement ring and added, "No offence."

"None taken," Susan replied. "Anyway, Jenny and Lucy are both lovely, so I'm sure they'll be really happy together."

There was a surprised silence.

"But… they're both girl's names," Tessa said slowly.

Susan looked around the room, somewhat bemused by the reactions of her group.

"I think it's lovely news," the usually reserved Sandra told them, as she left the room.

"Yeah, it's cool. Love is love," agreed Tessa as she started to cook some food.

As Susan walked to her room after her dinner, she encountered Mia in the corridor.

"Your friends. The two women," her flatmate said in the manner of a strict schoolmistress, "I mean, do you think they are entirely appropriate for you to associate with?"

"Why?" Susan asked in bafflement.

Mia responded, "What would your churches' elders say? I'll write out some bible verses for you."

Susan politely extricated herself from the lecture and continued to her room. As she passed Abi's open door, she stopped to chat.

"You didn't say anything back there," she said, referring to the conversation in the kitchen.

"That's because you don't know who's listening," Abi replied. "I don't want to get reported by some politically correct do-gooder for saying what I really think."

Scales fell from Susan's eyes and she returned to her room.

* * *

Susan returned to The Cherries for Christmas, ecstatic to be back home with Luke. She spent hours talking about her art and how her techniques were developing, showing him photographs of some of her pieces. They braced themselves for a very different celebration to previous years; Vivian had moved away, Dominic was with his father, and June and Peter had other commitments.

They even received a curious message from Marian, saying that she would be staying at the hotel at the country club, arriving late on the 24th December, and asking them to have Christmas Dinner there with her. The cost of the hotel was prohibitive, and Susan was worried that she must have somehow upset her mother in some way for her to not want to stay at The Cherries.

Luke and Susan decided to have a private celebration at home on Christmas Eve; they had baked ham, creamy mashed potato and moist, home-made dumplings, before heading out to Midnight Mass. They returned home in the early hours to mulled wine and mince pies before bed.

In the morning, they exchanged gifts and then drove to the hotel for morning drinks with Marian. When her mother descended the stairs, Susan was surprised to see her accompanied by a handsome man of about sixty, with groomed grey hair, tanned skin, manicured hands and a Gucci suit. Marian introduced her consort as Graham Thorn, a property developer businessman from Chelmsford, and her boyfriend.

Marian's self-confidence and general attitude had changed since she started her new career. She was still the same caring mother at heart, but she now had a new burning and consuming passion for singing, so she was a more distant, if refined, person.

The dinner was delicious and the wines excellent, though Luke did not indulge in more than a solitary small glass because he was driving. Afterwards, when they were comfortable in the plush chairs of the lounge bar, Marian explained to Susan and Luke that she had met Graham earlier in the year, when he was on a cruise for three weeks; they hit it off immediately but it wasn't until he turned up for a further holiday a few weeks later, that she realised how serious he was.

Marian went on to give some more unexpected news. While Graham was indeed originally from Chelmsford, he now lived and worked in Dubai. Moreover, he had a friend who had seen a video of her performing and who now wished to employ Marian as permanent singer at one of his Dubai nightclubs, on a very attractive salary. Graham had asked her to live with him in his condominium, and she had accepted. They would be flying out the day after Boxing Day.

Susan took the news with a veneer of pleasure on behalf of her mother, but an underlying sense of desertion and sadness. Why would her mother have so little time to spend with them? How well did she know this Graham? Would she be safe?

There was also a frustration that she would never be able to take her future husband to visit her mother; Luke could not possibly cope with the trip. Susan had tried on several occasions to explain his anxiety problems to Marian, but her mother had always either dismissed them or forgotten about them after a short while.

She did, however, ask how her nan had taken the news, and Marian looked uncomfortable.

"Graham and I will leave first thing and drive and see her tomorrow. We'll stay overnight and on to the airport in the morning. Graham has said your nan can come and live with us in Dubai if she wants."

Susan was stung – her mother was not even going to stay for Boxing Day! Again, she repressed her hurt, and simply commented that she doubted that her grandmother would like the heat in Dubai.

That night, Susan slept very little, and she rose early. She dressed and jumped into her car, driving to the country club to speak to her mother one more time before she left. She found her sitting in reception and Marian immediately leapt to her feet and apologised for everything, explaining that she was so excited about the new opportunity that she hadn't been thinking clearly the previous night. Both women laid bare how much they loved and would miss the other, and Marian assured Susan that she understood about Luke's travel issues and she would fly back to the UK twice a year.

This parting was happier and sadder, but Susan returned to The Cherries more at peace in her heart.

* * *

The workload on Susan increased hugely when she returned to the university after Christmas, but she kept her focus and produced some excellent pieces.

However, she found the time to attend Jenny and Lucy's wedding, a civil ceremony at a country house near to their home. Luke managed to overcome his travel anxiety to attend, though Susan again witnessed his struggles, and they stood arm in arm watching the two brides (wearing matching ivory dresses) pledge themselves to one another. "Us next," Susan whispered to Luke. Vivian was there, looking much slimmer, declining alcohol (save a drop of champagne for the toast) and cigarette-free. She needed a walking stick and stumbled a little over her words when speaking, but seemed to have regained some zest for life.

News from The Cherries and the village was limited, for things rarely changed. At one point, Luke told Susan that Dominic had been in touch to say that he had finished his agricultural course and was taking a job offer at a large farm in Hungary. The young man had been in very little contact with them since he had gone to college, caught up in his new life, so everyone was pleased to hear that he had such an exciting opportunity, though they feared that it may spell a final farewell to a good friend.

Susan also found the time to get even more involved with the CU. Tom was a charismatic leader, and he involved the team in many outreach programmes: supporting lonely students, helping drunk revellers spilling out of the union bar late at night by giving them tea and a biscuit, and reaching out to the community by befriending elderly people or assisting in a foodbank.

Every night, she called Luke and they would tell each other about their day and their plans for the next. They both felt that being together finally and completely was excruciatingly close.

* * *

Since submitting her final coursework and project for assessment, Susan had been shuttling regularly between The Cherries and the university and was feeling very torn. She still wished to support the CU in its activities, and she had formed a close bond with her flatmates, so she wanted to maximise her little remaining time with them. However, she also loved to be with Luke and to potter here and there in the house and garden, or to be with him in his studio, painting together purely for pleasure.

Now Susan sat in the kitchen with Luke, looking at the laptop and trembling. Tentatively she logged into her university email to see what the results of her degree were. She went into shock. Luke worriedly looked at the screen.

"First Class honours!" he exclaimed hugging her.

"What? How?" she stammered in disbelief.

"And you've been awarded the faculty prize for outstanding work!" he crowed, kissing her cheeks and head in a flurry of joy. "I knew you could do it, I knew it!"

Susan screamed and jumped up and down in a state of bliss. Then she calmed and looked at Luke.

"This is all thanks to you," she told him, "you made this happen. Thank you so much, my love."

"No," he said firmly, "I just prodded you in the direction. This is your own work and your own doing, and I am the proudest man on the face of this planet."

She kissed him.

"Now I'm going to call Mum and Nan!" she told him, skipping from the room.

* * *

The graduation dance would be held on the evening of the degree awards ceremony. Susan planned to wear her dress from the Christmas Ball, but Abi had nothing suitable and so dragooned Susan into helping her find one.

They wandered through the soulless shops of the vast mall, looking at outfits of different styles. While Abi was far from obese, her large frame, ample bosom and generous posterior tended to give the impression that she was; consequently, she declared that most of the dresses she tried on made her look like a marquee.

At length, Abi decided to try on a tight fitting black mini dress, which Susan silently considered to be the least ballgown-like outfit that they had looked at. Abi went into the changing rooms, passing a smartly dressed shop assistant who was posted at the entrance, while Susan browsed the nearby array of novelty socks with disinterest.

Her perusal of unwanted hosiery was interrupted by Tessa who was in the shop with another friend from CU.

"Hi, Susan! How are you doing? Are you looking for a dress, too?" Tessa asked in greeting.

"Hi," responded Susan. "No, I'm helping Abi – she's in the changing room."

“That’s nice,” said Tessa. “Say, are you going on this prayer retreat that Tom’s organising for the summer? I’m thinking of going.”

“No,” Susan replied with a slight giggle, “I’ve got a wedding to plan. Which I hope you will be coming to?”

“Try and keep me away, babe.”

Susan’s phone vibrated; it was a message from Abi.

‘Can’t do up zip. Help plz’

She rolled her eyes, and apologised to Tessa, who said she was leaving anyway, as the shop had nothing in her style.

Susan explained the situation to the shop assistant and entered the changing rooms. Surrounded by portals with curtains drawn across, she called out, “Abi?” in a tentative voice, to be rewarded by the appearance of her friend’s head and an, “Over here.” She slid into the tiny cubicle and examined the nature of the zip problem; Susan’s unspoken verdict was that the dress needed to be a size larger.

“If I hold the sides together, you pull the zip up,” she told Abi. They tried, Abi reaching behind her back to tug at the unwieldy fastener, but Susan couldn’t maintain her grip and the material slipped from her fingers. To improve her angle of approach, Susan knelt on the floor and this time the zip began to move, before shooting up in a quick movement.

“Yes!” crowed Abi.

“Ow!” cried Susan. “My hair!”

A fair chunk of her long dark hair was enmeshed in the teeth of the fastener.

“Undo it,” Susan squawked.

Meanwhile, in the kitchen of the store’s cafeteria, Jamey Pond was having a bad day. He had been late (again), he had got three orders wrong in quick succession (again), and he was in the process of being fired. Enraged at his unjust treatment he stormed towards the staff cloakroom to gather his things, and, as he did so, his eye fixed upon a small red box on the wall. A sharp movement with his elbow was all it took to break the clear plastic fascia.

“What’s that?” shouted Abi when the fire alarm went off.

“It doesn’t matter! Just pull the stupid zip!” screamed Susan.

As well as the ear bursting siren, they could hear the cubicles around theirs emptying.

“Is anyone in here?” a woman’s voice asked after a few minutes, during which their struggle with the zip fastener had been ever more frantic.

“Yes!” called Abi. “We are! What’s happening?”

“I need to ask you to leave the store and assemble outside,” said the shop assistant, pulling back the curtain.

“We can’t,” wailed Susan. “My hair is stuck.”

The assistant tried to pull the zip down and, when that failed, she tried to tug Susan’s hair free, again with no success.

“We can’t wait any longer,” she apologised to her customers, “I can get some scissors and cut you free if you like?”

“No time!” exclaimed Abi, who was convinced they were about to be consumed by fire. She launched herself at speed towards the fire exit, towing a stumbling bent-double Susan behind her.

“Ow, ow, ow, stop, stop, stop!” Susan squealed as she was dragged down the stairs.

When they reached the fire assembly point, curious eyes gazed at them. Some people laughed, but several kinder-spirited people gave assistance, and after several minutes of twisting and pulling and squawking (on Susan’s part), she was free.

Once the fire brigade had declared the store safe to re-open, they returned to get their things. To Susan’s eternal disbelief, Abi bought the dress.

* * *

Two days before graduation, Susan returned to The Cherries to collect her ballgown. Luke had arranged that he would travel up for the degree ceremony and would stay the night in her room at the flat.

“Are you sure you’re OK to come?” she asked. “I really don’t mind if you can’t make it.”

“I’ll be there,” he assured her.

Susan made her way upstairs to the bedroom, and lifted the ballgown off the rail in the wardrobe, where it hung. Holding it up to the light, she spotted a few loose threads, which she decided to snip off while she had the chance.

She looked for some scissors, but couldn’t find any in the bathroom or bedroom, and she was about to go downstairs to fetch a pair, when she recalled a small leather men’s vanity case that Luke had. She worked through his chest of drawers, moving clothes aside in her search, until she reached the bottom-most drawer and lifted out some heavy, seldom worn, jumpers.

Susan’s eyes alighted on two framed photographs which she stared at in disbelief as her world crumbled about her.

The first picture was of Luke in a morning suit and top hat, standing next to the mysterious blonde woman, who was wearing a puffy white wedding dress. The second was of the pair of them posing happily together, proudly displaying a pregnancy bump.

Chapter 16

In his study, Luke noticed that Susan was still not downstairs with her dress, so he made his way to the bedroom to see if there was a problem. As he entered, he saw what she was holding in her hands and his blood froze and his throat constricted. Susan looked at him with a face of rage, but she spoke calmly.

"Was this woman your wife?" she asked. He nodded his head dumbly. "And is she still your wife?" she pressed.

Luke shook his head slowly.

"I can explain," he managed to say from his choking gullet.

"I think these pictures are explaining quite enough, don't you?" Susan stated.

Luke didn't know how to answer.

"Was there a child?" she whispered.

Luke tried to speak, but words would not form.

"Did your beautiful wife have a child?" Susan suddenly screamed at him.

"Yes!" he gurgled. "But it's complicated."

"I'm sure it is bloody complicated!" she raged. "My father would have said it was complicated! Do you ever – ever – imagine that I could marry… that I could love a man who would desert a wife and child?"

Susan moved her hand with a rapid wrist action, and Luke felt a sting on his cheek. He put his hand to his face, as she stood up and grabbed her dress.

"Stay away from me!" she hissed as she marched from the room. Luke looked on the floor to see the engagement ring shining in the sunlight from the window.

"Susan," he called, "Susan, please."

Luke raced to the stairs, but his legs were unsteady. He grasped the banister and half ran, half stumbled to the hall. The front door was swinging open and he could hear the engine of Susan's car start up.

“Please,” he implored as he tumbled into the front garden; Susan was turning her car in the lane. Luke’s vision was blurring, the world spinning, he seemed to develop tunnel vision and he dropped to his knees, desperately holding out his hand, as Buttercup disappeared around the corner of the narrow road.

He struggled to breathe; rasping hideously, he crawled back into the hallway and reached for the phone. But blackness engulfed him, and he passed out on the floor.

* * *

Susan drove as she had never driven before, replaying memories in her head: of the last conversation with Luke, of her father’s leaving, of her broken childhood. She had no recollection of the journey, or of parking, or of climbing the stairs to her flat; she simply found herself sitting on her bed, ballgown draped over her knees. She was once again experiencing intense heightening in her senses; sounds seemed loud and harsh, colours garish, smell noxious and her very skin felt unbearably sensitive.

She cycled between anger with herself for not giving Luke a chance to explain and anger with him, because there was no plausible excuse. She was about to call him when Abi entered the room, and she tearfully told what had happened.

“All men are bastards, darling. I learnt that a long time ago. You shouldn’t give him the satisfaction of calling. If he cares, he’ll ring you,” Abi counselled.

Susan was visibly torn, so Abi confiscated her phone and dragged her out to get “rat arsed drunk,” though she spent the evening miserably cradling half a pint of cider.

When she returned to her room, Abi gave her back her phone, but there were no missed calls or messages.

* * *

Reverend June arrived at The Cherries in the early morning to borrow some garden chairs for a church function. She was surprised to find the front door ajar, so she pushed it open and entered, calling out softly, to be confronted with the sight of Luke sitting on the floor, propped up against the wall, unshaven and dishevelled, staring ahead blankly.

She rushed to crouch beside him, calling his name until he acknowledged her presence. She helped him into the kitchen and gave him some orange juice; the sugary energy revived him somewhat and he told her of the events of the previous day, of Susan's discovery, of her anger, the breaking of the engagement, his collapse, and that he had been sitting in the hallway ever since, half dreaming that she was coming back home.

"But, Luke, do you mean to say you never told Susan?" asked June in disbelief. "She is so kind and understanding, she would have understood."

"I tried to start so many times," he replied, "but something always happened or I would be afraid that she couldn't forgive me. It turns out that I was right."

"Luke, surely if she knew the truth…"

"The truth?" Luke interrupted. "That I was a failure as a husband?"

"That's not the truth!" June said firmly. "When you told me the story, I didn't think you were at fault."

"Well, you are paid to forgive people," he said dryly. "No, this has been a good thing. Susan has seen me for what I am and she will have a better life without me."

"I don't think so, Luke," the vicar corrected him. "Few people ever get loved the way you love Susan. Just tell her what happened. If you don't want to, I will."

"No!" Luke responded sharply. "It is my secret to tell or not. Do not speak to Susan, give me your word."

"OK," she placated him.

"It is best like this," he insisted, his voice trembling with emotion. "She can forget me and have a good life. Not be tied to a man who can't go ten steps outside his own front door without shaking."

June sat patiently with him for a while. At length, she persuaded Luke to shower and shave, and prepared him some scrambled eggs and a cup of sweet tea while he did so.

"I am adamant, Vicar. I don't want you speaking to Susan," were his final words, "I think it would be too much for anyone to forgive."

June, however, did not leave the matter there. She respected Luke's insistence that it was not her secret to tell, but he was wrong about one thing - it wasn't just his secret.

When she got to the vicarage, she leafed through her address book and dialled a long telephone number. After a few long tones, a sleepy American voice answered, asking if the caller had any idea of the time; she glanced at the clock – oops, it was still the middle of the night in the USA.

"Sorry to wake you, Jerry," she said. "This is June Leicester. It's about Luke; I need your help."

* * *

Abi kept guard over Susan all that day and forbade her to use her phone in any way. But no calls or messages came anyway. All the residents of the flat were back, ready for graduation the next day, and they passed the time chatting, playing cards or wandering around the campus. They had one last group lunch in one of the university coffee shops, and Susan began to find the emotion of parting with her friends mingled with her depression over her split with Luke, increasingly hard to bear.

She went with Tessa and Mia to a CU meeting, where Tom approached her to ask if she wanted to go on the prayer retreat that he had organised. It was at a remote country house on the edge of a moor, with no mobile phone signal, no Wi-Fi and no telephone. She told him that she would think about it, but that it sounded tempting.

She dropped into her faculty building to say goodbye to some of her lecturers and was delighted to also see Mercedes, who had travelled up from the college for graduation. The congratulations rang hollow in her ears, but they were at least a small distraction from her sadness.

By the time they were ready for bed, Abi could see Susan was once again wavering on the brink of contacting Luke, so she confiscated her phone and her laptop overnight to remove temptation.

* * *

Abi woke early in the morning, excited by the prospect of the day ahead. She was now the proud owner of a degree and she was going to enjoy it. She glanced at Susan's phone and computer sitting on her desk, and immediately felt sorry for her friend; moreover, she realised that Susan used her phone as an alarm clock and may therefore need waking up.

She knocked loudly at Susan's door, which was a good thing as Susan had only fallen asleep in the early hours and could easily have slept through. As Abi tramped to the kitchen, she passed a sleepy Tessa in the hallway, who was heading to the flat's front door. "Someone rang the bell," Tessa explained.

Susan lay awake in bed, dreading what should have been one of the happiest days of her life. But Luke was not in the bed beside her, he would not be at the graduation ceremony later, nor would he escort her to the ball that evening.

There was another knocking at the door, gentler than before.

"OK, Abi!" she yelled. "I'm getting up!"

There was another knocking. Susan angrily opened the door, to be confronted by a stranger. Or not quite a stranger, for she recognised the beautiful face and long blonde hair.

"You must be Susan," the mystery woman said with a slight foreign accent. "I have a story to tell, and I think you need to hear it."

Susan mutely held open the door for her and gestured to the solitary chair in the room. She closed the door and sat on the bed in her pyjamas, shaking with shock and nerves.

"You're Luke's wife," Susan stated flatly. "You're very beautiful."

"No," the woman replied, "I am not his wife, nor was I ever. My name is Elsa and I am the younger sister of the woman you saw in the pictures that you found. Many people have made the same mistake as you, I can assure you. I should apologise for arriving unannounced, but your phone is going straight to voicemail."

"Oh, sorry, I think my friend Abi turned it off," Susan apologised.

"It is of no matter. I was glad in a way, because you might have said 'no' to meeting me. I have a long story to tell – do you have time?"

"Yes," replied Susan in a small voice.

"The lady in the photograph was my sister Agnes. People thought we were twins growing up, as we looked so alike, but she was eighteen months older than me. She and Luke met at university and married soon after, when he was working in a bank with Jerry – that's how I found you by the way, Jerry called me – and they made a lovely couple. My family loved Luke almost as much as she did, but, well, we did a terrible thing."

Elsa broke off, struggling to find a way to continue.

"Go on," Susan encouraged her.

"My sister had mental health issues – what you call bipolar - from her late teens, but she was on medication. She seemed so well, and she was so happy, that to our shame none of us told Luke before he married her. It was foolish, because he wouldn't have changed his mind, but maybe some things would have turned out differently."

Elsa coughed a little, so Susan fetched her a glass of water, which she sipped before continuing.

"Our family is from Sweden, and at that time only Agnes lived in the UK. Maybe if one of us had been here too, we would have realised… but things are what they are. Luke had always wanted children, so Agnes wanted to make him happy; she wasn't enjoying her job much anyway, so she decided to get pregnant. The trouble was, she worried that her medication would affect the baby, so she stopped taking it without telling anyone. Luke said he noticed some minor changes in behaviour, but when she told him she was expecting a child, he put any mood swings down to that. When the baby was born, everyone was ecstatic, but… there was something wrong."

"What?" asked Susan.

"Would you like to see a picture of my nephew as he looks now?" Elsa said. Susan nodded, so the blonde woman took out her phone and brought up a picture of a teenage boy posing in his football strip; he had black hair, brown eyes and dark skin.

Susan's reaction to the picture was exactly what Elsa was expecting.

"Yes, we all thought he doesn't look much like Luke," Elsa said. "But, well, all babies look alike, don't they? His name is Mark, and when little Mark was a few days old, your NHS carried out some tests and it turned out that he had a condition called Phenylketonuria, or PKU."

"Poor boy," said Susan, with feeling.

"You can have a normal life with it, but there are some things you can't eat and you have to be monitored. Anyway, it turns out that it is an inherited disease which requires both parents to carry the gene; Luke insisted that they both be tested, ostensibly to check to see the risk of any future children having it, but I have always wondered if he was suspicious. Anyway, the tests revealed that my sister carried the gene, but Luke didn't."

"So?" said Susan, being slow to realise the import of this information.

"So, Luke couldn't have been the father. Well, Agnes broke down and confessed everything, her bipolar diagnosis, not taking her meds, and the affairs she had been having. You can imagine that Luke was devastated, but he was also a real gentleman. He insisted the real father be contacted and allowed to meet Mark; it turned out to be a work colleague of Agnes's, and he is a great guy. Mark lives with him now - in fact he took him in when he was a baby, because Luke could tell that Agnes's mental health was deteriorating."

"That must have been hard for your sister," Susan commented.

"It was. We all agreed with Luke's thinking, but he blamed himself for inflicting a cruel blow to a sick woman. He was acting in Mark's best interests, but my sister was angry – who could blame her? Luke didn't. Anyway, it seems that she stopped taking her meds again, without anyone knowing. One night she and Luke had a huge argument and she stormed out of the house. Luke went looking for her, ringing everyone they knew, but gave up the search and went home at dawn."

Elsa started to cry, so Susan handed her a tissue.

"They found Agnes's body at the railway tracks. She had taken some pills and lain down to wait for a train."

Now Susan was crying, too. She wondered how Luke must have felt when he saw her storm off from The Cherries.

"So, Luke buried his past," Elsa continued. "He tried to go on working at the bank, but after a few years it got too much for him; too many memories."

"I am an awful person," Susan thought aloud, "I can't believe how I treated him. I should have known."

"You thought what any of us might have done," Elsa consoled her.

"Do you think he can forgive me?" Susan begged to know.

"Luke is the most forgiving man I know," Elsa told her. "And now I must get home. I live close to Mark now, to be a part in his life. He is a sweet boy, and I promised to take him ice skating this afternoon."

"Thank you for coming," Susan said as Elsa left.

Susan hurried to Abi's room, told her that it was a misunderstanding and asked for her phone.

She sped back to her room and started to call Luke, but nerves got the better of her. She would say it all wrong. What if he wouldn't forgive her? She couldn't bear to hear those words.

So, she sent a message:

'My darling. I have met Elsa and I know the truth about Agnes and Mark. I am sorry that I misjudged you and was angry. Is there any way you can forgive me and love me?'

* * *

Luke ignored his phone for some time. He wasn't expecting to hear from Susan, and he did not care to hear from anyone else. When he did pick up the phone and read the message, his heart leapt with joy.

He started to type a response, but hesitated. There was too much to say. Should he ring? No – he would go to the university. He could still make the degree ceremony and see this wonderful woman in person, this wonderful woman who could forgive him for his secret past, and tell her what he wanted to say.

He dressed in his best suit, with a crisp shirt and smart silk tie, and slipped Susan's engagement ring into his waistcoat pocket. He hurried into the garden and cut a selection of blooms, wrapping them in coloured paper, before getting into his Jaguar, so elated that he felt no anxiety at the prospective journey.

Sunshine turned to rain on the motorway and he joined a queue of slow traffic, edging forward. If it cleared soon, he should still be able to make the ceremony.

The road ahead did clear, and Luke started to make good progress once more. He was only about ten minutes from his destination when the engine suddenly started to cough and splutter. As the power died away, he had no option but to coast to a halt on the hard shoulder. Luke climbed out and lifted the bonnet, but there was no obvious problem. He called his roadside recovery company, just managing to make himself heard over the roar of the motorway traffic as the rain soaked through his jacket.

Then he wondered what to do – he wouldn't make the ceremony in time, even though the university was cruelly close. Susan could well be in the hall by now, so he couldn't ring her even if he was willing to, given the noise of the passing cars and lorries. He started to type a message - "Blast!" His finger slipped in the rain and the text disappeared. He climbed into the passenger seat of the car and tried again.

'I'm so sorry, I've tried but I cannot get to the ceremony – the car has broken down. I will try to get there as soon as possible. I love you so much, I can't wait to be with you. Thank you for understanding and I have nothing to forgive. Ever yours, Luke.'

Luke was still reading the text through when the lorry hit the back of the car. He never felt the impact, never heard the noise of the truck, and he never pressed send on the text. All that had been sent were those first few words that had disappeared in the rain.

Susan's phone buzzed in her bag as she gathered with her friends after the ceremony. The last message Susan Jones would receive from Luke Cartwright in apparent response to her question 'Is there any way you can forgive me and love me?' was 'I'm so sorry, I've tried but I cannot'.

Chapter 17

It was not until she was back in her room that Susan found and read the message from Luke. She went cold with shock and distress welled up inside her; with a primal scream, she hurled the phone across the room, and it shattered against the wall.

She sobbed so deeply that she could not breathe. Her mind raced with self-rebuke and inward loathing. How could she expect him to react otherwise? She had acted disgracefully, and now she had thrown away her chance of happiness forever. Of course, Luke would try to forgive her, try to love her, but he could not. Who could? And she did not deserve forgiveness or love. Susan collapsed onto her bed and sobbed until exhaustion took over and she slept; but still she dreamt of Luke and of all the accusing faces of people that they knew.

A knocking at the door brought her into the real world.

"Susan, are you ready? It's almost time to go to the ball," Abi called.

"Oh," she responded numbly, "I'm not feeling like it."

"Come on! You've got to come – you can't let us down!"

Susan became an automaton; not wanting to let anyone else down she would go through the motions. She replied that she'd be as quick as she could. Going into her little bathroom to look in the mirror, she suddenly found herself leaning over the toilet, vomiting. This seemed to wake her up a little, and she managed to make sure she looked presentable.

Opening her wardrobe, she looked at her beautiful blue ballgown, but removed the dress her mother had given her for her birthday three long years before. She slipped it over her head, and felt its gentle caress, wishing Marian was with her now.

When she emerged into the hallway outside her room, the rest of her flatmates were gathered.

"What happened to your posh blue frock?" Abi asked.

"It doesn't fit," Susan lied.

"Why not?" Abi asked. "You're so skinny."

"Look, are we going to this thing or not?" asked Mia, to Susan's relief.

Later that evening, Susan stood at the side of the dancefloor watching Abi dance while kissing a newly graduated Physicist, who was clearly out of his depth and loving it. Distress had now turned to a melancholy acceptance on Susan's part, and she felt calm and composed.

Tom and Tessa spotted her and moved across the hall to chat.

"Have you still got a place at the retreat?" Susan asked when they reached her.

"Yes, but the minibus is full," Tom replied.

"I'll drive up in my own car," said Susan.

"Great! Can I hitch a lift with you?" Tessa requested. "Better than being sandwiched in the minivan."

"I'd like that," said Susan. "What time do we leave?"

"Seven in the morning," Tom told her.

Susan was grateful for the early start; the sooner she was gone from there, the better.

* * *

The retreat was in a place called The Grange, a large grey country house with an assortment of red bricked outbuildings, and a large walled vegetable garden. To the sides and the rear were rough, tussock-filled pale fields with rippling long grass, and to the front was the yellow, brown and red bracken of the moor, stretching into the distance, with purple hazed hills rising on the horizon.

A long, potholed, cement drive led to a car park (of sorts) for the residents. Susan lugged the suitcases and bags that contained all her worldly goods through the front door and up the stairs to a large bedroom, with a high ceiling and wooden shutters at the sash windows. There were two comfortable single beds on either side of the room, two wardrobes and dressing tables and an old white porcelain basin in one corner.

Tessa appeared in the doorway, and announced that they were roommates, which pleased Susan. They spent a pleasant half an hour settling in and exploring the corridor to find where the bathroom was (it transpired to be directly across the hallway). Then they were summoned downstairs by a gong being rung to announce dinner, which was a choice between vegetarian lasagne and spaghetti bolognaise; neither appealed to Susan, so she nibbled a bread roll.

Leading them in grace was the owner of The Grange, a bespectacled young man in his late twenties, slight of build with an attractive smile. He introduced himself as Spencer Taylor and welcomed them all to the retreat.

For the next few days Susan earnestly threw herself into the activities: group prayer, meditation, bible study, and silent reflection. But still neither her mind nor soul could elevate her mood, and her appetite remained non-existent.

She decided to go for a walk on the moor. Spencer met her in the hallway on her way out and advised her to be cautious, as the weather was closing in and conditions on the moor could change rapidly. Susan took this advice on board and decided to stick to the little road, which ran as a black ribbon of tarmac snaking through the heather.

She lost track of how long she had walked and she did not know the time, as her phone was broken beyond repair, but looking behind her she could no longer see The Grange. A fine misty rain had started, dampening her clothes, but the temperature was still warm, so she decided to walk a little further.

The sound of a solitary vehicle came from behind her and she moved onto the verge to let a small blue van zoom past. Continuing her walk, she could see the vehicle a little way ahead; for a moment, its brake lights flicked before it went on its way, but she could see that it had struck something.

Susan hurried to the crumpled form and found a young deer lying at the edge of the verge, stunned. She squatted, stroking its head and trying to see if there was any injury to its legs or body. She made soothing noises, and the creature seemed to be calming down when it suddenly leapt up and ran off across the moorland.

"Wait!" called Susan. "Please wait! I need to check you're not hurt."

She broke into a canter across the heather, tripping every so often and scratching herself on the unforgiving gorse. It was to no avail, for the little deer was now lost in the mist. It was a mist that Susan hadn't noticed coming down, and it was now disorientating and claustrophobic. She realised within minutes that she had no idea which direction would lead to the road and she made the practical decision that the wisest thing to do was to stay put.

Her cries for help sounded feeble in the blanket of grey, but she persevered until she had no voice left. It was getting darker and colder and Susan calmly decided it was her time to die. She fell to her knees, the bracken digging in to her skin and bone.

“Oh God,” she prayed, “oh God let me die. Let me come closer to you and to leave this world and its pain. Forgive me for all that I have done wrong, though I know that I don’t deserve forgiveness. Lord, I hurt so much.”

By now she was bent forward so far that her face was touching the harsh moorland plants, and they tangled in her hair, pulling her down to the earth.

“Lord, I don’t want to be Susan Jones, who gets everything wrong,” she whispered, her eyes tightly closed. Her breathing slowed and slowed until it seemed to stop, as if her very existence in time ceased, and she lived in the moment, and through the moment and outside of the moment, hearing the life of the moorland and inhaling the scents.

Had she died? For a time, all pain stopped, all thought suspended. Yet suddenly she was awake and alive. She stood up, the plants freely releasing her, and realised that it was night. The mist had cleared, and the stars were bright in the sky, making her feel giddy at the enormous expanse above her. Then she looked around her. On the horizon was a bright light.

“Well, that has to be something man-made,” she reasoned to herself, and she started to tramp across the moor towards it.

It was much further away than it looked, or it was moving, but ultimately, she was at the front door of The Grange and then in the hallway.

“Susan!” exclaimed Mia, who came to see who it was. “We’ve been so worried. People are out looking for you.”

She looked closely at Susan, who was looking on the point of collapse. Mia led her to a chair.

“Look at the state of you,” she said tenderly. “Oh, you’re burning up.”

Mia called for help, and Tessa came hurrying. The two women assisted Susan upstairs and ran her a bath. After she had bathed, Tessa helped her into bed, and gave her some paracetamol; Mia arrived carrying a tray with some soup and bread which Susan managed to eat, while the girls tended to her open cuts with antiseptic.

She stayed in bed for the next day, and was touched that Spencer came to sit with her, reading aloud or talking about faith and his life. The Grange was a family home which he took over when his parents retired. His father had been a preacher before setting up the retreat and when Spencer had finished his own theology degree, he came home to learn the business.

He was highly intrigued when Susan told him she was an artist. She had a small portfolio of her work in her suitcase, which she showed him, and he invited her to use a studio that he had set up in one of the outbuildings.

The next day, she was up and about and the day after she went into the studio. While it was quite well equipped, she used many of her own materials, including the watercolour box that Luke had given her. Her style was darker and bolder, but the finished effects were pleasing – she signed the pictures 'Susan C' as she reasoned to herself that she had so nearly been Susan Cartwright.

* * *

Spencer was very enthusiastic when Susan showed him her work and had a proposition for her. He had always wanted to offer guests of the retreat courses in art and spirituality, giving them the opportunity to paint as a method of exploring faith. Would Susan be interested in being the artist in residence?

"But I'm not a teacher," she objected.

"We don't want a teacher, just someone who would be a kind of mentor, working alongside the guests and giving suggestions," Spencer explained. "We can't pay much, but you can live at The Grange and have your meals for free. Take a day or two to think it over and pray."

Susan did give the matter careful consideration and she could find only positives in the idea. It was her opportunity to disappear, to have a safe place to live among kind people, to continue painting, and to try to become a better person. She accepted the offer and was also pleased to hear that Tessa would be remaining for a while, too, as organiser of youth retreats.

The next day Susan drove into the local town and bought a new smartphone. She decided to keep the new number, and only messaged it to her mother, her nan and Jenny. She registered at the local doctor's surgery and the dental practice.

Back at The Grange, she took her laptop into the office and plugged it into the aging router to access the internet. She set up a new email account and imported the address book from her old one. She notified her bank, her car insurance, and DVLA of her new address and contact details. She didn't use social media, so had no accounts to change.

Susan was an expert in vanishing from her past – after all, she had done it before years ago, when she arrived at Hayfield Barn.

Chapter 18

Susan spent a peaceful year at The Grange. Her art sessions went well; many guests bought work from her and she also supplied several galleries in the surrounding towns. Having no bills to pay, these sales meant that she had soon built up a comfortable nest egg.

She and Tessa continued to share the large bedroom with its panoramic view of the countryside, and both women contributed hugely to the running of the organised retreats. Spencer's business grew well, its diary chock-a-block with events.

Mia was a frequent visitor, and the three women invested in walking boots and outdoor wear, and took to exploring the moors, often accompanied by Spencer, showing them prehistoric settlements, or rare birds and butterflies. Susan carried a sketchbook with her wherever she went, needing to sketch and paint as much as she needed to breathe. And every night in her prayers, she prayed for Luke.

* * *

Mia's regular weekend visits to The Grange meant that she often got roped into activities as an unpaid volunteer. She was a natural organiser, so she assisted Spencer in improving the operation and planning of the retreats, and her mathematical skills and job (training as an accountant), meant she was a huge help with the bookkeeping.

Spencer tended to arrange planning meetings to coincide with Mia's visits, so on Saturday evenings the team would squeeze into the small office and perch on desks and brainstorm. People put forward ideas, gave updates on progress of projects, or pointed out problems they had spotted.

On one such occasion, Mia put forward a suggestion that The Grange should host an outreach programme for LGBTQ Christians, to give them a safe place to explore their faith. Given Mia's previous comments when learning of Jenny's and Lucy's wedding, Susan was surprised by this change of attitude, so she drew Mia aside for a quiet word.

"That was a change of heart," Susan said.

"It was. I've thought about it a lot lately, and I have changed my position substantially."

"So, what persuaded you?"

"You, Tessa, and your friends did, Susan," Mia replied simply.

"Me? What did I do?" Susan said, surprised by the answer.

"Your example as a Christian," Mia told her. "Your acceptance of everyone, well, it made me feel pretty small. And you speak so fondly of Lucy and Jenny, too, which got me thinking. Look, Susan, I guess I just want to have an open mind and listen, but at the same time, I love my scripture. It is a struggle, but I guess faith is a journey and I am certainly not in a position to judge others."

After everyone else had left the office, Susan returned having fetched her laptop and plugged it into the router; she felt as if she were betraying the spirit of The Grange if she used her mobile phone to access the internet. She opened her emails and sent a message to Lucy, telling her of the new outreach programme and that it had come about because of her and Jenny's marriage.

* * *

Eventually, Susan and Tessa moved into a flat in the town near The Grange; Spencer needed their room for guests and his growing business was now able to pay them both a proper salary. Susan's contract was part-time allowing her to focus on selling her own work; 'Susan C' was getting quite a following, and she was invited to exhibit in larger galleries further afield, in addition to receiving a growing number of commissions.

She also volunteered for one afternoon a week at a special needs school, helping the children with their art and craft; her students' enthusiasm and uninhibited laughter were highly infectious, so these were some of the rare occasions that she too laughed.

Susan was not depressed; indeed, she felt an inner peace and was serene, but she simply didn't change her emotions – she was rarely up or down, just reliably consistent, and this suited her. Her lifestyle was a simple one; her limited social life revolved around The Grange, her cooking was basic but nutritious, and her dress sense conservative. She wore little or no makeup, with hair pulled into a loose pony tail most days, though she still liked to let it hang free sometimes.

She kept in touch with Bonita, both women exchanging long handwritten letters and photographs of their work. Bonita spent a year in teacher training before travelling home to Java to be married; she and her new husband, who was a television producer, settled near his job in Manchester, where she taught in the local primary school. She sent Susan and Tessa each one of her home-made head-scarves as housewarming gifts, and as a wedding present, they sent her an ornate vase, which they had spotted in a local antique shop.

Abi was less good at keeping in touch, but Susan made a point of emailing or calling her. She moved back home with her parents for several months after university while she looked for work. Eventually, she relocated to Leeds and a career in Public Relations and soon after moved in with a boyfriend, at which point her calls and messages became even less frequent. Tessa and Susan were both determined not to let the friendship disappear, and Abi was grateful for their tenacity.

Tom regularly visited, and after a little prodding by Susan, he and Tessa began an old-fashioned courtship, with walks on the moor, fish and chip suppers on a park bench after seeing a movie, or sometimes going to a concert.

Marian was loving Dubai, but she did return to the UK, staying first with Vivian for a few days and then with Susan and Tessa. She looked well, tanned and relaxed. She and Graham were in a comfortable relationship, living together, but with no plans to marry.

Jenny and Lucy were in semi-regular contact, but were very absorbed in their own lives. However, Susan was one of the first people to receive the happy news that Jenny was three months pregnant, and she was honoured to be asked by Lucy to get ready to be a godparent.

* * *

Spencer was a regular caller at the flat, and Susan also saw him at services and charity events. He was a very serious man, a little literal in his understanding, but with a kind and generous heart. Often jokes would pass him by, and Mia (when she was there), or Susan would rephrase them in such a way as to make them clear, at which point he would laugh loudly.

His scriptural knowledge was detailed, and he had an amazing memory for details. His intensely logical mind meant that Spencer was a poor evangelist, unlike his father, as he simply couldn't comprehend why someone didn't follow his argument; at times, he could come across as abrasive or uncaring, but it was an unfair impression.

He had a love of music and worship songs, and frequently organised small concerts at The Grange, which spilled out into the grounds in the fine weather.

What Susan found challenged her most about Spencer was his earnest treatment of everything that happened to him, and every person he met, as a challenge that he was being tested on. He seemed to believe that in some way everything had a correct answer which God was expecting him to find. If he believed he had erred and sinned, he was distraught and would seek penance for days, but if he thought he was right, he would be convinced there had to be an even better answer.

While she found his ways worthy of admiration, they were alien to her, which was ironic, for Susan privately still believed that she herself was almost beyond redemption for her treatment of Luke.

Spencer was very pleasant company though. She enjoyed their walks together, his tastes in music and even his football fandom, allowing him to drag her to several games in the draughty stands of the local non-league club.

But while he could recite long tracts of the bible, he could not quote poetry or Dickens or Thackery; she had lost the only one that could.

* * *

Tom proposed to Tessa at Christmas, and they married in early April. The wedding was in the university chapel, as it was a place of many shared memories, and was a fusion of traditional and gospel sounds. It was an emotional day for Susan, who, standing with Mia in the pew, missed Luke's presence more than ever.

Susan rattled around her flat after Tessa's departure, but she focussed on her work and her reputation grew, especially as she had now expanded into oil painting. Then, an offer from a large gallery came for her to put on an exclusive exhibition at their premises, along with several commissions from a prestigious London-based interior design company, which promised a long-term contract to supply works for offices in major City firms. Two publishing houses contacted her to start producing prints and calendars based on her work.

Susan was soon earning more money than she wanted or knew what to do with. She saved her money carefully, but also gave much of it away to worthy causes. With regret, she knew that her job at The Grange was becoming incompatible with her workload, so she began, with Spencer's agreement, to taper it off, while he found and introduced a replacement.

She worked with a fervour to get a large body of work together for the exhibition, and she tried to suppress one fear that was manifesting in her mind. The gallery was based in a city not far from the town that she had grown up in and the idea of returning to the area, even after five years, was almost crippling, but she drew on her strength and focussed on painting.

One afternoon, she had a knock at the door. Wiping her paintbrush on a rag, she hurried to answer it, and was pleased to see Spencer standing in the corridor. He seemed rather uneasy as he sipped the tea that she had made for him, and he struggled to make easy conversation.

"I think we should get married," Spencer suddenly blurted out. Susan was stunned.

"I beg your pardon?" she said, though she had heard perfectly well and her brain was racing.

"I think we should get married. It makes perfect sense," he asserted.

"It may to you, Spencer, but this is… well… a bit out of the blue from where I'm standing," Susan responded, struggling to regain her mental equilibrium.

"It is a logical thing to do," he stated. "We are both the right age, we like the same things. My parents would like grandchildren and, well, a man shall leave his father and his mother and hold fast to his wife."

Susan stared at him, deeply flattered, but also mildly insulted.

"Do you love me?" she asked.

"Of course, you are a sister in Christ."

"No, but do you love me? Do you want me?" she pressed.

Spencer's major weakness in this argument was his honesty.

"I admire you. I'd do everything I can to make you happy," he replied. "Isn't that enough?"

Susan discovered that she was seriously considering the proposal – he was a good man, he would put her before himself, and he would be a patient father. But then Margaret's words from years ago manifested themselves into her mind: 'We only had three years together, but they've lasted me a lifetime. You know, when you meet the one for you, well there's no point in second best'.

She smiled sadly at Spencer.

"I'm so sorry. I am honoured by your offer, but I cannot accept it," she said gently.

"Why not?" he asked, rather stunned to be turned down.

"Well, for one thing Mia might not like it."

"Mia?" he asked, taken aback. "Mia…," he repeated slowly.

"I think she is rather hoping you would have asked her that question," Susan said. "And I think you want to ask it."

Spencer was lost in introspection. Susan stood patiently.

"Susan," he said suddenly. "Thank you for the tea. I must leave now… I… I think I have a train to catch."

* * *

Susan decided to let her flat go and rent a furnished place near to the gallery where she would be exhibiting. There were practical reasons for living there, including a direct train line to London for her other work, but it was also very intimidating. She still had few possessions, so she made the move by loading Buttercup with her clothes and personal items, while Spencer and Mia followed behind in The Grange's minibus, carrying her art supplies and paintings.

Once settled in, she continued to focus on work and the exhibition, which was to run for several weeks. Within the first few days of the show, nearly all her work had sold, so Susan started a production line, finishing pieces and driving them to the venue as quickly as she could, sometimes with the paint still damp. Every picture she dropped off seemed to sell before she got back to the flat.

After the exhibition ended, she decided to relax. Susan had more than sufficient funds to take some time off, to just paint a little for pleasure and do some voluntary work. Marian was constantly messaging her to come to Dubai, where there were good opportunities for artists, and Susan certainly did miss her mother. She also made a point of spending a weekend with her nan, who was starting to look very frail.

Through the local church, she had started to volunteer in a foodbank, assisting people in desperate need by giving them the basic essentials, which had been donated by the public. One late afternoon she was going through the shelves, checking best-before dates, when she became aware of a minor fracas between one of her fellow helpers and a client.

"I'm sorry," said Susan's colleague, "but you have to have been referred here by someone before we can give you anything. A doctor, or Citizens Advice."

"Please!" implored a young woman, who was cradling a baby in her arms, while a toddler clung to her leg. "I have nothing for the kids."

The assistant sighed, and stuffed a few items into a carrier bag.

"I shouldn't do this," she said, "but this should keep you going for today. Then you need to get over to the CAB, alright?"

Carrier bag in one hand, which also clutched the toddler's, baby in the opposite arm, the young woman left. Almost hypnotised, Susan mumbled her apologies to her colleagues and followed her.

She trailed the young woman until she stopped at a battered hatchback in the corner of a car park outside an empty industrial unit. She put the children inside the car before looking through the bag – whatever the contents were, it was enough to make her burst into tears.

"Oh, no!" she sobbed over and over.

Susan walked quietly behind her.

"Hello, Katherine," she said.

Katherine Willis spun around and looked at Susan in shock and (for the first time in their acquaintance) fear.

"You," she whispered.

Susan gestured to the bag.

"What's wrong with that? It's just pasta and stuff," she asked, peering past Katherine to the children in the car, who were surrounded by dirty sleeping bags and blankets.

"Nothing," was the taciturn response.

"Is this where you live?" Susan asked bluntly. "Is your problem that you don't have a cooker to make the pasta?"

Katherine nodded, so exhausted that she didn't have a fight left in her. Her hair was thick with dirt and grease and her clothes stained; she was simply beyond resisting.

"Come with me," Susan instructed quietly but firmly. She bent to look inside the car and said brightly to the toddler, "Do you want to come with Mummy and see where I live?"

The toddler's head nodded, with large eyes staring at her.

"Come on," Susan said, lifting the baby out. "Is there anything you need to bring?"

Katherine pulled a huge holdall out of the boot and locked the car, before following Susan for the few hundred yards to her flat.

Once inside, Susan put the television on to a children's TV station, and the toddler was immediately transfixed. She handed the baby to its mother and went into her bedroom, returning with underwear, leggings and a t-shirt. Then she pointed to a doorway.

"The shower's in there," she said, taking the baby back. "Put these clothes on when you're finished and chuck your dirty ones out when you've taken them off."

Katherine, almost in a trance, complied and went into the bathroom. A few moments later, a sticky mass of dirty clothes was pushed out of the door.

Susan put them in the washing machine. She popped some bread into the toaster, poured a large tin of baked beans into a pan, and scrambled some eggs. Then she rang the curate from the church, with whom she had become good friends and who lived with his young family a few doors away, and asked if he could spare some nappies and baby wipes. He dropped a bag over almost immediately, before Katherine emerged from the bathroom.

When she did appear, Susan pointed Katherine to the table and turned off the television. She put out three plates of eggs, beans and toast, though she only took a little for herself, and some glasses of fruit juice. The toddler immediately started eating, but his mother was torn, almost as if she feared the food was poisoned.

"Why?" Katherine asked.

"Isn't it enough that I am?" Susan answered, spooning a little egg into her mouth. "Maybe I just like to have company when I eat."

Katherine ate her food, at first tentatively then with ferocity. Susan made a second batch of toast, which she brought over with some pots of jam and a selection of fruit. Katherine was crying silent tears as she ate.

"I wasn't sure what the baby can have," Susan said. "Can I mash a banana for her?"

"Yes."

Susan fetched a bowl, mashed a banana with a fork and fed it to the baby on her lap with a tea spoon.

"You can give the kids a bath after tea," she told Katherine, "I've got some nappies and stuff in a bag, but not clothes. Have you got any clean?"

"Some t-shirts, pants and a babygro in the big bag."

Susan nodded.

“And what’s your name?” she asked the toddler, who remained mute.

“Nathan,” his mother answered for him, before smiling at the baby, “and this is Kelly.”

“Hello, Kelly,” Susan said brightly, causing a banana-smeared smile.

While Katherine bathed Nathan, Susan watched Kelly and changed the sheets and duvet cover on her bed with fresh linen.

“You three sleep in the bedroom, I’ll take the couch,” she told them. “No arguments.”

Nathan went to sleep in Susan’s bed, while Katherine sat on the sofa breastfeeding the baby.

“It’s cheaper than formula,” she explained.

Susan made two large cups of tea and opened a packet of chocolate digestives, which Katherine couldn’t stop herself from eating, one after another.

“I don’t understand why you’re helping me,” she said, with a mixture of pathos and bafflement. “You must hate me?”

“I don’t hate anyone,” Susan answered truthfully, “and you can’t change the past. It’s what you do with the future that matters. I have enough to be sorry for in my own life. Anyway, it seems like you’ve had a bad enough time without me adding to it.”

“Chucked out by Mum and my stepdad when Nathan was born, went to live with his dad,” Katherine told Susan. “When I was pregnant with Kelly, he beat me up so bad I thought I’d lose her. After she was born, he got worse, so I did a runner a month ago. Tried to get help, they put me in a hostel with a bunch of junkies, so I decided to live in my car. Ran out of money last week.”

By nine o’clock, Katherine was struggling to stay awake, weeks of hardly sleeping had taken their toll, so she went to bed. Susan lay on the settee, mulling over the events of the day and praying for guidance.

* * *

In the morning, Katherine found Susan making coffee. The baby and her big brother were both awake and full of energy, but calmed down when Susan served up breakfast.

“I have some jobs I need to get done today,” she told Katherine when they had finished. “Here is forty quid, it is all the cash I have. You need to get to the CAB today and try to organise some benefits. This should be enough for you to get a bus, have some lunch and pick up any essentials that you need. I'll meet you back here at six this evening. OK?"

Katherine agreed and made her way out with the children. Susan flew into a flurry of activity. She went to a self-storage unit and put all her paintings and art materials in a large locker; then she ran some other errands, before returning home and lugging more stuff to her car.

When her three guests returned, Susan had dinner waiting, including jars of baby food. When they had eaten, and Nathan was in bed, she stood up, pulled her coat on and handed some keys to Katherine.

"This flat is a rolling monthly let," Susan stated. "I have pre-paid the next four months and put it in your name."

"I don't understand," Katherine responded as if winded.

"This is your home now," Susan explained, "at least until you can sort something permanent." She placed a page torn from a notebook on the table. "Any post that comes for me, please forward to this address – it is my good friends Tessa and Tom."

"But…" Katherine stuttered.

"I've stocked the fridge," Susan continued, handing a thickly packed envelope to Katherine, "and in here is enough money to keep you going until you get some benefits, or a job, and my email address is on the back if you need to reach me."

Katherine started to sob.

"I don't understand why you're doing this. I don't deserve it."

"Everyone does and nobody does. That's what I realised last night," Susan answered enigmatically.

"Where will you go?"

"Dubai probably, but first I am going to see if I can have one last chance at forgiveness for myself."

Susan walked to the door.

"Goodbye, Katherine and God bless you and your family."

Katherine stared at the floor, droplets of tears patting on the carpet.

"Thank you," she called as the door shut.

Chapter 19

Susan stayed the night at the halfway point of the journey at a comfortable budget hotel. She had a nervous breakfast before returning to her room and showering, blow drying her hair and taking time to get her makeup and outfit just right. She planned to call on Luke and apologise for her behaviour one last time before leaving the country; she had no expectations of a romantic reunion but hoped that they may part friends. She at least had to see him one more time, and know that he was OK and happy.

She drove the remaining distance rehearsing the impending conversation in her head again and again. Almost all too soon, she was on the familiar leafy lanes, finally turning the corner to see the never forgotten sight of The Cherries and Hayfield Barn side by side.

Except, as she neared the buildings, she saw a sight that she simply could not understand. Where the cherry trees had once stood in beautiful blossom, there was an area of oily back tarmac, with a Range Rover and a large BMW parked on it. The sign which had read 'The Cherries' had been replaced by one saying 'Nirvana'. As she slowed Buttercup down, she saw a young boy kicking a football between the cars with an expression of boredom on his young features.

She stopped the car and got out.

"Excuse me," she said to the boy, "I am looking for Luke Cartwright. Doesn't he live here?"

The boy ran to the open front door and called out. An older girl of about fifteen came out.

"Can I help you?" she asked Susan suspiciously.

"Yes, please," Susan replied politely. "Sorry to trouble you, but I'm looking for Luke Cartwright. He used to live here."

The girl thought for a moment, and then she remembered something.

"Oh, yeah. Mum and Dad did say something about it. We used to get loads of post to him, which they dropped up to the vicarage. Sorry, I think he might be dead – a car crash or something."

These words struck Susan like a sledgehammer. She took a step back and put her hand to her heart. She would have known; someone would have told her… but how? She hadn't been in contact with anyone. But wouldn't she have known anyway, to have somehow felt his absence from this world?

In a daze, she returned to her car and drove to the village, straight to the churchyard. She ran up and down the rows of headstones, looking for a new one, looking for his grave. There she would lie down with him for one last time, there she would be with her love again.

She stopped at a familiar one.

"Oh, Margaret! Where is he?" she begged her absent friend to tell her.

Reverend June walked out of the church and saw a young woman running among the graves. She was a familiar and unmistakeable figure.

"Susan!" she cried hastening towards her. "Oh, Susan!"

Susan looked up and saw her, racing to meet her. June flung her arms around her long-lost friend.

"Oh, Susan. Where have you been?" she asked breathlessly. "We tried so hard to find you."

"I'm so sorry," Susan replied, "I didn't want to be found."

June held both of Susan's hands.

"You look well," she said, "I'm so glad. I feared the worst had happened."

Susan wasn't in a state to talk, but could only say one thing.

"Where is he? Which one is Luke in?"

"Which what?" asked June, confused.

"Which grave?" Susan said in a frustrated voice. "I asked down at The Cherries and they told me he was dead."

"Susan, Luke was in a terrible accident," June said slowly, "but he isn't dead."

Such joy as she had never felt before filled Susan's heart.

"So, where is he?" she begged.

"Well," June answered hesitantly, "he lives in Blossom Cottage. Margaret's old house. But he –"

Susan was already running full pelt to the road.

"Susan, he isn't who he was!" shouted June.

Susan didn't listen, she was running hard, pausing only to remove her heeled shoes so that she could run faster. Clutching the shoes to her chest, her lungs felt they would burst, but still she ran, up the lane to the little row of cottages, up the path and to the familiar front door.

She rang the bell, and waited desperately for the door to open. Gradually, her wish was granted and Luke was standing before her.

"Susan!" he exclaimed in shock.

June was right in her warning. He leant heavily on a walking stick with his left arm, and his right seemed to only have a limited range of movement. Most shocking though was a thick scar zigzagging down his brow to his right eye. He now wore a pair of thin-framed metal spectacles.

"Oh, my love," she said softly, trying to reach her hand out to touch him, but withdrawing it, uncertain how to act.

"I expect you'd like a cup of tea," he said, moving stiffly down the hall. Susan followed him inside the cottage, closing the front door behind her.

* * *

Susan watched Luke move about the kitchen; when once he made complex meals with ease, he was now clumsy with cups and saucers, his damaged arm having an almost permanent tremor. She ached to help him, and he did at least allow her to carry the cups through to the living room.

There was an easy chair next to the fire, and next to it a table with a photograph of Susan in her blue gown which he had taken on the night of the Christmas Ball. The walls were now lined with shelves of books, and over the hearth hung the watercolour she had painted of the doorway to The Cherries.

Luke saw her looking at the picture, reminiscing how it had been bought by him to fund her purchase of a bicycle.

"I still have the stuff you left behind," he told her. "Your bike is in the shed, your art supplies and pictures are crated in the spare room. There are some clothes, too; oh, and I found what appears to be a Batgirl costume stuffed in the corner of a wardrobe. I'm sorry I never managed to arrange to have them restored to you."

Susan nodded as her eyes took in the familiar room, now filled with Luke's furniture, but she said nothing.

"You look well," he remarked, "I'm so glad to see you're OK. And I'm very proud of your career."

"What?" she replied, surprised.

"I may not be as sharp as I was, but a talented artist called Susan C? I recognised your work immediately. Of course, I didn't tell anyone else. I realised that you wanted your privacy. Perfectly understandable after my behaviour."

"Your behaviour?" Susan was confused. "What do you mean?"

"If I had just replied to your message when I got it… well, things would have been different. It must have hurt you terribly to have no reply. Of course, you were long gone by the time they tried to contact you."

"I am getting very confused," she said, "what do you mean?"

"I was travelling up to surprise you at your graduation when my car broke down on the hard shoulder. I was texting you, but the accident happened before I could send it. Not that I recall what happened exactly, but when I came out of my coma, I asked Peter to check and he found my last message unsent."

"But you did send a message," she enunciated slowly, as if to remind him. "It said you couldn't forgive me or love me."

"I would never have sent such a thing!" Luke objected with feeling.

"I remember the words exactly," Susan stated, the pain evident in her voice. "They were: 'I'm so sorry, I've tried but I cannot'."

Luke gaped at her in astonishment.

"What I typed was: 'I'm so sorry, I've tried but I cannot make the ceremony' – then there was a whole lot of stuff about nothing to forgive and loving you... I still have the phone somewhere."

He tugged a drawer open and started to look inside.

"Don't bother, I believe you," Susan said, slightly tartly.

She was angry with him. Angry for being so ridiculous as to have to send complicated text messages, angry that she hadn't been told of his accident, angry for not having been able to care for him, angry for the lost wasted years. Or had they been wasted? Spencer and Mia, Tom and Tessa, Katherine and Nathan and Kelly – would those people's lives have been the same if she had not followed the path she did?

"Why didn't you contact me?" she asked. "I'd have wanted to know. To come to you."

"June and Peter tried to find you at first, but they had very little to go on," Luke explained. "When I regained consciousness in hospital, I insisted that they not try to find you. The doctors had told me of my physical… limitations… I didn't want you to come back to this."

"But, I'm here now," she said simply.

"Ah, but I have so very little to offer you now," he replied sadly. "A lover with a broken body, poor eyesight and much reduced financial circumstances. Before I could give you The Cherries and a good living, but now all I have is this."

"Do you think so little of me that I only wanted those things?" she asked. "Do you think that that was what made me love you?"

"No. You're too good for that," he replied, "but now…"

He gestured to his scarred face.

"You're beautiful," she said simply.

"No I'm not."

"I'm the artist, remember?" she stated, echoing his own words to her of many years ago. "I know what's beautiful. Now... do you love me?"

"Please, Susan, don't. It's not fair!" he moaned.

"Do – you – love – me?" she demanded to know.

"I always have, I always will, with all that I am and more. Yes, I love you, I adore you. And I'm sorry," he stated.

"Stop being sorry and kiss me," she instructed.

"Oh, my Susie, can it be true?"

"Oh, my love," she murmured, tiptoeing to kiss him.

* * *

Luke and Susan were not apart for a single day until they married just over a month later, surrounded by friends and family.

Marian and Graham flew back from Dubai for the ceremony, picking up Susan's nan, Rose, on the way from the airport. They came with news that Marian had decided to buy a property in the village, so that she could come and stay for long periods nearby, and have a home to retire to. While she was still enjoying her performing career, there was much about the UK that she was beginning to miss, not least her daughter. Graham, ever an amicable man, was perfectly content with the arrangements, and would very probably retire with her.

Vivian, Jenny and Lucy and a little baby girl called Milly, came, as did Tom and Tessa, Spencer and Mia, and Abi and her boyfriend. Susan had asked Jenny to be her matron of honour, but recent motherhood meant Jenny said she preferred a lower-key role.

Jerry was Luke's best man. He and Tina flew back into the country for a month, staying at The Cedars for old time's sake, and their twin daughters were Susan's bridesmaids. Dominic came back from Hungary to be chief usher and surprised them all after the wedding by announcing he was moving to Canada as he had met someone online like himself, who also wanted companionship.

A very pregnant Bonita designed a veil for Susan's dress, but she and her husband were barely home from the ceremony before they had to dash to the maternity unit.

Susan's dress was an ornate ivory bodice with a rose-gold Celtic pattern on it, a matching long skirt and train, while her veil and headdress had an exquisite design in silver, gold and crystals.

The Reverend Peter Leicester escorted Susan down the aisle before he joined his beloved wife, Reverend June, and they jointly officiated at the ceremony. Luke managed to walk Susan back down the aisle without needing his walking stick, which Dominic discreetly carried out for him.

At the reception, held in the village hall which had been decorated and festooned with flowers by their friends in the village, the speeches were mercifully short. Luke and Peter were both firmly instructed by their wives not to ramble on with long quotes from literature. Hence, Luke had turned to his bride as he cited from War and Peace, "All, everything that I understand, I understand only because I love." Peter, however, had turned to the groom and paraphrasing P.G. Wodehouse said, "Susan has enough brains for two people, which is exactly what she's going to need now she's married you," to the amusement of all present, particularly Luke.

Susan couldn't stop smiling the whole day, and they honeymooned at the country club hotel, where Marian and Rose were also staying. They had a perfect week enjoying fine food, beautiful walks and Susan even tried horse riding.

It was not long before the garden at Blossom Cottage was equipped with a tiny plastic slide, and a scattering of children's toys; a couple of years later, a Wendy House appeared.

At the very end of the long back garden, past the lawn, past the vegetable patch, in the bank under the trees separating it from the fields behind, was the burrow of a little family of rabbits.